FILTRATOR

FILTRATOR

THE MARTENSEN CHRONICLES - BOOK III

1950-2076

JOHN GERTS

John Streg Publishing

Acknowledgments

Cover art: John Gerts
Contributing Editor: Steve Gerts, Margretta Dumas
Research: Steve Gerts, John Gerts
Archive Collection, Copy Editing: Marda Gerts, Steve Gerts,
Thanks to Terry Gerts, my life mentor.

Thanks to my wife, Margretta, who is my inspiration, love, and life.

Printed in the United States of America
First Printing, 2021
ISBN 978-1-7326034-7-9
John Streg Publishing
Ludington, Michigan 49431

CONTENTS

1

EXPLORER

Martins Army ants of the subfamily Dorylinae are nomadic and notorious for destroying plant and animal life in their path.

1950

The pacing man smacked another pack of smokes against his left palm before tugging the red band, tossing cellophane in the waste basket, popping a cigarette into a corner of his lip, and matching it, adding more smoke to the haze floating in the room. The aura surrounded the two-foot diameter, white, upside-down saucer-shaped globes of light suspended from long electrical poles hanging from the twelve-foot ceiling. The two-tone beige checkerboard linoleum flooring helped echo the footsteps of the pacing man.

The waiting room at Allegan General Hospital in June 1950 contained three leather couches in a horseshoe arrangement. A door in the southwest corner led to a hallway connecting four delivery rooms and a surgical operating room. Behind the center couch, a wall of bookshelves well stocked with Popular Science, Popular Mechanic, Outdoor Life, and other magazines awaited expectant fathers. Life, Good Housekeeping, and Better Homes and Gardens magazines in a separate section enticed occasional expectant grandparents. Used hardcover books packed on several shelves and dog-eared mystery and sci-fi paperbacks lined two shelves.

A second expectant father sat reading the fifth chapter of *The Case of the Baited Hook*, a Perry Mason mystery. He did not pace, this being his third birth, although the first in Michigan. The first child had been born in '44 near the base in South Carolina. The second was in Chicago four years ago. This man appeared to conspicuously regard the page, eyes moving across and down, focusing and maintaining steady breathing, as relaxed as possible to not let the Chicago birth creep inside his head. The smoke in the room was somewhat annoying. He had quit his pack-a-day habit when his wife had stopped smoking in '49. The lung cancer death of his stepfather in '45 and his wife's father in '46 and the Popular Science cancer warnings had made a lasting impression.

The corner door creaked open, and both men turned as Nurse entered.

"Harry Martensen," Nurse queried, "You are welcome to come with me now.

The reading man stood tall and thin in face and hair. Bending, he collected his coat and replaced the paperback on the shelf before following Nurse through the door and into the third delivery room.

His wife smiled, sweat and red blotches bordering her forehead and neck, her right arm surrounding a baby in a blanket.

Harry stared first at the baby for a time and then into his wife's eyes, attempting to read the emotions behind her smile.

Healthy?

The nurse picked up the baby and handed it to the man. He hefted the bundle, parted the blanket, pinched hands and feet, and scratched under the chin, the baby active but gentle and soft in his arms.

Boy! His third son. He again turned to his wife to read her smile, breathing the release of suspense that Chicago had not repeated. This child might forever be distinct due to that sigh and immediate bond.

Healthy!

The wife swallowed, looking back at the grinning, affable, six-foot-one-inch man holding the baby boy. Not a baby girl.

F our years later…

Today is the day. The sun, high and road warming. Waves rose off the asphalt at eye level to the boy standing in the east gully, fifteen feet from the occasional flash of a car along M43. The boy turned to check the farmhouse behind him, far to his left. All quiet. Mommy stretched out, napping on the couch; baby crib silent, and little brother in Granny's bedroom sleeping. The boy had bare-footed down the stairs, studying Mommy's pudgy arm hanging off the edge of the cushion, still; the back of her hand brushing the floor. He had cautiously swung open the pump house screen door, so the spring would not give him away and escaped into the July 1954 warm summer day: again. The boy focused on the road and the concrete drainpipe that ran underneath. The decision had been made; he just wanted to enjoy the moment. Mommy's invisible wall stretched left of the boy to the corner of the 40-acre farm. It turned ninety degrees, running the requisite 1,320 feet to the southeastern corner before turning again, paralleling the border in front of him, and then turning to meet the property's northwest corner to the boy's right. The wall, rising in front of the boy to the infinite, might as well have been electrified. The rule of not crossing beyond was etched in his mind by Mommy's repeated warnings.

"You must never cross...." But down the slope, he saw the shadowed concrete tunnel he knew he could navigate and the bright summer on the other side. He stepped forward, cooled within the confines of the pipe, crouching, barefooting around pebbles left over from the last storm. The rough texture of the tube registers a new memory, but not much on the other side. Cattails stretched before him, nothing he had not seen on his side of the invisible wall. To the left and right were just tall weeds, but it did not matter. He crouched in the bit of sand at the pipe's exit and relaxed, breathing and listening. Red-wing blackbirds whistled amidst the cattails clicking in the breeze.

No need to go further, the boy scrambled up the gully and stood on the edge of the road, studying the farm before him from this new angle. Forty-foot-tall boxelder trees stretched over the house in the backyard, lilac bushes blooming blue on the side of the living room window. He could see the alfalfa field stretching acres to the north from the road. The barns are visible through the trees up the long dirt driveway.

The boy stood tall along that road and made up his mind again. The street was quiet, with no cars. He walked back across the road and down the gully to safe territory.

What stirs a baby to start to crawl or take the first steps? A small adventure, but the boy believed in its importance. He would certainly not tell Mommy or Daddy. He did not care to tell his nine-year-old or eleven-year-old brothers. No, this first adventure would forever be his and his alone. But the boy's eyes brightened, and his smile touched his soul as he reached the backyard and began climbing his favorite tree, lost in thought. *What to do next?*

Two years later…

The family called their home a farm, but a swamp occupied a third of the northeast corner. Sarah chided her children, "Stay away from the farm's 'Mosquito Haven.'" Harry arranged each year to have fifteen acres of the northwest corner leased to a working farmer. The farmer grew alfalfa in exchange for turning over an area for a family garden and enough bundled hay in the fall to fill the barn.

Beyond the alfalfa, the railroad tracks marked the border of the farm. The sound of the train whistle carried to the farm twice a day, early in the morning and after dark, as the train prepared to cross M43. The family hardly heard the train rumble after a while.

After the war, Harry worked full-time as a door-to-door salesman and inside sales representative. He obtained employment as a bookkeeper. Each employment step depended on the progress of his correspondence training under the G.I bill and his ability to find better jobs in Kalamazoo, a twenty-minute drive.

In addition to the vegetable garden the family maintained every summer, they raised chickens in a coop attached to the small barn. They owned a cow, Janet, that Harry or Robert milked every morning and night. The garden always produced corn, potatoes, many tomatoes, squash, watermelon, cucumbers, pumpkin plants, string beans, and straggly radishes that never grew round or tasty. The children trekked out to the garden twice a week to hoe. Even Stephen, as a four-year-old, tagged along and hoed half a row assigned to him.

A fence surrounded the football field-sized yard in the back of the house, but the boy paid no attention to that limitation. The gate remained open. The yard contained the swing set, a tractor tire filled with Lake Michigan sand, and two seventy-foot-tall boxelder trees, perfect for climbing. The boy spent much of his days shinnying up first one tree as high as he dared and then crossing over in the upper branches to the other tree.

He took an emptied Kleenex box high up into the tree and broke a branch, leaving a sharp point to stick the carton onto the pointed twig, leveling it in a crook. The package would contain his treasures. His older brothers could not be bothered with tree climbing. Stephen could not reach the first branch, so in between rain storms, the box remained untouched by others. The boy did not like to play army with toy soldiers, so no soldier inhabited the box. He never zoomed little toy cars around on the floor, so no toy cars rolled around in the container. A small rubber ball may have been a good candidate, but what can you do with a ball in a tree? No, the box contained an unusual piece of driftwood and a smooth stone brought back from a Lake Michigan beach outing or a cocoon he would hope would hatch into a butterfly or moth and, of course, string. String is always helpful to have on hand.

Outside of the backyard fence, the gravel driveway stretched seventy-five feet from M43 to the rear of the house, transitioning to hard-packed dirt and grass running another hundred and fifty feet up to two barns. At the fence corner, Toni's doghouse provided another climbing challenge for the boy. Toni, a border collie mutt covered with beautiful black curly hair and a white patch on his chest, roamed the entire forty acres and never came into the house.

Harry constructed the doghouse from scrap wood and shingled the roof at a matched pitch to the farmhouse. The hole in the front allowed Toni and the boy inside. The boy left the wet-dead-animal-smelling space to the dog. A wooden floor protected the dog somewhat from cold winter nights. Toni rarely stayed around the yard during the day. As the boy explored the forty acres, Toni would appear suddenly and rub his leg and then be off again, vanishing in the weeds or cattails or sloshing in the swamp. At dinner time, Toni would show up at the house for food. Frequently Toni would come bounding up to the house with a possum that could no longer play possum in his mouth. Toni rarely barked, even at strangers. The boy, who liked to run as much as Toni, turned six that summer, so the family understood that the dog somehow belonged to the boy.

With a running start, the boy could jump up to the roof of the doghouse, his forward momentum allowing him to reach out for the roof's peak and haul himself up to a standing position on top. He would jump off the roof, land, and roll, brushing dirt. That summer, the boy often looked up at the sky, an ashen blue, soundless sky, from the top of the doghouse roof. He would steel himself and decide he could fly off the roof, Superman style, instead of jump. He did fly once. Amazed, the boy did not hit the ground when expected. That fraction of time before he touched the ground, longer than all the other times he had jumped from the doghouse roof to the ground, proved to the boy that he had flown like Superman. He had flown. The boy tried repeating that flight many times that summer and the next but never captured that fraction again. It did not matter because it had happened, and the boy remained forever, ready for it to happen again someday.

Three more boxelder trees grew between the backyard fence and the dirt drive, then two cherry trees and a pear tree. The fruit trees never received insecticide spray, so eating half a pear before encountering a worm meant good fortune. The cherry trees provided a red-wing blackbird feast for the flock nesting in the cattails in the ravine on the other side of the drive. Along the south side of the dirt drive up to the barns, a hundred-foot-long fencerow ran east/west, covered by Concord grape vines. The boy would pinch a grape into his mouth as a youngster, spit out the pulp, and then chew and swallow the skin. When older, he also liked the pulp, getting proficient at pinching the seeds with his teeth before eating the entire grape. Next to the fence, the raspberry bushes would await being attacked each summer by the whole family as the raspberries turned from green to pink to red. South of the raspberry bushes and beyond the shallow cattail ravine, the land turned sandy to the fence row on the south side of the forty acres. Strawberries and blackberries covered a portion of the field. The size of the boy's toe, the blackberries came in after the raspberries ran out, and they, too, made it to the family table for dessert with ice cream.

Further to the south, Johnson's farmhouse, visible in the middle of the parcel next to the family farm, intrigued the boy. The house appeared more worn down than the boy's house. Rusty machinery and a couple of cars with only half of their tires formed a sculpture garden in the weeds next to a single barn with a sway to the roof.

The inside of the boy's barn at the end of the drive became dim and dusty with the barn doors closed. Hay bales stacked two stories high in the fall provided more climbing and jumping fun for the boy. The milking shed, attached to the barn, reeked of manure. A smaller barn/garage covered the orange tractor that Robert drove around the farm on chores. The upstairs in this barn offered storage and a studio for Edward and his art. A basketball hoop mounted against one side of this barn permitted Robert to practice foul shots. The chicken coop slanted off the back of the small barn. Behind the barns at the end of the drive to the east, a small corral held the cow ready for milking. Two craggy apple trees produced other wormy fruit a few feet from the corral. Beyond the fruit trees, the forest led to the southeast corner of the forty acres marked by the tallest pine tree on the property. The tree was too big in circumference for the boy to shinny up to the first branch twenty feet over his head, besides being too sticky and sappy. The boy ventured on his own many times to admire the giant scotch.

Forty-acre safaris filled the days of summer. The boy, adept at being lost in the family shuffle, went his own way. Stephen and baby girl, Laura, consumed the eyes and ears and hands full of

Sarah. At ten and twelve, the boy's older brothers rode their bikes miles each dawn to another farm where they picked gladiolus or detasseled corn to earn money. The boy never felt alone or lonely in the people quiet outback of the farm far away from the house. Always accompanied by rustling grass fields or pine trees whistling, Toni bound up to him through the weeds only to turn and leap out, his rear and tail full of matted burrs. The boy ran from one far corner of the farm to another, barefoot in a brightly striped hand-me-down t-shirt and jeans to avoid sticker scratches: the grass and the forest underfoot were soft and cool. Only when he returned to the house in the late afternoon did he need to be careful where he walked, of man-made hot sidewalks, gravel drives, and the heat wave rising asphalt of M43. Sweeping off hundreds of mosquitoes from his bare arms picked up from the swamp and turtle hunting, he entered the house, banging the pump house screen door and sniffing dinner preparations.

Upon settling on the farm, Harry undertook to build a pump house, recalling all the skills he learned in Chattanooga while helping to develop his stepfather's resort. The boy had seen pictures of the windmill and the original farmhouse, almost unrecognizable now in comparison. The boy's older brothers had witnessed the framing, siding, and roofing of the attached eight-foot by six-foot shed. The pump house served as the farm's mud room, housing the water pump, electric hot water heater, washing machine, and a workbench that supported the pasteurizing equipment. Cold concrete made up the floor several steps down from the kitchen. Hooks for work clothes and coats pegged the wall next to the door. A pipe ran from the pump to the windmill wellhead buried below the Michigan frost line. Harry dismantled the four-inch angle iron, rod, and turnbuckle windmill and converted it into the sturdy swing set in the backyard.

The boy ran from the pump house through the kitchen, heading for the bathroom to pee. The outhouse moved into the house and became a bathroom upon completing the pump house.

Harry partitioned/split the bedroom on the northwest corner into a much smaller bedroom and the bathroom, housing the bathtub, toilet, and sink. Unaware of this challenging home improvement project, the boy shivered with clattering teeth each evening, awaiting his agonizing turn in two inches of lukewarm water left over from Stephen's bath. A laughing, unsympathetic mother called the skinny toothpick boy "Freeze-pot" while wrapping him in Stephen's wet towel. Almost no cold water would be added to the bath water mix for the first bath. Avoiding third-degree butt burns when stepping in and sitting down; is equally torturous.

The small bedroom leftover from the bathroom project held Granny's bed, dresser, and a second small junior bed. The boy slept there until he turned four. Moving ever slower around the house, Granny, noticeably quiet, slept soundly. They respect each other's status in the family structure, the boy being the guest in Granny's bedroom and Granny perceiving herself as a guest in the farmhouse. Stephen needed to move from the crib in the parents' bedroom to make room for the baby girl, so Stephen took over the junior bed in Granny's room.

The boy shifted to Robert's room, a marvelous and exciting milestone. After stopping at the bathroom, the boy sprinted upstairs and flopped on the bed in Robert's room. The smaller room to the right at the top of the stairs, Robert's, faced north, with a window between the built-in desk on the west wall and the shared double bed. Both sides of the room slanted down with the roof pitch, and in the closeness of the room, the boy imagined he lived in a tree house with his oldest brother. He respected his guest status in Robert's room, just like with Granny. Robert assigned the wall position in the bed to the boy. Getting up at night to go to the bathroom, he would crawl over his brother, trying not to bump him. Robert worked late on his homework at the built-in desk that also served as their dresser.

The boy thumbed through Superman or Batman comic books in the dim light from the desk until dropping off to sleep. Robert, for his part, never complained once about sharing the room with his foot shorter, blond-haired brother, forever simpatico, even with six years of an age difference.

The boy cooled down from his afternoon adventures with the bedroom window open and lights off. Minutes later, checking the hands on the desk clock, the boy raced downstairs to the living room using both hands to change the channel to three just in time for the beginning of "The Mickey Mouse Club." Harry had added the living room to the south side of the farmhouse. A doorway had been cut into the wall between the dining room and Harry's and Sarah's bedroom next to the farmhouse front entry and stoop. Built as a single-story addition two steps down from the basic bungalow, a carpeted, linoleum over slab on grade, fourteen by twenty-four-foot space held the entire family, Christmas tree, and all the presents in season.

After singing the "M-O-U-S-E" mantra today, Jimmy introduced the next thrilling episode of "Spin and Marty." In the early episodes, Marty played the city dude on the show's ranch. Spin, an accomplished equestrian and roper, tried to befriend and then mocked Marty, a sullen loner. But in episode three, after a scuffle outside the corral, the counselors put boxing gloves on Spin and Marty. The ranch teens surrounded the two, watching two scrawny shirtless kids punch each other with bulbous, huge, soft leather gloves. Spin's reach and skill never slowed Marty's feisty, head-down adrenaline. After the fight, a begrudging friendship began to cement between the boys. Horses and cowboy hats on a ranch out west enthralled the boy, as did roping calves and solving mysteries, standing tall, offering friendship, not backing down, and earning respect; the boy yearned to be as tall as Spin and have his own horse. He resolved to ask for a horse yet again during supper.

Discreet amid the family activity around him, the boy absorbed every adventure on the twenty-four-inch diagonal, black-and-white screen. T.V. defined and shaped the boy, ultimately shaping generations in an unprecedented audio/visual bombardment. Harry and Sarah grew up influenced by serial movies in their thirties and forties. Robert had been mesmerized by Hopalong Cassidy and the Green Hornet radio shows. T.V. added anytime visual hypnosis.

The boy became hooked on T.V. like his mother. Regular weekday afternoon movies on T.V. captivated Sarah and became her favorite pastime. Movies came to be her respite from child and baby fussing, studying for her college courses, and supper preparations. She also spent time doodling hairstyles and woman's portraits on the borders of the Chicago Sun-Times, arriving daily in the mailbox. The new daytime "Soap Operas" held little interest to her or the boy. Sarah denounced the adult-coded dialogue of love and cheating as boring. But a Charlie Chan or Sherlock Holmes movie captivated both of them; the boy surrounded by Sarah as she lay on the couch. The boy cherished movie time with her. Not so much for the hug, the couch barely accommodated his expanding mother pre-childbirth, but for the shared adventure of the movie.

The movie star always solved the mystery through logic and clues that the secondary characters missed or misdiagnosed. The number-one son or Watson affably stumbling along, assisting in the riddle, or acting as the sounding board for the masters of mystery. The thrown knife or gunshot in the dark thrilled the boy. The heroes may be tied up or knocked out for a time, but they never suffer or die, and the bad guys always end up caught in the end due to quick wits instead of fisticuffs. Sarah taught/instilled problem-solving and a love for seeking and learning in all her children without opening a textbook or standing at a chalkboard.

Harry arrived home from work just as The Mouseketeers chorused, "Why? Because we like you!"

Robert sloshed milk from the evening milking into the vat for pasteurizing, and Edward finished painting for the day and sat down at the dining table smelling of turpentine. His "studio" consisted of an old table upstairs in the small barn where his oil paints and brushes would not stink up the farmhouse.

Harry transported food from the kitchen to the center of the table while the boy set the table; fork to the left, knife, and spoon to the right, as instructed, napkins nonexistent. The boy used the lick and suck of greasy fingers instead. Sarah steered Stephen to his booster chair and lifted Laura into the highchair. The boy eyed the sweet ketchup smothering the meatloaf but, obliged by family rule, took a small portion of green beans, a sizable portion, and a baked potato. He prepared the potato by assigning butter to each fork-mashed section. Salt and pepper patient, the boy started on the meatloaf, portioning out each bite to maximize the ketchup topping. After being passed and pouring his milk, salt, and pepper seasoning his potato, the boy continued eating until only the beans adorned his plate.

Conversation at the table dropped off when the family filled their plates and consumed the presented food, chewing noisily. Sarah allowed no snacks except summertime fruit off the vine during the day. At meals, portions vanished, and serving bowls and platters scraped clean.

The green beans were the exception. The boy caught glances from his father and Robert and reluctantly followed through, choking down his green beans. A clean plate meant desert. Sarah did indeed award the boy a sizable piece of yellow cake with chocolate frosting, his favorite. Unlike the rest of the family, the boy begged off adding ice cream. The frozen vanilla made his teeth ache. The cake vanished in measured enjoyment.

The boy looked to Harry, recalling an episode of "Fury," about a boy with a horse, set his fork down, *"When can we get a horse?"*

Robert laughed, "You don't want a horse; they are dumber than stone. Janet is smarter than any horse and worth at least something because of the milk!"

The boy, a sarcastic corner of his mouth turned up, said, "You don't ride a cow." Harry nipped the discussion, "You are not old enough to care for a horse."

"When do you think I'll be old enough," the boy said, "When I'm six?"

Harry didn't hesitate, "When you are old enough to care for the horse like Robert takes care of Janet. You have to clean the stall daily, feed the horse, and brush the horse."

"I think I could do that now!" the boy said.

"When you carry two buckets of water from the pump house to the barn, you will be ready for a horse. Then we'll see." The boy envisioned the barn, far away. The certainty that he could not carry even one half-full bucket of water with two hands half that distance ended the conversation.

He had a dream and a goal, but just like the clean plate rule for dessert, he knew his plan would turn real someday. When he could carry those two buckets of water, a horse would again be up for discussion, and his father, who had never failed him, would follow through, and somehow, someday, there would be a horse.

Supper finished, and Harry and Sarah headed for the living room. Harry picked up his current book and the Sun-Times from the raised hearth. He sat in his comfortable chair, angled near the red brick fireplace stretching along the south wall. Harry put one foot on the lower mantle, straightened his right leg, crossed the left at the ankle, and unfolded the newspaper. He had fashioned the hearth and laid the entire fireplace over a year ago. The cement mixer sat outside next to the fireplace chimney awaiting the next project, stairs down to the coal storage basement. Saturdays and Sundays after church and at weekday dawn to milk the cow, Harry would dress in his brown, front pleated pants, handkerchief in his right rear pants pocket, belt cinched above his slight pot belly, making him appear even taller and lankier than his six-foot one-inch frame. He would also put on his beige short sleeve dress shirt, stained with varnish and paint, over a sleeveless t-shirt. Paint-splattered old dress shoes and a cocked fedora completed the outfit, ready for farm work. During the week, after supper, tie loosened, and collar unbuttoned, his reading time.

Sarah sat in a chair on the other side of the fireplace and sorted through the piled-high stack of books, notebooks, and disarrayed papers, her homework for her child psychology course. She would have at least forty-five minutes to add to the essay before steering the younger children toward their baths. Laura crawled on the floor at her feet. Stephen piled blocks in front of the TV.

Back in the dining room, without a word of direction, the three older boys cleared the table and stacked the dishes next to the porcelain sink in the kitchen. Robert scraped; there were no leftovers for the refrigerator, not in this family. With the dishware stacked, Edward left for his room, not his night to wash. The boy dried the dishes with a towel, putting them away in accessible cupboards since he could not reach the sink or control the faucet. Same with the silverware. The sink lined up with the archway from the dining room, and sounds from the TV drifted into the kitchen.

Standing at the sink, Robert looked past the combination stove/oven and cupboards to the pasteurizer on the workbench in the pump house. The red indicator light had not switched to green. Behind the two brothers, next to the arch, the breakfast banquette with built-in benches on either side provided tight seating for the entire family. They rarely all ate breakfast at once. The pantry next to the banquette filled out the south side of the kitchen. On Robert's left, the countertop formed the short leg of an "L," ending at the refrigerator with rounded top corners.

Both boys wasted no time and completed the chore silently, Robert heading up to his room to study. The boy followed at a distance. The stairs to the two upstairs bedrooms began/ended in the dining room, but after five steps, a landing forced the boys into a ninety-degree turn to the left to continue up the remaining stairs. The landing created a small cubby underneath accessible from across the bathroom. By convention, the family threw or kicked dirty clothes into the space; to be collected and taken to the pump house and the washing machine. The boy grabbed his P.J.s from his designated drawer in the built-in desk in Robert's room. He intended to return downstairs to line up for his bath, but the lights in the bedroom to the left of the landing, Edward's room, kept going on and off again. When the boy wandered into the darkened room, he noticed small stars covering a portion of the ceiling, shining like real stars in the night sky. A magical effect. "Wow!" the boy said, awed.

"Pretty cool, huh?" Edward said. The boy agreed.

Edward turned the light back on. Like Robert's room, this bedroom had the same sloping sides to the ceiling on the east and west sides. This room measured about fourteen feet long to

Robert's ten-foot by ten-foot room. The room's furniture included a dresser, a small desk, and a bed. Edward had no built-in desk like Robert's room, and it did not seem cozy to the boy. The boy thanked the stars he had been assigned to Robert's smaller space.

Edward went back to the center of the room, where several sheets of stars were spread out on the floor as well as a map of the night sky. He cut out an applique with scissors, dipped the star in soapy water and picked up a razor blade, sliced underneath the star, lifted it off the glossy paper backing, submerged the decal in a rinsing bowl of fresh water, Edward climbed on a chair and reached the ceiling, applying the star and dabbing it smooth. The biggest stars, the size of dimes, graced the east slope of the room as well as halfway across the flat part of the ceiling, scattered among seventy-five stars of various sizes. Edward turned off the light again.

"Can you find the big dipper?" he asked. The stars glowed in the dark. The boy came to the center of the room, looking up, and as he turned, he recognized patterns to some of the stars; and yes, on the northern part of the ceiling slope, he recognized the big dipper. Edward had not applied the star stickers randomly.

Millions of stars sprinkled the sky on the farm on a cloudless night. With no city lights as a hindrance, the wonder of the heavens thrilled the boy and filled him with questions; answered by older family members. Edward reached to the ceiling, pointing at the constellation, and traced an imaginary line from two stars up to another star. "That's the North Star, and that's how you find it." That 'W' over there is Cassiopeia, and this one is 'Leo' the lion." Leo looked like a mouse to the boy, not a lion, but the stars' effect on the ceiling amazed him. Edward sliced off another deal as the boy heard his mother call him to his bath. Edward would take days to meticulously complete the panorama, but the boy admired Edward, the family artist, for creating an inside night sky.

Once downstairs, the boy shucked clothes and kicked them into the dirty clothes pile under the stair landing. Near the end of his bath, with tightly closed eyes, he blindly reached for the washcloth held by his mother. He used the rag to wipe and open his eyes, thus avoiding a soapy sting.

In bed that night, he reached for one of the Batman comic books littering the floor, studying each frame and the words captioned below. He began to guess the meaning of some words in the clouds next to Batman's mouth, matching them to the action in the frame. He could not wait for school to start in the fall.

After the excitement of attending school wore off, kindergarten, first, and second grade disappointed the boy. Reading about Dick and Jane skipping around the page with their dog and cat seemed babyish. By the time the boy began his first day of first grade, he had deciphered most of the words he had come across in Batman comics. One word popped up a lot in the comic book, the green Martian Manhunter and had the boy stumped. The word: "alien." The boy told himself the word would be pronounced with a long "a," followed by the same sound as the word "line." Indeed, every time he saw the word, he thought "aline" with a long "a" and a long "i." No one in the boy's sphere of reference ever used the word in a sentence or in casual talk, so a year and a half went by before Robert corrected the boy. He happened to read one of the dialogue bubbles in a comic book containing the word out loud, and Robert laughed and made him repeat it three times before accurately pronouncing the word.

The comic book world used vivid colors to express the city of Metropolis and Superman flying. Batman's cape streamed in the wind as he swung down on the bad guys; much more thrilling than Dick in blue jeans and a blue and white striped shirt throwing a "ball" to "Spot."

Third grade provided an adventure in just getting to school. The boy took the morning bus with his brothers, including Stephen, who headed to first grade. Upon exiting the bus, he walked to another bus containing a gathering of the rest of the third-grade class. The new elementary/high school building in Gobles, planned just before the baby boom bubble, did not have enough classrooms to hold all the students. The administration decided the third graders would attend the schoolhouse in Kendall, ten minutes east by bus from the Gobles school. The schoolhouse in the tiny town of Kendall provided two classrooms. The third graders were split evenly so that the same number of boys and girls occupied each room.

A glorious year for the boy as friendships grew since no one older or younger distracted their class. The boy and Larry Champion were the fastest runners in the whole school and best friends. Bill Stanton, Larry Champion, and the boy caught frogs and crickets during recess. The majestic old trees could not be climbed, but hiders could avoid seekers by sneaking around to the other side of a tree when the seeker walked by.

Perhaps being the fastest boy in the school went to the boy's head a little. Every morning he carried his lunch to school in a metal lunchbox brightly painted in a Zorro motif. Sarah's fortes did not include sandwich making, especially when the boy compared lunches the other boys brought to school.

"Mom," the boy chided, "can you see how Jimmy's mom makes his sandwiches? He always has the best in class and a Twinkie or something for dessert."

"I always throw in two cookies," said Sarah.

"Yeah, but I just don't like cookies that much."

Sarah turned to the boy, perplexed, "You don't like my sandwiches?"

"Well, they're OK, I guess," the boy said, deciding to backpedal, but too late.

"Just OK!" Sarah removed the wax paper from a kitchen drawer.

"Great, here's the wax paper; make your own sandwiches."

That settled that. Every morning from that day on until forever, the boy made his own lunch. He abandoned the Zorro lunch box as childish, but not Zorro. He did not have the luxury within the hectic time and space in the kitchen to make sandwiches for himself that were any different than the ones his mom used to make. He became an expert at what he proclaimed a "Zorro" sandwich.

The boy rushed to the kitchen each school day to grab four slices of Butternut white bread and lay them down in a row. Grab the ketchup and make a heavy "Z" on the first and third slices. Squash the second piece of bread on the first, spreading the ketchup to both sides of the sandwich. Squash the fourth piece against the third. Open both sandwiches up, slap a piece of bologna from the fridge in between, and re-close the sandwiches.

Rip a piece of wax paper just the right size and stack the two Zorro sandwiches, placing them at the center of the wax paper sheet. Fold the wax paper sheet once, then fold again from the opposite side, overlapping at the middle of the sandwich at least one inch. Fold into triangles the two corners on the left and the two corners on the right and fold under, making the assembly an airtight origami sandwich.

The boy ignored his metal lunchbox now in favor of a quick and easy paper lunch bag: take a brown paper bag from the paper bag container by thumb and middle finger at the mid-point cutout in the bag. Snap the bag in a wide swing, catching air and expanding the bag into shape. Slip the sandwich bundle into the bag, wrap two cookies in wax paper, and slip it on the top of the sandwich so nothing can shift or slide around. Fold the paper bag over at the top in a straight, even crease about one-half inches from the top. Fold and tuck again to create a three-quarter-inch, neat handle for his lunch bag.

Done! Total time, less than sixty seconds.

When the class sat down to lunch, the boy would trade one or two of his cookies for a gorgeous mom-made sandwich with lettuce, turkey, and the works. He enjoyed sandwiches as much as his little brother Stephen liked cookies. The boy enjoyed even his Zorro sandwich if he could not trade up. Of course, he never mentioned his strategy to his mom, encouraging her to buy the fancy cookies at the grocery store.

On rare occasions, Mom drove the boy to spend the afternoon at Billy Stanton's farm. The Stanton farm appeared more extensive than the boy's forty acres. The barns, the house, and the fields; are bigger. Workers on tractors are coming and going. Billy's father worked with the men. Larry Champion lived in a tiny home in Gobles compared to Billy Stanton's farmhouse. An only child, Larry, and the boy would play a board game at Larry's house. On his birthday in June, the boy reciprocated by inviting several boys from his class to his first-ever birthday party. Sarah inserted a leaf into the dining table and spread the white lace tablecloth over the top. Places for all the boys (no girls allowed) surrounded the table. The boy unwrapped presents as his friends wolfed down the cake and ice cream.

Six boys piled into the back of the station wagon while Dad, Mom, Robert, and Edward sat in the front and rear seats, and Dad drove to Paw Paw for a double feature at the movie theater. The first science fiction movie, *20 Million Miles to Earth,* starred a hatched little creature from outer space that kept tripling every day until it became as huge as a three-story building, terrorizing the city and tossing people this way and that.

In the creepier second movie, a scientist developed equipment that allowed him to pass through solid walls. *The 4D man* could not touch anyone without their molecules speeding up, aging them until they shriveled and died of old age. That drove the scientist mad, and he could not resist killing his friends and co-workers.

The boy thought the movie was fantastic. Three days later, he asked Edward something about the film.

"Are you kidding? Robert and I didn't even see most of those movies."

"Why not?" The boy asked.

Said Edward, disappointed, "Some of your friends were so scared of the monster and the 4D man we had to take them out into the lobby for most of the movies. They cried and carried on, so we had to babysit them while you finished the movies."

"Gee, I didn't know," the boy said, "I didn't notice anything wrong."

"That's because we took them to the lobby so fast."

That birthday party was the last time the boy saw his third-grade friends.

One night In July, at dinner, Dad suggested the family take a trip to Kalamazoo to see a house the family might move into. The following day the twenty-minute drive brought the station wagon to the house at one fourteen Sage St., in Kalamazoo.

The boy loved the farm, but the farmhouse could not compete with the fancy three-year-old house on Sage Street. The garage is connected to the south side of the house. A short white fence squared off some plantings in front of the walk between the garage and the home. An old-fashioned light post with an electric light lantern on top anchored the corner of a sandstone walkway leading up to the front door. The house sat on a three-quarter acre lot with fields all around. Across the one-hundred-foot driveway, the only close neighbor's house appeared to be a baseball center fielder's throw to home plate away.

Entering the front door of the Sage St. house, the boy noted the open stairway, complete with wooden spindles and a rail to the left and a hallway with a front closet just to the right. After the closet, Sarah converted a bedroom to a den. The main bedroom came next, and then the stairs to the basement, a quick turn to the left. Across from the basement access door, the bathroom In the northwest corner of the house, the kitchen led off to an enclosed back porch that headed back to the garage. Space in the corner of the kitchen allowed for a small breakfast table. The open railed stairs to the second floor overlooked a dining area and the living room on the south end of the house.

Upstairs, a bathroom with a tub/shower, a sink, and a toilet separated two more bedrooms. The east bedroom had a built-in closet and could hold four or five beds and a couple of dressers. The west bedroom had a little nook for a desk. This room also had a built-in closet. The basement had a walk-out to the slope of the backyard. Outside the enclosed porch, a towering maple tree provided shade for the house from the afternoon sun.

Back on the farm, Dad waited for everyone to receive dessert at the dinner table.

"We're going to buy the house we visited today. We will move in a month. Mom has been hired to teach fifth grade at West Main Elementary School. We'll be able to put away money for you kids to go to college and take some family vacations."

"What about the farm?" the boy asked.

"We're selling the farm. In fact, we have a buyer that wants it on a land contract." Sarah stood behind Harry, excited.

"Kalamazoo has better schools," she said, "Robert will attend Kalamazoo Central High School. They have excellent science and math teachers. Edward will start at Hillside School. This brand-new school only handles seventh, eighth, and ninth-grade students.

"You three will attend Grand Prairie Elementary School. Laura will start kindergarten this fall."

The boy had questions.

"Is it a long bus ride to our school, Mom?"

"No," she said, "You'll be walking to school, eight blocks, about a mile. Harry will drop off Robert and Edward on his way to work, and they will take a bus home.

"My school is close by as well."

That night in bed, the boy thought about the move to the city. Leaving his Boxelder trees, raspberries, and farmhouse concerned the boy, but the new place generated great excitement with plenty of space and fields to explore and trees to climb, and the prospect of a new school, new friends, and brand-new adventures.

In August, the boy planned one last safari to the far corners of the forty acres. *Goodbye to the barn, goodbye house*. Janet, the cow, had been taken away to the butcher. The chickens had dwindled down to nothing, having provided many dinners. The raspberries and the rest of the fruits had been stripped and desert-topped. Goodbye, favorite climbing tree. The family piled into the station wagon, and the boy waved goodbye to the farm and Gobles.

In September, the boy, brother Stephen, and sister Laura (heading to kindergarten) checked both ways before crossing a busy street, a thoroughfare through Kalamazoo. Main Street met the highway at the far western edge of the city. The three siblings walked seven more quiet blocks down Piccadilly Lane to the end, taking a left turn for a block past the playground to the school.

The school had been planned and built before Kalamazoo experienced the same baby boom crowding that Gobles dealt with. The boy's classroom held a third-grade/fourth-grade split. Miss. Desautells, his teacher, appeared incredibly young and scrawny, like she could not have lifted a corner of her desk. A split classroom is impossible for an inexperienced teacher to control, and the boy became bored after finishing his assignment while the teacher taught the third graders.

John Dutton and Jeff Rollason soon took the boy under their wing, and friendships and trouble brewed and grew. Several fourth-grade boys shot tiny spit wads through milk straws at the back of the girls' necks. After a couple of weeks, that escalated to straight pins that could be shot five or six feet with a mighty breath to stick in the cork boards around the room.

Miss Desautells mysteriously vanished from the classroom after Christmas break. A new teacher, Mrs. Cox, appeared. Whether rumor or fact, Miss Desautells suffered a nervous breakdown from the chaos in her classroom and abandoned teaching altogether, according to the story whispered from student to student. Whatever the reason, Mrs. Cox had eyes in the back of her head, and she organized helpful lessons. Her name became all the boys' source of amusement. John Dutton, Jeff Rollason, and the boy huddled at recess, laying out crude scenarios about the teacher's name, despite not knowing what they were discussing. John Dutton had found a magazine on his father's bedside stand.

"I had to look real quick 'cause my mom came home," he said, "The naked man lay on the back of the naked woman with his thing in her. That must be the way they do it. I've seen dogs doing that."

The boy had never even imagined what his parents did in the bedroom. His friend's story fascinated the boy.

John Dutton continued, "Underneath the picture, it said the man's cock moved deep inside her."

"I wonder if Mrs. Cox likes cox," Jeff commented.

"No, it's cock, 'C O C K,'" Dutton corrected. Her name's funny, though."

The next day John Dutton came running up to his two friends. "I got it wrong," he said, "I had more time to look last night. Most pictures show the man and the woman front to front, not the man on her back. That must be the way it works with people.

Alone at his house, the boy rifled the bedside nightstand beside his parents' bed. Sure enough, he found several back issues of *Playboy* in the drawer. His mind raced as he thumbed through the one on top. First, he found no pictures of a man and a woman coupled together. He did find all sorts of images of beautiful large-breasted naked women. Secondly, the boy wondered what role his mother played in the magazines. She sure did not look like any of the pictures in the magazine. His mother had no figure at all anymore. The boy did not get it. He did not get his dad. As far as the boy could tell, Harry and Sarah loved each other. His dad seemed very attentive to Sarah. The magazines initiated the first of many quandaries about sex that the boy had to leave unanswered until he gathered more information.

Mid-winter, the boy's stomach ached, and he stayed home from school. The boy thought it a weird sort of stomachache. He did not feel like throwing up. He did not feel like moving at all. The next day the pain worsened. His dad checked his forehead before and after work and told the boy to hang in there; it would get better the next day.

Harry had no remembrance of his near-fatal bout with the Spanish Flu when he turned five years old. A stomachache meant just that in his experience. Concerned, of course, but maybe the boy would improve. On the third day, Harry came home from work at lunchtime to check on the boy.

That morning the boy thought he might indeed be dying. He could not help but moan to distract himself from the pain. He experienced more pain than he had ever experienced, like a knife pressing hard into his side. Pressing and holding the spot himself did not help. Nothing helped the pain.

At noon Harry decided to take the boy to the doctor. The boy walked hunched over. Dad helped him into the passenger seat. Ten minutes later, the boy sat on the white paper roll of the doctor's examination bed. Dr. McFadden came bustling in.

"Can you stand and let me take a look? Where does it hurt?"

The boy struggled to stand, but he could not straighten. The doctor put two fingers on the spot where the boy pointed and pressed firmly. The boy grimaced.

"Harry," the doctor said, "If you can drive the boy over to the hospital, I'll meet you there, and we'll get the boy right in. We will take care of you, son. I'll see you in a bit."

Harry drove to the hospital calmly, not saying a word. Within twenty minutes of leaving the doctor's office, Harry and his son had arrived at the hospital, the boy had dressed in a gown, and Dr. Mcfadden had pulled back the curtain and examined the spot as the boy lying on the gurney bit his lip.

"Not to worry, son, we will remove your appendix. It is a little organ the size of a finger, and for the life of us doctors, we cannot figure out why it is there in the first place. You have heard of getting your tonsils out. The same thing happens with your appendix; totally useless and OK to remove. You'll be asleep the whole time and won't feel a thing."

The boy woke up from surgery in a hospital room. Harry stood over the bed. The pain in his side had left, replaced by the feeling of a bruise on his side where the pain had been. He gingerly felt around that area. He found a gauze bandage and tape that began to itch. The boy dropped off into sleep. That first night in the hospital, the boy woke up several times. Nurses woke him up. The itching woke him up. He sipped water and ice. Throughout the night, Harry sat in the chair next to his bed. He smiled every time the boy woke up.

"Doing fine," his dad would say, "How are you feeling," he would say, "Do you need anything," he would say. After suffering alone on the couch for three days while his parents went to work, Harry stayed at his bedside, incredibly out of character for his hard-working father and totally comforting to the boy.

The boy stayed in the hospital for a week. Sarah came to visit. She asked the boy if he recognized the nurse taking his temperature. She had been their neighbor back on the farm, Doris Johnson, and she used to babysit the boy. Her dark complexion startled the boy. The boy remembered the house with the rusty cars, but he never realized until that moment that a colored family lived next door.

Nurse Doris changed his gauze bandage three times a day. She would pull on the tape. Ouch. Then take away the gauze, which had turned a little green. A beige tube stuck about an inch and a half out of his stomach. That is where the green ooze came from. Nurse Doris said the drainage tube helped remove infectious fluid where his appendix had been.

The boy's appendix had burst at home or the doctor's office. If Harry had waited another ten minutes to bring the boy in, he probably would not be alive now. Did his father stay all night out of guilt for not getting the boy in sooner? The boy understood that the illness had been life-threatening, but being fine now, he appreciated spending time with his father. He vowed that if he ever experienced a similar situation with a sick child, he would never play doctor but swiftly find a real one.

On the day of his release, the nurse came in to change the bandage for the last time. She told the boy the drainage tube would be taken out. The boy had made enough potholders to last a lifetime on the little loom Sarah had brought as a hospital present. He could not wait to go home. Uncovering the tube, the nurse started to pull. That hurt. Hurt like crazy. Like his guts were being pulled out by a monster. The boy assumed the tube extended two or three inches on the inside of his stomach like the part that stuck out. The nurse kept pulling. At least two feet of tubing had been buried in there. The excruciating pain of the pull at last subsided. Time to go home.

The boy moved on to the fifth/sixth-grade class in the fall. Mrs. Wilson, his new teacher, had a slight smirk that curled the corner of her mouth as she smiled, which she did a lot. Her eyes twinkled bright and piercing, and she enjoyed challenging the class with questions or inquiries the boy had to consider. There still existed the problem with what to do with the fifth graders while the sixth graders learned a grade-level lesson. For the boy, one day in November, Mrs. Wilson brought a workbook to his desk, asking him to try some exercises. The workbook involved learning and practicing the "new math." In addition to his regular arithmetic work, Mrs. Wilson said the boy could progress at his own pace through the workbook.

The boy thought the theories on sets and algebra fascinating. Within his fifth-grade attention span, he progressed in the book. It kept him busy in class and did not require additional homework. Mrs. Wilson made school enjoyable.

Sarah taught a fifth-grade class at West Main Elementary School, and before the school year began, she asked the boy if he would like to attend school and ride to school with her. The boy thought the idea insane. What would the other kids think? The worst kind of teacher's pet came to mind. *No. No. Absolutely not.* Since Sarah and her son attended fifth grade simultaneously, she knew about the possibilities for his age group in the district. After school started, Sarah told the boy about Junior Civic.

"A program sponsored by the school administration involves acting and stagecraft. Is that something you might be interested in?"

"That sounds cool!" the boy said.

"Well, you have to audition. The program takes two students from each elementary school and junior high, so there would be about fifty kids. You would take the bus downtown every Tuesday after school, and Dad would pick you up when you are done."

"What do I have to do for the tryout?" asked the boy.

"You have to recite a poem you have memorized and perform a short pantomime for a panel of teachers. Then they select two to go downtown and be members of the Junior Civic Theater."

"When are the tryouts?" the boy asked.

"Two weeks from now."

The boy remembered the night a few years ago that he saw Harry in a play on the small stage in the Gobles School Gymnasium. He remembered vividly, even the name of the comedy. *My Three Angels*. Harry had played the lead character, the leader of a band of three escaped convicts, hiding in plain sight from the police as servants at a wealthy family's home in some foreign country. Even though one of the convicts used his little pet snake to bite and kill some scoundrels attempting to hurt the family, the audience laughed. Harry played the straight man, the leader, the smart one, and the hero. He had so many lines in the play. The boy sat mesmerized from the opening to the curtain. How did he know all those lines? The boy had never seen him working on them. His father made the dialogue sound like when he talked over the dinner table. Natural. He moved on stage with the grace of a hero. In character, Harry was a different person. The boy did not recognize the man on stage. The crowd laughed and applauded like crazy. The experience thrilled the boy. The boy did not recall his father saying much other than he had fun being in the play.

Two weeks later, the boy considered himself ready for his tryout. His pantomime involved driving a car and changing a flat tire. He had memorized A. A. Milne's poem *Missing,* one of his favorites from the *When We Were Very Young* book. The poem describes the escape from the shoebox of a boy's pet mouse. The boy in the poem keeps asking his family members if they have seen the little creature. Harry had read the poem to the boy since he turned three, so he almost had it memorized when he chose it. Four girls and a boy signed up for the tryout. The girls all went first, and the boy, standing behind the judges' table, could hardly hear the girl's poems. Sarah, experienced from her years as a high school thespian, had coached him not to be soft-spoken on stage.

At his turn, the boy began in a loud, clear voice with a bit of a whine.

"Has anybody seen my mouse?"

His pantomime followed the poem. He imagined a station wagon, rolled the tire from the trunk to the front left axle, loosened the lug nuts, removed the flat, replaced the tire, and tightened the lug nuts on the spare. A week later, he received a letter inviting him to join the Kalamazoo Junior Civic players.

The boy had a banner year. New friends everywhere; Gobles and the farm were cherished dreams.

The boy, his younger brother, and his sister either walked or rode bikes to school along the now familiar Piccadilly to Canterbury street path, joined by additional kids, also on their way to school. New to the school that year, Valerie Cantos, for some reason, often walked down her short driveway at the same time the boy walked by. As they walked, Valerie pointed to a house on the next block.

"Remember the bomb drill last week?" asked Valerie, "Marjorie Shaer says she's been in the Von Clompen's bomb shelter in their basement. It is supposed to be a secret, but everybody knows about it now. It has an air filter, and it is made out of thick concrete. You can't see it from the street at all."

The third bomb drill had occurred the previous week. Fire drills occurred about four times a year, and tornado drills three times in the spring. Bomb drills involved students crouching behind their desks, covering their heads with their arms, and keeping their eyes closed until the bell rang. The boy could not see how much that would help if a bomb hit the school. The boy's class had viewed a film strip on what actions to take during a nuclear attack, and of course, the boy had seen several clips on T.V. of the hydrogen bomb explosions. The gossip about the Von Clompen fallout shelter prodded the boy to check with Mom what the family would do in case of an attack. "Mom, have we thought about building a fallout shelter?" Sarah stopped analyzing the fifth grader's theme she held.

"Your Dad and I have discussed what would happen, and we will not build a bomb shelter."

Perplexed, the boy said, "I know of one over on Piccadilly Avenue. Von Clompens have one."

"Look, think it through," Sarah said, "You've seen the pictures, haven't you? Nothing is left but burned ground after a hydrogen bomb. The United States has thousands of them. Russia has thousands. You can bet Chicago is not that far away and a prime target; Grand Rapids is probably a secondary target. "The probability of having enough time to gather here in a fallout shelter seems remote. Your father and I both work, and everyone else is at school. Robert is at Michigan State. Those fallout shelters cost thousands of dollars, and we would not be near enough to get to them.

"But what if we could all gather there, or maybe some of us could make it there. Then what. How long can people stay in fallout shelters? The food will run out, and the water. Then what?

"You come out to the surface and look around at burnt rubble. Or maybe the bombs do not hit anywhere near us, but the radioactive cloud blows across the lake in our direction. So, you die of radiation poisoning because radioactivity last years and decades.

"If you're old enough to ask the question, you're ready to hear that a fallout shelter is ridiculous."

"I guess I see what you mean, Mom," the boy said, "The drill at school seems pretty ridiculous, for sure."

"Harry and I think if it goes that far and we are stupid enough to get into a nuclear war, we wouldn't care to be around to see what comes next. That is one reason I donate to the United Nations. The world is too small now to be thinking in terms of countries. We should be thinking about the world, the earth. Harry and I are optimistic. People have to move beyond war to solve problems."

The boy thought the chances were slim that Mom would be right and there would be no more war. Sometimes, in the middle of the night, the boy would awaken. In a nightmare, he would be looking west and see a mushroom cloud in the sky above Chicago, across the lake. A minute later, he would be vaporized into dust.

The boy tackled one exciting adventure after another. Kathleen, a sixth grader, and her sister Patricia cornered the boy one morning before the second bell to start school. "I found this pack of cigarettes on the road as we walked to school. It is almost a new pack. It just lay there on the side of the road."

"Hey," the boy said, "let me see those. You are right; they have not been touched. What are you going to do with them?"

Kathleen shrugged. "Throw the pack away, I guess."

That seemed like a waste to the boy. "Can I have it? My parents don't smoke."

The bell rang. The boy shoved the pack in a jacket pocket, hung his jacket up on the hooks outside his class, and sat down. His hands had the not unpleasant odor of fresh cigarettes. He could not get his mind off the cigarettes all morning. At lunch, he decided he wanted to try smoking one. He wandered around the front of the school and came up with the idea of using Mrs. Wilson's car. She smoked. Surreptitiously, he opened the car door, punching the cigarette lighter button. In twenty seconds, it popped out, and the boy lit the cigarette and got out of there. He kept the cigarette near his leg while walking to the farthest corner of the playground, where no one appeared to be within eyesight. He tentatively took a first drag of the cigarette. He did not want to cough like all the kids on T.V. did when they took their first drag. The boy walked the four corners of the playground, far away from all the other students, smoking the cigarette surreptitiously down to the filter before stomping it out. The bell rang, so he headed back in toward the school. The principal walked up to meet him.

"You are smoking on school grounds. Come into my office."

"Really, Mrs. Hanson," the boy argued, "it is no big deal; I just wanted to try it."

"I will call your parents. You will be expelled from the lunch program."

The boy could not believe his misfortune. Had he hurt anybody? He did not think anyone had even seen him. Somebody had, for sure. He could not believe they had run and tattled on him even then. Throughout the grilling, the boy could not develop a pinch of remorse for breaking all the playground rules. He did not tell them he had ventured into Mrs. Wilson's car for the lighter. That would have just been dumb. He still felt justified in trying the cigarette for the experience. That is what it was, an adventure. Some adventures have consequences, and this one did. Harry picked him up, took him home, and used his belt on him. That hurt like holy hell. The boy felt excruciating pain that multiplied upon each whack, eight of them. Yes, he cried; anybody would. Still OK with what he had done, the question was: What would be his next adventure?

From then on until the end of the school year, Harry picked him up at lunchtime, and they drove to the house. Dad would fix split pea soup or some other kind of exotic soup (any other than traditional Campbell's tomato soup,) and the two would eat lunch together. The boy regretted the inconvenience for his father. At the same time, he enjoyed learning to like weird soups.

Sixth grade played out like a yearlong nightmare. According to school administration recommendations, the sixth-grade class count at Grand Prairie Elementary School expanded by three students from out of town: too many students per split classroom. To solve the problem, all the sixth graders from Grand Prairie had to attend Indian Prairie Elementary School, about three miles from the boy's house.

The boy knew several of the boys and girls in his new classroom at Indian Prairie from attending the Westwood

Methodist Church. He also knew all the boys from his fifth-grade class, but they had been split between two sixth-grade classrooms. If he had stayed at Grand Prairie, his teacher would have been Mrs. Wilson again. As it was, he sat in a classroom at Indian Prairie dedicated to sixth graders and a teacher named Mrs. Lazenby. Once the cold weather descended on Kalamazoo, it became impractical for the boy to ride his bike, so Harry had to drop him off early in the morning on his way to work.

Mrs. Lazenby may have modeled for the "Old Maid" in the "Old Maid" card game deck. She had a perpetually straight back (must be a stick in there someplace) dripped stifling lavender perfume; her hair permed and short, never a tight curl out of place. She displayed her worst trait when using a lace handkerchief to noisily honk her nose several times daily. Then Mrs. Lazenby would take the snot rag in her right hand, stuff it up her left sleeve at the wrist, and leave it there. The boy decided she must be so old she did not know about Kleenex. The boy clashed with Mrs. Lazenby; the generation gap is too extreme.

Classwork bored the boy, a real letdown from the new math of fifth grade. Called out by Mrs. Lazenby for not paying attention, raising her voice, Mrs. Lazenby yanked out the handkerchief from her sleeve, blew her nose, and tucked the snot rag back up her sleeve. The boy used his newly acquired acting skills to demonstrate to the other guys an imitation of their teacher, dramatically stuffing a make-believe handkerchief up his sleeve. When the first report cards were sent home, the boy received average grades and minus marks on his attitudes and behavior.

Safety Patrol presumably taught the sixth graders in the school responsibility. The class elected a Captain and a Lieutenant, and Mrs. Lazenby passed out white safety belts to selected sixth graders to wear. Everyone in the class would have a turn. Safeties left the classroom eight minutes early at lunchtime and at the end of the school day to put on their safety belts, taking up their position at street intersection corners to prevent the younger kids from unsafely crossing the road. Some kids could not wait to wear the white belts and hold the more youthful kids back with outstretched arms. Some vied for being elected Captain and Lieutenant.

The boy waited for his turn to be a safety for only two reasons. First, he would get out of Mrs. Lazenby's classroom eight minutes early at lunchtime and eight minutes early at the end of the school day. Second, anyone who performed their safety patrol duty received a commendation certificate. The document could be used as a ticket to the Harlem Globetrotters basketball game when they came to Kalamazoo and played at Western Michigan University's field house. The boy waited over half the year for his crossroad assignment in the sixth-grade rotation.

The boy received his white safety patrol belt to wash and wear at the corner of Seminole and Pontiac. He could now earn his commendation. He could not wait. The Harlem Globetrotters would be coming to town soon. The boy had ogled the Globetrotters on TV. They wore red and white striped gym shorts and a blue tank top, running rings around the opposing team.

The team's star, Meadowlark Lemon, could make baskets from the foul line facing away from the basket without looking. He could trick his opponent by stuffing the basketball up the back of his shirt. When the other players glanced away, Meadowlark let it drop out. He would turn and, in one motion, make an easy layup. Hilarious. Everyone on the Globetrotters team had fantastic basketball skills. The Globetrotters had all colored members, and the players on the other team had all white players who wore white uniforms. According to the announcer on T.V., the white team lost every game. The Globetrotters inspired the boy to learn and practice basketball. Someday, maybe he could be half as good as a Globetrotter.

The day the boy would begin as a Safety, it poured down rain at lunchtime, so the whole school held recess in the gym. The boy shot baskets and played a little dodgeball with his friends. Near the end of the after-lunch free time, the boy kicked one of the red rubber balls high. Amid the chaos in the gym, he hoped to see if the ball could reach the ceiling. While swinging his leg in a big kick, the lunch supervisor blew the whistle. Everyone stopped what they were doing at the shrill piercing noise.

The boy could not stop the kick, his foot connecting with the ball an instant after the whistle blew. In unison, the eighty kids and teachers in the gym witnessed the ten-inch red ball flying high up to the ceiling, banging the metal cage protecting one of the lights fastened to the gym's peak.

Silence reigned in the gym as the supervisor called the boy over and instructed him to go to the principal's office. He tried to explain to the gym monitor that he could not stop his kick. At the office, he attempted again to explain to the principal that he did not mean to continue after the whistle. He did not mean to do it. The lunch supervisor told the principal the boy would no longer be welcome in her lunchtime program. The principal complied with the lunch supervisor's request and banned the boy from the school lunchroom.

Things went from bad to worse when the boy returned to Mrs. Lazenby's classroom. The lunch supervisor called Mrs. Lazenby out to the hall, and the boy sensed additional trouble, despite the laughter of the rest of the class at the boy's ultimate bravado in kicking the ball.

Before the end of the day, Mrs. Lazenby called the boy up to her desk.

"I've warned you before about behavior that reflects badly on your classmates. It would be best if you thought long and hard. You are in trouble, young man, and I will not tolerate such behavior. You will not be getting a ticket to the Harlem Globetrotters game. Go and sit down."

The boy turned away, too flabbergasted to speak. Sweat chilled his forehead, and his hands went cold. He unclenched his fists, a wry smirk relaxing the tenseness on his face. He turned back to the class and walked casually back to his desk. He would not let his friends see his extreme disappointment, and he made damn sure Mrs. Lazenby would not see how much she had gotten to him. That evening he approached his father with the letter from the principal explaining his suspension from lunch. The boy described the whole episode in honest detail. Yes, he had kicked the ball, which ricocheted up in the ceiling after the whistle, but he did not go beyond the whistle on purpose. Other boys kicked balls just like him. The boy choked out sorrow at getting kicked out of the lunch program. He did not mean to cause more work for his father, who would need to pick him up for lunch and return him to school for the rest of the year, just like in fifth grade.

Harry believed the earnestness of the boy's explanation.

"Looks like it's soup and sandwiches again, starting tomorrow. We'll be OK, I guess."

The boy swallowed and continued, "The worst part is that Mrs. Lazenby won't let me go to the Harlem Globetrotters game next month over this. I did not mean to make it hard on you, Dad. I do not see what I did deserves banning me from that game."

Basketball meant a lot to the boy. Harry knew just how much. Harry had played pickup games on Iwo Jima.

"It does seem a bit strange. Do you want me to speak to Mrs. Lazenby?" he asked.

"No, Dad, I don't. But I think I have no reason to be a Safety now. Is it OK if I do not? It always seemed silly to me. No cars travel by the corner I've been assigned."

"It's OK with me," said Harry, "Just stay out of trouble with Mrs. Lazenby."

"I'll try, Dad, but that's hard too. I do not like her, and she sure as heck doesn't like me."

Harry smiled, "Like her or not, she's the teacher. You will have good teachers, and you will have bad teachers. That is the way the world works. Do the best you can."

Just before the beginning of class the following day, the boy walked up to Mrs. Lazenby's desk without calling attention to himself and laid down the white safety belt in front of her.

"I do not want to be a Safety. Here's the belt."

He returned to his seat before what had occurred even registered with Mrs. Lazenby. She did not say a word.

Dad dropped the boy at school every morning once the cold weather hit, and for a time, the boy just sat in the hall reading a library book for a half hour before the other kids started showing up. The gym teacher asked if he wanted to help her in the gym. They put up the aluminum volleyball poles and strung the net, repeating the process for a second court. When the gym teacher saw the boy sitting in the hall a second day, he agreed to help her again.

"Say, how about we give this job over to you to do every day? It looks like you can manage the poles and nets."

The boy eagerly agreed, "That would be fine. I would like that. Can I shoot baskets when I get done?"

"Certainly, the gym teacher said, "Just take off your shoes and put away the basketball when the first bell rings. Do not let anyone else in the gym. This is your job; no one else can be in the gym."

The boy had the gym all to himself for the rest of the winter mornings. He measured slightly shorter than most boys in the class, yet he ran a quick fifty-yard dash. Basketball guards could be small if they were fast. He concentrated on his dribbling, foul shots, layups, and outside set shots. He loved it. He went to class sweating from running up and down the court practicing layups.

Bob Prader and the boy joined the Westwood Methodist church team and played against other church teams at the YMCA. The team practiced once a week, and the two fathers that coached divided the boys into two scrimmage teams, with one of the fathers on each team. The two men impressed the boy with how fast they could move up and down the court for being old. He had never seen his father run, although Harry did have an enormous, rapid stride.

Three weeks later, during a pea soup lunch, a week before the Globetrotters game, Harry slapped the kitchen table with two tickets to the game. The boy read the tickets and beamed. Good seats, away from the school kids. Dad came through again.

Just about every evening after dinner, with the dishes done, the boy wandered down into the basement. The makeshift ping pong table, made from a four-foot by eight-foot piece of plywood purchased at the lumber yard, took up most of the space between the stairs and one of the block walls. A net purchased at the sporting goods store stretched across the middle of the table. The plywood rested on the family's old dining room table from the farm. Sarah had bought a new dining table, four chairs, and a bench to match the rest of the new furniture in the living room. The boy picked up a ping-pong paddle. He found a ping pong ball that had rolled beneath the table. As he held the paddle out horizontally in front of him, the ball bounced a foot in the air. While the ball arced in the air, the boy twisted his wrist, turning the paddle over, and the ball bounced on the opposite side of the paddle. The boy repeated this pattern for several minutes without the ball hitting the ground. This self-prescribed exercise increased his dexterity in using the paddle. The sound of the ball rapidly hitting the paddle enticed Robert down to the basement to play ping pong. Out of the four boys in the family, the boy and Robert gravitated to the table and the game.

Stephen, just a bit young still to handle the paddle, had other interests. Edward, not on his life. Mom had told the boy one day that Edward had been born with a cleft palate and lip. Several operations had diminished the effect below Edward's nose, and the boy never noticed it until Mom discussed it.

The boy had never witnessed Edward playing any physical game or sport. Edward the artist, pure and simple. He no longer had to paint and draw in the cold barn. Instead, Edward and his art occupied space next to the toy closet under the basement stairs. Harry had made Edward a "makeshift" drafting table. He attached a thirty-inch by thirty-six-inch store-bought drawing board to a plywood and one-by-two-inch maple frame. The surface could be tilted, raised, and lowered. Edward always sat at that board, drawing hands, feet, ears, and eyes. Drawing women. Drawing landscapes. Sometimes he cut out and painted miniature dress designs he had created and hung them on women models he had drawn in detail and cutout. Anything to do with art, Edward became accomplished in any media or sculpture material. Edward worked on his projects in summer or winter, spring or fall, his complexion pasty white from never seeing the sun. The boy called Edward's desk his "Hermit Hole." Asking Edward to play ping-pong would be unthinkable. The boy wondered if Edward even knew how to hold the paddle.

Robert came down the basement stairs, crossed to the other side of the table, picked up a paddle, found another ball, and served. The boy had learned the game from playing hours and hours with Robert. They each had their individual style. Robert, an offensive powerhouse, had a wicked slam, and if the boy had a chance at a return, he had better place the ball on the opposite corner. Robert's proficiency at forehand and backhand slams made for uneven scores in the early years of the boy's ping-pong experience. The boy, on the other hand, played defense almost exclusively. He had to since Robert slammed nearly every play.

The boy lost every game the two played, but slowly, he improved his score into the teens to Robert's winning twenty-one. He did not care. As long as Robert would play, the boy wanted to be right there, losing. Sometimes, the boy would surprise his oldest brother and return a slam. Another slam usually finished the boy off. Someday, the boy's quickness and advancing technique would turn the tables on his brother. Playing ping pong provided hours of fun.

Despite the boy's efforts to stay below the radar in Mrs. Lazenby's classroom, she still found a way to deride his lack of enthusiasm. He consistently received the comment, *not working up to his potential* on his report cards.

Bob Prader and the boy somehow ended up on the wrong side of Mrs. Lazenby's day. Her mockery of the boy came in the form of comments directed at Bob, even though Bob might be just as likely to be the culprit and instigator of trouble as the boy.

"I do not understand, Bob, why you are friends with this boy, and you, Mr., are going to end up in an alley with a switchblade in your back. Class, you mark my words."

The boy marked and vowed to himself never to forget those words.

On the first day of Hillside school in September, the boy walked three miles from the Sage Street house. On a windy, warm fall day, the modest homes on the quiet west side neighborhoods helped block the worst gusts.

Dressed in brand new crisp jeans, a brightly colored pullover, a t-shirt, and new white Converse gym shoes, the boy carried his old pair of Converse gym shoes, the laces tied together, strung over his shoulder for the gym. He also brought a new blue cloth notebook with three rings and tagged dividers for each class.

The glossy smooth, expansive hallways in the school showed no scuff marks. While the boy walked in relative silence due to his gym shoes, the overall effect of hundreds of students clattering to their homerooms deafened and excited everyone. Multiple wings and corridors lead to classrooms off a central thoroughfare stemming from the cafeteria and the front entrance to the school. The administration wing housed the principal, vice principal, and secretaries' offices to the left of the front doors. Next to the cafeteria, along one whole side, a hallway open to the cafe contained six new ping-pong tables permanently set up for use during the lunch hour. The diner included a stage. South of the administrative offices, a section of the school contained the art and music rooms, weight room, gymnasium, shop, and home economics studios.

Bob Prader and Steve Holland leaned against the row of lockers as the boy approached. All three friends headed to the same homeroom. The first bell rang, and everyone filtered into their respective homerooms. Homerooms assign lockers, review school rules, discuss absentee procedures, fire, and tornado procedures, and review upcoming school events such as the school dance and

Halloween party. Too much information to fit into the ten minutes allowed for homeroom before the first bell rang.

The rest of the first day of school is universal; textbook lists are handed out, the first three chapters are assigned, supplies needed are noted, bathroom procedures are gone over, and some short writing assignments or math table reviews fill the hours. You cannot beat the first day of school.

The gym period occurred right before lunch. A fifteen-foot partition closed off half of the gymnasium; boys on one side, girls on the other. The boys' gym teacher, Mr. Rousseau, was four inches taller than the boy's father, who stood six feet one. The coach had long legs and bounced a basketball while reviewing the procedures. When he blew his whistle eight minutes after the bell, he expected students to be in their gym outfits (red shorts and white t-shirt with the Hillside logo) and ready for the day's activities. Before explaining the lesson for the day, the coach pointed to a paddle hanging in his office, a deterrent for inappropriate behavior or delinquency. He required all students to shower at the whistle near the end of class; the paddle was referenced again. A half-size gym locker stored the gym outfit and a towel brought from home for drying off. The gym outfit and towel must be taken home on Friday, washed, and returned to school each Monday.

After lunch, the boy lined up on one of the ping-pong tables. Seventh, eighth, and ninth graders surrounded all the tables. Two players volleyed, vying to win two points. The loser of the mini-match put the paddle down and went to the end of the line to the right. The winner stayed at the table and played the next person in line at the left side of the table.

Used to playing his twelfth-grade brother, the boy spent the first few weeks picking out the best players and ensuring he lined up at their tables. The other students were no match for the boy. Only one player came close to the boy's skill level. John Gordon, a likable seventh-grade athlete perhaps two inches taller than the boy, could slam consistently. He did so with a controlled sweep of his arm, maybe even more adept at attacking the ball than Robert at home. The two seventh graders remained evenly matched. The boy could anticipate where the slam would land and shift to that side of the table, stepping back and tapping the ball to the player on the opposite end. Gordon slammed, and the boy returned the ball, shifting on the balls of his feet, sometimes up to eight feet away from the table's edge. This drew looks from players around the other tables. The boy loved the challenge of returning a slam, and his ability improved throughout the school year.

At Gym time each day, the boy ran/walked (running in the halls meant suspension) to the locker room, dressed, and grabbed a basketball, shooting layups until Coach blew his whistle. The boy could practice for three minutes before each class.

Hillside School supported two basketball teams that played the other five Junior highs in the city and junior highs in neighboring school districts. The tryout-based, eighth-grade, and ninth-grade basketball teams had fancy polyester shorts and reversible jerseys. The boy practiced during school to prepare for next year's tryouts.

Dick Grilles approached Bob Prader and the boy to play for his church's basketball team, a Baptist offshoot on the north side. The team practiced in a rickety gym connected to the church. Two negros played on the team, and with the boy and Bob added to the team, they won most of their games downtown in the YMCA church league. The games were a lot of fun, but the boys had to attend Sunday School the Sunday before the game to play. The Sunday School teacher, actually, kept track. Sunday school seemed more severe than the Methodist church Bob and the boy usually attended. For a chance to play on a good team, both boys suffered in silence through the Sunday School lesson.

Church, in general, had fallen out of favor with the boy. Most Sundays the year before, he had been one of the acolytes at Westwood Methodist church on Nichols Street. The boy performed the duties of an acolyte, lighting the candles on the candelabras at the beginning of the service, helping to gather the collection plates, sitting behind the pulpit, and snuffing out the

[45]

candles as the Minister exited the sanctuary. Two acolytes performed these duties on their respective halves of the church. Boring, boring, boring, and the boy had to wear a short white pullover blouse with puffy sleeves. Horrifying. It was, however, less tedious than sitting with his parents and siblings through the entire service. At least as an acolyte, he moved around during the service a little.

As an acolyte, the boy sat next to one of the two tall windows in the front of the church. The cars outside zipped by. Birds or the occasional dog from the neighborhood wandered by. He checked the neighboring houses for cat burglars or Sunday kidnappers.

While the boy's mind wandered on a sunny Sunday in April, he considered the hypocritical nature of religion. He imagined a colossal crash happening out the window. What did it matter that he sat in church? The people in the collision would be dead. Nothing he could do about that. Fate, chance, God's purpose? That last did not seem logical. Would God prevent the accident? The boy knew that God did not act like that; otherwise, there should be no accidents.

Right then and there, sitting in church, the boy concluded that he did not believe in religion or church.

Heaven arrived in the form of seventh grade. Compared to Mrs. Lazenby's sixth-grade class, all his teachers were courteous, and most knew their subject matter. Miss Manis, the Math teacher, had the added attribute of being attractive; extremely attractive. She wore tight-fitting pencil skirts and heels daily; the material of her blouse was so thin every curly etching in her lacy bra showed through. In the boy's opinion, Miss Manis wore too much lipstick. Among the boy's friends, she became the subject of wet dream discussions. Always upbeat, Miss Manis seemed oblivious to the eyes that feasted on her.

Everyone said Mr. Scranton was an excellent social studies teacher. Unfortunately, the boy had him for the fifth-hour science class. In the middle of the second marking period, Mr. Scranton assigned the chapters dealing with the solar system. Space fascinated the boy. He dreamed of reaching the stars like Adam Strange in his comic books. Mr. Scranton explained the elliptical paths of the planets around the sun.

"The earth tilts on its access to this position on June twenty-first. On December twenty-first, the earth has tilted back the other way, so at that point, the sun is farther away from the northern hemisphere and Michigan," said Mr. Scanton, pointing to a full-color chart on the front wall.

The boy, hand raised and called on, said, "Mr. Scranton are you saying the earth tilts back and forth on its axis."

"Yes," said the teacher, "that's how and why we have the different seasons. Look in your book on page two hundred fifteen. You can see in the illustration the relationship of the sun and earth in summer. On the next page is the illustration of the relationship between the sun and earth in the winter. You'll note that the angle has flipped or tilted slowly to the winter position during the year."

The boy, startled, could not help himself, "I just have to say that must be wrong, Mr. Scranton. The earth doesn't tilt back and forth on its axis."

"Young man, I've been teaching science for eight years. The book shows it plain as day tilting back and forth."

"I'm pretty sure the earth's axis doesn't move like that."

The boy bit his tongue and allowed the teacher to move on.

During the third week of school, as the boy headed to Math class, three ninth-grade boys approached him, one of which went out of his way to stumble into the boy and push him hard. The boy did not lose his balance and stood defiantly as the pusher walked up close again.

"Listen, squirt," said Pusher, "when you see us coming, you get way out of our way. Do you understand that? What do you say, guys?"

As the pusher turned his head to watch the other two boys nod in agreement, the boy took a step closer, swung, and caught the pusher right under his chin, sending him into the arms of his companions. The pusher recovered and tore into the boy. They were at close quarters and wrestling more than slugging. The boy struggled, losing badly against the bigger, more muscular boy until Mr. Roth, another social studies teacher, pulled them apart. The bell rang simultaneously, and the three boys ran down the hall. Mr. Roth still had a hold of the boy.

"I know who you are. You are Edward's younger brother, am I right?"

The boy nodded.

"Edward never got in trouble in the three years he attended Hillside," said Mr. Roth, "Edward became the student council president last year and a credit to your family. Here you are, getting into trouble. You had better start minding your p's and q's. Now straighten up and get to class."

In the six-hundred-student school, talk of the fight spread. The seventh-grade class heard the details from Sharon Stinson, a seventh-grade girl in the boy's homeroom who had been passing by and witnessed the battle from the initial push. The boy had been lucky to get that first punch in; otherwise, the fight had been one-sided in the pusher's favor. To the boy's amazement, they ignored him whenever he saw the three boys in the hallway after the fight, even if he walked shoulder-to-shoulder with them in either direction. They never bothered him again; no eighth or ninth-grader did.

Many of the same seventh graders were in all his classes. Mom explained that Kalamazoo schools practiced tracking, grouping kids in the same category according to their standardized test scores. That way, the brighter kids would not be held up in the learning process by the average and below-average students. The boy was in the more challenging classes based on his sixth-grade performance. He must have done well on the tests because his grades had been far from great.

There were well-off kids in his class. Charlie Tolliver's father had been a US congressman, and his family owned one hundred acres in the heart of Kalamazoo. Their property backed up to Sage Street by the boy's house. Others in the group the boy hung around were not as rich as Charlie, but they did not seem to lack anything. His friends all purchased lunch instead of packing lunch as he did. He still made two bologna sandwiches for lunch, but he had difficulty trading up for an authentic mom-made sandwich.

Bob pulled him aside one day.

"Hey, when are you going to get some pants? You'd think you were living on a farm or something."

The boy, taken aback, had never even noticed what the other kids wore. The five children in the family were called awake by Harry every morning, and each got dressed on their own in a hand-me-down from an older sibling. Stephen, Edward, Laura, and the boy shared the bedroom upstairs, while Robert occupied the smaller west bedroom, allowing him to study long into the night at his desk in the alcove. Robert, a "National Merit Scholar," had been offered a scholarship to attend Michigan State University in the fall. He excelled in science and math, besides being a great ping-pong player. The boy wore jeans, a shirt, and shoes each morning as he had done since kindergarten.

That day, when he scanned the room, all the boys in the class had on creased pants except him. They all wore button-down collared shirts. They were not wearing gym shoes but shiny loafers instead.

The minute his mother walked through the door after her school meeting, the boy cornered her, asking for something new to wear at school. Explaining that he had been called out for wearing farmer clothes. The following Saturday afternoon, Sarah returned from grocery shopping and handed the boy a shopping bag.

"I found you a pair of pants on sale and two shirts. We will see what the Thom McCan store has for shoes for you tomorrow after church. Try the pants on, and we'll see how you look."

The boy calmly walked the bag upstairs to his bedroom to try on the new clothes. After all, Lynda Silks had a birthday coming up, and he had heard he would need to ask a girl for a date to the party at her cottage on the lake.

He opened the bag and pulled out the outfit Sarah had purchased on sale. The pants were a burgundy color. Purple. The boy sat on the bed holding the creased new purple pants in his lap. How could she pick purple? Crazy! Why not navy, or khaki, or black. Where did Mom even find purple pants? The plaid shirt with purple pinstripes running through the weave did not match the pants. In fact, the shirt and the pants clashed.

What to do? Maybe they would not fit. He tried them on. They fit. Great, except they were purple, bright purple. He knew what would happen if he went downstairs and told his mother he had hoped for a dark navy-blue pair of pants. After all, Sarah had never made another sandwich for him after the slight criticism he had offered over her lunch preparations. Besides, the pants had been on sale, non-returnable. He put on the shirt and the purple pants and descended the stairs to show his mother. As he suspected, Sarah beamed with satisfaction at the beautiful ensemble. The boy masked his cringe.

"I'm probably going to need at least one more pair of pants, I think, for when this pair is in the wash. Maybe we can look for a second pair when we try on shoes tomorrow."

"I suppose that would be a good idea," Sarah said, "You look very handsome indeed, son of mine."

No classmate said anything for or against the boy's purple outfit. At the end of the week, he had decided to ask Sharon Stenson to the party. He wanted to ask Lynda Silks, a petite Greek goddess. Lynda had long black hair, a cute figure, and sophistication. Ann Clemens, perhaps Lynda's best friend, kept her nose up in the air, both girls out of reach to the boy. A bit plainer but more voluptuous, the boy deemed Sharon Stenson approachable. He asked, and Sharon said yes.

The boy, ecstatic that evening after dinner, mentioned the arrangement to his parents.

"Oh no, you are not, young man," Harry said, "You are way too young for a boy/girl date."

The boy had not anticipated an objection, certainly not an outright veto.

"But Dad, it's too late," he said, "I've already asked Sharon Stenson to the party. The boys are supposed to go with a girl to the party."

"You are welcome to go to the party, but you will not be taking a girl," Harry said, adamant.

The boy tried again.

"I don't see what the big deal is. It's just a birthday party."

"The answer is no. Tell the girl."

The boy agonized over his quandary all night. Ultimately, he did not know what he would do at a party with a girl. He spent the whole time at the school dances playing ping-pong or basketball or watching movies in the music room. He never went into the cafeteria to dance.

At school, he approached Sharon to withdraw his invitation to the party.

"I can't take you to the party next Friday," the boy said, "I told my Dad, and he said no. No way. I am sorry, Sharon; I wanted to go with you."

Sharon smiled, sympathetic. "That's Ok. I understand. It's not your fault."

"No, it is not. I wanted to take you. I'm sorry."

No bridges burned. Maybe the boy would see if his father thought him old enough next year. Bob Prader asked Sharon Stenson to the party the next day. The boy decided to go to the party. Dad dropped him off the following Friday at Lynda's cottage on Fisher Lake, ten miles west of Kalamazoo.

The boy/girl pairings were evident walking into the cottage from the porch. Some couples were sitting awfully close to each other. In other cases, the boys had their arms around their girl's waist or shoulders. Surprisingly, out of the fourteen people at the party, only the boy and Charley Tolliver did not have girl dates. The dancing started, and Lynda stacked slow dance forty-fives on the RCA portable record player. Lynda's parents were nowhere to be found.

The group sat on the rug for "Spin the Bottle," a kissing game that mystified the boy. He and Charley hung back outside the circle to watch and learn. The game could not be more straightforward. One person spun the bottle on the floor. Whoever it pointed at when it stopped spinning, if they were of the opposite sex, the spinner had to go over and kiss them, generally on the cheek. If the bottle stopped on someone of the same sex as the spinner, the bottle passed to the next person in the circle for another spin. If the bottle stopped spinning, pointing to that person's date, they would lead their date into the closet, emerging a couple of minutes later, flushed and smiling. After everyone chanced on a turn in the closet, the couples resumed slow dancing.

The boy wished he had not come. Seeing Bob Prader lead Sharon Stenson into the closet devastated the boy. That would have been, should have been him. He had no idea what he would have done in the closet, but the boy knew he missed a fantastic adventure. The boy stepped out on the porch during the Leslie Gore song, "It's My Party," lamenting his fate. After the party, boys carried the girl's books from class to class. The boy decided that meant "going steady."

The boy did acquire two more pairs of pants. With his Mom teaching, getting home late from meetings, and having to grade papers until all hours, one of the boys fixed a simple meal for the family during the week. Each of the boys also managed their own washing and ironing of clothes.

The boy learned to use the mangle in the basement to crease and iron his pants and the sleeves of his long sleeve shirts. By the end of seventh grade, he could iron a shirt perfectly in short order. He also vowed to get some job in the summer to pay for his own selection of clothes and barbershop haircuts. He would then be done with his father, who used cheap dull electric clippers that pinched his hair into an uneven mess.

Seventh grade offered just too many distractions. The boy's priorities were basketball, ping pong, gym class, Junior Civic Theater, girls, and homework, in that order. Concentrating on his studies could not hold his attention. His grades were not good, and he somehow found himself in trouble more than a few times in class.

[52]

The first few days of eighth grade shocked the boy. Except for homeroom, he shared none of his friends' classes besides the gym class. He elected to take shop as an elective that year. No future college-bound kids took shop. The biggest shock came in English class.

English is the boy's favorite subject, and reading is one of his favorite activities. He did not recognize anyone in the class. After two weeks, the boy realized he had been moved from the top track to the bottom. Had he been that much of a behavior problem in seventh grade? Had his test scores tumbled?

The boy made the most of it because of the simple classwork. Day after day, the students read a collection of short stories aloud from the textbook. The teacher began class by asking a student she would name to read a page or two of the stories. Then she would stop the reader and call on her next victim.

After eight days of other students reading, the teacher called upon the boy to begin reading. By that time, he had read the entire book. The book had some interesting stories, but it drove him crazy reading them at a snail's pace with the rest of the class, so he just read ahead. No other student in the class read close to grade level. It made no sense to the boy. Harry's adage haunted him, "You'll have good teachers, and you'll have bad teachers."

So, at his turn to read out loud for the class, the boy politely asked what page she wanted him to start on?

"We're on page forty-seven. You are to follow along with us, or the next time you will receive an "F" for your classroom participation for the day."

At the end of the fourth week, he finished a second book, laying the book the rest of the class worked on on his desk in case he needed to read it aloud. Then he spent his class time watching the squirrels outside the window wall in the back of the room. In two marking periods, he accumulated seventeen "F"s. He received a "D" for the first marking period in English and an "F" for the second marking period. He promised Dad he would bring up his grades for the rest of the year.

The boy felt lost at school, almost like in another dimension, the *Twilight Zone*. The school library offered some solace. He decided to start at the "A"s and work through the library one book at a time.

The first book on the shelf was *Flatland: A Romance of Many Dimensions* by Edwin Abbott. The book is about a two-dimensional world where the king existed as a straight line and different geometric shapes, like circles and squares, his obedient subjects. The only way one form could tell the differences between the various other structures was by the way light faded at the edge. A sphere from the three-dimensional universe entered the King's world. It mystified the residents because the globe appeared as a circle that could grow and shrink depending on what part of its circumference passed through the two-dimensional world. As he read the small book, he thought of Mrs. Wilson in fifth grade and her "New Math" workbook.

At night he read everything in the house and whatever he found at the public library during Mom and Dad's weekly trip. They would each bring home a stack of books, and Harry read five or six books a week. He had no TV addiction like Mom and the boy.

One book, *The Source,* by James Michener, modified the boy's religious views. The thousand-page book recounted the history and heritage of the Jewish people from the time of early cavemen to the present day. The boy decided he missed the heritage and pride acquired in passing down ancient and contemporary traditions. Harry did not help much in that regard.

"I think we are Polish, son. Our last name is short for Martenslowski or something from Poland. I really do not know. We're American."

"But what about your dad and grandfather? What about them?" said the boy.

Harry retrieved a small box from the bedroom. He handed the box to the boy, who found a ring inside.

"I do have a ring from one of my relatives. The brothers supposedly went to the California gold field during the rush and found only enough gold to fashion this ring. Maybe someday I will pass it on to you.

"My father died of pneumonia in Canada just before I turned five. I became sick as well. Then Nana and my sister, and I moved back to Chicago. My mom met my stepdad there and married him. I resented him at first, but I learned to appreciate him. I believe I met him at twelve or thirteen."

The boy examined the ring.

"That's cool, Dad. What's this inside the ring?"

"It says something about a Mason's Lodge. It's pretty hard to read."

"So, the relative that owned this ring belonged to the Masons; I can look that up. That is a heritage, like The Source. Thanks, Dad."

The boy read everything from science fiction to historical fiction to detective stories. He read Westerns by Zane Grey and all the Tarzan books by Edgar Rice Burroughs. He read purported non-fiction books about UFOs and every book about ping-pong technique he could find. He read most weeknights until one-thirty or two-thirty to suffer through half asleep the next day in school.

Basketball tryouts for the eighth-grade team were held the last week of October. The boy had played church ball all summer and spent September and October working on his shooting skills. His knees began to bother him in early October. He had started to gain some height. The eighth-grade team had won over fifty percent of their games the previous year. The coach had recruited three players from the seventh grade who would be experienced this year. John Gordon, Rick Johnson, and Paul Verhaegen would surely be shoe-ins for this year's eighth-grade team.

The boy could understand why his friend, John Gordon, played with the team as a seventh grader. A natural athlete, he dribbled like a gazelle on the court. He made baskets, a great shooter. The other two seventh graders that had played with the eighth-grade team were tall for their age. Rick Johnson galumphed down the court, an embarrassing ball handler, tall. The boy figured that Rick and Paul had been recruited for the team because of their size.

The boy had attended a high school basketball game the previous year. James Gordon, John Gordon's older brother, started the game at the forward position. James played smoothly and effortlessly like the boy's friend, another reason John Gordon had been given special treatment.

The first day of tryouts consisted only of conditioning exercises. The players were divided into two units. On the coach's whistle, the first unit sprinted from one end of the gymnasium to the other while the second unit lined up on the baseline. As soon as the first unit crossed the opposite baseline, the coach blew the whistle for the second unit to sprint. Sweat soaked through the boy's shirt by the end of the practice, and his knees hurt like hell.

The next day of tryouts replicated the first, except the hopeful players dribbled basketballs while sprinting. The less accomplished players lost their dribble, and the ball floundered in the middle of the court. The boy did not have any trouble with the dribbling exercises, but his knees began to swell halfway through practice, and by the end, he came in last in the wind sprints. He went home that afternoon and rested.

On the third day of practice, his knees swelled to the size of grapefruits within twenty minutes. Sweat poured from the boy as he attempted to win his unit's wind sprint. He did win twice, grimacing in pain, but after that, his knees would not bend; they were so swollen. He never said a word, even as he cried inside. He kept hobbling up and down the court for the rest of the practice. The boy felt a terrible emptiness in his stomach when Coach called him into his office. His shirt literally dripped sweat on the floor. Coach motioned the boy to a seat opposite his desk. The office and the desk were out of proportion with the size of Coach. He awkwardly folded his legs under the desk. Coach's oversized chair was the only thing in the room that fit the man.

"You have heart, son; I'll give you that. It is almost painful to watch you run. But my teams are known for fast-break basketball. In virtually every practice, half the time is spent on wind sprints and ball handling at a full-out run. You did well with your ball handling. Your shot shows good form.

"Let me put it this way. If your knees were up to the punishment, you might have had a shot at being part of the team. Take that to heart, but I cannot let you go on and risk real injury to yourself or the team, so as of today, you are cut from tryouts. Maybe next year."

The boy, crushed, looked down at his knees, understanding.

"Thanks, Coach, Maybe next year."

The boy could hardly swallow. His eyes reddened as he struggled to get out of the chair. Coach reached across the desk with his hand out, and the boy met it for a handshake, his palm dwarfed by the tall center's hand. Bob Prader and John Gordon gave the boy "tough luck" gestures as he dressed in his street clothes and left the building to await his ride home.

Two weeks later, Dad and the boy met with Dr. McFadden, who examined his swollen knees.

"It's called Osgood Schlatter's syndrome. Your body is growing, and your knees are struggling to keep up. Coupled with extreme physical workouts, the area around the knee swells. Take heart. This is not a permanent condition. You will grow out of it."

"What can I do to get well, Dr. McFadden?" the boy asked, "I love basketball."

"The treatment for this syndrome is patience, Harry. The boy should rest the knee when it swells and take it easy. The coach is correct. We do not want to do permanent damage by pushing the knees to the extreme. Rest those knees for now when they swell up."

The boy sighed, resigned. "When do you think I'll be done with this doctor?"

"Can't say for sure. Every case is different. Six months to a year, typically. It depends on how tall you grow."

So much for basketball; normal gym activities pained the boy's knees, but he handled it. Perhaps he could still play church ball. He kept working on his shot and layups.

The boy was invited to a hayride and games party just before Halloween. This time he approached Harry first. He had no expectations that his father would say yes, but he did. A year made the difference. Or did the boy look older and taller?

Regardless, the boy asked Carol Hempen to be his date, and she agreed. Carol, a petite, quiet girl, cute, had black hair that curved under her chin, just brushing into her neck. She appeared to be a couple of inches shorter than the boy. Carol wore conservative wool skirts and excelled as a top student. She did not seem to be pursued by the other boys. The boy could not understand why. She and the boy found space in the back of a station wagon with two other couples.

The hayride filled the boy with expectations. He dreamt ahead to carrying Carol's books at school, going steady. The hay felt scratchy, and a night chill made for huddling close to Carol without presuming kisses and embraces. The bouncing of the tractor-pulled wagon soon made the boy need to pee. He tried not to think about it. The tractor moved too fast for him to jump off, go into the bushes, and jump back on. What would Carol think? At the end of the hayride, everyone started loading back into the station wagons to travel to the game party.

The boy looked around desperately for a bathroom, but everyone hurried to the car, and the parking lot offered no facilities. The boy sat in the rear of the station wagon next to Carol. If the drive had been only a few minutes, the boy would have been fine, but the ride stretched longer and farther than the boy anticipated. He squirmed and wiggled. He thought hard about a bright summer day. Desperate, he could not even look at Carol. Should he say something? *Weren't they there or almost there?*

Then it happened. The boy's bladder let go, and he soaked his pants, smelling of concentrated piss evident to everyone in the car. He had to confess.

"Mrs. Cordell, can you drop me back at my house? I have had an accident back here. I need to go home."

No one laughed or said anything. The boy had never been so embarrassed. He still could not look at Carol. At least he no longer squirmed in agony.

Mrs. Cordell followed the boy's directions to his house. When he walked through the front door, Sarah asked about the party.

"I wet my pants!"

"Oh no," she said, "what a shame. Well, go on up and change."

The boy climbed three steps, turning back, "Can you tell them to go on without me, Mom?"

"No, go up and change; you'll feel better."

"Are you kidding, Mom? I cannot go back out there. Carol, I can't face her Mom!"

"You certainly can," Sarah said, "and you will. I'll tell them you'll be down in five minutes."

"I can't, Mom. It's too embarrassing."

"That's why you have to go back out there. No more talk. Get upstairs, go!"

The boy did clean up and changed his pants. He did get back in the station wagon with Carol. The station wagon continued on to the game party. Carol hardly said a word, and the boy became even more subdued. He thought his Mom had been right to make him get back into the car and finish the party. The boy did not want to be known as a coward, after all, and the experience could happen to anyone; humbling but not the end of the world. His friends never spoke of his nightmare unless he brought it up and laughed.

In November, the boy caught a bad cold and stayed home alone from school. In the den, Walter Cronkite interrupted the program on TV to announce that President Kennedy had been shot.

News and comments about the assassination ran on every channel for the rest of the day. The boy knew that Kennedy had been a young president. Known for his status as a World War II hero on some boat in the Pacific, Kennedy and Khrushchev had blustered back and forth over Cuba and missiles. Beyond the fact that the boy's parents had voted for Kennedy, the boy had no interest and turned off the TV to read his book.

When Mom returned from school, she rushed in and switched the TV on again, and within minutes she began crying and sobbing. The boy had never seen his mother cry before. Kennedy had been Sarah's beacon of hope. She spoke to the boy about the potential John F. Kennedy represented to America in Civil Rights, Viet Nam, and the economy. In the following weeks, the boy understood the momentous event more clearly. The assassination of the president of the United States was a step in the wrong direction for the country, perhaps even the world.

In February of 1964, a song played on the radio that caught the boy's ear. The boy believed "I Want to Hold Your Hand" by the Beatles was different than any music he had ever heard. He listened the rest of the morning to hear it replayed. The boy's quirky brother, Edward, spent Saturday mornings recording the top thirty singles on the billboard chart broadcast by WLS out of Chicago. Edward had purchased a high-quality reel-to-reel tape recorder. Edward did this religiously, every Saturday, every top 30 songs; cutting out the ads and the silly DJ jargon between the records; labeling and indexing each tape.

The Beatles, their hair, and their attitude infected the boy. One Beatles song after another became number one hits. The boy thought the Beatles had great voices that harmonized as if they had sung together since they were young. The songs they wrote were innovative right from the beginning. After sixth grade, the boy had given up the saxophone but became interested in guitar. Robert had a cheap acoustic guitar the boy began to plunk.

Near the end of the summer of sixty-four, the boy met up with Terry Timmerman and Mike Belkis in downtown Kalamazoo to shop for school clothes. The three were in a euphoric mood. Soon they would be ninth graders, big shots at Hillside. The former friends of the boy had remained with the high achievement track of seventh grade. After all, no National Merit Scholarship awaited the boy, unlike his two older brothers. Terry, Mike, and the boy were working class "brothers in apathy" with paper routes and lawn jobs instead of fat allowances. The fall outfits for guys involved peg-leg white jeans, white Jack Purcell canvas shoes, and V-neck sweaters. The boy had found some Jack Purcell knockoffs at the K-Mart store he could afford that would make do.

The boys visited a small department store in the Kalamazoo mall. After wandering around for ten minutes, the boy landed at the belt racks. He examined the selection and then tried on the one he liked. It was made of beige canvas, tan leather in the front, and a cloth-covered buckle. The boy looked everywhere on the belt for the price tag. All the different styles were at different prices. While Terry and Mike laughed and jostled in the aisle, the boy looked up from the belt rack and around for a sales clerk to ask about the price.

Mike shrugged, impatient, "Let's go. I have to start thinking about getting home."

"Yeah," Terry agreed, "let's go."

"I can't find the price," the boy said.

"You're wearing it," said Mike, "let's just go."

Terry again agreed, "Yeah, let's go."

The boy looked at his two friends, grinning and laughing, and he laughed as well. He looked around and did not see any salesman coming to his aid.

"Ok!" he said, "Let's go."

The second the three boys left the store, a man came out of nowhere after them and grabbed the boy by his jacket.

"All right, you are arrested for shoplifting; come with me. Now!"

"Listen, officer," the boy said, "I looked for a salesman to ask about the price, and no one came around. I can pay for the belt."

"Too late for that. You are under arrest; come with me. You two boys, go."

Mike and Terry shuffled off. In the office at the back of the store, the boy sat in a chair while the man called the police. The boy could not believe it. He had never stolen anything in his whole life, not even a piece of bubble gum.

The policeman arrived in about fifteen minutes. The man who had grabbed the boy handed a written description of the incident to the policeman who walked the boy to the police car. The policeman opened the back door of the police car and directed the boy to get in.

At the police station, the desk sergeant ordered the boy to sit while his parents were called. The boy's fingers felt ice cold, his hands numb, and his stomach burned with the knowledge he had screwed up. He kept thinking about the stupid belt he did not even like. *How could he have been so stupid*, showing off to his friends?

The desk sergeant escorted him into an inner office where Harry sat across from the police officer who had transported him to the station. The policeman offered the boy a seat next to his dad. The officer stood and looked down at the boy as he sat down.

"This incident will go on your juvenile record. This is your first offense, so we are releasing you into the custody of your father."

The boy sighed.

The police officer continued, "Give me the belt. Take this to heart and do not show up in this station again. You may go now."

Harry stood, embarrassed, not saying a word. He led the boy to their car, parked in the police station parking lot. He drove home in silence, never looking at the boy. The boy sat silent as well. He anticipated, with trepidation, belt swings across his backside when they arrived home.

No beating occurred. Harry went to his easy chair and buried himself behind the Kalamazoo Gazette. In the kitchen, Sarah made dinner. She ignored the boy as well. He went up to his room to lie down on his bed and tried to read his book. Robert came in from his room and pulled up a chair.

"What were you thinking!" Robert said, "Whatever were you thinking!"

The boy stated the obvious, tears forming, "I didn't think!"

"I've never seen Dad like this." Robert just kept shaking his head. "I don't think I've ever even seen him sad. What were you thinking! How could you do this to him."

The boy had no other explanation. "I just wasn't thinking!" crying, "It was stupid."

After several meaningless exchanges, Robert walked back over to his room. The boy continued to cry alone. Never in this world would he wish to disappoint his older brother in this way, let alone his father. His throat closed; hard to swallow. Robert meant the world to the boy and his dad even more. But the truth could not be disregarded. He had disappointed both of them. He had lost their respect. After a while, he stopped crying, realizing there was nothing for it. He would have to get on with his life.

Getting on with his life turned out to be complicated. Robert returned to Michigan State in the fall. Until leaving, he had checked on the boy and played a little ping-pong with him. Support in the family occasionally came from Robert.

On the other hand, Harry had not said twenty words to him since the incident. Father totally ignored the boy; shut him out from any discussions which involved the family if the boy stayed in the same room. The rest of his siblings must have noticed this cold shoulder. Harry finally had enough of the boy, wanted no more to do with him, and left him to sink or swim alone. The boy waited for a thawing between them month after month that did not occur.

The boy knew and abided by the new law of the household. Nine times out of ten, he took the city bus if he needed a ride, paying out of pocket. He made his own lunches and washed and ironed his clothes as always, but now everything but the food on the table and the bed where he slept was up to his own resources.

Even with different classes, school seemed the same as the year before. The gym class included a six-week weight training unit that kept the boy going. Basketball tryouts were out of the question because his knees were still problematic. Even the squats with weights caused knee pain. However, the boy rapidly added pounds to the bar for curls, deadlifts, and bench presses in the workouts.

This would be the last year he could be involved with Junior Civic Theater. He earned parts in each of the two plays the group offered. Play practice kept him downtown, Monday through Thursday for rehearsal, away from the house and his family. He took the city bus downtown after school, but Harry had to pick him up for a ride home in silence.

Harry and his son had been close the year before the belt incident. The boy had wanted to make a Tesla Coil for his fourth-year electrical project in 4-H. The boy had to wind a cardboard core with fine wire to build it. That part of the project alone took three hours at the shop in the back of the electrical supply house where Harry worked. The larger coil wire wound around a wooden core the boy built. The copper wire measured a quarter inch thick. Two antennas were constructed from thin copper tubes with metal bulbs soldered on top. The boy and Harry baked the smaller cylinder covered with shellac in the basement oven, stinking up the whole house and infusing any future turkey roasted in that oven with shellac. After the cores were assembled on a one-by-ten by thirty-inch maple base, Dad found old automotive parts to complete the assembly. When the lights were turned out, the sparks from the Tesla coil made fluorescent bulbs glow, and his sister's hair fly wild. The two-inch spark looked like captured lightning when anyone's finger approached one of the bulbs. All in all, a hell of a project.

The year before the belt, Harry had also asked the boy for advice on the design and layout of the sixteen by thirty-two foot in-ground swimming pool the family put in. The boy had suggested that the filter and heater could be out of sight under the corner. The pool contractor staked out the corners just beyond the Maple tree and the back porch; cut into the slope of the hill that allowed for the basement walkout. The boy had helped build a three-foot-high by forty-foot-long retaining wall along one side of the pool out of two-inch flagstone.

The year before the belt incident, the boy had asked his father to help him buy an electric guitar to replace Robert's cheap acoustic guitar he had been using to take lessons. The boy had checked it out in the window of the pawn shop downtown after school. The boy told Dad he had cash for half of the guitar and would pay Harry back with earnings from lawn mowing.

Harry and his son had entered the pawn shop and asked to look at the guitar in the window. The salesman brought it back to the rear of the store, where the boy fingered silent chords, checking the action of the strings. The salesman plugged the guitar into an amplifier, and the boy tested all the controls, tuning the guitar and playing a bit of *Pipeline*, one of the first songs he had learned. Excited, he could hardly put the guitar down. Harry looked over at the salesman.

"The tag says one hundred twenty dollars. We'll give you ninety for it."

"No, sorry," Salesman said, "the price is one hundred twenty."

"Well, the boy has ninety dollars to spend," said Harry, "What do you say?"

The boy leaned on the counter in agony. He knew between the two of them, they could fork over one hundred twenty; his dad said as much in the car ride.

"Well, the boy really seems to like it," Salesman said, "I guess I could go down to ninety on it."

"OK, great," said Harry, "ninety dollars with the case."

"Oh no, the case itself is twenty bucks. The original leather case is fur-lined, heavy-duty, and in perfect shape. No sir, I'm sorry."

"You're sure?" Harry said.

"I am sure. If you want the case, it will be one hundred ten plus tax."

Harry shrugged. "Ok, let's go, son."

The boy could not believe it. A new guitar of this quality would cost at least two hundred fifty dollars and the case another seventy-five. He gritted his teeth, acting the calm hero. He stood expressionless, on weak legs, putting the guitar back in its case and following his father toward the door. Inside he screamed. Dad opened the door, holding it for the boy. They were both halfway out the door.

The salesman hailed Harry. "Alright. I am losing money, but I hate to disappoint the boy. Ninety dollars out the door."

The boy took home a used gold-colored, solid-body Gibson Les Paul guitar.

Sarah offered some respite from the wall of silence by allowing the boy to join her folk-dance group. Sarah loved anything to do with performing arts. She had led the Van Buren County Folk Dancers when the family lived in Gobles. Using Robert and Edward and 4-H kids from Kalamazoo County, she had gathered a new group when the family moved to Kalamazoo, The Kalamazoo County International Folk Dancers. The boy could replace Robert, who had graduated from high school and departed for Lansing. Sarah bought all the records and worked out the dance moves from the diagrams that accompanied the folk music. About twelve kids danced with the group.

The group danced for various rest homes, variety shows, competitions, local TV stations, and fairs. The boy first danced in a one-night performance on the Ionia County Free Fair grandstand stage, about eighty miles from Kalamazoo. A fair official directed the group to a tent assigned for costume changes with a canvas partition hanging down the middle of the tent. Boys changed on one side, girls on the other. The sagging canvas partition dropped to about four feet in the tent's center. The boy kept a peripheral eye on the girl's side and received his first view of bras and petticoats.

The older high school girls were not giving a second thought to modesty as they changed. The boy could not believe his luck and sightings.

The boy partnered with Karen Radner, a striking redhead with light freckles a year older than the boy. Within a few months, the boy and Karen became fluid partners, anticipating wild polka spins and waltzing in broad circles around stages. The boy yearned to be more than a dance partner, but Karen stuck to the business of dancing. However, she never danced with anyone else.

Nothing in his last year at Hillside School motivated the boy beyond ping-pong, basketball, and girls. He found out that the girls accepted his invitations to dance at school parties in the cafeteria. After all, he could dance above and beyond the simple steps the other boys had to rely on, and the girls liked to dance with him. Folk dancing skills were quickly applied to slow and fast dances.

At the end of the summer, the boy attended MYF (Methodist Youth Fellowship) camp as a teen camper for four days at Crystal Springs Camp near Dowagiac, Michigan. According to his mom, he did not have much choice. Yes, it had been his favorite summer pastime when the Clement brothers and he contested who could make the most giant bubblegum bubble. His whole family attended, and his dad had been his cabin counselor.

The campgrounds, cabins, and buildings were familiar to the boy, having attended choir camp there seven years in a row. But without his family and friends, the place echoed the emptiness of his year estranged from his father. Two other boys looked in the same straits as the boy: attending camp rather than juvenile home. He fell in with them.

The camp activities were boring to the extreme. The campers, all teenagers and all ninth graders, wandered the camp during their free time a significant portion of the day. There were only a few circle sessions where the bible or social justice was discussed. He and his new acquaintances ensured they were on the other side of

JOHN GERTS

camp when those activities occurred and missed most of them. No one cared.

The only thrill during an incredibly dull few days came on the suggestion by one of the boys that the three of them sneak out of their cabins and meet in the middle of the night. Sure enough, when the boy heard the cabin counselor start to snore that night, he dressed, grabbed his shoes, slipped out, and walked to the camp store, the designated meeting spot. For a time, the boy stood alone in the dark of the night, the trees rustling wildly in the wind. About to head back to his cabin, the two boys appeared. Their counselor had taken forever to turn out his reading light and fall asleep.

The three boys wandered the camp for an hour, skirting the edges of the light of the buzzing halogen streetlamps hung on poles high overhead. They entered the rear of the enormous replica tabernacle featured at the camp. The stage at the front of the auditorium held one hundred-plus singing campers during each year's concert, closing out the week of choir camp. The sides of the tabernacle were open, and over eighteen hundred rickety old chairs were set up in rows sixty across.

With the wind roaring, the boys lost all their inhibitions, testing the echo. The structure had a thirty-foot-high ceiling made of wooden beams and spider web-filled rafters. When the noise did not elicit any movement from the cabins across the way, one of the boys grabbed one of the chairs, the back of which wobbled because the spokes had pulled out of the base, and slammed the chair against the rest of the row, splintering the broken chair as well as the chair next to it. The second boy laughed, wrenched another chair free of its tie-in to the row of chairs, and broke that one to pieces.

The noise from the smashing of the chairs was deadened by howling winds high in the old maple trees surrounding the tabernacle, forested cabins, and camp.

The boy felt somehow out of body, out of mind as he picked up a chair, raising it high over his head. He brought the chair down against the row, and it broke apart with a bone-jarring crash the boy felt all the way to his shoulders. He joined the others in the

[68]

smashing of the place where he had spent so many summers. The boys destroyed two and a half rows of chairs before throwing down the last spokes, exhausted from their efforts.

The boy surveyed his handiwork. The ancient Tabernacle must be nearly a hundred years old. The chairs were all gray and worn for lack of paint, essentially sitting outside in the weather for years. The Tabernacle itself seemed as old as the bible. The boy could not muster much guilt at putting the chairs out of their misery.

But it began to gnaw at him. *Why does he do such things?*

It began to sprinkle, and the boys agreed to call it a night. The boy wandered back to his cabin, crept in, and slipped into bed, exhausted and empty. He whispered to himself, *what was he thinking!*

There were no repercussions; the broken chairs were never mentioned. The boy went home in another day and a half. He did not go out foraging again while the camp slept. The other two boys mainly kept to themselves. He had forgotten their names.

Eighteen hundred students attended tenth, eleventh, and twelfth grade at Kalamazoo Central High School. There were over six hundred thirty students in the boy's class. He considered hiding in mediocrity within his classes a skill. While the advanced track kids were studying college algebra, the boy blended into the background in geometry class. The boy had an innate ability to understand geometric shape relationships. Anything to do with drawing shapes and comparing sides or angles was a breeze for him. He could do his geometry homework so fast that it wasn't drudgery. In study hall, he gave passing attention to his other assignments and rarely, if ever, took any homework home.

The second semester the boy signed up for driver's training. The training course consisted of a half-city block circular track, a few cars for practice, and spaces for parallel parking practice. The instructor, Mr. Bolton, also coached football. The course was four blocks from Kalamazoo Central and about eight city blocks from downtown.

On the second training day, the students were lined up, ready to get in the cars, when Mr. Bolton approached. He pointed right at the boy.

"I need you and Jane to take the first car into the dealer's; downtown. They'll give you a ride back."

The boy opened the car door and started to step in behind the wheel.

Turning back to the instructor, he said, "Mr. Bolton, this car is a stick shift. I just practiced yesterday with an automatic. I have never driven a manual transmission car before."

Mr. Bolton, smug in his disbelief, said, "Come on, don't give me that. You come from the farm, don't you, boy? Don't tell me you haven't been driving for years."

"That is what I am telling you, Mr. Bolton. I have never driven a car before yesterday, and I have never driven a stick shift before."

"If I believed that," said Mr. Bolton, "I'd buy swamp land in Florida. Now take the car downtown and be back here before class is over."

The boy caught on. He did not play football. He acted in plays. Mr. Bolton waited for the boy to cry and make a scene like a chicken wuss.

Instead, the boy shrugged, "Alright, Mr. Bolton, hop in, Jane."

He shut the car door and turned to Jane. "I've never done this before, so buckle up and hang on."

The boy stalled the car twice, letting the clutch out in front of all twenty-two kids. The vehicle jerked along to the stop sign at the gate entrance to the training lots. The boy stared straight ahead, forehead sweating, and jerked out into traffic. He had about four blocks to practice before being in mainstream downtown traffic. Jane white-knuckled the passenger armrest, but she smiled and encouraged the boy.

Downtown, heavy lunch traffic flowed around their car, a light blue Ford Fairlane labeled "Student Driver" on the side. The boy thought Mr. Bolton an idiot for putting him in an automobile in real traffic after one day of driver's training without a supervisor riding along in the shotgun seat. He had the clutch/gas/brake timing figured out halfway to downtown. He even turned and climbed a hill with a treacherous stop sign halfway up.

After pulling into the dealer's lot, Jane and the boy had to wait ten minutes for a ride back while the boy's armpits dried.

In May, the boy started scanning the want ads for summer employment. He found a notification asking boys his age to apply for camp counselor openings at YMCA Camp Aharah. The next afternoon the boy walked downtown from the high school, filled in an application at the YMCA, and walked home. The following week, a secretary at the YMCA scheduled him for an interview after school.

When he arrived for the meeting, Dave Thymes, the camp director, called him into a small office lined with bookshelves along the north wall. Piled in a corner opposite the books were various pieces of sporting equipment; bats, gloves, rolled-up badminton nets, a bin of basketballs, and three baseball bases. Furniture in the room consisted of three chairs pulled in from other offices. Mr. Thymes sat in the far chair and motioned the boy into another empty chair. As the boy entered the room, a second man, seated in the third chair, stood, smiled, and offered a hand for the boy to shake. Mr. Thymes introduced the man with a steel grip as Gene Duclair, the camp's assistant director.

Mr. Thymes had the manner of Santa Claus in a suit; soft, smiling, the camp's father figure. He looked to be under forty. Mr. Duclair looked like he had just descended from an eighty-foot-tall Sequoia or maybe a two-hundred-foot-tall high-voltage power pole. In either scenario, he would be wearing a worn leather tool belt. Mr. Duclair wore a short-sleeved dress shirt and slacks for the interview. His jet-black hair hung beyond his ears, combed back in a gentle wave. Curly black hair sprouted from the neck of his shirt. He looked ready as a stalking cat to finish a bar fight or to lift beers, whichever the occasion demanded. His shoulders were broad, his body narrowing to a tight, slim stomach. His smile was incredibly disarming. The boy thought the man might be anywhere between thirty-two and forty-seven. He wore a five o'clock shadow at the four o'clock meeting.

Mr. Thymes referred to the boy's application and paragraph on why he wanted to be a camp counselor. The boy answered his questions in an easy, confident manner. He had been an officer and president of the Westwood 4-H group, held down the same lawn mowing job for over a year, and participated in the Kalamazoo Junior Civic Theater for four years. He had attended a two-day leadership seminar at Camp Kett, a 4-H conference center, before gaining experience as a 4-H camp counselor for two weeks last summer. He professed to be exceptionally good at ping-pong and had played basketball on church teams for three years. The adults began addressing the needs of the camp and asking if they might match the boy's skill set.

The camp needed an archery instructor. The boy beamed and explained he had purchased a used, semi-recurved bow, read how-to books on archery technique, and considered himself a fair shot but did not hunt. He felt he could explain safety procedures and demonstrate the proper method to campers. He did not tell the men how he envied Errol Flynn in the movie *Robin Hood*, but he did describe the impossible task of hitting a chipmunk popping up from his hole with his bow and arrow.

Then Mr. Duclair asked the boy if he could describe how to build a campfire.

"First, I'd search for twigs and small sticks and build a little teepee," explained the boy, "next, I'd gather some larger sticks ready to put on the fire. Once they caught fire, I'd build the fire up with larger logs."

The boy did not hesitate and explained the steps until the fire stayed lit, demonstrating his confidence. He thought he described a respectable fire. Both men laughed and looked at each other.

"I think you would have a fire," said Mr. Duclair, "that's good. Of course, the forest might be burning down around you. That is not good. But you would have a fire.

"First, you want to clear a brush circle, anything that could catch fire, and dig a pit for your little teepee."

"Yes," the boy admitted, "that would be a good idea."

"How much canoeing have you done?" asked Mr. Duclair.

"Quite a bit on the lakes around here and at 4-H camp," the boy added.

"Any river canoeing?"

"No," admitted the boy.

The conversation dropped off while Mr. Thymes and Mr. Duclair looked at each other with some silent signal. Mr. Duclair nodded to Mr. Thymes.

Mr. Thymes explained the position.

"Gene needs an assistant for the second half of the summer. He leads the advanced campers on a wilderness canoe trip in Canada. He takes two trips each summer. Gene has an assistant for the first trip. We will need you to help on the second trip. You would be the archery instructor for the first part of the summer. What would you think of that arrangement?"

The boy tried to remain calm. Inwardly, his stomach flopped.

"I'd say it's incredible, Mr. Thymes. I would love to spend that much time at a shooting range. I know I could handle that part of the job. The canoe trip sounds amazing. I can only say that I can learn. I will give anything a try and work hard. I couldn't ask for a better opportunity, and I hope I get the job."

"You'd have one night off every two weeks," the camp director said, "you'd be signing two contracts, one as Archery Instructor and one as Assistant to the Canadian Bush Voyager Director. That is Gene here. The pay is fifty dollars every two weeks, plus room and board, of course."

The two men looked at each other again, and the boy caught a nod from Mr. Duclair.

"Alright," said Mr. Thymes, "if you stop down tomorrow afternoon, I'll have the contracts ready. We meet here at three o'clock on June 15th, and we'll give you a ride up to Camp Aharah in Walkerville, about two hours north of Kalamazoo."

Mr. Duclair handed the boy a list of necessities.

"You'll need a sleeping bag and your bow if you wish. Here is a list of clothing, tools, and supplies you may want to pick up. Good boots will be at the top of the list. Rain gear, your own mug, waterproof bag. The outfitters provide canoes, backpacks, and food at the Ranger Lake Lodge. Any questions?"

The boy looked over the list. "No," he said, 'thank you, I'll be there!"

The boy could not believe his good fortune. The canoe trip sounded like an adventure of a lifetime. He would be away from his family, on his own, and being paid besides.

On June fifteenth, the boy carried his suitcase and a waterproof bag filled with the items on Mr. Duclair's list over to the group of twenty counselors and the four station wagons and vans that would take the group up to Camp Aharah. He tried to engage Mr. Duclair to let him know his readiness and excitement for the job, but Mr. Duclair continued his conversation with two other boys, and if he had seen the boy, he did not indicate it.

The mountain man acted like a distant stranger to the boy.

On the evening of the first day on the new job, the evening before the counselor's canoe trip, the boy sat on the outskirts of the campfire while a counselor challenged Gene to wrestle. The counselor, Rod Tongan, a friend of Gene's, rumored to be a state competitor at the one hundred forty-five, one hundred fifty-pound weight class, crouched a short distance from the older man. Tongan stood a good six inches shorter than Gene, so when Tongan went for Gene's legs, Gene pushed Rod away by the shoulder or forehead. Both laughed, semiserious, but the boy knew Rod tried hard to beat their boss. In a moment of distraction, as he pushed Tongan away, Gene caught Tongan's wrist with one hand and spun him sideways. Then Gene took hold of that hand with his other hand, and suddenly Tongan knelt awkwardly in pain. Gene pinched Rod's hand with his thumb, pressing Rod's palm in a judo hold. Tongan cried; uncle and Gene let go, friendly fight over. Sitting next to the boy, Dale Garten leaned close to the boy's ear, "Special forces Korea. You do not mess with Gene."

The summer's experiences met the boy's expectations in every way. During the first half of the summer, he held court at the far end of the camp, watching campers shoot and teaching archery safety procedures. Because he had time between cabin groups, he became a marksman at fifty and seventy-five-foot target distances.

In July, the boy joined Gene Duclair and ten campers in the Bush Voyager camp on the other side of Lake Aharah. He learned and practiced portaging with a canoe and pack. The group ran a mile each morning before breakfast to get in shape. He went on a shakedown river trip from Bolton to Lake Michigan and camped on the Lake and in state forests.

Once in Canada, he learned how to navigate rapids, compassing his way along lakes, streams, rivers, and forests. He became adept at making freeze-dried campfire dinners and scrubbing pots and pans after each meal, putting up taught tents, and breaking camp.

Before leaving for Canada, Dave Thymes opened a cardboard box on the picnic table bench beside the van. Dave pulled out brand new dark green Stetsons with embroidered patches stitched to the front, handing them one at a time to Gene, who checked the size and handed them out to the campers, including the boy. The patch depicted a flaming campfire with the words *Bush Voyager* forming a crescent over the flame.

The hats needed breaking in. The boy hoped his hat would one day look like Gene's: clean yet comfortable. Wearing the ten-gallon hats beyond Texas should have been dorky, but as a Bush Voyager heading for the Canadian wilderness, it just felt right. Dave wished the Bush Voyagers a safe trip. Gene broke out in song:

Oh, we're the Bush Voyagers you hear so much about.
People stop and stare at us; don't ever count us out.
We are not a bit stuck up about the clever things we do.
Most everybody likes us, and we hope you like us too.

The Bush Voyagers shoved off from the shore on Ranger Lake, fifty miles northwest of Sault Ste. Marie, Michigan. The lake was more significant than all but two lakes in Michigan, the wind creating one-and-a-half-foot waves that rocked the canoes. For two hours, they paddled against that wind. The lodge looked as small as a doghouse when the boy looked back. No other cabins were visible on the shore. They had passed a couple of islands and were again in open water. Gene motioned to the group to gather for a moment. His canoe approached the port side of the boy's canoe, and he handed the boy the map.

"Which way now?" Gene asked.

The boy looked at the map and the shores and terrain surrounding the canoes. Forest to the left, forest to the right, and forest straight ahead. Maybe an island graced the horizon way to the left, or it could have been just a bay of the mainland. The only reference, the lodge, now a dot on the shore behind him. He studied the map.

What direction were they heading, northwest, north, or northeast? Who knew? The map showed that Ranger Lake formed a sort of triangle. One angle included the bay with the lodge. A second angle marked their return route off to the west on the map. The Voyagers wanted to take the bay at the third angle to the north. Which way? Should they go to the left of the island and then head north, or should they head for the shore on their right? At this point in open water, the lake looked like a round fishbowl with a coast all around them. He could not distinguish the angles ahead, only the bay and the lodge behind them.

The boy surmised the importance of the map test on Ranger Lake. He studied the map a half minute more, then pointed ahead a little to the right.

"That way, we head toward the right," said the boy.

He held out the map for Gene to take back. Gene ignored the gesture. Gene looked in the direction the boy indicated, smiled slyly, and began paddling. The boy, of course, had no idea if he guessed correctly or not. Gene gave no indication either way. If he were wrong, the boy would lead the group to "God knows where," hours out of their way. They may have to double back and head off on the other side of the island or peninsula or whatever the land to the left hid. The boy debated his decision, yet an hour and a half later, the bay started narrowing on both sides of the canoes. To the boy's stupendous delight, in another five minutes of paddling, he noticed a definite opening in the trees and a red mark on a tree overhanging the water; the first portage lay ahead. Gene's way, learn by doing, mistake or not. In his manner, Gene mirrored the boy's father. You must make your decision and live with it.

The canoe trip settled into a fantastic time of forests, lakes, rivers, and sky. The Voyagers transported their gear out of Ranger Lake in short portages through a series of lakes heading north, camping the first night on an island in Gong Lake. They made a freeze-dried beef and noodle dinner over the fire.

Everyone brought their porcelain or aluminum mugs to the rock table, and Gene spooned the dinner in each cup, one spoonful at a time. After the first round, Gene managed a second-half spoonful for each. The beef noodles were gone. The boy took a second helping of bug juice to fill up. Gene rationed some of the birdseed grain for breakfast into a pot to cook. Raisins were passed out to mix into the cereal. The group started out paddling north up the Aubinadong River, portaging through to more lakes and backwaters of the river. Lunch consisted of a hunk of bread topped with a generous spoonful of axle grease (two parts peanut butter, one part honey, one part strawberry jam: mixed.) The bread looked like it would last one more day. Then lunch would be the thick rye crisp wafer squares with axle grease spread on top. Another freeze-dried dinner left the boy hungry again the second night. There were no complaints. The boy supposed the food had been limited as part of the wilderness experiences. The boy hungered for lunch in the morning, an hour after breakfast.

The boy could not get enough of the emptiness of Canada. In the first two days, they did not see even a cabin, let alone people, other than their fellow Bush Voyagers. This, the boy thought, exemplified life as it should be. Canada was all rock. Rocks the size of islands with moss and lichen and trees growing out of crags. A breeze on an isle kept the mosquitos and the flies offshore.

In the morning, after Gene called "Wakey, Wakey," the boy and Gene jumped naked into the cold northern waters, scrambling out wet to soap up, then jumping in again to rinse. Each morning loon song echoed across the lakes. In the distance, moose grazed near shore or swam across their path, a calf struggling to keep up from behind. Paddling in the canoe caravan, the boy might break the silence of a lake with a string of songs. Songs from his choir camp days when Dad supervised the bus ride from Crystals Springs to the lake where the campers swam. The boy suspected Dad's songs were left over from his Army Air Force days. The campers soon learned the words and joined in.

"Just plant a little watermelon on my grave, let the
juice trickle through.
Just plant a little watermelon on my grave; that is all
I ask of you.
Well, I have had fried chicken, and its mighty, mighty
fine,
But what could be better than a watermelon rind,
So just plant a little watermelon on my grave. Let the
juice trickle through."

Lost in the paddle, paddle, paddle. The boy often told his bowman Mike to relax, and he would steer and paddle the canoe by himself. Mike might then take up his fishing rod, and they would troll along. If the group thought they had found a good fishing eddy, the boy would pull out his book, relax and read while the fishermen tried to catch bass or trout. No hurry, no hustle or bustle, just water and sky.

The days in Canada of sweat, paddle, portage, and more sweat, finally ended. Mid-morning, the campers would return to Rockway Lodge; Gene demanded that everyone wash and dry their muddy trip clothes. The Bush Voyagers kneeled or stood in a close group for a before picture, looking grim and tired. After a half day of scrubbing themselves and their outfits, the boy and some of the others changed to their backup clothes for an after-trip picture, all smiles and bright sunlight. With the wind at their backs, the canoes flew across Ranger Lake. The Lodge kitchen indicated dinner would be ready in an hour, so the Voyagers crowded into the sauna in their skivvies and let the dirt pore out. Once the sweat became unbearable, they ran out of the sauna along the dock and jumped into the fifty-five-degree Ranger Lake waters. Most of the group repeated the process several times before dressing for dinner.

The boy devoured the meat, potatoes and gravy, beans, green salad, milk, apple crisp, and ice cream dinner.

As they packed the Camp Aharah van, Mr. Eliot approached the boy.

"Maybe think about hiring on up here as a guide next year. Take canoe groups around. Be a guide on fishing trips, that sort of thing."

"I'll think on that, Mr. Eliot. Thanks!" said the boy.

Then Mr. Eliot turned to Gene.

"Our school bus needs to be taken to town for service. Could the boy drive it in for us? It must be dropped off at the Standard Station, about sixty miles. It is a five-speed manual on the floor."

"Sure, we can spare him," Gene said, "up to him, of course; what do you say?"

The boy thought *Great, another challenge.*

"I'd be glad to!" he said.

"Great," said Mr. Eliot, "I'll show you the controls and the gears."

Grinding into second out of the Rockway Lodge driveway, the boy realized he had done it again, probably way over his head driving the clunker into town safely without ending up in a ditch. Navigating the narrow road in the rusted yellow monstrosity became a dangerous chore. Once out of the valley, he drove into the foothills on the curvy gravel road. There was nothing for it, though, so he unwrapped a stick of gum to chomp and kept going.

The gears were stripped, the clutch loose, and the brakes nearly nonexistent. The boy lost sight of the van up ahead. He worked through the gears as he steered the bus back to the highway. The road consisted of loose gravel for at least forty miles.

[79]

The road curved around to fit the terrain of the Canadian bush, rivers, and hills. Slowing down or speeding up became treacherous on the curves. The boy could feel the rear end slide. He wanted to stop to adjust his rear mirrors again. As they were positioned, he could not tell if the back end approached the ridge of the road. He did not dare stop as he continued going uphill. He feared that working the clutch/brake combination on a steep incline after stopping would be too tricky.

The boy white-knuckled the steering wheel to the paved road, coming awfully close to sliding off at least three times.

When he pulled into the Standard Station, Gene and the boys in the van had been waiting for a half hour. The boy did not say a word about the harrowing trip, but one look by Gene and the boy knew his shirt sweat gave him away.

After returning to Camp Aharah two days later, the boy said goodbye to the other campers and Gene as they prepared to head to Kalamazoo. The boy stayed at the camp at Dave Thymes' request to be a lifeguard at the week-long family camp. Gene and the boy shook hands goodbye.

Still grasping the boy's hand, Gene said, "Dave and I have been working out a different trip for next summer. Advanced, older campers are looking for more challenges. Twenty days instead of ten. A route no one has traveled. Rockway Lodge people have some ideas. Probably blaze our own trails. If you're interested?"

"I'm more than interested," said the boy, "count me in."

The boy returned to Kalamazoo Central High School in the fall, wandering from class to class. He was an expert at completing the least amount of homework by faking teachers out if called upon or in a pinch, just admitting that he did not do the assignment. He managed to pull "B"s or "C"s in most of his classes. He ate lunch at the bakery around the corner from the school.

Outside of school, the boy's rock group, "*The Lost Souls,*" practiced and performed in battles of the bands. The boy danced in the school musical, partnering with Connie Grazer again in "*Camelot.*" He had a small part in the school play, "*The Mouse That Roared,*" a stupid farce about a fictitious European monarchy. The Director of The Kalamazoo Junior Civic Theater asked the boy to perform as a panel member in a sex education documentary produced and filmed by the State of Michigan.

The boy could not pinpoint when Harry warmed to him again. He had not been in trouble for over a year and had worked independently, first at Camp Aharah and now as a janitor five days a week at Kalamazoo Spice Extraction Company. The boy emptied wastebaskets every evening after five o'clock and dust-mopped the floor. On Saturday morning, he swept, mopped, and waxed the offices. A great job. He cleaned the offices late at night if he had to be at a rehearsal. The job paid well, keeping the boy in date money.

Harry brought home an old pinball machine for the boy to tinker with. When the boy plugged it into a wall outlet, nothing happened. Harry showed the boy the electrical schematic on the back of the machine's cover and left it to the boy to follow and determine the problem. The boy traced the wiring in the machine's base through all the relays and switches and "tilt" mechanisms until he found the short, and the machine whirred, clang, clang, clanging to life. The boy bypassed the coin drop and set all the tilt switches to a liberal position. The boy's picture appeared in the Kalamazoo Gazette with the pinball machine lid propped up, showing all the electrical intricacies.

For this year's electrical project, the boy built a Heathkit amplifier following the soldering and assembly instructions in the one-hundred-fifty-three-step manual.

Dave Thymes sent the boy a Kalamazoo YMCA summer contract. It denoted two Bush Voyager trips, a beginner's trip similar to what the boy had accomplished the previous summer and the advanced twenty-day trip Gene had outlined when they parted company last summer. The boy signed and returned the contract, arranging with his brother Stephen to take over the Kalamazoo Spice Extraction Company janitorial job for the summer.

Two days before heading up to Canada from Camp Aharah, the boy took his entitled night off. A van full of counselors, including the boy, headed twenty miles west to the shore of Lake Michigan for the Pentwater Yacht Club Teen Dance. Emboldened by his Canadian achievements, the boy asked a short, long-haired blond girl named Janet to dance. She was petite except for genuinely perky breasts. After several dances, he asked her to walk on the dock. He spent a half hour necking with a very responsive Janet before a fellow counselor hollered at him that the van would be leaving. He had told the girl he worked at Camp Aharah and asked her to visit him on the Sunday after he returned from Canada in a month. Janet said she would.

The boy's new, mail-order down sleeping bag had arrived at the camp while he traveled on his early summer canoe trip. Along with new calfskin gloves, a package of wine-soaked slim cigars, lifesaving Juicy Fruit Gum, and MacIntosh Toffee, he felt outfitted and ready for the advanced trip.

There were only four campers that arrived for the advanced canoe trip. Dave Benin, Curt Sanderson, Ted Rice, and Ryan Tempura. Dave and Curt looked capable. The boy knew Ted from folk dancing. Ted had three gorgeous sisters, Connie and Judy, and the eldest, Ann, who could have been a model. Ted was a mouth breather, a little slovenly when he walked, but good-natured and ready to try.

Who could tell about Ryan? Inches shorter than the other campers, he extracted every gadget known to man from his expensive-looking suitcase. He found space on the nightstand beside his bunk for his electric toothbrush, fancy transistor radio, alarm clock, and an awfully expensive-looking waterproof watch that looked ridiculous on his skinny white arm. Ryan made it clear to Gene within the first hour that he might have to bow out of some activities due to his hay fever. Gene gave him a withering look and said nothing. Ryan seemed not to notice.

Gene accelerated the training and doubled the strenuous physical tasks from what the boy experienced on his other trips. Dave and Curt were up to the challenge. Ted was usually far behind but managed and even smiled when he completed each exercise. Ryan complained about everything. He could not lift the lightweight aluminum canoe. The backpack straps cut into his shoulders. He could not swim across Aharah Lake, "too big," he said. The rest of the campers, Gene and the boy, finished breakfast in the mornings before Ryan sauntered in from the morning run. The boy never saw evidence of Ryan's hay fever, like a runny nose or sneezing. He never saw Ryan even breathe hard. Ryan would give up before he worked up a sweat.

On the second day, Ryan began to complain. The rest of the group ignored the complaints, following Gene's lead. Gene never gave Ryan extra work, laps, or portages for quitting before completing a task. It is Gene's way to show the campers once, perhaps twice, how something is done. He tied the paddles to Ryan's canoe for portaging once and then once again. After that, Ryan or any of the campers had to figure it out on their own. If they came up with their own way to tie their paddles, more power to them. Ryan gave up and started dragging his canoe on the portage rather than carrying it. As Gene and the rest of the campers pushed on, Ryan sat down on the canoe he pulled and waited for everyone else to be long out of sight. Then he left the canoe and walked behind the rest of the group, careful not to catch up.

On the third day of training, Ryan mysteriously vanished in the afternoon. He appeared later with Dave Thymes and collected his gear, stowing his toothbrush, transistor radio, and alarm clock in his suitcase and strapping on his waterproof watch before leaving.

[83]

The Bush Voyagers investigated the whirring of a helicopter landing in the parking lot near the Lodge, arriving in time to watch the rotors stop. When they did, Ryan came out of the lodge with Dave Thymes carrying his suitcase and sleeping bag. The pilot met Ryan and took his baggage to stow, and another man led Ryan over to a seat in the helicopter. Then the stranger returned to have a conversation with Dave. The bush campers could not hear anything that the two men said. Dave stood tall, nose to nose with the stranger in an unapologetic stance, arms crossed, shaking his head at anything the man put to him.

When the helicopter left, Dave came over to Gene and the boy.

"Wanted a refund," he told Gene, "said it wasn't what the kid expected. I almost laughed. No way is that man getting a dime back."

Gene did laugh, "And the kid just learned his daddy will spend the price of a helicopter hire to give his little boy what he wants."

After Ryan's departure, Dave, Mark, and Ted clicked into a unit. Ted received a bit of teasing; Dave and Curt were friends before camp. Ted good-naturedly held his own. The three of them would have to take one canoe: the only unfortunate downside of Ryan's departure. The boy and Gene would be canoeing and tenting together for the first time.

When the Bush Voyagers arrived at Rockway Lodge on Ranger Lake at the end of July, a group of girl canoeists returning from a three-day trip and staying at the lodge organized a dance party. Dave, Curt, and Ted were kept entertained while Gene and the boy packed the food and equipment.

The plan entailed two food packs. The second pack would be dropped off at Mekatina to supply the second ten days of the trip. The Voyagers would start from Rockway Lodge as Gene and the boy had done in the past, paddling up through the Aubinadong River lake chain and continuing north from the hellholes for a few days until they reached the Cow River. The Cow River feeds the great Montreal River running west to the coast of Lake Superior.

The group would flag down the Algoma Central train at the massive hydroelectric dam at Montreal Falls and ride the rails down to Mekatina. From there, the Voyagers would follow lake chains hoping to pick up the Goulais River. The Goulais River/lake chain feeds into the farthest west bay of Ranger Lake, ending the canoe trip with a half-day paddle back to Rockway Lodge.

Gene had laid out the trip on a contoured map he handed the boy for safekeeping. The boy would be the navigator. He had purchased a small army surplus surveyor's compass with a cross-line sight lid. Since no one had canoed the planned route before, Gene hoped the group would accomplish the trip in about twenty days. If they guessed wrong on the first part of the trip, they might run out of food before reaching the second food pack in Mekatina. The same would hold true about the second part of the uncharted trip back to Ranger Lake.

The Bush Voyagers, eager and optimistic, started out early the following day. The wind at their backs made for easy paddling to the north on Ranger Lake. After the first portage to Saymo Lake, the wind turned against them for hard paddling into the waves. When the boy and Gene pulled into the shore to pee, a strong wind gust scooped their canoe, sending it out into the lake. With Ted (sitting in the center of their canoe), Dave and Curt gave chase, tracking it down and towing it back to Gene and the boy who waited amongst a field of raspberries. After lunch and their fill of raspberries, the group portaged the two canoes to South Anvil Lake and Gong Lake, where the Voyagers set up camp.

The boy helped Gene pitch their tent the first night on the river. The boy's new down feather sleeping bag promised a huge sleep improvement. They both enjoyed the remains of their cigars within the tent, the smoke shooing away the mosquitos for the night. When the glow of the cigars died, the tent became pitch-black. The boy heard Gene settling into his sleeping bag.

"You should try to keep your distance a little in the tent," Gene said, "I sometimes may seem a little restless, but don't worry, and don't try to shake me or anything."

The two-man tent allowed for not more than two inches between them. The boy cocked his head and replied, "OK, no problem."

Gene explained.

"As a drill sergeant in Korea, a soldier disliked me. I slept in my cot, I swear, dead to the world, when for some reason, I have no idea why, I woke up, and the guy swung down at me with a knife. If I had not woken up, I would not be here today."

"What did you do?" the boy asked.

"He never came close to me again, knife or no knife. Since that time, I have become an exceptionally light sleeper. Just try not to touch me."

The boy could not imagine how Gene had survived a knife attack while lying in a cot. Having seen Gene cripple Rod Tongan with one hand, he had no doubt Gene's attacker that night had been as lucky as Gene to survive, but he did not ask. The boy positioned himself as close to his side of the tent as possible without touching the canvas. He did not fear the man, nor did Gene intimidate him anymore as he did when they first worked together, but he felt no need to test the mountain man either.

The next day included thirteen portages as the Voyagers hustled up to Megason Lake: arriving late in the evening. They met the owner of the Megason Lake Resort. He and an Indian guide were fishing to supply breakfast for their resort guests. The Voyagers camped on the opposite side of the lake.

In the morning, the group bypassed the first hell hole portage, staying on the Aubinadong chain, north, into territory Gene had never traveled. The portages from then on were much less traveled, impossible to spot, and sometimes leading in unintentional directions. Under the boy's leadership, the two canoes had followed a series of portages west through a chain of three lakes before realizing they were off course.

Smaller lakes are somewhat indistinguishable from a map's shape and shore configurations. There were hundreds if not thousands of lakes within the five hundred square miles the Voyagers were trying to navigate. A missed can on a stick or a red slash on a tree sends a traveler off course by miles. By comparing the three lakes they crossed with various groups of three lakes on the map in the vicinity, the boy could admit his mistake and recommend the hour-long backtrack.

After the two-hour delay, the group set up camp at six o'clock, portaging from Beacon Lake to Gord Lake. On one of the lost lakes, an enormous moose exited the water on the opposite shore and tromped into the woods.

A light rain grayed the sky, making camp cleanup difficult. The group pushed on. In the late afternoon, the sky cleared, drying the campers off. They continued camping on Lake Haya Went Ha and decided on a freeze-dried dinner new to Gene and the boy. They also fixed soup. Gene baked biscuits in the reflecting oven for dessert and divvied up applesauce.

Fixing meals on the trail is a somewhat complicated process. Gene packs plenty of Ivory soap in the pots and pans kit to aid cleanup. The cook for the meal cakes ivory soap on the underside and sides of the containers and pans before setting a water pot or frying pan on the fire. The fire must be hot and steady, coals crackling orange before setting up the wire grate and boiling the water. After the meal, the principal pot is washed out offshore, re-soaped if necessary, and set back on the fire to boil water. The rest of the dishes are cleaned off in the lake, washed in soapy hot water, and put on a rock beside the fire. The cleanup crew then sterilizes and dries the dishes, including each camper's mug and spoon. The sterilizing pot is washed and rinsed in reserved sterilizing water. The cleanup process is repeated for breakfast. Lunch is just axle grease and rye crisp wafers.

As with all chores, meal preparation and cleanup become familiar and rote. Hard work seems to ease with repetition.

On the morning of August first, the boy, Gene, and Curt stripped off, dove into the lake, soaped up using their bar of Ivory soap (unlike Dial and other soap bars, Ivory soap bars float,) and dove in again to rinse off. The sun shone warm and bright, the day cloudless. Gene asked the boys to consolidate packs to four in preparation for what appeared to be about a five-mile portage to Farewell Creek.

Gene and the boy began the portage at eleven forty with their canoe overhead. Both of them were of a mind not to stop until the end of the trail. As he walked, the boy rested the front thwart on his neck and shoulders. When the pain of the thwart became intense, the boy shifted forward into the bow and rested the gunnels on the ends of his shoulders as he proceeded. Between these shifts, the boy held the gunnels as long as possible in the air off his neck and shoulders. The boy refused to think about the distance, looking out from beneath the canoe at the path and, peripherally, the woods surrounding them.

With miles to go, the boy began to rest one gunnel on a shoulder and hold the opposite gunnel in hand while dangling an arm, blood circulation returning to the resting hand while continuing the portage. Then he would reverse the arrangement, resting his opposite arm. Suddenly, they saw the creek ahead and set down the canoe at the water's edge. The boy kneeled and rinsed his sweat-drenched face in the stream. He dipped his hat in the water. When he put it back on, the headband cooled his forehead for a time. His shirt and sweat-splotched jeans began draining as he and Gene trekked back for their backpacks. They passed the other three boys trudging with their canoe about halfway back to the start of the portage. Due to the consolidation, the packs were heavier, around fifty pounds each. They proceeded again along the five-mile trail to their canoe. Gene and the boy were in their canoe in the middle of the cooling creek by three thirty in the afternoon. The other canoe joined them at three-fifty.

Farewell Creek turned out to be much narrower than indicated on the map. Unlike the boy's previous ten-day canoe trips, which are kept clear of debris by the Rockway Lodge staff, obstacles on this trip abounded. The Bush Voyagers crossed over between twenty and thirty beaver dams or fallen logs blocking the creek. The canoe's bow would be pulled onto the beaver dam. The bowman then scrambled onto the embankment and held the bow with his legs braced while transferring the packs from the canoe to the top. With the canoe nearly empty, Gene and the boy could pull the canoe over the dam. Gene held the stern with his legs while the boy replaced the packs into the canoe, and they took off. Sometimes they found the next beaver dam around the very next bend. They camped that night on a wide spot in the creek, noodles and beef for dinner with orange bug juice and toffee for dessert. The dishes were completed by eight-thirty; their beds were a blessing.

Next to the creek, camping in the thick of the woods, the boy listened to timber wolves and a howling moose. Squirrels scampered back and forth across the top of the tent. All these noises were underlaid by the background sound of the creek rushing by the tent. The boy could not imagine a better bedroom.

The next day the Voyagers crossed over more beaver dams and lined the canoes along the edge of several rapids. They came upon the remains of a bridge over the creek, logs tipping into the stream. A logging road ran up to each side of the left-over bridge. The route consisted of a ten-foot-high, fifteen-foot-wide jumble of massive logs bulldozed together and flattened to form a somewhat straight line. The road in summer could not be navigated even to walk on.

The boy imagined a four-foot snowfall packed on the sides and on top of the log jumble, smooth and hard-packed enough to allow a logging truck to barrel along, transporting logs to the mill or the train. It messed up the forest. The enormity of the Canadian wilderness, its ability to hide this ecological blight, amazed the boy. A huge raspberry field surrounding the logs provided dessert for lunch. Filling a coffee pot with raspberries, the canoeists continued down the creek until it merged into the Cow River. They stopped for the day at three forty-five, pitched tents, and set up the reflecting oven. They prepared a pie and filled it full of raspberries using Bisquick mix. Two hours later, after supper, the campers feasted on the hot baked raspberry pie.

The swift Cow River measured more than twenty feet across. At eleven thirty, Gene and the boy in the lead canoe back paddled while Gene tried to decide whether to portage, line, or run the set of rapids ahead. The river, too swift, made the decision for them. They were sucked into a quick run faster than anything they had experienced. They maneuvered down and through one white water churn after another. Rounding a bend, fighting not to be thrown into the swirling eddy on the right, the current forced them to steer left of a "V," cutting next to a rock. That river path led them into a wedge between two boulders further down in the rapids. The boy, paddling like a madman in the bow, thought they might make it past the boulder on the left and, with luck, the boulder on the right. With Gene's powerful "J" stroke, they did almost get by. Then the midpoint of the canoe swung, smashing into the boulder, jarring the boy, and snapping his neck.

The power of the river rush began to wrap the canoe around the boulder, and a crunching, cracking sound alarmed Gene and the boy. They both scrambled out of the canoe into armpit-high water. The torrent of water slammed the boy against a boulder. As he entered the river, he grabbed the precious food pack out of the canoe, filling rapidly with water and heaving the bag up on the boulder on the right. With his left hand, he grabbed his backpack and heaved it onto a boulder while his chest remained pinned against the rock. Gene did the same with his pack as the canoe slipped off and around the boulder, straightening out, coasting, full of water, down and out of the remainder of the rapids. It came to rest caught in a bush at the side of the river.

Dave, Ted, and Curt came down on the other side of the river and made it through unscathed, although they had swamped earlier. With all the gear and paddles recovered, Gene and the boy tipped the canoe over and assessed the damage. The water line would fall a good four inches above the gash in the side of the canoe. After the slashed area dried, Gene mixed the epoxy tubes from the repair kit and began to apply fiberglass patches and epoxy to the gash. Without the repair kit, or if the outfitter had provided aluminum canoes instead of fiberglass, a signal bonfire would have been lit. They would have stoked the fire, hoping a Mountie from a fire lookout station spotted their emergency and helicoptered them out of the bush. Either that or Gene and Curt would have canoed on for three days in search of a Mountie to help. The patch looked crude and thin to the boy, but it worked.

The boy spent the patch drying time stripping down to skivvies and drying his clothes on the rocks at the side of the river. Gene did the same. The drying time for the clothes on the hot boulders by the river equaled the fiberglass patch drying time as the two dressed, optimistic that the patch might continue to climb. Gene knocked the boy's right boot into the river when he grabbed his hiking boots. Within seconds the river rapids carried the boot around the bend, the boy struggling in the heavy bush at the river's edge to keep it in view. They all lost sight of the boot after a second bend, and no one could determine even an approximation of where it might have gone under the water. Still stripped back down to his underwear, the boy searched a wide swath of the river, stepping barefoot on the rocks and stones to recover the boot.

The boy dug out his extra pair of black, low-cut Converse gym shoes and helped Gene load the canoe wearing one boot and one gym shoe. Even with the two-hour patch delay, the group made it to the more expansive Cow River, preparing a campsite downriver at around seven o'clock.

The granite boulders along the river at their chosen campsite stretched back into the bush. The trees were further apart, and the moss was deep, providing an excellent and roomy layover area. The boy and Gene slept in, recovering from the previous day's ordeal. The other boys explored downriver a bit and fished an eddy around the bend. The rest of the day, the boy read his pocketbook.

By nine thirty on August fifth, the two canoes were paddling rapidly down the Cow River, reaching the Cow River falls by early afternoon. The group portaged around the falls. A short while later, they paddled up to a log jam. Huge cut twenty-foot-long, fourteen-inch or larger diameter logs packed the one-hundred-foot-wide Montreal River, stretching at least a quarter mile downriver and out of sight around a gentle bend. Some of them bobbed and crunched together, but none of them moved downstream.

There was nothing for it. The group prepared to double portage around the log jams. The boy tied his ammo box to a thwart, secured the bag of kitchen utensils to another thwart, and pulled on his backpack. Gene and the boy lifted the canoe overhead and started off through the woods, keeping the bank of the river and the log jam in sight. The Canadian bush is well-described as dense and challenging to push through. The boy, leading the canoe, struggled, watching for fallen logs to step over, listening to Gene's directions as they navigated around and through the trees. The stabbing ache between his shoulder blades from carrying the heavy canoe, combined with the extra weight of the heavy pack, approached his bearable limit. Still, he sloshed along in one boot and one soaked, slippery gym shoe, muttering his watermelon song to himself as a distraction. He knew the silent mountain man behind him would not rest. The man from the Korean War never complained. He must have endured much worse. The boy silently began Dad's Amy Air Force marching mantra.

I left my wife and forty-three children in starving conditions with nothing but gingerbread,
Left, right, left, right, left,
I left my wife and forty-three children in starving conditions with nothing but gingerbread left.

The boy looked ahead at each bend in the river, seeing a continuation of the log jams. He kept moving, one foot, then the other, until he saw the open water three hundred feet ahead. Made it.

The cool waters of the lazy Montreal River calmed the boy and the rest of the Voyagers. They ate lunch right in the canoes floating downriver. The day turned gray, and a light rain turned heavy. For such a large, navigable river, the group saw few cabins. Gene stopped paddling, and they both pulled out their rain gear.

As the river widened to two hundred feet, the group paddled for four hours in the rain and finally beached the canoes to the right of the tremendous Montreal Falls, which drops over two hundred feet down over a hydroelectric plant. The Voyagers set up camp in a field about forty feet from the Algoma Central Railroad train tracks. The dinner that night included freeze-dried beef steaks and potatoes.

In the dark of early morning, the boy dreamed he heard a rumble. Awaking to a rumbling roar, the boy could not identify, his chest tightened, panic mounting, thinking the group had pitched tents on an airport runway. The roar kept getting louder. Surely a plane taxied toward them. The propellers would slash the tents and the inhabitants to a bloody pulp.

The boy thought to shake Gene awake so they could get away from the tent, but he remembered the story of the Korean soldier and thought better of it. Terrified, he remembered setting up the campsite next to the railroad tracks. In a moment, the train whistle screeched, and the boy settled back with a huge sigh, sweat dripping from his forehead.

In the morning, Gene hung a red bandana on a post planted up the rail from the bridge spanning the river. The backpacks and gear were readied close to the tracks a quarter mile south of the pole. Then the group waited. They saw no sign of the train at the prescribed scheduled time at two-forty-five. The boy began to worry, thinking, *What the hell. What made Gene think the train would stop for two canoes and five passengers.*

At three-twenty, the boy heard the train whistle in the distance. When he saw the train, it began slowing to a stop. A coachman came from the caboose and opened a freight car door, and the canoes and backpacks were loaded in. The Voyagers walked to a passenger car, and the train left the bridge. Dave, Ted, Curt, and the boy headed to the dining car. Pooling their money, they could buy a sweet roll, a soft drink, and a bag of potato chips. In forty-five minutes, approximately thirty miles from where they loaded the canoes, the train stopped in Mekatina, and the Voyagers unloaded their gear.

Gene inquired at the Mekatina station master's office, and the postman produced the second food pack from behind the counter. The small amount of food in the first pack and the canvas backpack was packed into the second food pack. The trip map indicated a long portage out of Mekatina to Thompson Creek.

The group completed the two-hour portage by seven-ten, reaching Gavor Lake and camping at seven-fifty that evening. From Mekatina on, the route would be rarely traveled by canoe or backpacker. The boy knew where they were on the map, but they would have to pick their way among the chain of lakes down to Teepee Lake and the Goulais River.

For the next three days, the five travelers wandered through the woods and hills southeast of Mekatina: at times, way off course. Compass readings and trails were tried and many times backtracked. Minimal distances gained on the map each day caused the boy to doubt their return to Rockway Lodge within the twenty days planned. On the twelfth day out of Rockway Lodge, the small creek they were canoeing suddenly ended at another crude road of piled logs.

Scrambling up to the top of the road, the boy called back to the group. "Nothing comes out on the other side, Gene. The creek filters to nothing beneath the logs. I can see a long way down the road but can't see a lake or water anywhere."

"What does the map say?" asked Dave.

The boy checked the topo.

"The map shows a small lake and creeks running in and out. Then there should be more small lakes down the way."

All the Voyagers climbed the log embankment to take a look.

"You can see by the foliage how this logging road has screwed up the water flow here," Gene said. "No way of telling, but the map is useless."

"Really," said Ted, "they can just do that?"

[94]

"When the bulldozer comes through," Gene noted, "it knocks down everything in its path, piling the logs into a road. This one, they smoothed and graveled the top. Cars can't get down it, but the monster trucks can."

"Shouldn't they have to fix it?" Ted questioned, "No one is using it!"

"Next winter, it'll be busy, I bet," said Gene.

"So, we go back?" asked Curt.

Standing in the center of the flat top of the tree heap, Gene looked left, then right.

"This thing goes as far as we can see in both directions," he said, "We pick a direction and start portaging until we find water on the other side of the road. Then we'll have to guess where we are on the map and find our way from there."

Within a few minutes, the gear and canoes had been carried to the flat gravel top of the logging road. Since they had no idea where or when they would find a lake or stream, they had no choice but to double portage until they found water. They strapped on the backpacks, hefted the canoes overhead, and trudged off down the road heading southerly through the thick forest.

In forty-five minutes, the sun, reflecting off the gravel unimpeded by overhead leaves and branches, scorched the boy's foot through the thin rubber of his gym shoe. The larger stones were sometimes unavoidable, reminding the boy why Gene insisted on boots for these trips. Gene called for rest, and the two canoes and backpacks were dropped onto the gravel. The boy walked further south as Gene backtracked, both in search of a flowing water source.

After fifteen minutes of rest, the double portage down the road resumed. The boy spotted a small creek paralleling the road off to the left, and the canoes were lowered for a better look. The three boys plopped down on their backpacks on the road. The boy continued walking, hoping to spot Hanes Lake. Instead, he found a crossing road at a collapsed section in the logging road and a white Valiant parked on the side. Three friendly wrinkled men, having no luck fishing the stream, pulled a map out of the car. The boy laid his map side by side with the fisherman's map on the hood of the Valiant. The fisherman pointed to a spot on his map that the boy transferred to his own map. They had, in fact, found Hanes Creek much further along than the boy expected due to their extensive walk.

The water flowed, and the Voyagers were in good spirits during several beaver dam portages and lining along rapids. The group made it down to Teepee Lake and, from there, found the outlet to the Goulais River. On either side of the river, the banks were high. A forest fire had burned to the river on one side. The boys in the second canoe pulled over to the bank to investigate. Gene and the boy beached their canoe as well. The forest fire had devastated the forest into stubble as far as the Voyagers could see. The fire damage must have occurred some time ago, nothing smoldered, and the charred wood smell had passed. Tiny green shoots were beginning to pop through the blackened earth. The group pushed on, not thrilled at the idea of camping among the bleakness.

With the meandering Goulais River, it took two hours of paddling and two more portages for the canoes to emerge from the edge of the forest fire to Ragged Lake. The island offshore on the far side of the lake pushed the forest fire out of the minds of the travelers. They made camp at eight that evening.

By ten thirty, the group had canoed to the bank of the Goulais River outlet of Ragged Lake. No trail or portage markings existed. They would need to blaze a trail to a small pond, canoe to the opposite side, and then portage over to Poem Lake. Their scaled map indicated two half-mile stretches to portage.

As this would be their first blazed portage, they decided to mark the trail and return for the canoes. Using the compass, the boy blazed the first tree; spotting the next tree along the compass line up ahead, he marched off and swiped a healthy swatch at the same eye level as the first tree. Curt became the blazer as the boy pointed out the trees along the compass line to be marked.

Sometimes, in the valleys, the brush grew so thick the boy struggled to break through with his pack to maintain the direct line of the compass. The compass took the group up a ridge before returning to the distant small pond. The half-mile map distance turned into one mile up and one mile down. The five backpacks were set down at the pond's edge, and the boy turned back along their trail to fetch the canoes. Crashing through the semi-cleared Canadian bush was far from previous canoe trips' manicured and well-trodden trails.

Reaching the canoes, the group turned uphill with the canoes overhead, making it to the lake where they had left the backpacks early afternoon. After lunch amongst the mosquitos on the pond, a pond that had never been seen by a human being, the group paddled for five minutes to the opposite shore and began to blaze another trail out of the thick bush. This time the trailblazers knew better; they hacked a wider path. The compass again led them uphill and down. At four thirty, they set backpacks down on the shore of Poem Lake and returned for their canoes. By seven thirty, the Voyagers were exhausted and setting up camp on Poem Lake.

The meal served and dishes completed, the group lazed around the campfire. The boy extracted one of his three last wine-tipped cigars from his ammo box and sucked all the wine off the tip before lighting up. Gene did the same.

Dave groaned while shifting to his other elbow. Then he said, "I don't know how I'm going to tell anyone about this trip; how hard it's been."

"How far did we get today?" Ted asked.

The boy studied his map before answering, "About one inch on the map, if that tells you anything. Compare that to five inches on that long day we canoed along the Montreal River."

"I cannot tell you how sore I am," Curt said.

Gene stretched and stood. The boy noticed Gene moved as stiffly as Curt. "Take a dip tomorrow morning, and you'll feel good as new," said Gene.

"It seems like every day we have to do something a bit tougher and a lot harder than the day before," the boy said.

After sleepy nods from around the fire, each of them, in turn, rose in slow motion and moved off to bed.

For the next two days, the Voyagers picked their way down East Goulais River, through Gujac Lake, over a myriad of beaver dams, and under or over fallen trees as they made their way southeast toward Laughing Lake and Upper Laughing Lake, preparing for the last push into Ranger Lake and home to Rockway Lodge. The territory is little traveled by canoes. Trails needed blazing, and the forest was thicker in areas and swampier on some of the portages. Most of the day, they played hippity-hop over obstacles in the river.

On the morning of August thirteenth, after a portage from a lake named Betz Lake, the group found a portage that led them one and one-half hours off course yet again. There, a small pond at the end of the portage led to another lake and portage, easy to navigate, that took them in a roundabout way back to Upper Laughing Lake. The next lake would be Ranger Lake. The last legs of the canoe trip. The Voyagers ate lunch. Depending on the direction of the strong wind, the lake might have two-foot waves running against or with them. They would not know until the other end of the last portage.

The five canoeists gathered for a grubby end-of-the-road picture. The boy and Gene stood on either side of their three companions, sitting on a fallen tree. Gene and the boy chomped cigars and snarled at the camera. The boy had his gym shoed foot planted on the log with his arm resting on his thigh. Gene established a similar pose on the other side of the group. Then they all dug out their backup outfits. The boy put both gym shoes on and tied his remaining boot to the thwart.

The differences between the two gym shoes were startling. The left shoe looked OK, practically new, but not the shredded right shoe the boy had worn since the canoe swamp. The shoe still had a thin sole with a hole at the ball of his foot where the boy took each step. He could put his pinky through it. The white rubber front of the shoe remained intact, and seven eyelets ran up to a patch of the black canvas where the boy could tie the laces around his ankle and hold the shoe on his foot. The black canvas on either side of the eyelets had rotted away in the wetlands of the portages. The reinforced black heel revealed that the shoe had been made of canvas. Of course, the shoe was worthless, but all the boy owned until he arrived in town and he could buy some flip-flops.

Still, the voyagers smiled, shoulders straightened, hands palming paddles standing up as straight as Voyagers, facing the sun. Click!

Ranger Lake turned out to be a swift and smooth hour-and-a-half paddle. Over the real meat and potatoes dinner at the Lodge, the boy made his final entry in his trip journal:

Five hundred miles by canoe.
Portaged sixty miles.
Completed a twenty-day trip in seventeen days.
First, to take the route.

Nothing seemed impossibly hard anymore.

Sunday, the Voyagers arrived at a deserted Camp Aharah. New campers would register for the "Family" camp late in the afternoon. Janet, the girl the boy met at the Pentwater Yacht Club Teen Dance, also rolled into Camp Aharah around one o'clock. The boy hung around the lodge, fingers crossed, hoping she would still remember him after being out of touch for four weeks.

Janet toured the camp with the boy, walking out to the archery and gun ranges, around the lake to the wilderness cabin, and back to the docks and lodge. He led her to a deserted cottage on the east side of the lake. Three musty bunk beds lined two of the walls. The cabin also sported a single bed for the counselor, positioned away from the door under the window. The boy cracked the window to air out the place, turned to the girl, and embraced her. To the boy's surprise, Janet decided to skip the rest of the tour and pulled the boy over to the counselor's mattress.

The next fifteen minutes confused the shit out of the boy; Janet writhing against him, kissing so hard the boy worried his lower lip might bleed. Janet's legs captured the boy's right thigh, undulating suggestively while the boy tried to keep up. He rolled Janet partly off and explored the top of her pants with his right hand, finding a way down the front to her satin panties. Janet never stopped their kiss, and the boy's fingers felt a wet spot at the crevice of her legs. That shocked the boy, and he pulled his hand back a bit and reached inside her panties, feeling her feathery pubic hair as his hand ventured further down.

Hot and stiff, the boy could not believe Janet let him delve into her secret garden, at a total loss for what to do next. After a minute of gentle exploration, the boy attempted to slip Janet's pants down from her hips. She suddenly rolled off the bed, straightened her blouse, pulled and tugged her pants back into position, and swept her long blond hair behind her ears.

"I have to get back home," Janet said, "thanks for the tour."

"I'll see you at the Yacht Club on Tuesday," the boy sputtered.

"Sure, see you," she said.

The boy, stunned, walked Janet to her car, and she drove away without a goodbye kiss. In the past half hour, the boy had experienced more sex than all the hours spent with all the different girls he had dated the previous year. He felt foolish that he had not tried more or taken off her blouse. He began to think when and where he might attempt more with Janet. He needed to buy a package of condoms.

On Tuesday evening, four counselors, including the boy, rode to the Pentwater Yacht Club in the van. The boy distanced himself from the group, waiting for Janet. In a half-hour, Janet walked through the front door draped all over a boy with curly long red hair. She, the redhead, and two other couples walked by the boy's table, and Janet never even glanced his way.

He might have been more upset if the boy had not returned from fighting and conquering the Canadian Bush. He had never discovered Janet's last name. He did not lose much to the redhead but a girl that played the Pentwater field.

Families arrived from Kalamazoo for the end-of-the-season family camp. The boy was a lifeguard and drove the speed boat for water skiers. Rod Tongan had hired on as a counselor for the week, driving up in his sixty-two blue Volkswagen Beetle. On Tuesday, Rick Johnson and the boy rode with Tongan in the Beetle to the Pentwater Yacht Club Teen Dance. The boy girl-watched and enjoyed the music in a sublime, serene mood. After the dance closed, Rod drove a mile and a half outside the city limits before the Beetle ran out of gas. All the businesses and the two gas stations in the village of Pentwater were closed. The three boys leaned against the side of the car.

Rod apologized, "Sorry, I thought I had at least enough to return to the camp."

"What now?" Rick said.

"We start work at eight o'clock tomorrow," the boy said, "We're all supposed to be there."

The three were silent for a minute.

Rick broke the silence, "I guess we'll walk back. How far is Walkerville?"

The boy calculated, "Eighteen miles to Walkerville, then two miles more to the camp."

"So, we walk," Rick concluded.

Rod could not see it, "No way, I can't leave the car. The first car passing by here will be State Police. My Dad gets a call from a towing company, and I'll never get the car again."

Rick had another idea.

"I guess we sleep in the car," he said, "and early in the morning, walk to the gas station, buy a gallon, and get to camp by eight."

"Right, Rick," Rod said, "You're six feet two and a football player. You take up the whole back seat of the bug by yourself."

Silence again.

The boy kicked the dirt on the side of the road and then looked at the other two. "Let's push the car back."

"You know," said Rod, "That might be the best way to go."

"You two are crazy," Rick said, "push a car for twenty miles? There are hills and gravel roads. Someone has to steer. That means just two of us to push."

The boy crossed his arms and leaned back against the Beetle.

"Listen, Rick," he said, "I'm going out for football this year. I know I have never played, but it is a no-cut sport, and I figure even if I sit on the bench the whole time, I will have been a part of a Kalamazoo Central team. I could contribute. I've been in training all summer."

Rod Tongan, a former Bush Voyager Counselor, nodded.

"Rick," said Rod, "you've stayed in camp all summer, but we know what it's like up in Canada. It is as hard as football practice any day of the week. We know we can do it."

The boy clapped Rick on the back.

"Let's go, the boy said, "Rod, you're the lightest; you steer first."

Rick reluctantly took the right rear bumper, the boy, the left. Rod put the car in neutral and steered. It proved not that hard to push the Beetle, at least for the first mile and one half on the road running along the bank of Pentwater Lake, flat and paved.

Then came the first hill. The boy lowered his body and shoulder on the fender and tried for a running start before the incline. The car slowed to a crawl, and pushing became torturous. Rod jumped out and put a shoulder to the door frame, steering with his right hand. They had slogged a quarter mile up the hill when the boy spotted the top of a half mile off. The boy knew they would make it to the crest. When they did, Rod jumped in, and Rick and the boy jogged to keep up as the car picked up speed on the downside of the hill. How many hills were there on the way to the camp? The boy did not consider it again. He just pushed.

Hour after hour, hill after hill, they pushed the car on the damp August night. Halfway there, they rolled onto the gravel country road to Walkerville. Loose gravel cost the boy a slipped step for every two his feet held on the inclines.

Tongan and the boy never stopped. To rest would be to allow defeat to slip in. Rest at the end of the portage. Sometimes the boy pushed alone while Rick walked beside the car.

Walkerville was even smaller than Pentwater. They turned the car north in two blocks for the last push to the camp. Nothing stirred in town. At five forty-five, they rolled the Beetle down the mile-long entrance to Camp Aharah. Exhausted, they leaned against the side of the car as they had back in Pentwater, watching the sun rise above the tree line. Rick looked over at the boy.

"I wouldn't have believed it," he said, "But we did it. Not sure how. You would be welcome on any football team. Welcome to ours. See you at conditioning practice in a week. Bye, Tongan. Bye." Tongan pounded the boy on the back, thanking him. The end of another Bush Voyage. The three went off to separate cabins for an hour's sleep.

According to league rules, high school would start in two weeks; therefore, football conditioning with no pads or equipment could begin. The boy, ready to go, waved to Rick Johnson, one of the bigger linebackers. Being on the football field felt strange when he had been in the stands. The first day consisted of sprints and distance running. The boy more than held his own. His knees had recovered from the Osgood Schlatter's syndrome that he had dealt with in eighth, ninth, and part of tenth grade. His legs and arms were strong; his shoulders widened from carrying that god-awful heavy fiberglass canoe. His chest had also expanded, yet he weighed a light one hundred sixty-five pounds.

He finished all his wind sprints in the top three positions, and he finished first a couple of times in the distance runs. He knew that with equipment on, everything would change, revealing his inexperience. No matter, he felt ready and eager to try.

The second day duplicated the first. Coach Bolton pulled the boy aside three-quarters of the way through the practice. They

[103]

walked to the coach's office. The man had tried to make a fool of him during driver's training, directing him to drive downtown in a manual transmission automobile on the second day. Perhaps resentment drove the coach now.

The coach sat behind his desk. He did not offer the boy a seat.

"This will be your last day on the field," he said, "You're done."

"What do you mean done?" the boy said, shocked.

"Just that, you won't be playing on the team."

The boy stood silent for a moment, not understanding. Did Coach Bolton think him cocky? A showoff?

"I don't mind sitting on the bench," said the boy, "even for the whole season."

But the Coach, in a raised voice, became more adamant. "Nope, you're done. You can't just come out here as a senior and expect to play football."

The boy tried to stay calm.

"Football is a no-cut sport, is it not?" the boy said.

"I'm not wasting time on you. The rest of these guys have worked out here since tenth grade. My time is valuable, and you would never catch up. You will not replace a guy I've worked with for three years."

"I'm sure I can do it. I won't quit on you," the boy said, still in disbelief.

"You're done," Mr. Bolton said, "Don't come back."

Coach Bolton looked down at his desk, checking names on a clipboard. The boy walked out and never looked back.

The boy started the school year relaxed, cavalier, and relieved. This would be his year, his senior year of high school. At the end of school last spring, the boy had tried out for the school's "A" choir and been accepted for his senior year. For his elective, he chose Creative Writing with Mr. Kundera. His elective the year before had been Drafting. For his final project, he drew a perspective of a house he had dreamed up; complicated, but the geometry of vanishing points made sense.

The boy had been intrigued a couple of years ago when Edward moved through his architectural phase, designing and drawing structures and plans for weeks. The boy's brother never did anything halfway. His ideas looked great, and when Edward depicted people and trees, the boy became excited about a career in architecture.

"These are floor plans," Edward explained, "You project the corners of the plan to the sides of the sheet and imagine elevations. Then you draw a perspective of the building and make it look realistic with landscape and people."

The boy had been intrigued.

"That type of drawing maybe I could handle. Straight lines, mostly," the boy had said.

"With the T-square and the triangle for vertical lines, it's not too tricky," Edward said.

Edward's drawing, of course, looked elegant and beautiful.

"You should be an architect," the boy urged, "They must make good money."

"Whoa," Edward said, "this is just for fun for me and for my portfolio for college."

The boy, still curious, said, "You don't like it enough to become an architect?"

"I like it a lot," said the boy's older brother, "But a real architect needs a lot of math and calculus. Those studies are beyond me. I'll stick to fine art."

That one statement by Edward made the boy drop the thought of becoming an architect like a hot potato. If his Merit Scholarship-winning brother thought the math too hard, the boy needed to avoid architecture like the plague.

But what would the boy do after high school? Harry and Sarah would pay the tuition, room, and board for the college of his choice. Robert went to Michigan State University. He had just received an additional scholarship in Statistics for graduate school. Edward would be attending the prestigious Kalamazoo College, majoring in fine art. Edward dreamed of attending the Pratt Institute of Art in New York.

The boy dreamed of building a log cabin in a remote area of Canada. No one would know he had not bought or surveyed his lodge and land. They would never know it existed. In the vastness of the Canadian wilderness, constructing a home and positioning his bed near the rapids of a sleep-inducing stream fit his limited abilities. If he did go to college, the boy felt confident he could handle the recreation courses for a degree in counseling and camp administration.

Creative Writing class offered an awakening for the boy. Mr. Kundera exemplified an avant-garde teacher even though he wore a tie and had short curly hair; the sleeves on his white shirt rolled up. His suit coat, rarely worn, hung on a hook on the back of the door. The class studied poetry, but not the boring rhyming stuff other English teachers had classes recite. Mr. Kundera taught the boy how to dissect a poem with word association to clarify the line or phrase as a part of an entire story. They studied and listened to all the Simon and Garfunkel songs.

Mr. Kundera taught the class how to shotgun thoughts onto the page, exploring virgin ideas that wandered within the brain in uncensored explosions. He did not care if the boy wrote fifty swear words if it led to a germ of a story or poem. The boy liked the class so much that he shrugged off his slide-by philosophy and wrote as much as possible.

Mr. Reynolds, the Drama teacher, approached the boy during the third week of the semester. The fall play would be "*Raisin in The Sun.*"

"The play tells the struggles of a black family moving into a white neighborhood in Chicago. Would that interest you?"

"What part could I try out for?" the boy asked.

"The cast consists of several members of a black family and their wives or boyfriends. I need someone to play the white man that tries to talk the family out of moving to his neighborhood.

"It's a serious drama. Some of the parts will be played by community members, not high schoolers."

"When are the tryouts?" the boy asked.

"I don't have anyone else in mind for the part. I doubt if anyone else would show up for a tryout. We will begin rehearsals a week from today if you can handle it. Here is the script."

The boy read the script in bed that night. He could not put it down. Karl Lindner, a bigoted mouse of a man, would be the role the boy would portray. The opposite of a Bush Voyager. A challenge: the most challenging character he could ever hope to attempt. Sidney Portier played the lead black man in the movie version.

By the third week of rehearsals, the boy knew he would be performing a small part in something incredible happening in Kalamazoo. The black actors had little, if any, stage experience. Stage directions for blocking scenes created a challenge. Mr. Reynolds patiently waited for everyone to write the movements in their scripts before moving on. The group's passion for the play and the characters was evident at every rehearsal. From the first day to opening night, everyone worked and reworked the scenes, memorizing, moving with purpose; tension. The boy worked with the same intensity. Karl Lindner had to be sincere and honest. His prejudice had to come through his words without sarcasm. Well, perhaps with just a touch of irony.

The small part was a gem. Off stage, the other actors treated him like family. They sensed his true feelings. Feelings he had to subjugate the minute he stepped on stage. The part involved two small scenes, both powerful.

The whole experience amazed the boy. His fellow actors were all exceptional, despite never being on stage. The scenes, the climax, everything; electrifying. The boy could not have been prouder to participate in the production.

Opening night challenged the boy's past theater experience. The theater had a balcony and an eighty-foot fire curtain, world-class. All eighteen hundred students could be seated for school assemblies.

The seats were not sold out for the opening night, but at least four hundred people attended. Most of the audience consisted of black men, women, and children who had never viewed a live performance of a play before. Backstage, the boy kept hearing gasps and "Amen" scattered among the audience.

The boy's surge of adrenaline as he paced backstage for his first entrance intensified. He concentrated on calming his breathing, listening for his cue. The scene concluded with just the right amount of tension, preparing the audience for his second scene near the end of the second act.

The audience vocalized respect for the matriarch and disdain for the cowardly actions of the male lead. When the boy entered for his second scene, the crowd booed the white guy with slicked-back blond hair. The boy carried on with even more mousey intensity, and when the male lead found the balls to kick him off the stage, the audience roared approval and applauded. The actors waited for an appropriate beat before continuing.

The boy came off stage feeling more satisfied than in any previous performances he had delivered. After the curtain, everyone congratulated everyone else. They all thought he had done the part justice.

The boy did not mingle with the black students at Kalamazoo Central during the day.

The boy attended the cast party held on the north side of town, the "colored" section. He did his best to act like he fit in but knew he did not. He wished he did. Great people, all. He would try harder in the future.

Two weeks into the basketball season, the tension in school boiled over. The frustrations from the summer Detroit riots migrated west to Kalamazoo. It began with the basketball cheerleaders.

The school's varsity basketball team held the top spot in the league. John Gordon, at six-one, played shooting guard, and Sam Simmons, a six-three all-state senior, played center, dunking the ball after bullet passes found him in the lane. John Gordon, the boy's ping pong competitor, and another white player off the bench supported the rest of the black guards and forwards, shifting in off the bench. During timeouts, the cheerleaders ran out in white and maroon skimpies onto the court and led the cheers. The boy thought cheerleaders were a waste of time. After all, they never made a basket.

The boy began to hear rumors about disgruntled black students wondering why the cheerleading squad for the primarily black basketball team was all white. Of course, the cheerleading coach pointed to the fair tryouts that had been inclusive and that the group had been chosen on talent. Feelings escalated, and a walkout during school hours ended with a protest at the administration building. At first, the march had little effect. But after several such protest marches and community meetings, the cheerleading squad coach conducted additional tryouts, and two black cheerleaders joined the squad. At the next basketball game, the black cheerleaders, as capable as the white cheerleaders, quashed the argument of superior white cheerleading skills.

Although the boy never made a school basketball team, he again played church basketball at the downtown YMCA as a senior. The old gym downtown had a curved running track suspended from the ceiling that angled up at the corner curves to facilitate running. Bob Prader, also on the team, sometimes attracted two or three girls from Kalamazoo Central who saw the game from the track above, although neither Bob nor the boy urged them to attend. As the boy glanced up, he noticed the girls were watching him as much as they considered Bob. He had grown shoulders and height over the summer as a Bush Voyager and now turned heads as much as Bob.

The boy took to writing during his senior year as he played basketball and ping-pong in junior high. He published one of his poems in "Echoes," the bound booklet of all the best work in the class. His stories were read often in class and met with appreciation.

The boy deliberated on the school and the rising racial tensions between his weekend dates. He felt the strength of confidence he had gained as a Bush Voyager underlying his entire senior year. Perhaps, he thought, he could do more, be more. He would never be a merit scholar, but he knew how to carry his weight and survive.

He took inventory of his strengths. The list included acting, speaking, writing, and, yes, carrying a backpack and a canoe simultaneously. Pausing one day at the trophy case in the first-floor front hallway, the boy read and reread the posting about the senior class speech at graduation. He knew that the valedictorian or another high achiever gave the address. But the more he thought about the hypocrisy of his small experiences at Kalamazoo Central High School, the more he believed he had to try.

He wrote the speech entirely on his own. He did not pay any attention to graduation speech conventions or the standards he had been bored with at graduations: "We seniors will go forth and do great deeds, blah, blah, blah." The boy wrote what he wanted to hear.

The speech had to be typewritten and submitted to the graduation committee. Five judges would listen to the presentations, grade them, and post the results.

The boy had signed up for Typing Class too late in eighth grade; all the classes were full. Just typing the speech turned into a bush voyage for the boy, but he submitted the paper on time, a first for him.

He gave the speech to Mrs. Seward, a teacher unfamiliar to the boy. As he laid the paper down in front of Mrs. Seward, he looked at it on the desk, satisfied.

The title at the top: *"Raisin in The Sun."* The boy signed the speech in cursive in the bottom right corner:

Author: **Sean Martensen**

Kalamazoo Central High School Senior Class Speech submission, April 24th, 1968.

The tryout schedule called for the boy's live delivery in front of the five judges on a Thursday afternoon in late April. The echo of the empty auditorium bounced his words back at him. He knew he presented well. The committee sat in the fourth to the last row of the darkened hall and clapped at the conclusion.

> Good evening seniors, administration, and parents. The senior year in high school is unique. Some choices need to be decided about college or work, getting married or staying single, Vietnam or peace, or where to live. Seniors anticipate being more unrestrained than ever before.
>
> These things are thought about by all high school seniors. That is high school U.S.A.
>
> Kalamazoo Central is different. All those decisions I noted must be resolved senior year, but they do not embody us until next year, so that is our future.
>
> However, the most significant conflict in American history did not wait until next year to define us. It did not involve the adult community or occur in the next city but in our halls and lunchroom. We that went to Central had to make definite decisions about "race" and act on them this past year.
>
> Making decisions, acting according to those decisions, and living with the consequences; is a teacher's definition of growing up. That is what your parents send you to school for, so that is what I am going to talk about tonight.
>
> First, the cheerleading incident. It is incredible to me that adding two girls or adding fifty girls to a school cheerleading squad could upset the entire city of Kalamazoo. There were walkouts from classes and five to ten fights a day. For two days, policemen patrolled the halls.
>
> On the third day of the cheerleading incident, I felt confident that a fight would not break out with a policeman in the front hall. Imagine a yell and a scream and everyone tearing to the front lobby, where a crowd of white and black students stood on either side of a

policeman. The officer attempted to control a black sophomore wrenching on his tie, trying to do some damage before being subdued. The policeman stuffed the boy into the wastebasket against the wall.

Two friends jumped out of the white crowd, exchanged a few blows with black students, and jumped back when no one followed their example. The teachers dispelled the group of students when the bell rang, and we went to class. At the end of the day, I heard that my two friends had been found and beaten during one of the fights.

I talked to one of the more neutral boys involved in these skirmishes who had been to the office and had talked to one of the officers. The officer encouraged the boy to clean up on those so-and-so blackies. "Just so you don't throw the first blow," the policeman had told him.

The next day the school board requested that the whites and the blacks have separate meetings during school to discuss problems and reduce tensions. And boy, did they let go. I heard such white statements as:

"One of them works with me and spends all his money on getting drunk every night, and, well, colored people just don't want to keep up their homes or work to feed their children."

Or "They don't want equal rights; they want our rights too."

And "They want cheerleaders according to population, not ability."

Some quite different views were:

"Give these kids a couple of cheerleaders so they feel like yelling for the black basketball team as much as we like to win with it."

"When your father hires them, they'll have enough money to paint their house."

These comments were drowned out by the many and louder voices of the "I say to defend ourselves" white students.

I left this all-white meeting so disgusted at the things I never thought to hear so openly that I said as much to my counselor. He is black. He told me what came out in the black discussion groups.

One boy claimed his teacher had told him he would flunk her American History class if he participated in the protest marches in front of the school on the cheerleading incident. Another boy said that one of his teachers had caught him talking in the back of the room and said, "Shut up, you damn dirty nigger." Yes, white students, this is what the other side said in those discussions where you claimed no prejudice existed at Kalamazoo Central.

Things calmed down. Two black cheerleaders were added to the squad, and a negro history class to the curriculum. The two new cheerleaders were uniform when I attended the next basketball game. They sat halfway up in the bleachers and came down to cheer twice during the game, turning on the smiles. Even the skeptics had to admit they were as good or better than the rest of the squad. The Board of Education stepped in again, and the black cheerleaders cheered a whole game.

Months passed in relative calm at school.

On April 4th, 1968, Dr. Martin Luther King died. Assassinated. I went to school the next day upset, perplexed, and cynical about the future of our country. No thoughts of violence entered my mind. But violence erupted. First, the fire drill bell rang, and when I looked out the open window of the fourth-floor window, I saw some black students chasing a white student, hitting, and cursing him as he ran.

We spent five minutes in Government class discussing the "Gold Shortage." I heard someone yelling and a general uproar down the hall. A group of fifty or more black students marched past our classroom. Someone passing by opened our door from the outside, and the noise increased. A few boys stopped outside our door, peering inside at all our white faces. They asked if

[113]

any of us wanted to come outside and start something. The teacher went to the door, explaining to the boys outside that the door had been closed, he had been conducting class, and he wished not to be disturbed. He tried to close the door, but they would not let him. The teacher said to let him close the door because it had been shut, and he wished not to be disturbed. The students said it had been open. The teacher said, "The door was closed." The students said it had not been. Then the teacher turned to the class and asked sternly but democratically, "Class, was this door open or closed?"

Everyone in the class said in unison, "CLOSED," but I, frustrated by the hypocrisy of a race incident arising over a wooden door, yelled out, "OPEN." The teacher expelled me, but the boys outside the door laughed, pointed at me, and moved on. During lunch, I headed for the bakery. Outside the front doors, some black girls came out of the door and accused a white friend of mine who was standing there of going out with their boyfriend. They started hitting her, knocking off her glasses. I said, *"Hold It!"* and bent over for her glasses. Surprise! The girls stopped, but when I looked up, I found four of my soul brothers in front of me.

I tried to smile when they hit. I stood my ground, unmoving, and tried to smile. It did not hurt much, just my jaw, my left ear, and my right eye. I stayed standing.

I went to the fourth-hour class a little shaky that day. My teacher knew right away that I had been in a fight. She is kind of short, big, old, and black. She is known as Central's master of sarcastic humor.

She congratulated us on making it back from lunch. She told us to read while going into the now terrifying halls. Everyone begged her to stay in the room. She left anyway but came running back in, pushing several white girls before her. Laughing, she got out a key and locked the door. Next, we heard gunshot sounds, but the teacher said the rascals were turning over the lockers. An announcement from the principal sent us all home.

The senior class council hired a soul band for the senior prom, but some of the classes' parents thought a soul band would be an outrageous way to end the year, so they decided to have a "nice, private party." They held their party the same night as the school-sponsored prom in a fancy room with a traditional band. The all-white attendance at this party, tagged the "Mini-Prom" by the seniors, was very light.

We seniors made it through the last year at Kalamazoo Central without death or serious injury from riots, despite the rumors about kids being thrown out of third-floor windows.

I wonder what adults would have done if our incidents had blown up into a city-wide or state-wide conflict. You have homes to lose and shotguns to protect them with. Could you boast a similar record of continuing communications between the races?

The connections between the races this year at Central put us years ahead of the other schools in this area and years ahead of other communities across the United States; because this connection will influence our thinking for the rest of our lives until the conflict is resolved.

I may never understand the pressures forcing the black man to fight for his rights instead of waiting patiently under the white foot until we give them to him. I have never known these pressures. I am not black.

And I will not say that I sympathize with the black nation, for they do not want my sympathy, only my acceptance and respect.

And I will not confuse or muddle the issue by leading a white revolution to coincide with the black one that may erupt in our summer cities in the U.S. You do not know how easily that could start over a cheerleader or death of a leader or neighbor shot.

But I will not take up arms against them, or against anyone for that matter. This is the education that I received at Kalamazoo Central High School. I found that I would just as soon shake hands with a black man with a gun as I would with a Viet Cong with a weapon or a Friend with a firearm. If they want to kill me, that is their decision, I will be dead, and it will not matter to me.

But I do not think it will come to that. I say that Kalamazoo Central is turning out the best community members to deal with this conflict.

To those whites in the audience who do not understand how anyone can promote violence or riots, try to understand through this poem by Langston Hughes.

What happens to a dream deferred?
Does it dry up?
Like a raisin in the sun?
And fester like a sore?
And then run?
Does it stink like rotten meat?
Or crust and sugar over
Like a syrupy sweet?
Maybe it just sags
Like a heavy load.
Or does it explode?

Three days later, Mrs. Seward stopped Sean in the hall, and he accompanied her back to her office. She handed him his speech.

"You did a fine job on this paper, Sean. You should be proud. You delivered an excellent speech; I thought the content was relevant and poignant.

"Two of the five judges gave your speech the highest marks and lobbied hard for it to be presented. Most of the committee believed the administration would not allow a controversial speech.

"Still, you presented an exceptional speech."

The boy would not be giving the senior class speech at graduation. He had expected no less from the day he started writing the speech. It did not matter. Just as he knew he could push a Volkswagen for twenty miles, he knew his address to be good. Just another Bush Voyage.

2

ARCHITECT

An ant superorganism has multiple colony members that cooperate to accomplish extraordinary feats. This social behavior significantly advantages ants over solitary insects and other animals.

1969

With the door open to his dorm room on the evening of December 1st, Sean became annoyed with the sound of turned-up radios echoing along the hall. At eight-thirty, rereading a paragraph in *Cat's Cradle* for the third time, he gave up, threw the paperback on the bed, and casually took the stairs from his third-floor dorm suite to the lobby. Five guys lounged on various chairs and couches, watching CBS. Occasionally, Roger Mudd's voice would make a short comment on the progress of the lottery.

The big windows lining the north wall of the lounge area dripped condensation as the outside temperature in Marquette, Michigan, dropped below thirty degrees. The weather that day had alternated between snow and rain, melting, dirty snow lining the always clear sidewalks on campus.

Sean stood behind one of the couches as one of the students, listening to the announcer, commented, "And there it is." The student got up off the couch and left the room.

Two minutes later, Sean heard his birthday announced, June 27th, number 64, guaranteeing that he would be drafted as soon as his college deferment expired. He shrugged, Vietnam out of the question.

He headed back to his room. His roommate, Craig Barden, sat hunched over on the bottom bunk to avoid the wooden support of the top bunk.

Sean began the year with two roommates. Craig Barden could have walked out of *The Legend of Sleepy Hollow* Disney cartoon as the embodiment of Ichabod Crane. Skinny enough to blow over in a Northern Michigan gale, Craig's hair appeared greasy (the shower was rarely used;) his face was covered with popped zits. His nose had the same hook as Ichabod's. Shy around girls, Craig did not play any sport. He mailed his dirty clothes downstate to be washed and returned.

Steve, the third roommate, had demanded the bottom bunk back in September underneath Craig, making Craig move to the top bunk. Steve, a hulking high school football player from the Milwaukee area, walked with a blank expression, making it easy to imagine he would need help tying his shoes. Steve spent the first three days away from their dorm room. Upon his return, Steve found the time when Craig had left their dorm room to approach Sean.

"Hey, what do you say we get da skinny guy out of here. We's would have a lot more room."

"Really," Sean said.

"Ya, eh, I give him a week, no more than two."

Sean did not respond, but Steve assumed they were in alliance.

From then on, Steve harassed Craig at every turn. Steve tried everything, from short sheeting Craig's bed to calling him names. Craig took the abuse. Sean finally confided Steve's ultimate goal to Craig while making it clear he would play no part in Steve's plan. Craig just chuckled.

The next day when Steve entered the room and plopped his massive frame on the bed, his head hitting the pillow hard, he found a bowling ball underneath. Rubbing the bump on the back of his head, he sprang up and wrestled Craig to the floor, turning

Craig into a pretzel and pushing his face into the linoleum. Sean thought Craig's arm might break.

Steve yelled at Craig, "Give up, give up,,,,, say Uncle."

"No," said Craig.

"Say, Uncle!"

"No."

"Say, Uncle," Steve said even louder.

"No, I won't," said Craig, through teeth mashed into the floor.

Abruptly, Steve let go of his human pretzel. Craig rose from the floor and hopped up on his bed. Amazingly, Steve left the room. Sean witnessed this routine two more times. During the third occurrence, Sean had had enough.

"Let him go, Steve," Sean said, "Just let him go. You know he's not going to say, Uncle."

Steve left the room in another huff. Craig and Sean returned to the room three days later to find that Steve had moved out. Where? They did not care.

When Sean returned from watching the lottery show on CBS, Craig, sitting on his lower bunk bed, mashed his cigarette in the ashtray on the nightstand. Room rules, no smoking; ignored by the ungainly roommate. Craig looked nonplussed about the lottery. Perhaps he would be lucky and draw a high number. Sean kept his own drawn number to himself.

"I'm off to the frat house," Craig said, gathering his cigarette pack and standing up, knocking his head again. He had taken up smoking to "look cool" to the officers in the only fraternity on campus that accepted his pledge.

Sean laid down on his own bed and opened his book.

Sean sometimes dreamed of living in a cabin in the wilderness of Canada next to a swift river. He pictured a rugged girl resting beside him in bed, listening to the rapids. That is where the dream always went awry. *Where in hell would he find a girl willing to live in the Canadian bush with him.* Not even the slightest bit likely.

Still, the second Kennedy assassination last June solidified Sean's cynicism for the American dream, nearly driving Sean to the Canadian wilderness despite a lack of sympathetic female companionship.

Instead, he followed in both brothers' footsteps and applied for college. Academically, Sean did not qualify for Michigan State University, Robert's alma mater. Neither could he see himself attending a fancy private college. Edward finished his degree at Kalamazoo College last May. Sean did not feel worthy of that kind of college expenditure. Harry and Sarah believed in providing the funds for all five children to attend a college of choice: which was risky in their middle son's case. Perhaps Harry believed in the importance of education due to his missed opportunity during the Depression. Her years in college provided Sarah with some of her most memorable memories and lifelong friends.

Sean had taken the college entrance exam (ACT,) receiving higher scores than expected. Still, his high school grades were so poor he applied to only two schools, the University of New Mexico in Albuquerque and Northern Michigan University in Marquette. Both schools accepted him under an open-door policy before they received his test scores or high school transcripts.

Marquette is a pleasant old-fashioned small town with two-story brick buildings built during the mining age. The sprawling campus of Northern Michigan University, built on the high ground to the north, overlooked the city. The three-story dorms and a classroom building hid amongst a carved-out second-growth pine forest. The freezing waters of Lake Superior, a half mile to the east, enhanced the atmosphere of learning and living with nature. The vast northern peninsula forest began steps from the campus. The area had the feel of the Canadian bush Sean treasured, a place to make a new start.

Sean worried he would flunk out of the classes his parents had paid for. On the first day of his Humanities 110 class, he sensed a difference from high school. Mr. Martell's gentle voice outlined the requirements for the course. Slight of build, Martell had black hair covering his ears and a trimmed beard. Smiling, he looked not much older than thirty. He wore a pullover gray sweater and a tie with dark slacks instead of a suit.

Professor Martell did not push or demand, or try to persuade the class. He presented the material and his thoughts fearlessly, which intrigued Sean. After class, Sean hurried to the bookstore to purchase the first novel they would explore; *A Farewell to Arms* by Ernest Hemingway.

To be on the safe side, Sean declared his major: *Outdoor Recreation Leadership and Management* with a *Theater* minor. An eventual position as a director of Camp Aharah, his bush voyaging base camp, would be ideal. He knew he would be able to handle the course of study.

Sean read *A Farewell to Arms* and wrote a paper about it ahead of the due date. He typed the theme with two fingers on the cheap portable typewriter he had brought up north, using more than half a bottle of whiteout. The discussions between the "Yoopers" and the "Trolls" from below the bridge amused the freshman in class. Mr. Martell related the book's themes to the times' political climate and the Upper Peninsula's sociologic climate.

The rest of Sean's classes were just as enjoyable. Sean completed assigned papers on time, ready to turn them in before hanging out with his girlfriend to play cards for the evening. Freedom to fail awakened in Sean a desire not to.

Sean kept up with the homework and papers in all his courses. He discovered a profound principle. Sean had been incredibly good at faking out his teachers in high school, sliding along, doing just enough to get by. He discovered in college that if he did the assignments required, he could pass the tests and receive excellent grades. As it turned out, studying took much less effort and stress than coming up with excuses.

That fall, Sean's girlfriend told him she wanted to date a sophomore fraternity man who asked her out. Even though he knew he could never convince her to live in a log cabin, he could not let go of the thought of her soft skin, the feel of her breasts and nipples.

Sean hung out with some of his high school buddies attending NMU. Chumming with them for a week, he drank too much cherry vodka and smoked his share of pot and hashish. They asked for help constructing a log cabin they were building on the weekends about seventy miles west of the campus. Sean agreed.

Early Saturday, Sean threw his down sleeping bag and camping gear in the truck bed. Amidst the October snow, Sean helped put another row of logs on the cabin. His friends had done just what Sean had intended to do if he had gone off to live in the Canadian bush. They had taken the highway until they were in the middle of nowhere, turned off the road on a lightly traveled two-track, and randomly turned again into the woods, finding a very isolated spot to clear and build their cabin.

The cabin was far more ambitious than Sean had imagined for himself up in Canada. He suspected that none of the other boys had experienced living in the wild as he had for two summers. He doubted the boys would complete the cabin before losing interest, but the work took Sean's mind away from the girl.

When he returned to campus on Sunday evening, he decided to survive without his girl. As he walked back toward his dorm room, he crossed paths with the frat man and the girl, nodding as he passed them. A minute later, his girl ran up to him from behind, confessed her love for him, and asked if they could be together. Sean nodded, but something deep within him had changed. He could not put his finger on the difference. A feeling, a broken trust, the letting go of love, the contemplation of a different than expected future; whatever it was, Sean buried it.

At the end of the first semester, Sean earned a grade point average of 3.78. He made the honor roll.

Beyond his studies, a fascination with sex occupied most of his thoughts. In the forest north of campus, Sean staked out a collapsed two-man tent covered by particle board over a two-by-four frame, leaving it covered with snow in the forest. Trekking out on Friday afternoon with three sleeping bags to erect the tent, he and his girl would stomp out in the snow after dinner, fooling around for a couple of hours at night, drinking cherry vodka or smoking pot before the dorm curfew.

In the second semester, Sean's grades were even better; he attained a four-point.

Sean learned of Michigan State University's twenty-four-hour open house rules that spring. Men and women visited any dorm room at any time. RAs did not watch every move. No weekend sign-outs to worry about. No PDAs (Public Displays of Affection.) At Northern, allowable visits occurred on Sunday afternoons; the dorm room door had to remain open, and at least one foot of each person had to stay flat on the floor at all times. If a couple accumulated three PDAs, the girl stayed confined in her dorm for a weekend: idiotic.

MSU became an obsession. Sean and his girlfriend had performed well in their college courses, and Michigan State University approved their transfer applications for the fall term. Sean anticipated far more challenges at the more prominent university.

In April, the wife of a former U.S. Representative of the Sixth Congressional District approached Sean to direct a day camp for several of her youngest son's friends. One hundred percent of the camp fee (set by Sean) would be his salary. At thirty dollars per week per camper, he figured six enrolled campers would net him $180.00 per week. Excellent money: the job was right up his alley.

Since the days of sliding by through junior high school and the time he stole the damn belt, Sean's life steadily improved, even to the point of regaining respect from Harry, his father. Now he wanted more sex, additional responsibility, regard, money, and freedom. Especially more sex.

Sean had taken a heavy course load at NMU and planned to take an even heavier load at MSU. By taking twenty-one credits per quarter, he could graduate in three years.

Sean switched his major to English Education with a concentration on creative writing. The Creative Writing class consisted of six students. The other students and the teacher received Sean's stories and poetry with appreciation. The Twentieth Century American Literature class inspired the nascent author. Sean read Hemingway, Fitzgerald, Dos Passos, and Steinbeck. He also found his Chaucer class amusing. The Professor who taught Sean's Shakespeare section convinced Sean of Shakespeare's genius.

On May 4th, images of the Kent State massacre flooded the Michigan State campus. On May 6th, SDS organized a boycott of classes and a sit-in protest on campus. Sean supported anything that might help stop the Vietnam insanity. He joined the march to the capital and listened to the speakers at the rallies. He decided to boycott class. Sean's seventy-two-year-old linguistics teacher made it easy. His anger over the Vietnam conflict resulted in an offer to extend every student's current grade in the class, canceling all further lessons until the strike ended.

Sean's creative writing professor declared the opposite; keep writing, create, come to class, and discuss ten poems due next Tuesday. Sean could not reconcile the hypocrisy. Either he would strike, or he would write. He quit writing. The sit-in and the class boycott ended when the quarter ended, and the students went home for the summer.

Sean and his brother Stephen were co-directors of the day camp that summer. The money reward increased as more kids signed up.

When the camp ended in August, Sean took the Kalamazoo city bus downtown each morning to the Manpower office, waiting to be assigned a day job. His jobs varied from cleaning up a burned-out drug store to corporate lawn work. The men Sean met in the Manpower waiting room all needed money; all ready to work. Except for the "ingot job." A black man, Percy, sat next to Sean one morning, moving away from the other men.

"Watch out, young fella," he said, "The third week of the month is when the foundry needs extra help. If you get that assignment, just run out the door."

"You have to take the job that comes up, don't you," Sean asked.

"I'm just telling you, the "ingot job" is the worst. Sometimes the blocks slip off the track. They give you these big heavy asbestos gloves so's you can grab the ingots as they slide out of the foundry oven. White hot. Believe me, you will think you are inside the furnace on that one."

Sean imagined third-degree burns on his hands.

Instead, that day he and another scrawny white guy in his fifties accepted a week-long assignment at a dorm on the Western Michigan University campus. The short white guy named Stacy had eyes that tracked funny. His pant cuffs puddled at his ankles. He shuffle-walked. When the two were dropped off on campus, the construction site foreman pointed to an elevator contraption anchored outside a seven-story dorm. They were directed to stand on the nine-foot square platform while the operator rocketed it up to a window on the fifth floor.

The operator could jerk stop the platform at a window on each floor that had been removed, frame and all. Two men were waiting to hand Sean and Stacy a wooden desk with drawers on the side. The desk needed to be tipped on its side and placed in the corner of the wobbling platform. A pipe railing on one side of the platform provided a handhold. The other three sides were open, with no barrier. Every movement on the raised floor sent it swaying back and forth. Sean helped set the desk down. Gung-ho Stacy started to muscle it over to one of the open edges of the platform. Sean helped the best he could while holding the rail for dear life with his other hand.

Five more desks were handed out the window, packed tightly on the platform leaving little space for Stacy or Sean. Stacy signaled the operator on the ground, and the platform jerk started, dropping a foot before the gears caught and the stage wobbled down. Stacy and Sean helped two additional workers offload the desks from the platform to a truck headed for a storage warehouse.

Sean and Stacy hopped back on the platform for another harrowing ride up to the fifth floor to repeat the process. Stacy leaned against the rail. Sean held on with one hand, trying to act nonchalant. Stacy tried to fix both his eyes on Sean. The left eye wandered left.

"I'm a roofer by trade, you see. This is nothing. You'll get used to it," Stacy said.

"Yeah, I guess so," said Sean, "That man operating the elevator, I've never seen a man as sunburned as that."

Stacy glanced down over the rail. "He's an Indian. Full blooded by the look of him. Lots of Indians are heavy construction operators. On the first try, he stops this crate within two inches of the window. They know their shit about heavy equipment," the short man said.

Wow, that is one very red man, Sean thought.

By mid-morning, Sean no longer held onto the rail. He moved much more cautiously than Stacy, minding the platform's edge. Stacy and Sean sat under a tree during a break, eating their sack lunches, a Zorro sandwich for Sean, an apple, and about six crackers for Stacy.

"You're getting it now, I guess. Hell," Stacy said, "I have roofed for sixteen years. I only fell once so far. Three stories, commercial. Broke a leg, cracked my head a little."

Thus, the slight limp Sean had noticed.

On the second day, the elevator began to stop on the sixth floor. It took Sean an hour to acclimate to the higher height. Stacy had been right; Sean did get used to it. He manhandled the desks on the platforms with little regard to the elevation at which he worked. He concentrated on the nine-foot square platform, its edge, its wobble. Sean worked the seventh floor on the third and part of the last day. He could see a lot of Kalamazoo from that height. He felt sorry to see the final desk loaded on the truck,

The following week, Sean worked at the Kalamazoo County Fair as a parking lot attendant, six hours a day in the sun until the day before the wedding, August 29th, 1970.

Weddings were not Sean's cup of tea, to say the least. He left all the details to his fiancé and her family. Whatever she wanted, Sean just nodded; OK with him. Her Uncle, Orin Criswell, would officiate, a very conservative minister from the state's east side. Sean had met him and socialized with the cousins at a few family gatherings. The eldest teenager, a socially awkward nineteen-year-old, interjected bible verses in every conversation. The dinner prayers from Uncle Otto went on forever. In short, Sean regretted the choice, given his agnostic, if not atheistic, beliefs.

Uncle Orin insisted on two sessions of marriage counseling. The first such session dealt with religion and the duties of husband and wife. The second session became torturous. Uncle Orin looked like a swarthy mafia boss. He spoke with the same authoritative voice that he used in his pulpit, even in a casual social situation, painful to listen to.

"I would like to cover the topic of sex," began the minister, "You will be unschooled the night of your wedding, but with patience, everything will work out for you just fine."

Sean concentrated on not widening his eyes in surprise and disbelief. Uncle Orin continued, "God allows experimentation, but you will want to settle in on the missionary position."

Sean, startled into giving the reverend a sour look, thought, *What the fuck business is it of yours?*

Uncle Orin noted Sean's quizzical demeanor, taking it to mean he did not understand. Uncle Orin illustrated his point by putting his left hand out, palm up, and then placing his right palm down over his left, patting it.

"Like this," he said.

Then Uncle Orin switched his left hand with his right, placing his left palm down over his right knuckles.

"Not like this."

Sean nearly burst out laughing. Glancing at his wife-to-be, they said nothing, relieved when the session concluded.

The wedding rapidly became Sean's worst nightmare. There were way too many people. Before they took their places at the altar in the front of the sanctuary, the men in the wedding party waited in the dressing room off the chancel. Uncle Orin leaned in, giving Sean quiet, last-minute advice.

"Now, Sean," he cautioned, "don't be a bull in a china shop."

Sean could not figure out the pertinence of that idiotic comment. He stood at the top of the stairs in front of the altar in tip-top shape, in a white tux, hair bleached from a week making change at the fair, a nice tan to boot. Sean had been in a dozen productions in front of audiences. He was not nervous, scared, or trying to show off. *What the hell did a bull in a china shop have to do with him?*

He repeated the words of the vows in a loud, sincere voice, listening to himself as if acting in a play.

",,, from this day forward, for better, for worse, for richer, for poorer, in sickness and health, to love and to cherish, till death do us part."

Sean, twenty years old at the time, had just committed to "forever." After all the months of planning, working, studying, and anticipating, those final words hit Sean like a hammer. *How could anyone say that? Death could be fifty years away. Could he do what he had said, really? Why hadn't he reviewed and modified the vows for the realities of the twentieth century?*

At the reception, due to a one-hour, ten-minute picture-taking delay, the guests (famished) waited at the wedding party to shake hands and hug the bride and groom. There was no booze at this reception; the bride and groom were under twenty-one. The reception, sponsored by the Ladies Auxiliary, held in the church's basement, sported white paper tablecloths taped to six-foot rectangular folding tables, complete with brown metal folding chairs, and a bouquet of pink tea roses in a small vase in the center.

Sean anticipated a two-week honeymoon full of sex; however, his bride came down with a terrible cold the first week. Amidst the sniffles and nose-blowing, the couple stayed in a friend's beautiful cottage on Lake Michigan near Petoskey. The couple spent a second week at a romantic resort east of Windsor, Canada. Per Sean's plan, the couple could drink legally there, which Sean did, proceeding to make himself sick with a two-day head and stomach hangover.

The couple settled in a one-bedroom apartment in the married housing complex at MSU. They ate through Sean's wildly unrealistic thousand-dollar cushion within months. Sean's student teaching requirement for graduation precluded his search for a job. His wife found part-time work as a waitress at the Woolworth's soda fountain but insisted they buy a car for transportation, even though the city bus route went right by the Woolworth's mini mall. Sean could walk two miles from their apartment to the Frandor Shopping Center and Woolworths in about a half hour. The monthly thirty-five-dollar car payment added to the couple's financial troubles.

Sean car-pooled with two other students to Owosso Junior High School for his student teaching internship. The drive to Owosso, a small berg northeast of the MSU campus, took forty minutes one-way. Sean's supervising teacher taught three sections of Theater Arts and two sections of English. Ms. Costner reminded Sean of his sixth-grade teacher, Mrs. Lazenby, in looks and manner. At least she did not stuff her snot rag up her sleeve. Sean stood in the back of the classroom each day while Ms. Costner told the students to open their theater textbooks and read or answer questions from the end of their assigned chapter. One disruptive theater section contained students that historically misbehaved. Sean wrung his hands behind him while watching Ms. Costner's absurd teaching technique. During his second week, Sean could no longer remain silent.

He approached his supervising teacher. "Ms. Costner, I suggest I try teaching all your drama sections starting next week. I believe I am ready. I have a lot of ideas I would like to try. Would that be possible?"

A surprised Ms. Costner said, "Really? All three sections? Are you sure?"

"I'm sure," Sean replied.

"Well, alright. I will confess that I have never seen a theater production. It is against my religious beliefs."

"If you allow me a free hand, Ms. Costner, I'll be ready Monday morning." He could not believe she had agreed.

Monday, Sean took over the three Theater sections. Ms. Costner stayed out of the room. Sean gave her a lot of credit for turning the sections over to him, a neophyte student teacher. But on Monday, Sean explained the history and concept of stage directions instead of reading out of the book. Within ten minutes, the students took turns in front of the class while Sean quizzed them.

"Jim, cross downstage left. Nicole, cross to center stage. "

All three sections of Theater Arts responded with surprise and fascination at Sean's prepared lesson. Even the trouble-making class absorbed the lesson and activities enthusiastically. In the smoke-filled teacher's lounge, Sean heard of all the problems his "bad" students created in their other classes. Sean could not stand the smoke or the conversation and never returned to the teacher's lounge, instead eating lunch with the music student teacher in the classroom.

The principal stopped him in the hallway one morning and asked to see him in his office. Sean anticipated recognition for his ability to take over three hours of classroom teaching with positive results. Instead, Mr. Jackson admonished Sean for wearing jeans to school. Sean remembered sitting in the principal's office in sixth grade. He got along with his supervising teacher, Ms. Costner. She allowed space for Sean to succeed or hang himself. He respected her for that. Sean did well. He had no disciplinary problems, even with the students with the worst reputations. He poured all his experience and theater training into his lessons. His students began to experience the fun and reward of theater.

Sean planned a breathing and warm-up exercise involving Yoga. The principal again stopped him in the hallway before class.

"I thought I made it clear that jeans were not to be worn by school staff," the principal said.

Sean stood firm. "I am wearing attire appropriate for the lesson I am teaching today, sir. We will be on the floor working on breathing and relaxation. I believed jeans were necessary, so I am wearing them."

"I see," said the principal, "Just for today."

Sean lost all interest in the man. He could not imagine what the principal would have said if he had mentioned his breathing and relaxation exercises involved yoga. Sean also kept the "yoga" label out of his explanation of the class lessons. He set aside the last fifteen minutes of each class to practice his prescribed exercises and body positions. Sean spoke softly, soothing the students from toe to fingertip and willing them to relax.

The last class containing the so-called underachievers hurried to their positions on the floor, receptive to the rhythm in his voice. A pin drop could have been heard in the hall outside of Sean's classroom when he finished his relaxation small talk. No one moved. The bell rang for the students to move to their next class. No one moved. Twenty-eight students were so relaxed (some had fallen asleep) that they ignored the bell. Two minutes later, Sean roused the class and sent them on.

By the end of his ten-week internship, Sean understood that he would not do well with the administration that ran the schools where he might work. He had ignored the Owosso bureaucracy but sensed he would not have that luxury as a legitimate employee in another school district. He knew he would be isolated from a high percentage of the other teachers. Sean realized he could not give up "doing" for "teaching." He still wanted to be in the plays, write stories, or create a novel. Students should not have all the fun.

Sean never looked at his evaluations or grades from his student teaching experience. Instead, he began to think more and more about the possibility of architecture. He began his quest by studying the catalogs of architectural schools and listing the prerequisites he would need to obtain. Mostly math, physics, and basic design principles. Remembering this was why his brother, Edward, had avoided architecture, he enrolled in advanced algebra, a subject he had avoided in high school. Sean discovered his principle of actually studying the material worked in Algebra. Each succeeding precept relied on comprehending the previous one. Building blocks. He received an A In the class. Laying out a fourth year of college to pick up the prerequisites he needed, Sean signed up for Calculus and a physics class. There were three levels of physics classes at MSU. Students who would be physics teachers in high school took the most accessible set of physics classes. Serious science majors enrolled in a more rigorous physics series. Physics major requirements included an even more stringent series of physics classes.

Sean decided on the physics for science majors' path. These classes were self-taught. Sean followed a course outline, read a chapter, completed the homework assignment then took a written test involving solving several problems. Upon passing the test, he would move ahead to the next chapter. If Sean failed the test, additional study of the chapter's material and a retest were required. The retests involved different problems but covered the same concepts until all the questions were solved correctly. It meant self-discipline and concentration, but Sean had dreamed of architecture since he was twelve, watching Edward dabble and doodle house floor plans.

The household money situation became dire by the end of Sean's student teaching experience. The couple could no longer afford the rent in married housing. Sean's wife discovered a want-ad for a live-in housekeeper and handyman at an estate in Williamsburg. Room and board are provided as well as forty dollars a month. Sean, skeptical of his wife's commitment to washing and folding clothes for a stranger's family, agreed. They took the job, moving into the basement of the colonial-style home. The father, Mr. Stott, and the three children, all horribly overweight, were directed by the six-foot-tall, stocky Mrs. Stott, who harangued the family about their *Weight Watcher* diets. Sean guessed the father weighed four hundred pounds. He drove a custom-modified Lincoln Continental with the front bench seat welded back from the furthest standard position so his stomach could fit in front of the steering wheel. A tax consultant, Mr. Stott, received half the money he saved for a client company as his fee.

On Sean's first day, he spent seven hours cleaning the garage. Six St. Bernard puppies kept in the two-stall garage for six weeks had been sold. No one bothered to clean the improvised doghouse. Mounds of poop peppered the floor like a small mountain range. Nothing for it. He shoveled what he could and then began scraping, washing, and scrubbing the floors and the walls three feet up where the puppies had jumped and scratched.

The boy's wife, the housekeeper, had to clean up after the youngest son's wetted bed every night. Carl, a fourth grader, weighed more than Sean. He flooded the bed every night. The boy, charged with stripping the bed in the morning, somehow managed to elude that task, leaving it to the housekeeper. The oldest boy, a sixth grader, sometime during the night, snuck the peanut butter jar to his room and fingered it clean, leaving the family-size empty JIF jar for the housekeeper to find under his bed. The teenage girl stashed some of her father's San Francisco porn magazines in her sock draw; hidden? Apparently, Mr. Stott did not miss them.

The family underwear, shit-tracked and huge, required multiple tubs of laundry each day. The housekeeper also made a healthy dinner for the children on the days Mrs. Stott helped at her husband's office and real estate holdings. The father repeatedly broke the toilet seat in the upstairs bathroom.

Sean knew they would not last long at the Stott house, but he did his best to cheer up his wife. Sean took care of the teenage daughter's neglected horse as well. The teenager's responsibility, Sean never saw the girl ride the horse or lift a finger to brush it. She forked hay into the horse pen on rare occasions. Sean mucked the stall every day and fed the sway-back horse regularly. He did not care to ride the horse but enjoyed tending to it. He never learned its name, but the two bonded over the occasional apple he fed the horse.

That Christmas, while visiting Harry and Sarah in Kalamazoo, Sean's spouse, carrying an armload of presents, slipped on the ice on the way to the car. Harry Ace bandaged her leg, and the couple left to celebrate Christmas at the other in-law's house. When they reached her parents' home in Portage, her leg throbbed. They drove to the hospital. She returned sporting a knee-to-toe plaster cast and crutches.

The couple returned to the Stott home after Christmas. Sean assumed the housekeeper and handyman duties for the five weeks his better half limped around on her crutches. When the crutches came off, the couple asked for and received a raise to fifty dollars a month to better cover the thirty-five-dollar-a-month car payment. The couple hung in with the Stott family while they desperately looked for alternative housing. The couple found a cheap basement apartment in Lansing in late spring with two one-foot-high basement windows. Sean's wife took a job waitressing at the Lansing Country Club, and Sean found work that summer at Allied Van Lines in Lansing. They had endured seven months working for the Stott family. The tips from the country club felt heaven-sent.

A decent hourly wage accompanied the heavy work at Allied. Sean packed book boxes, wardrobes, and dish boxes, carrying the household items and packages to the semi-truck under the direction of professional movers. Usually, two men pack while the driver three dimensionally jigsaw puzzles household goods into the semi: stacking and cramming from floor to ceiling, wrapping each piece of furniture in blankets. The skill of the movers amazed Sean. The driver walked through the house a couple of times during the loading. He packed the truck, remembering which furniture pieces he wanted to use for the base of the following stack in the trailer. Belts and ropes tied off each stack. The driver wedged small items like an ironing board behind a completed stack.

The movers never stopped, even on the hottest days. In general, the middle age men appeared slight in build but wiry, never distracted with unnecessary talk. They worked their shift and headed to the bar. A couple of the workers had their paychecks held in the office over the weekend. Otherwise, their pay would be pissed away in alcohol, and the company could not count on them the following Monday. No sluff-off men worked at Allied.

Sean and a twenty-year man, Tim Sloan, went out on a job to move a piano in an apartment. That is all the work order said. Move the piano. The lady opened her door, and Tim introduced himself. He showed the thin lady in a below-the-knee, tiny fleur-de-lis sprinkled, green dress the work order and, nodding to Sean, pointed to the polished grand piano that took up at least half of the small living room.

"Where are we moving it, Ma'am?" he asked.

The lady wistfully scanned her small apartment.

"Down a floor," she said, "I've taken the two-bedroom apartment below this unit. You'll see it is much nicer."

She looked about to cry, skeptical that the two movers could safely move her piano. Tim stood a scosche over five foot seven. Sean appeared to be just a kid to the lady in her seventies. Tim looked at Sean while the lady gathered sheets for the men to walk on in their dirty boots.

Tim muttered, "Three-man job. It does not say on the work order we are changing floors. That is a three-man job with a 'grand.' It does not say 'grand' either. We've been fucked."

Tim paced the floor, sputtering again and again under his breath about how the bastards should have sent three movers out for the piano.

Said Sean, "You want to call it in? They can send someone."

Tim slapped the furniture strap he carried against his thigh. "Nope."

Tim folded the top board prop, carefully setting it to rest. He covered the piano in furniture blankets and belted them tightly. Sean and Tim, straining, turned the piano on its side. The piano was heavier than anything Sean had lifted to date. They unbolted the four legs, wrapped them in two blankets, and set the legs aside. The movers hefted the piano onto a four-wheel dolly and wheeled it to the landing outside the apartment. They removed the cart and snuck the carrying strap beneath the piano.

Their first goal was the landing between the third and second floors. The landing did not look big enough for the piano to make the turn. Tim glanced down as well.

"Ready?"

"Ready," said Sean.

Tim wrapped the strap around his right wrist and forearm. Sean followed suit. They lifted the piano, tightening the tension in the belt. Sean tilted it toward Tim, who took the piano's weight into his chest, shoulder, and back leg as best he could on a stair. Sean kept a solid hold of his end of the strap, holding the end of the piano up off the stairs, waddling down each step to the landing. The glossy black curves of the damn heavy thing made for a problematic handhold. Sean's strap arm took all the weight, awkwardly keeping the piano off the edge of the stair that would cause inevitable damage.

Once Tim reached the landing, the weight shifted to Sean continuing down the stairs.

At the landing, the movers rounded the corner in small increments, sure not to scrape any part or piece of the piano. The piano made the turn with an inch and a half to spare. The mover's mantra: "Once started, do not stop, do not put the item down; finish the move." With sweat pouring down his forehead, cheeks, and neck, Sean kept tension on the moving strap as Tim backed down the next flight of stairs. They reached the landing for the new apartment. The lady held the door open. Tim kept backing up.

"Show us where it goes, will you?"

The lady pointed to the corner of the much larger living room. Finally, the movers set the burden down and unstrapped the protected piano. Sean folded the blankets while Tim re-bolted the legs to the piano. The lady signed the bill of lading, and Tim ripped out the customer copy and handed it to the lady. The movers left the apartment building within minutes of setting down the piano without waiting for a thank-you tip. Sean, awed at their accomplishment, his left shoulder socket stretched and sore, decided the professional mover could probably figure out a way to move anything. If they had not been able to make the turn at the landing, they would have somehow lifted the piano over the rail to the second set of stairs. Tim, the quietest man that worked for Allied, climbed into the truck.

"Should have sent three men," he said again.

A man looking a bit older than Sean walked up to the Allied dock holding delivery bills of lading. Sean took the papers to the office and returned with orders to assist the driver and unload his truck full of family items from Kansas for storage on the second floor. The home receiving the furniture and belongings in Lansing would not be cleared out for another week.

The driver said, "OK." He scoped the paved parking and turning area connected to the dock. The driver walked the length of the one-hundred-fifty-foot alley adjacent to the north side of the Allied building. Because of the narrowness of the passage, Sean could only see the truck's cab as the driver climbed in. Sean heard the air brake release, and the semi roared away, only to return from around the block in a better position to back down the alley. Sean could see a full-size, fifty-three-foot-long Allied Van Lines semi-truck, and trailer, trying to back into the ten-foot-wide alley. After ten minutes of maneuvering, the truck inched down the lane, with three inches of leeway on both sides between the side mirrors and the buildings.

Twenty minutes later, when the trailer reached the clear space in front of the dock, the driver jackknifed his rig to align with the landing. Except there was no way he could swing the rear of the trailer back to parallel the dock. It looked to Sean that the space to make the double jackknifed semi nearer did not exist. The two other dock workers who would help Sean unload the truck sat in chairs at the edge of the dock and leaned back to be comfortable, balancing the chairs against the wall of the Allied building.

The van driver pulled ahead and tried again, the air brakes hissing and the cab lurching forward and turning. On the second try, the trailer still could not align with the dock. The driver adjusted his thinking, angles, and side mirrors, pulled back into the alley, and tried again; six more times. To Sean, this all seemed pointless. It would not be much more work to park the van, use the trailer's aluminum ramp to unload the truck, and another ramp up to the dock to load the goods on the elevator. No one ever even whispered that option. An hour went by. The hissing brakes sounded like ten trains pulling in and out of a train station.

After an additional twenty minutes, Sean went over to Drew and Bruce.

"Do you think he needs help," Sean said, "Bruce, is it possible with a trailer that size?"

"Sure," Bruce said, "Takes me about ten minutes to back in here. Do it all the time."

Drew chuckled a bit.

"Everyone's got to learn. We have all been there."

Fifteen minutes later, the aligned trailer tail simultaneously hit both dock bumpers. The driver stepped down from the cab and climbed the ladder to the dock. He unlocked the swing doors on the trailer and swung them open, asking where the nearest soda machine might be. Drew pointed the way, and the driver headed off. No one blinked or said one disparaging word then or during the whole two-and-a-half hours it took the man backing to the dock. Sean helped Drew and Bruce unload.

A world away, Sean's brother, Edward, sat at his desk in Major Waltham's outer office at the Long Binh Post in Saigon, Vietnam. Ten handwritten memos awaited Edward's corrections for grammar and spelling. The major's assault on the written word astounded Edward. He suspected his commanding officer, a lifetime career army man, had dropped out of school before sixth grade.

Edward attended several of the senior officer's monthly meetings, taking notes. If called to testify, Edward would warrant that Major Waltham's intelligence surpassed the other officers in the room by a narrow margin.

In September, Sean received a letter from his brother Edward stationed in Saigon.

Brother Sean,

I am writing to convince you to stay away from Vietnam and out of the army. This place is a disaster. I work for Major Keller, a man who cannot spell school (he always writes skool.) The memos coming forth from the meetings of the officers are equally illiterate. My job is to make the chicken scratching seem presentable to the press and the troops. The servicemen are generally of the same caliber, high school dropouts that could not get student deferments. The tension between black and white here keeps boiling over.

There is no way to distinguish between a friend and an enemy. They are all poor, mostly shoeless, and selling the same drugs. Both groups wander the streets making money off the black market.

The endless jungle is two miles away from my office. Vietnamese and Vietcong melt into the wilderness without regard to malaria-carrying mosquitos, snakes, or booby traps made from needle-sharp spears. So far, my desk job has kept me on the pavement. My guard duty at the gate is scary enough for me. They issue me a revolver for guard duty which I have not used, but I have heard gunshots nearby.

I did not go to Canada because Pat and I would never be able to return. I did not think that fair to ask of my wife. I can return to the Pratt Institute of Art after twelve months.

The risk is significant, the place is a nightmare, the officers have no clue, and the boys in the jungle are either lucky or dead. We should not be here.

Do whatever it takes to stay away.

Edward

Before receiving the letter from Edward, Sean had completed two of the four questions on the application for Conscientious Objector status. Sean had already decided that Vietnam, or for that matter, any war which could lead to the nuclear holocaust, would be a mistake. He knew his student deferment would end the following June when he received his bachelor's degree. His low lottery number, sixty-four, would ensure he would be drafted.

Becoming a Conscientious Objector involved submitting answers to four questions to the local draft board. Sean wrote extensive responses to the first two questions under Series II – Religious Training and Belief.

1. Please describe the nature of your belief which is the basis of your claim, and state why you consider it based on religious training.

Sean could not write that he belonged to the Religious Society of Friends (A Quaker.) Quakers refuse to participate in war. Sean did not believe in organized religions. His four typewritten page answer revolved around personal freedom and his personal beliefs.

My religious belief is in the struggle for personal freedom for all men. Since war can only provide personal death and possible world death, I reject war as something I cannot participate in.

[141]

Instead, I will work in a positive direction for individual freedom, remembering that the struggle for personal freedom is the struggle for human freedom.

2. Explain how, when and from whom or from what source you received the religious training and acquired the religious belief which is the basis of your claim. (Include here, where applicable, such information as the religion of parents and other family members.; childhood religious training; religious and general education; experiences at school and college; organizational memberships and affiliations; books and readings which influenced you; association with clergymen, teachers, advisors, or other individuals that affected you; and any other material which will help give the local board the most complete picture of how your belief developed.

Sean wrote another four-page response that involved family, exploration of the world, outdoor survival living, and the walkouts and riots during his senior year in high school, culminating in the submission of his graduation speech.

Sean asked his father for a letter of recommendation and the Congressman's wife, who had hired Sean to direct her day camp.

Sarah, Sean's mother, became an adamant supporter of the United Nations after the advent of the hydrogen bomb. She feared the cold war and had become an avid supporter of avoiding Vietnam. Harry aligned with Sarah in objecting to the Vietnam War. Sean hoped his dad's letter would be persuasive since he had been in the Army Air Force during World War II.

In December 1971, Sean wrote a preliminary letter to the local selective service board, a head's up on his intentions.

Mid-December, Sean's mother-in-law called to his attention an article in the newspaper that suggested that the Secretary of Defense, Melvin Laird, might not be drafting any more soldiers in

December. If a man did not have a deferment, he could be selected for service for twelve months. The January to December eligibility requirement for those with no student deferment extended through March of the following year for those who would drop their student status at the very end of December. The article indicated that Laird would not call up draft-eligible men in January or February. Sean decided *What the hell,* dropping his deferment via registered letter to the local selective service board on December 31st, 1971.

As predicted, Laird called no one up in January or February. March came and went, and Laird still felt he needed no replenishments. Sean had found a loophole that prevented his going to Vietnam. Later in 1972, Laird called up additional draftees with lottery numbers well beyond Sean's number 64. Sean thanked his mother-in-law and no longer pursued Conscientious Objector status.

How many tens of thousands of men had not been able to play the system as Sean had, missing the fateful newspaper article or unable to read it or understand the process? The loophole was a clear example of an unfair, unjust system. Out of Sean's siblings, Robert, Edward, Steve, and himself, Edward fit the image of a serviceman the least. Robert and Sean were fair athletes who enjoyed team sports such as basketball. Steve, perhaps the best athlete of the brothers, captain of the swim team, and a long ball hitter in baseball, would be 4F due to his blood disorder. Edward, the opposite of an athlete, disliked team sports. A true artist; sensitive, quiet. Edward should have been the last of the brothers chosen for duty in Vietnam.

Sean landed part-time work as a shoe salesman at Nobel Shoes in Meridian Mall, Okemos, Michigan, a few miles east of the MSU campus. After a few weeks of learning the stock, Sean began to make more money from his commission than his hourly wage. Part-time was not a living wage, but brainless work allowed him to concentrate on his studies.

Larry Fleenor managed the shoe store. He had blond hair, tinged orange because of cheap hair color, which he wore in a pompadour style with enough goop in it that not one hair ever strayed out of place. From Kentucky, the twang in his voice went with his plaid leisure suit. Mr. Fleenor thought himself on top of the world as a manager of one of the thirty-five Nobel shoe stores nationwide. As soon as Sean arrived for work, Fleenor left the store to wander around the mall and jabber with whomever he could find to avoid the work there.

Most of the woman's shoes that Nobel Shoes carried looked like patent leather but were, in fact, plastic. If a woman wanted a quality shoe, Sean would sometimes even suggest the store fifty feet across the mall that carried genuine leather shoes at a much higher price. Women always ask for a shoe size smaller than they should have. Sean toyed with the customer's vanity, bringing out more expensive models in the correct size. Sean's suggestion looked great when he slipped on the shoe and was more comfortable.

On many occasions, the customer would insist the new shoes were fine, just a little tight.

"That's the way I like shoes to fit," the customer might say, "They're just a little snug in the toes. Do you have one of those machines that stretches leather? Could you stretch the left one a little in the toe? Might as well do both shoes for good measure, then I'll take them."

"Yes, ma'am. I'll be right back."

Sean took both shoes through the doorway to the shoe warehouse stacks and the leather stretching machine. Sean crammed the left shoe on the handle of the broom Fleenor kept in the back for stretching purposes. The broom handle fits into the toe of the shoe enough that if the shoe were repeatedly pulled down hard on the handle, the toe would bow out a little. Sean had to work fast because the plastic shoes would collapse back into their original shape within minutes. The customer, always right, left the store thinking her feet were skinny and short instead of fat and exceedingly long.

The whole philosophy of the New York Nobel Corporation grated Sean as much as the student teaching school administrators. The New York designers provided store window layouts that Mr. Fleenor had to follow in minute detail. The problem with the design was that the Midwest women had different sensibilities than the women in the East. Sean would have featured several better-selling shoe models that would have attracted more women into the store.

One day when Sean arrived at the store, he found Mr. Fleenor buttering up a couple of the Nobel vice presidents visiting from New York. They were stiff, arrogant, and condescending to Larry. Then they turned their attention to analyzing Sean. Sean sold customers three pairs of shoes right before the two corporate suits. After bringing out two pairs of shoes for the next customer that did not fit, Sean brought out a third and fourth pair he thought she might like. The customer did, in fact, like one of the pairs and told Sean she might be back later to buy them. She left.

One of the vice presidents called him over.

"What happened there?" he asked.

"She may be back," Sean said, "she liked the shoes, but the customer has some shopping she wanted to take care of first."

The VP became stern: "There is no excuse for letting anyone walk out of the store without shoes. Do you understand? You should apologize if you cannot find the shoes the customer will buy. Say, 'I'm sorry, let me get my manager to assist you. I'm just a part-time helper here.' Always get the manager involved if you can't make the sale."

'Uh, yes, sir," said Sean, hiding a smirk.

Sean knew the sales method espoused by the VP would only piss off the customers. The VP just wanted to show the other VPs his superiority. Sean understood the stock as well as the tastes of the Meridian Mall shoppers far better than Larry Fleenor, the

[145]

Kentucky leisure suit guy, who spent little actual time in the store with customers. Sean could locate three pairs of shoes to show the customer in less than a minute. His sales numbers at fifteen hours a week were just shy of Fleenor's, who worked full-time at the store.

As the year progressed, Larry suggested that Sean could make serious money in the shoe business. If he came to work full time for him as an assistant sales manager, he would have his own store in no time. Sean did the math. Only a few would gain their own stores if thirty-five stores had one or two assistant sales managers. Nobel Shoe's plan included" five new stores over the next two years. Sean told Larry, "No, Thank you."

Every week a corporate truck dropped off a load of shoes to replenish the inventory on the shelves in the back of the store. If a shoe sells well, the replacement shipment may not fit in the same space. Shoes were shifted together on the shelves to make room at the end for the new model shoes in the delivery. Sean could see no rhyme or reason for the organization of the warehouse shelves, which drove him crazy. He began to analyze the incoming shipment and the shoes on the shelves. Sean noted that the manufacturer's label on the tongue had a definite pattern as to color and style. He formulated an idea for making the store more efficient but kept it to himself. Any corporation that would not allow a local manager to vary the position of a shoe in the display window by an inch would not be receptive to inventory efficiency.

As he learned calculus and physics, Sean enrolled in art courses from the Art and Landscape Design colleges at Michigan State. He absorbed concepts of color, shape, and composition. He practiced two-dimensional and three-dimensional drawing. Sean designed a stylized bird wing-shaped house built on two massive concrete stilts; the wings cantilevered out, making the house appear flying away. He built a model of the house, covering it with cream of wheat sifted onto the spray-glued surface to look like stucco. Sean drew the floor plan of the house and, along with some sample drawings from the two-dimensional design class, put together a portfolio of his work. He applied to the University of Michigan Architectural School. In the middle of his last term at MSU, Sean received a letter of acceptance to the College of Architecture and Urban Planning at the University of Michigan.

Sean graduated from Michigan State University, receiving a bachelor's degree in Secondary Education with an English major, a teaching certificate, and a minor in science and math. The couple prepared for their move to Ann Arbor. Sean's wife gave notice at the country club, and Sean did the same at the shoe store. They had both been working full-time for the summer. Fleenor became agitated.

"Wow,' said Fleenor, "OK, but I better take my two weeks of vacation before you leave. I will be busy training after that. You'll be fully responsible for the part-timers and opening and closing the store."

Sean said, "Not a problem. Have fun."

The day after Larry left on vacation, Sean gathered the two high school part-timers and explained his idea.

"I want to rearrange the inventory in the back," he said, "I want to rearrange all the shoes in numerical order based on the serial number on the tongue.

"First, we'll take all the shoes off the shelves and set them down numerically. Then we will load shelves back with spaces at the end of each type of shoe, say the women's black heels, etc... That way, we will not have to shift the whole store to fit a new model, just that section."

Sean and his crew worked for four days straight on organizing the inventory. Sean showed the other part-timers how it worked.

"Say the customer hands you a shoe and says she needs a size seven. Look at the tongue and head for the shelves. We've placed signs that will lead you to the right section, and then find the shoe based on the number."

After two days, the part-time help could bring out shoes as fast as Sean. If the customer wanted to see a similar shoe, the salesman would find a similar style on the same or nearby shelf. Sales

[147]

actually went up during the second week. Mr. Fleenor, upon his return, expressed displeasure.

"You did what," Fleenor gasped, "You're kidding; you did what?"

"See for yourself," Sean said, "Here, look at this display shoe; look at the tongue. I bet you can pick it out in less than thirty seconds."

"Corporate won't like it," Fleenor said, looking panicky, "You're going to move them all back, aren't you?"

"No," said Sean, "It's a better system. This is my last day. If you don't like the new system, which is helpful for the part-timers, then good luck moving everything back."

Sean moved to Ann Arbor in August of 1972, renting a new, two-story low-income townhouse on the north edge of town. Sean's spouse found employment at Win Schuler's, an upscale restaurant on the east side with the potential for great tips. Sean did not work. Instead, he concentrated on his studies of structure, acoustics, heating and ventilating systems, and design. Sean bought a used drafting board, four feet by six feet, and installed it with a parallel straight edge in the townhouse's basement. He drafted for hours late into the night, working on his design projects.

Sean worked for a pickup truck camper manufacturer north of Ann Arbor during the summer. Sean used air tools to help create the frame, screw on the aluminum siding, install windows and the door, and attach the interior seating. The worst task involved packing the frame with pink scratchy fiberglass insulation in the ninety-degree temperature in the shop.

On a good day, Sean accompanied the awning installer, building frames over back porches that could take the weight of the twelve feet awnings. At night, Sean worked as a busboy at Win Schuler's.

Whereas Sean's first four years of college had taught him how to study and allowed him at last to absorb interesting material, architecture now became an obsession. Sean created. He always had an idea about how he wanted the assigned project to look. He spent hours on detailed drawings or models to bring the project to life. At the end of each semester, Sean presented his final project to a jury of four or more instructors and architects for review. In two years, Sean received a Bachelor of Science in Architecture.

In the fall of 1974, Sean's wife began her contract to teach fifth grade at Hamburg Elementary School, twenty miles north of Ann Arbor. The couple celebrated the contract signing in July at the Gandy Dancer in Ann Arbor. Over his wife's second glass of wine and his own gin and tonic, Sean toasted her contract signing. Sean, the confirmed cynic, also toasted Nixon's June departure from the presidency. The shaking jowls of the man who proclaimed, "I am not a crook," had not helped Sean's abstract view of the world.

In 1975 Sean's wife moved down to third grade. In January 1975, she became pregnant.

Sean continued on in the Master of Architecture program. The instructor in his design class, a prominent young architect from the Detroit area, began to demand Sean explain the concept of the building or project Sean produced. Sean drew his projects the way he wanted them to look. Professor Daniels wanted to know "why" they should look like they did. The concept should be defined first. All decisions about design, structure, interiors, exterior landscaping, and everything should reflect the original idea. When someone questions the look of some portion of the building, the architect should be able to refer to the concept and explain how it fits. A revelation for Sean and his guiding principle moving forward.

In the second semester of his third year of school, Sean participated in an internship program for architecture students. He worked at the firm of Patterson Architects out of Jackson, Michigan. He and another intern rode in a carpool with two designers who traveled from Ann Arbor to Jackson each morning.

On the fifteenth of October, after an eighteen-hour labor, the couple's first child arrived; a girl named Kelly (after a song by a British pop group.) The cephalohematoma caused by the obstetrician's tongs squashed Kelly's head a little. Sean thought she looked like Jiminy Cricket.

The couple had taken Lamaze classes on how to birth a baby naturally. Sean had breathed with his wife for the last three hours of the delivery, speaking softly and encouragingly to his wife. After the birth, Sean's wife had so many popped blood vessels dotting her face that she looked like an empty pin cushion. Sean's wife handled the birthing process well. A Bush Voyage like no other, Sean gained even more respect for women, particularly his wife.

Kelly screamed the loudest of all the babies brought down the hall from the natal care room to where her mother waited for her to nurse. Kelly squealed all the way home in the car. She screamed and cried most of the night.

Sean had always pictured a Gerber baby, smiling and happy, occasionally crying when hungry or wet. Baby Kelly slept or fitfully nursed; otherwise, she would scream and spit up. On the third day, Sean picked up his daughter when his exhausted wife could no longer stand Kelly's screams. He carried Kelly around the townhouse, downstairs from the bedroom and around the living room, and into the kitchen, turning into the hall and taking the stairs down to the basement. He walked around the ping-pong table and then up the stairs two floors to the bedroom and began the circuit again. After twenty minutes, Kelly stopped crying. Sean continued to pace, afraid that Kelly would awaken again if he stopped. Looking down at her in his arms, Sean decided the screaming little cricket, the loudest baby in the maternity ward, had been born to cry. If that was his daughter's nature, so be it. He would love her, he would walk her, and he would always be there for her. Her life; his life; OK.

The small firm where Sean interned in Jackson designed most of the schools in the county. When Sean arrived to work at the firm, the designers were working on a 1500-seat auditorium connected to two smaller adjoining theaters for Jackson Community College. Designing such a prestigious project created an excellent opportunity for the small architectural firm, specifically Sean. Sean worked on the grand stairway from the lobby to the balcony, mezzanine, and common areas on three floors above ground level. The exterior of the building consisted of a series of pentagon-shaped spaces. Sean held to that concept with the staircases he drew. He also designed the grand courtyard approach to the front of the building.

Mr. Patterson kept a watchful eye on the designs his team produced. Patterson balanced engineering with design. He ensured that no roof drain took rainwater anywhere but to the outside edges of the building. He never allowed an interior drain that could clog with ice, snow, or debris and cause damage to the building. The same went for the cut-and-fill calculations on the land and parking areas surrounding the Center. Water must always drain away from the building. No catch basins or sump pumps; too risky.

After his internship, Sean stayed at Patterson Architects part-time for the remainder of his last year in architectural school. For his final project in his design class at U of M, Sean drew a perspective of the residence he designed for his father and mother-in-law on Feather Lake, south of Kalamazoo. Located at the end of a man-made peninsula., the property boasted water views on three sides. Sean proposed a home in which every room had multiple views of the lake. Those same views turn bleak and cold during winter, so Sean designed an atrium in the center of the house to provide green space and internal views throughout the winter. The house accommodated all the areas requested by the client, including three bedrooms. Sean proposed a deep crawl space instead of a basement due to the high groundwater level at the end of the peninsula. Soil samples taken at the site necessitated a floating slab foundation. The lot had been formed with dredged marl, so standard footings might slowly sink. Sean drew a complete set of architectural drawings and oversaw the construction bids based on the schematics.

Sean believed in his concept. His thirty-one working drawings explained every detail. He had met all the client's requirements. The bids all came in higher than what Sean's father-in-law wanted to spend. Sean destroyed his concept to save fifteen thousand dollars from a two hundred sixty-thousand-dollar budget, a six percent overrun. Sean's father-in-law hoped to retire after the completion of the house.

The atrium was cut from the design, and the brick exterior became vertical cedar siding. Sean redrew all the pertinent drawings, sending them out for additional bids. Upon acceptance of the proposals, Sean turned the project over to the residential construction company, which made another drastic change. Instead of the floating slab foundation, the construction company used a standard footing broader and deeper than usual.

At the end of the semester, Sean plastered a wall in the Architecture and Urban Planning building with both sets of drawings. The drawings covered every inch of the nine feet tall, thirty feet long space. Sean's design, when constructed, consisted of a low-slung one-story structure with integrated porches and decks that melted into the lake.

Patterson Architects offered many design opportunities for Sean but little in terms of future advancement. The two principals who reported to Mr. Patterson were under thirty-five. It would be decades before more partners would be needed. Besides, Sean wanted to experience different design environments. He began to apply to firms along the I-94 corridor. Cornell and Associates of Grand Haven, Michigan, responded to his application. He interviewed with Mr. Cornell, who hired him after reviewing his portfolio.

The College of Architecture and Urban Planning at the University of Michigan reviewed a thousand applications for admission a year. They accepted one hundred new students a year: Sean was one of the fortunate students in 1972. Of those one hundred, only fifty percent completed the program of study and received their Master of Architecture; Sean was one of the fortunate graduates in 1976. Of the approximate fifty graduates in 1976, Sean knew of only four graduates that found jobs.

Sean, his wife, daughter, and Sheltie moved from Ann Arbor, a city that had legalized the use of Marijuana, to Holland, Michigan, a town where no one mowed their lawn on Sunday. Sean would have preferred moving to Grand Haven, an upscale city on the Lake Michigan shore between Holland and Muskegon but found no available housing that accepted both a toddler and a dog.

The work in the small firm of Cornell and Associates differed vastly from Patterson Architects. Mr. Cornell wanted evidence of "lead on paper," urging Sean to work faster and produce more drawings. Projects Sean worked on were drawings to be submitted to building inspectors for moving houses or cabins back from the crumbling shores of Lake Michigan before they toppled down the cliff. Sean made no design decisions whatsoever. The monotonous work forced Sean to become much faster at drawing, dimensioning, and labeling official-looking working documents. Mr. Cornell seemed pleased with Sean's progress. Only one other apprentice worked in the office. He labored on a fast-food restaurant to be built in Plainwell, Michigan. Occasionally, he would have window or door details needed for the building, which were assigned to Sean.

To take his mind off the repetitious boredom of the day-to-day foundation drawings, Sean began to look for a building site and work on plans for his own house in his after-hours spare time. Sean approached the First National Bank, secured a loan, and purchased a small lot on the east side of Grand Haven. He and his wife signed the paperwork on a Thursday in early September of 1976.

The next day, Mr. Cornell asked Sean to meet in his office around three o'clock. Sean believed he had progressed satisfactorily in knowledge and speed. He anticipated a raise in pay.

Instead, Mr. Cornell said the work had run out, and Sean would no longer be needed. This would be his last day. Sean returned to his desk, stunned. The other draftsman would not look him in the eye. Sean had worked energetically for Cornell and Associates for eighty-five days, shy of the ninety days required to collect unemployment. Cornell's modus operandi: he hired summer help to capture the business of cabins inevitably needing to be moved back from the erosion of the cliffs around Grand Haven. Cornell let the summer help go when the season ended: clear to Sean now. The other draftsman could have warned Sean when he had taken Sean on a tour of some of the residences Cornell had designed in Grand Haven. Sean had been dutifully impressed until he happened on pictures in an architectural magazine on his lunch break that mirrored the design of Cornell's most impressive accomplishment. Sean also continued to find other examples in the magazines of ripped-off designs. Compared to the ethics displayed daily at Patterson Architects, Cornell and Associates dove to the opposite end of the scale. Cornell indicated he would give Sean an excellent recommendation.

After achieving a Master of Architecture, a designer needs two years of experience with a licensed architect before being allowed to take the incredibly challenging state board test for architects. After passing all the requirements, a designer became a licensed architect in Michigan.

Now Sean had lost his job. He went to the bank and withdrew the purchase of the lot in Grand Haven. Since the three-day grace period had not expired, he received a return of his down payment, and the real estate transaction was nullified.

Then Sean began the grueling task of locating another job with an architectural firm. He wrote letters of introduction to over sixty firms in Michigan, as far north as Escanaba and Houghton in the upper peninsula. He drove to the UP and knocked on the doors of every architecture firm in every small town in the phone book. Most told him they had no openings. Sometimes he would be given a courtesy interview. He sat next to two other applicants waiting for appointments in several instances. Sean felt he carried an impressive portfolio. He had samples from his work at Patterson Architects and Cornell and Associates. His complete drawings were rolled up from the house he had designed for his father-in-law.

Sean discovered that the portfolios of the men he sat next to in the lobbies of the architectural firms he visited were as impressive. In 1976 the oil shortage and a building recession weighed on the architects he met. A slowdown in construction meant a downturn in design opportunities. Sean finally grasped the fundamental issue of becoming a licensed architect. It would take a magnanimous architect indeed to hire an apprentice. An apprentice who, in two years, could take the state licensing exam and become a licensed architect, competing for the limited amount of business in the state. The system appeared stacked against Sean.

The driveway and parking lot of the company located in Holland, Michigan, did not impress Sean Martensen. Neither did the squat, weathered office attached to the Butler building shop. The receptionist made an impression. She took his coat, opened Stuart Arbeider's office door, and signaled her boss sitting at his desk.

"Mr. Martensen, come in; thanks, Petra," said Arbeider in a high-pitched voice. "Why don't we sit at the table."

Sean, sitting, noted the shabby surroundings and furniture that matched the worn-out building.

"Thank you for the interview, Mr. Arbeider," he said. "The ad says you need a sales engineer, someone unafraid of getting their hands dirty. Someone to help with conceptual drawings of your custom equipment."

"My name is Stuart, but everyone calls me Blade," said the president. "You have a degree in Architecture, is that right?"

"That is true, Mr. Arbeider; here is my portfolio, if you care to see," said Sean.

Sean had two degrees in Architecture, a Bachelor of Science degree in Architecture and a Master of Architecture. He also had a

Bachelor of Arts degree in English Education. Given the surroundings, he did not think bringing all that up would advance his cause.

Blade Arbeider took the portfolio from Sean, glanced at the cover, a beautifully detailed reduction of a drawing he had worked on for the Jackson Area School District, and set it down on his right.

Instead of looking through it, he retrieved and unrolled a drawing from his desk. The D-size drawing presented plan, front, and side views of a large piece of equipment. The crude representation would never have been acceptable in Sean's classes at the University of Michigan, but the drawing provided the machine's scale and concept. Sean noted the customer, General Motors, Cadillac division. Impressive.

"This is the kind of drawing I need to be accomplished. Not taxing for someone of your education, but I am on the road more and more, and I sometimes rush the drawings," said Blade, "the concept drawing is how I sell the machine to the client."

"Mr. Arbeider," Sean said, "I will tell you that I could add a lot of pizzazz to a drawing like this."

Sean looked again at the drawing. He would vary the weight of the lead to emphasize essential pieces on the machine. His lettering would be much more professional. He would take the time to add more detail. Detail impresses.

The president seemed satisfied so far. "Let's tour the shop," he said.

Welding dust covered everything in the shop. The pungent odor from the arc of the welder wafted through the warehouse. Blade showed Sean the area they kept the bags of media used in the machines. Glass bead, steel shot, and even crushed acorn shell. All in various abrasive sizes, diameters, and grit.

Assemblers in another bay fastened purchased and fabricated parts to three machines spaced twenty feet apart. In another area, green paint applied to completed equipment left a coat of paint dust on everything.

Cyclonic cylinders attached to the top of every machine had six-inch or eight-inch diameter steel pipes running down to the bottom of each unit. A three to five-foot cube of steel housed filter bags that automatically shook away particles picked up when the machine operated. Air regulators, electrical panels, and more provided air and electricity to the robotic equipment. Each device involved a conveyor in and out of it to automate the process.

After the shop tour, Blade introduced Sean to the engineering staff and Petra Thorne.

Sitting back at the table in the president's office, Blade leaned forward. "What do you think of the place, Mr. Martensen," he said.

Sean thought a moment, "I'm interested in the job. Certainly, this would be something new for me, but the duties and the dust do not bother me. What would be the pay?"

"This is a salaried position," said Blade, "$10,000.00 a year. We all work until the job is done, including Saturdays, if need be.

"Now, I must know, why are you here? Manufacturing is a far cry from architecture."

"Honestly," Sean said, almost fainting over the salary, "I'm here because I have a wife and baby girl. Since graduating, I have traveled all over the lower and upper peninsulas applying with architects. No one is hiring during the current construction downturn and high-interest rates.

"As I said, I'm interested," Sean said.

Blade tipped back in his squeaking swivel office chair.

"The job is yours under one condition. I will invest in you and expect you not to take another architectural position for at least a year. If you can commit to a year here, you can start on Monday. Give me a call when you decide."

Sean needed no additional time.

"Mr. Arbeider,,, Blade, I'll see you Monday."

Sean took his position as Sales Engineer at PMC seriously. Blade rough sketched a machine concept after interviewing the client's project engineer, touring the customer's plant, and understanding their process. Returning to PMC, Blade handed the sketch to his sales engineer. Sean converted the sketch into a professional drawing on vellum for Blade's approval. Then he ran the illustration through the Falcon Non-ammonia blueprint machine. He folded three copies, put the copies in a large envelope, and asked Petra to create address labels and attach postage.

All the custom machines produced at PMC contained several standard components. Cyclones separated dust and debris blasted off the client's part on the conveyor as it passed through the machine. Nozzles within the enclosure created a compressed air venturi force concentrating the media on the area to be blasted. Reusable media (glass or steel shot or steel grit of various sizes) fell out the bottom of the cyclone and circulated for reuse while the high-speed fan sucked the debris out near the top of the cyclone separator. The waste traveled into the five feet tall by four feet by four feet steel encased filter container. Filter bags within the filter enclosure trap the debris. Periodically, a cam attached to a motor and pipe threaded through the filter bags shook the dirt off the bags. The media dust collected in the drawer at the base of the filter box is to be disposed of. All these parts needed to be scaled to the difficulty of the process, but they basically looked the same from one PMC custom machine to the next.

Sean began to see areas of the company that he thought could be improved or modernized.

A 3M Thermo-Fax machine provided copies of official documents such as quotes or contracts. The resulting duplicate hardly seemed professional. The thin material often became mangled in the machine, wasting time. Making a decent copy meant multiple attempts, dialing in the darkness of the imprint to the point that the background might appear smudged or too dark.

As a sales engineer, Sean proposed acquiring a new Xerox 3107 copier. His proposal included a method to decrease the time spent on concept drawings with the help of the copier. Blade agreed to the concept and the copier, one of the earliest laser printers that allowed eleven-inch by fourteen-inch plain paper copies. The 3107 could reduce and enlarge images. It included a document feeder. A thirty-page PMC quote with specifications streamed through the copier.

The new copier revolutionized many of PMC's office procedures. Copies looked as professional as the originals. Staff no longer had to wait for the old 3M machine to warm up or wrinkle the result. Employees made their own copies rather than depending on Petra's time. The copier could make a copy on plain paper up to eleven inches wide by seventeen inches long (B size.)

When the copier arrived, Sean went to work making intricate, detailed, professional drawings of each component of a PMC machine. Then he made copies of the standard part, cut, and pasted as many on an eight-inch by eleven-inch master sheet. He purchased the sticky-backed transparent paper and copied his master sheet onto one of the sticky-back sheets.

He made a much more intricate drawing of the next client's custom machine concept. He cut and pasted the standard components onto a copy of the basic idea using his transparencies. Sean made final copies for Blade's approval when he finished pasting all the parts together.

A concept drawing constructed this way could be completed in four hours, including lettering, instead of two days. Sean used the same technique with typewritten descriptions rather than freehand labels. His approach, which Sean called his Xerographic method, turned out detailed concept drawings in a quarter of the time. The final copies measured eleven by seventeen inches, and clients appreciated the easy-to-read, easy-to-handle informative packets.

Sean kept a notebook of his building blocks ready for the subsequent request for a concept drawing using his cut, paste, and copy system. He began to look around for another business improvement project. He received a raise to twelve thousand dollars a year at six months.

Sean's brother, Robert, worked at the time for a company called KMS Fusion, a group trying to contain the sun's surface temperatures of the fusion process.

A fusion reactor is much safer than a fission reactor. Current reactors, uncontrolled, could accidentally run amok. The fission process used raw radioactive fuel and produced waste dangerous to humans for decades or centuries. Fusion reactors would use heavy water with a byproduct of hydrogen, which is helpful to the planet.

Robert programmed the company's mainframe to analyze and direct the scientist's innovative efforts. After graduating from MSU, he was recruited by IBM and, within a couple of years as an analyst, decided to stretch his abilities at KMS.

Sean wished to take advantage of computers at PMC. Payroll, accounts receivable, accounts payable, and purchasing were manual processes handled by Petra and Blade. When Sean queried Robert, the family's brain, Robert somewhat discouraged his younger brother.

"Computers are a lot of work," he suggested, "You can hire that out, but that would be expensive for a small company like yours."

"I thought I would try to program the computer," said Sean.

"I wish you luck, Sean."

The new computer arrived, and Sean unpacked his Christmas present. He set up the computer in the office he had just completed by enclosing a corner of the shop. One of the smaller boxes contained the user and programming manuals. Sean had researched computer manufacturers and models of computers on his own time for a month. "BASIC" programming, touted as easy to learn and work with, seemed an appropriate choice for a beginner. He showed the setup to Blade, and they discussed the project.

"We should back up each other on programming this thing," Blade said, "I see they provided two copies of the programming manual. What do you say we each take a manual home this weekend and, on Monday, see if we can get our programs to work?"

"Deal," said Sean.

On Monday, Sean produced his three-page program written in proper BASIC. Blade gave Sean his one-page program to input into the computer. One look at Blade's attempt and Sean could tell that it would not work, did not abide by the language rules, and that the computer would produce errors starting on the second line.

Saying nothing, Sean entered both programs. Blade's program elicited several angry syntax errors on every line. Sean's program ran error-free. On the screen, a paragraph appeared that included the name and address of the company. The screen also displayed the ubiquitous "Hello world!" exclamation. Blade's program attempted but failed to produce the same simple result.

Blade looked at the numerous red error codes as his program ran. Then he watched the smooth running result of Sean's program.

"I guess we know who will be programming this thing," Blade conceded.

"Not a problem, Blade; I'll start with a payroll program. I believe I can program the taxes and other withholdings in and also print the payroll checks."

Blade nodded, and the computer became Sean's baby.

The payroll program took five months to complete. On nights and Saturday mornings, Sean set aside media sorting, cleaning up, reordering, and concept drawing, concentrating on programming the payroll system. The program included tax tables and algorithms to calculate yearly salaries. Sean's algorithm utilized the accumulated historical wages paid and added a projection of compensation to the end of the year according to the current week's hourly total. The program then applied the correct federal and state income tax and mandatory and optional withholdings. Finally, the checks began printing out with the employee's name, net amounts, and detailed withholdings on each stub. Blade offered another raise of fifteen hundred dollars per year.

Within a year, the company leaped into the black.

The contractions preceding the birth of Sean's second child advanced to five-minute intervals. The couple decided to head for the hospital, eight minutes away. Sean pulled up at the emergency entrance and helped his wife into the wheelchair offered by the ER attendant. Parking the car took some time. Sean decided he had plenty of time, based on his experience with his daughter's birth, which was eighteen hours long.

Inquiring at the desk on the maternity floor, a nurse approached, verified his name, and hustled him to a room to wash his hands and put on a hospital gown.

"Your wife is moving along very rapidly with this birth," the nurse said, "She may be fully dilated by now. We should get in there."

Upon entering the birthing room, his wife's contractions peaked. This would be no eighteen-hour effort. After the next contraction, Dr. Milton, the obstetrician, entered the room, spoke to the nurses and Sean's wife, and began the birth procedure. Sean, stunned at the speed of this birth compared to his daughter's three years earlier, held his wife's hand. She did the rest. Twenty minutes after Sean entered the room, his wife gave birth to an eight-pound three-ounce baby boy.

Sean's many months of walking his daughter up and down and around in their townhouse to quiet her colic bound him to her, whether she liked it or not. His daughter's taut, jerky, tension-filled movements as a newborn transitioned with his son to unrelenting world exploration and experiment, a joy to watch and encourage. Sean's son soon smiled and giggled in the arms of whoever wished to hold him. Two different humans, both precious.

The computer now became a limitation to Sean's future plans. Only six files or tables could be opened at a time. If he wanted to reference the employee file for a name, and also an address file, a state file; possibly a UPS regional rate file for costs at different weights, a vendor file, a customer file, and a ship-to-address file; the BASIC language forced him to close one file to open a seventh file. Sean began to research a larger minicomputer capable of opening unlimited tables. He also wanted the computer to act as a word-processing system. Engineers and salesmen could type their letters with workstations on everyone's desk. Using a word processor to correct their spelling and grammar, engineers could print their letters with a button. Petra Thorne applauded the idea and moved up in the company to executive assistant to President Arbeider.

He settled on a Wang minicomputer with word processing software built in. He licensed Mini-Computer Business Associates (MCBA) boilerplate software as a starting point for customizing PMC accounting software systems.

Sean purchased eight workstations. The president, four engineers, one salesman, an executive assistant, and the sales engineer each had a workstation. The computer room housed the CPU cabinet and disk drive enclosures that contained two fourteen-inch diameter, ten-megabyte data storage platters. A reel-to-reel tape drive and cabinet for backing up the system and a three hundred line per minute band printer for reports completed the equipment list in the conditioned space. Letters were printed on the slower, high-quality printer near Petra's desk.

The new computer did not use BASIC. Instead, it used COBOL, a more sophisticated computer software language. Sean learned the language and began programming. He customized the old payroll program to the MCBA payroll module to ensure a PMC fit.

The accounts-payable and accounts-receivable modules needed only minor adjustments. With Petra's help inputting customers and vendors, PMC began printing vendor checks within weeks.

The MCBA inventory module did not fit a custom equipment manufacturer but rather a gadget on-the-shelf type of operation. Sean concentrated on customizing the inventory module to suit the custom equipment business.

The purchased parts for a PMC system are called out on the engineering drawings of each machine. An engineer inputs the part requirements into Sean's database. Sean's program determines the availability of the part on the warehouse shelf. At first, shortages would be listed on a preliminary purchase order sheet.

With additional programming, purchase orders are printed automatically to be sent to the vendor.

Raw steel makes up the bulk of material needed for custom equipment. At PMC, the drawings may call out tubular, sheet, or angled steel in various sizes. The steel may have to be cut out of four feet by eight feet sheets of a quarter or half-inch steel. Angle iron and tubular steel are sized with a cutoff bandsaw. Sean's program calculated the square inches of sheet steel necessary for the welding shop, compared the need to the steel in stock, and, if necessary, added sheets of steel to a purchase order. The steel algorithm Sean created handled the angle iron and tubing inventory.

A few golden leaves sashayed down to the patio from the river birch. The tree grew beyond the six-foot fence surrounding the deck and hot tub at Blade Arbeider's Grand Rapids, Michigan home. The weather in the autumn of '79 was in the 80s. The clear October day, hot and muggy, could not stifle the optimism of the principals of Pioneer Manufacturing Company rimming the hot tub. The preferred drink of each director sat within easy reach behind them on the sidewalk surrounding the seven-foot diameter bubbling pool.

Blade hoisted his neat scotch and saluted his employees, "Another milestone, guys, our first million-dollar paycheck. Good work, all."

The three men and Petra Thorne, Blade's executive assistant, held up their glasses. Sitting opposite Blade, Petra slugged down half of her Cabernet, her lipstick slightly lighter than the dark wine. Sitting to Blade's left, Ben Rademacher, Vice President of Sales, sipped his Baptist-inspired nonalcoholic Coca-Cola.

On Petra's right and Ben's left, Sean Martensen, Vice President of Systems and Planning, reached for his second gin and tonic. On Petra's left, seated next to Blade, Curt Hinton, Vice President of Engineering, grabbed his third beer.

"The gamble paid off, I have to admit," said Curt after the toast, "But I'm not sure the rest of the engineers will take to the new design stations, Blade."

Blade's freckled face began to redden, beginning to match his curly mop of hair. His eyes narrowed a bit.

"You'll get their attention when the new computers arrive next week, and we start their training."

Sean had researched Computer Aided Design systems. He set his sights on the engineers, now familiar with their word-processing workstations. They would need to be enticed to expand their computer skills. The custom equipment plans would be drawn on the computer rather than on a vellum sheet attached to a drafting board. The idea offered the engineers several benefits.

First, the standard components could be drawn once on the CAD workstation and copied into the drawings for the next client's custom equipment. The computer could work with overlays on the machine. Different levels within the cabinet could be shown. Clearances could be guaranteed. The electrical and plumbing diagrams could be overlaid as well. A 3D drawing of the machine could be printed that would be a thousand times more impressive than Sean's best conceptual drawing.

Blade purchased a computer-aided design station on Sean Martensen's recommendation for $62,500.00. The president worked three weeks on drawing two six-foot-tall by seven-foot-long by three-foot-wide robot-controlled automated shot peening machines.

The client, Pratt & Whitney, impressed with Blade's custom equipment's detail, accuracy, and idea, signed a purchase order for two machines the same week.

Arbeider charged the client $500,000.00 per machine based on the impressive drawing. Before the Cad system, he would have set the price at about $325,000.00 per machine.

Curt's staff translated Blade's CAD conceptual drawing into engineering drawings (using traditional pen and T-square.) The Pioneer fabrication shop welded the ½" thick steel cabinet and machined all the parts.

The shop completed the assembly of the machines on October 3rd. On the seventh of October, Pratt and Whitney's representatives participated in the runoff. The approval followed, and yesterday a check arrived.

Sean Martensen ordered four more CAD stations installed in four engineering cubicles. The eight engineers would be split into two teams working six-hour shifts to justify the $250,000.00 equipment investment.

"They better get with the program. Sean has already arranged to donate the old drafting tables to Calvin College's engineering department."

Stuart Arbeider (Blade) stood five foot nine inches. His red hair and angular face gave him a fox-like appearance. At thirty-eight, Arbeider had finagled ownership of the company by catching the previous owners embezzling company funds. He bought them at pennies on the dollar in exchange for not pursuing prosecution. Along with the look of a wild-eyed crazy fox, his razor-sharp instincts cut like a "blade" through the competition in the business world. Blade worked at breakneck speed daily, instilling his urgency for success in the rest of his employees.

Like the other engineers at Pioneer, Curt Hinton's career worked comfortably and fast on a four-foot by six-foot adjustable engineering table. He drew details with various Pentel drafting pencils for over twenty years. Curt's legendary speed in turning out machine drawings contributed as much to Pioneer Manufacturing Company's growth as Blade's wits and Sean's technological ideas. The president recognized Curt's reluctance to embrace computer-aided design. Attitude and enthusiasm meant everything to Blade Arbeider. The previous week the president had pulled Sean aside and told him he may have to take over engineering as Interim Engineering VP until Curt came up to speed on the new equipment. Sean knew that would mean the beginning of the end for Curt at Pioneer Manufacturing Company.

Ben Rademacher stretched his long legs to the seat on the other side of the hot tub, leaned his head back against the rim, and closed his eyes. A pure salesman (meaning he could sell anything he believed in) had recently joined the company. He would not be required to learn the new system. Instead, his plan included befriending his favorite engineer and encouraging that person to understand the CAD system inside and out. With drawings like the one Blade had produced on the new system, Ben knew he could sell big-ticket machines and look at salary increases and hefty bonuses.

In the short time since Blade Arbeider took over the company, the financial statement of the company had moved from three years in the red to being profitable for two.

Petra looked over at Sean, nodding with her glass as they both took another drink. Petra had black hair, cut to an inch above her shoulder, styled to flip under her chin. In high heels, which she wore religiously, her long legs put her eye to eye with Sean. Petra, tall, slender, ambitious, dedicated, and proficient, had green cat eyes and high cheekbones. She had a longish neck, workout shoulders, and a suitably proportioned chest, not small for her thinness. Slim in the waist.

Since Sean had brought word processing to the company, Petra had become more of an advisor to Blade. Sean installed computers on all the principals' desks. Everyone types their own letters these days. The company employed thirty-three men. Petra had moved up in the company much like Sean, providing "class" in joint client meetings. She was efficient and proficient. Petra learned new computer skills as fast as Sean provided the equipment and the software, grateful not to be retyping hand-scratched memos by the company executives.

Petra finished her glass of wine and poured herself another. Sean mixed his third drink with his gin and tonic fixings at hand. *Nothing like gin and tonic in the summer.*

[167]

Sean respected Petra as an equal. He admired her posture, her poise with clients, and her beauty. She had never caught him staring at her body in the four years Sean had known Petra. He always focused on her eyes. Respect! Inwardly, Sean yearned for the married Petra Thorne in the worst way. Day in and day out, watching this beautiful woman stroll with purpose by his office, dropping memos or mail on desks, always caused Sean to lose focus.

Sean set his drink back down and relaxed, laying back just like Ben, watching the flock of goldfinch flit back and forth from the feeder in the center of the patio and the birch tree on the other side of the fence. The birds, bright yellow against the blue fall sky, reminded Sean of his days wandering the forty-acre farm of his youngest days.

Like Blade, he could only relax in snatches.

Unlike Blade, Sean could concentrate on a problem for hours or days until he had a solution.

Curt splashed out of the hot tub, heading for the bathroom and a cold beer from the fridge. As he returned, he hailed Ben. "Ben, tell Blade the one about the two salesmen at the bar in France."

Sean slid back to a sitting position as Ben answered. "You mean the one about the Baptist preacher and the nun?"

Sean reached for his drink, took a refreshing slug, and set it down on the sidewalk again. That made his hands cold. He buried them in the bubbles again, sliding down so that bubbling water covered his shoulders.

When Curt climbed back into the crowded hot tub, Petra moved closer to Sean to avoid his splash. She sat shoulder to shoulder with Sean, legs innocently touching, as the group listened to the joke.

Sean did not hear the ending. Petra had placed her right hand on Sean's left hand and squeezed. She traced Sean's bulging member with her index finger through his swimsuit. He looked over at her. She stared straight ahead, managing a small laugh at Ben's joke.

Petra then guided Sean's hand to her lap, pushing his hand down the front of her bikini bottom, held open by her left hand. With everyone in the hot tub, the bubbler turned up, and Petra and Sean underwater to their shoulders, the conversation and drinking continued.

Sean thought he might have died. His heartbeat thumped in his chest like a base drum in a marching band. Petra spread her legs to accommodate Sean's fingers through her fine pubic hair. She held Sean's arm with both hands urging him to continue.

Had they really drunk enough for this to be happening? Sean never indicated to Petra that he longed to be doing just what they were doing.

He glanced at her again as he explored her, slippery, even as the water churned around her. Finally, she turned to him and smiled, mouth open, chin raised. Minutes later, Petra pulled Sean's hand away. He squeezed his dick and adjusted his swimsuit to try and hide his stiffness. Everyone scrambled out of the tub. Sean stayed another minute, willing his erection to subside. Thinking of ice cream.

Sean sprang from the hot tub, grabbed his towel, and vigorously toweled off, wrapping the towel around himself. Petra ran off to change into street clothes.

The men thanked Blade for the party. Sean could think of no excuse to linger until Petra returned dressed. He went to his car and drove toward home, teeth chattering, stone-cold sober.

His mind jumbled the episode in the hot tub, alertness for the traffic on Fulton, thoughts of his wife, daughter, and son at home, and the ache in his groin.

Sean already knew he would pursue Petra if she were willing. A new adventure. Was he ready? How had he arrived at this juncture? Could he succeed in this venture as he had in his previous survival of the Canadian river rapids?

"**P**etra," Sean said in his best business voice as she walked by his office. "Have you got a minute?" She did. Petra came through his office door and stood next to his desk.

"What's up," said Petra in a noncommittal voice.

"I want to know if you will go for a drink tonight?" Sean asked.

"Perhaps not a good idea, Sean."

"I think it is an excellent idea. Whatever happened in the hot tub, I want to see where it goes."

"Are you sure," said Petra.

"I've never been surer. I will meet you at five thirty in the Marriott bar across 28th Street."

Petra nodded and walked out. Now Sean had to somehow focus on work until five o'clock. Impossible! At noon he took off for the Marriott on a scouting trip. He checked out the bar. There were quiet booths (hidden caves.) The luxurious fixtures in the restaurant and bar looked appropriate for a sophisticated meeting.

He rented a room at the front desk, pocketed the key, and returned to work. He walked right past Petra. She was wearing a simple white blouse and a dark blue pencil skirt. She could wear anything well. She looked like a million bucks. Her makeup was exactly right, not too much. Diamond stud earrings. Two-and-a-half-inch heels.

At five-thirty, Petra walked into the bar. Sean stood and waved her to their booth. She slid in, and he sat next to her. They ordered gin and tonics, and when they arrived, she slid back against Sean and declined the cheese basket brought by the waitress. Sean did not know what expensive perfume should smell like, but Petra smelled like a dream.

Eight minutes of chit-chat later, they ordered two more drinks. When they had just about finished those, Sean called the waitress over.

"Can you please give us two more drinks and the bill?" he asked.

Sean pulled the room key from his pocket and placed it on the table. "What do you think, shall we go up?" he asked.

"You think of everything, don't you," she said.

"Systems and Planning, right," said Sean.

When Blade called Sean into his office to tell his Interim Engineering VP about yet another raise, he asked Sean to work on drawings for a new building in Grand Rapids. Blade no longer wished to commute thirty miles one way to work. Sean's efficiencies and the appearance of the professional sales drawings gave Blade an excuse to increase the price and, therefore, the profit of each system he sold. Ben Rademacher had joined the PMC team along with two more engineers.

Sean presented conceptual drawings for a building to house the expanding company. Moving away from the conservative city on the coast of Lake Michigan to a more cosmopolitan area suited Sean as well. Scorned for mowing his lawn on Sunday, tired of the Sunday ban on alcohol sales and the only movie theater in town, he put up his house for sale. The president used Sean's drawings to negotiate with a commercial properties real estate development company that had just finished a new building one block from the Kent County International Airport. The building, the location, and the deal could not be passed up, so instead of designing the external envelope of the building, Sean turned to designing and laying out the offices and shop spaces on the inside of the new plant. A central room conditioned to handle a new computer became the focus of the office layout. The salesmen used the new building and the glass-enclosed computer room as a showcase on client tours. An excuse to increase the price of the PMC equipment once again. Blade lived eight minutes away from the new building. Clients could be off and on a plane to their company headquarters minutes after five-hour machine runoff tours. Sean's relief at never having to walk into the dilapidated company building in Holland and the periodic salary increases eased Sean's regret at turning away from architecture. Petra Thorne and Curt Hinton hired Sean on the side to design new homes, so he kept his hand in that realm. The increases in salary allowed Sean to purchase a contemporary split-level home in East Grand Rapids,

Sean's kids were a source of joy. His daughter was driven and creative; his son continued to smile. As the boy grew, he laughed, even while allowing his big sister to put his blond hair up in curlers. When she neared five years old, she began to fix the boy's cereal on Sunday mornings by climbing on the counter and reaching the Cheerios box in the wall cabinet. She handled the refrigerator, retrieved the plastic gallon of two percent milk, and poured it. Only a drop or two escaped the bowls and hit the table. The boy watched, learned, and kept smiling. He was a joy to everyone that met him.

At the end of 1979, Sean discussed with Blade the possibility of exporting his software system and expertise to another company. The president of Calhoun Engineering, an injection molding company a few blocks from PMC, had approached Sean about the possibility. Sean suggested creating a separate information technology division of PMC; Blade agreed.

Sean's lived in a state of euphoria. His work on algorithms that would automatically strip out steel callouts and manufactured parts, electrical or mechanical, progressed each day.

Blade's bonus and generous raise meant he could buy a Mazda RX7. Sean, not usually a car person, could not resist the remarkably smooth-running Wankel rotary engine. The car had only two seats, but the kids were small enough to fit in a pinch on the shelf behind the seats.

The salesman had seen Sean coming. Sean tried to negotiate the price down from $9,300.00, but the salesman and sales manager measured the gleam in Sean's eye and did not drop the price. The car drove like a dream. When you floored the gas pedal on the highway, the RX7 accelerated beyond eighty miles per hour in seconds, and Sean never felt nor heard a difference in the engine. It seemed like silent power.

Sean played basketball as often as possible. At thirty-one, his stomach was taut, his legs basketball strong; his stamina matched anyone on the court. He still never professed to be a superstar, but he held his own with the good players down at the 'Y.'

With Blade's approval, Sean began to work on Calhoun Engineering's manufacturing resource planning system (MRP.) Calhoun Engineering produced plastic bumper linings, front console foundations, sound barriers, and more for GM, Chrysler, Herman Miller, and other end-product manufacturers. Companies sent eight-week projections of the needed parts based on their MRP systems. Calhoun Engineering owned fourteen thirty-foot-long injection molding machines. Sean devised an Infinite Capacity Planning system to show the Calhoun Engineering management team bottleneck weeks. The software could automatically extend the schedule of all client requirements so that the client could be notified of delivery dates. Shortages could also be addressed by farming out the production of a part so that schedules could be met.

With the success of two software systems for two different types of manufacturing companies, Blade offered Sean a ten percent stock ownership in PMC. The company equity now topped a million dollars which Sean assumed meant he had one hundred thousand dollars worth of equity.

Blade's generosity also extended to Petra, Ben, and Curt: ten percent stock ownership for each. Sean could not comprehend his good fortune.

He worked just as hard at PMC as he had in architectural school. Sean overcame a less-than-stellar high school education to learn calculus, physics, structures, acoustics, and design principles. A transformation had begun in Canada, fighting through the bush wearing one boot and one disintegrating gym shoe. The Canadian wilderness altered his perception of his own capabilities, and it helped him forget his father's disappointment over his shoplifting and arrest. Yes, he was capable of evil deeds, as well as a lot of positive accomplishments. Either way, he would never retreat from an adventure that came his way.

In January, the coldest in five years, the boot finally stomped down on Sean's neck, crushing everything he thought was going right in his world. His brother-in-law, Jason, asked to meet him for a drink at the bar after work.

Jason accused Sean of having an affair with Petra. He had followed Sean and Petra to a motel.

Sean denied any wrongdoing, then switched to indignance; it was none of Jason's business. Jason said it was his business as Sean's wife's brother. Then Sean asked Jason to forget about it. Jason said he would not.

Sean had helped hire his brother-in-law out of college for an inside sales position in spare parts at PMC. Jason, a natural salesman, had always done well with the company. Jason and Sean played on the same Wyoming recreation league basketball team. Sean had known Jason since seventh grade. Jason gave Sean two days to confess to his wife.

He could not do it. Sean could not give up Petra. He would quit his marriage, quit his job, and take up permanently with Petra. The next day Sean explained all this to Petra, asking her to join him. She turned away for not more than half a minute.

"No," she said.

"What does that mean?" asked Sean.

"I will not do it," said Petra. "You have kids. You can get a job anywhere. My job at PMS and the stock is the best thing for me. We have to call it quits."

Sean could not believe his ears. "But I love you," he said. "Alright, we will cool it for a month or three. I need you, Petra. I cannot give you up."

"You will have to, Sean," she said, firm, hard, strong as always; I won't see you again."

Sean reflected later that Petra could not have meant what she said. That night at home, his wife accosted him about the affair.

Jason had not given Sean the two days he promised. Sean battled his inner demons the entire weekend. His wife browbeat him incessantly. Sean finally conceded that Petra had been correct. She had reached an inevitable conclusion, being the stronger of them. Now Sean must do the same. He resigned himself to giving up Petra, the woman that dripped sex. That meant giving up his job and leaving the PMC work environment to Petra, who considered it her life's ambition. Looking at her, wanting her day in, day out, that would be impossible for Sean.

That night Sean's wife accosted him again in the living room, "Just leave. Why don't you just leave us," she said repeatedly.

"No," said Sean, "I am not going anywhere." He kept his head up, watching his wife wail. She picked up a hefty hardcover book and winged it at him as hard as possible. It hit him in the thigh, but Sean refused to duck or flinch. She threw another book, aiming at his head. That one connected as well. Then she sat down and cried into a pillow on the couch. Sean retreated, but he never left.

Do not do the crime if you cannot do the time, he thought. *What the hell was I thinking. Will I never grow up?*

Sean walked into Blade's office and quit. In a week, he accepted and signed a deal for thirty cents on a dollar for his stock, approximately $30,000.00. Sean planned on launching his own consulting business. He never saw Petra Thorne again.

3

PLAYMAKER

Thirty million years ago, the climate in South America cooled. Dry habitats became more abundant, and ants began to farm outside of a forest environment.

1983

Sean looked up at the fifth-floor bay window reflecting the morning sun in the Leighton building. He opened the trunk of his lime green Fiat 127. The tiny four-door sedan had set the family back $1,878.00. Gone was the RX7, which Sean had sold for $9,000.00, costing him only about $350.00 in depreciation. He carried the file folder box holding his meager office supplies under one arm and the Compaq Portable computer in his right hand. Upon entering the Leighton building, he approached the antique elevator. The elevator operator closed the steel accordion gate and the heavy metal sliding door.

"What floor," the operator said.

"Fifth floor," Sean replied.

The liftman wore a button-down shirt, open, with a white t-shirt underneath. The operator's goodwill pants had not seen an iron in years. Sean wondered if he doubled as the building custodian when the elevator traffic died. Sean did not expect clients to visit him; the elevator man's appearance was of no consequence. Sean always met with the client in their business.

He unlocked the door to his office, closing it behind him. The door missed the corner of the desk by an inch. Behind the desk, the surprisingly comfortable, lone office chair tilted and swiveled. A two-shelf bookcase completed the décor. The furniture fit awkwardly in the small office due to the angular walls of the bay window. Sean gazed out on the Heritage Hill area to the east, shading the low October sun with a salute. Then he sat down, retrieved a three-prong adapter from his supplies box, and plugged in his computer. Tool of the trade.

The quiet soothed his soul. Relaxed, he began laying out a program for Calhoun Engineering. He set the modem up and dialed into Calhoun Engineering's corporate network at 9600 baud. His vow to cut back to a forty-hour work week and positively no Saturday office work had kept him in balance.

He worked best in the mornings. Over lunch, he walked across the small park next to the Leighton building to the "Y" for an hour and a half of basketball.

In the afternoon, he either programmed via the modem connection to his client or visited Calhoun Engineering to gather new assignments. He billed by the hour, installing the ClientTrac software package on his computer to provide monthly statements to Calhoun Engineering.

Saul Calhoun, the president of Calhoun Engineering, struck Sean as an innovative future thinker, similar to Blade Arbeider. An analysis of the company procedures and paper flow offered several possibilities for improvement.

The three largest customers of Calhoun Engineering, General Motors, Chrysler, and Steelcase, used their own MRP software to predict inventory requirements eight weeks into the future. Sean had developed his own MRP system for custom equipment at Pioneer Manufacturing. His Infinite Capacity Planning module for Calhoun Engineering would use the raw data reported to Calhoun Engineering by the three large customers. Each company supplied a report detailing the part number and weekly requirements projected for the next eight weeks. The customer reports arrived on Wednesday to be addressed before the following week's production and shipment. The requests varied up or down depending on the demands of the marketplace.

Sean learned that large corporations used an Electronic Data Interchange (EDI) standard to communicate their requirements to

[177]

sub-contractors such as Calhoun Engineering. The idea intrigued Sean. He proposed an integration module to Saul Calhoun based on the EDI standard. Calhoun Engineering could use the application to communicate, computer to computer, with existing and future customers. The system would meet the strict specifications of ANSI EDI. The Calhoun Engineering production manager could initiate the computer-to-computer transactions by setting up a new customer in the database with a simple set of defined parameters. Manual input to Calhoun Engineering's customer order system for clients adhering to the EDI standard would become unnecessary.

The analysis and programming work at Calhoun Engineering caught the attention of Saul Calhoun Sr., the president of Superior Die and Engineering. Superior D&E cast the aluminum molds used by the injection molding machines at Calhoun Engineering.

Saul Sr. approached Sean about possibly converting CNC three-dimensional grid points to a visual 3D representation. Sean recognized that his brother Robert would better handle the complex programming involved. At the time, Robert managed the computer department at ChargeCard, Inc., the multi-state charge slip processor for millions of VISA charge slips daily. He would not have the time to devote to collaborating with Sean on a 3D imaging project.

Still, other areas of the Superior D&E software requirements fit Sean's programming expertise, and he tackled them.

The two companies piled on requirements beyond what Sean had time to complete. He needed more help; he needed to expand his business. Sean Martensen Consulting filed incorporation documents under SMC & Associates, Inc.

Sean hired two programmers, Jim Steller and Daniel Burgess. Both showed promise. Daniel Burgess left Sean's employ four months later, never having proven his worth as a programmer.

Jim Steller had striking blue eyes, curly back hair that he wore long to his collar, a Mediterranean complexion, and smooth baby face features.

On the brink of exiting the software field, Jim reluctantly accepted a position with Sean at SMC & Associates. Jim's former employer refused to give him the respect and assignments Jim felt he deserved. After a three-month trial apprenticeship, Sean handed Jim the next new client, Mill Steel Co.

Alexander Ruiz interviewed for a position in sales support a month after Jim Steller began employment. Sean encouraged Alex to market a turnkey, shrink-wrapped construction accounting package, taking advantage of Sean's architectural background. Timberline Software Company provided such a solution. Alex began studying the modules. He marketed the Timberline suite to small construction contractors in the West Michigan region.

Liam Cross, the president of Mill Steel, spoke with Sean on the phone a month after Jim began working on the software design for the steel roll form company.

"Sean, I need you on my project," the president said, "Jim is just too inexperienced to handle a development of this size."

"Liam, I can assure you Jim is right for your project," Sean said, "I vetted Jim thoroughly, and he worked with me for enough time before your endeavor that I know I can count on him.

"He graduated near the top of his class at Calvin. Isn't that your Alma Mater?"

"Yes, it is, but he is too young," said Liam.

"Listen, he looks young," replied Sean, "but he has the brains and the drive to see this project through. Give Jim three more weeks. I will take over if you are still uneasy, but I don't anticipate that happening."

"Alright, we'll see."

Jim presented his skeletal program and analysis to Sean in the office two weeks later. Pleased with the progress, Sean wondered if Jim might be a better information technology specialist than himself. Sean called Liam at Mill Steel a week later, who admitted complete satisfaction. Jim now had reference credentials. He continued on the Mill Steel Co. project for another ten months.

In the spring of '84, Sean visited Skytron LLC, an importer of variable and fixed-focused surgical lights from Japan. The accounting department had the difficult task of manually converting the yen to the dollar value of the shipments.

Sean automated the process. First, the ship containing the lights arrives at a port in the United States. The same day, the Japanese company generated a bill of lading and invoice transferring ownership to Skytron. The Skytron SKU number, description, cost of each light in yen, and quantity are sent electronically to Skytron via the TTY protocol.

Sean's program strips out the pertinent information from the file. According to a mutually trusted third party, the Bank of England, the algorithm also secures the daily conversion rate, yen to dollars.

The cost conversion is then calculated, and the received quantity is added to the Skytron inventory system, re-averaging the total inventory cost. Impressed with the system, the accounting department manager purchased inventory, invoicing, and accounts receivable modules from SMC & Associates.

At Michigan State University, Sean became friends with his neighbors in campus married housing. Harold and Connie Jasper remained friends beyond when Sean and his wife became domestics and moved in with the Stott family. Harold left Michigan State to assist his brothers in running the largest truck farm in Wayne County near Detroit. Before the birth of Sean's children, they invited Sean and his spouse to spend occasional weekends at the farm.

Hal epitomized the hippie stereotype while at MSU. He always wore jeans, navy style: no underwear or belt. His hair varied from long to longer. He typically sported a full beard and rarely wore shoes, even in cold weather. Harold had run a roadside market out in front of the farm from when he turned twelve until he could drive. From then on, he steered the tractor in front of the migrant pickers and trucked the farm produce to Eastern Market in Detroit. There he hawked vegetables to individual and commercial grocery buyers.

The Jaspers resided in the family farmhouse, a tilting one-hundred-twenty-year-old structure. At one point in the farm's history, the house had been rotated ninety degrees on its foundation to face the county's new gravel road. In their counterculture living room, Sean and his wife partied with Hal and Connie. Splotches of chartreuse, electric indigo, and hot-pink blacklight paint adorned the walls and ceiling. Three small end tables in the room provided places for setting down drinks. The four friends sat or lounged on the many four-foot square stuffed paisley and rainbow-colored pillows scattered about the room. Incense and marijuana clouded the house and the friends' senses.

Connie might be mistaken for a suburban housewife unless she stood arm and arm with Hal. She had short straight black hair and a petite athletic figure. Connie consumed gin and tonics with discretion and smoked weed with gusto.

When Hal and Connie visited Sean in their new townhouse in Ann Arbor, there were only a few large pillows and a sectional to sit on. Sean paid homage to the 70s by painting a twenty-inch-wide, free-form rainbow stripe up one wall, across the ceiling, and ending behind the sectional.

The Jasper brothers sold their valuable real estate in Wayne County and began another farm in Litchfield, Michigan. By then, although the brothers voted on each proposed improvement to the property, Harold, the youngest brother, drove the business with technological innovations, pricing models, and growing decisions.

It took Hal a couple of years to convince the partners to build greenhouses and concentrate on young plants for the wholesale perineal and annual growers.

Greenhouses cost a lot of money. In the second year of the transition, Hal pushed for glass and plastic greenhouses with automated ventilation systems and temperature control. Hal had grown frustrated with the expensive irrigation needed for truck farm crops and the farm's dependence on natural sunlight, which was never a sure thing in Michigan. He planted seed trays of hundreds of varieties of perennial and annual seedlings in the greenhouses. Hal found brokers to market the plugs. He worked out an agreement with Federal Express to deliver a box of five plug trays anywhere in the country overnight so that the tiny plants would be healthy and ready to plant with the opening of the box.

Under Hal's guidance, the company thrived, doubling the available greenhouse planting space every two years.

A year after Sean formed SMC & Associates, Inc., Sean and his wife visited Hal and Connie near Christmas. Hal sucked the last joint at midnight and rattled the ice in his empty gin and tonic glass, setting it on a table.

"Time to check the heaters," he said, standing up.

"I'll go with you," Sean said. The Spirit album finished with one of Sean's favorite songs, *Nature's Way*.

Sean donned his coat (Hal did not bother with even a jacket,) and they braved the snow and wind outside. Sean followed his friend into one greenhouse after another, floating behind Hal as he moved through one damp, warm, Eden-like ecosystem to the next, gasping for breath in the cold between the buildings.

As they wandered the glass houses, Sean remembered cherished times exploring a greenhouse business in Bloomingdale, Michigan, before the family moved to Kalamazoo. Row upon row of Cyclamen and Poinsettias filled every inch of the space at Christmas time. The owners, friends of Sean's parents, had three glass houses. Sean wandered the sweet-smelling, condensation-dripping, quiet environment while his mother dropped off choir music for Mrs. Dickerson, one of her bridge buddies.

As magical as Sean remembered, Hal's greenhouses circulated warm air via a large fan and heater suspended from the structure at one end of the building. At the far end, away from the fan, the background noise can calm a buzzed visitor nearly to sleep. Walking underneath the roaring space heater at the other end of the greenhouse, Sean could almost feel the greenhouse rocking from the powerful fan. The two friends checked the pilot lights of the heaters in all the greenhouses, listening to the structural metal expand or contract in the howling weather beyond the glass. The atmosphere of the quiet, human-empty greenhouses mirrored the psychedelic farmhouse living room. Hal knew how to live well and work hard.

Hal took Sean to the greenhouse attached office to talk business. Sean noted the TRS-80 computer on the desk. Hal gestured at the computer.

"I put our production plan into a Lotus spreadsheet, said Hal, "We track what gets sown and when, so we know when to pull it from the germination chamber and move the tray of seedlings to the warmer greenhouse."

"That's great, Hal," said Sean, "What's the red light next to the workstation?"

"That is how we signal the person in the office next to the germination chamber that they can work on the computer. When the red light is on, the grower can go in. Then they can turn the light off when they are done.

"OK," Sean said, "That's a little like using a sophisticated computer and typing on it with a pitchfork. That is the problem with MS-DOS; it's a single-user operating system."

"I know," Hal said, "before we turn on the light, we send the spreadsheet to the other office. Only one person works on the file at a time; otherwise, the file gets screwed up and out of sync."

Sean nodded. "Still, it sounds like the system is working and providing the tracking you want."

"How would you go about improving my idea?" Harold asked.

"Well," Sean said, "I would start with a multi-user operating system that allows two or more operators to work on the data simultaneously. That would eliminate the light switch.

"Beyond that, I would set up a database of all your plants. You say you produce more than seven hundred varieties, right?"

"Yes, perhaps close to one thousand varieties next year."

"Alright, you need a database that can extract individual requirements for growing times and greenhouse conditions and produce a scheduled start and finish date for each crop."

"Could you do that for us?" Hal asked.

"That would be a big project, Hal," said Sean, "You would be looking at a considerable chunk of change."

Hal patted the 'Trash 80' top and looked up at Sean.

"Send me a quote," said Hal.

Saul Calhoun, Jr. sat on the board of directors of The Michigan Council of Foundations (CMF) in Grand Haven, Mi. The council requested Sean's help setting up a multi-station word processing system and high-quality printer to output the monthly newsletter for their one hundred thirty foundation members. They also needed to track member dues, members' assets, contact information, and the state of their development. The project bore no relation to manufacturing, SMC & Associate's typical client, but Sean benefitted from reference accounts among the CMF members.

Sean worked on Hal's greenhouse software for nearly a year, once his friend gave him a contract. Then he installed it at Jasper Greenhouses, Inc. The Unix modules included General Ledger, Accounts Payable, Accounts Receivable, Payroll, custom Order Entry, Inventory, and Production planning systems. Sean created a database for production that used several growth factors to predict when the plants should be started, when they should be transplanted, and when they should be shipped.

One of the factors, a predicted loss, forced the growers to start more plants than were ordered, but if all the plants survived, brokers were allowed to sell the overage after all preorders were filled. Hal adamantly refused to lower the price of these plants, dumping them rather than giving them away in a fire sale. After all, the plants were just as good as those preordered. With this philosophy of quality first and always, Hal kept his prices high, and his reputation for quality was never questioned. With the software that Sean created, he acquired contracts with Federal Express and his customers to deliver the plants in an enclosed box in one day.

This meant that all orders had to be filled no later than 3:00pm on any given day to be delivered to the customer the next morning without fail. No boxes were shipped on Sunday when the greenhouse closed.

Hal's business grew, and so did SMC and Associates, Inc. Sean named his software VeriCell Greenery Production Software, Veri (green), and cell (smallest unit of a planting container.) A tray contained three hundred fifty cells in a fourteen by eighteen-inch tray. Hal sold millions of plants a year and would soon multiply that into tens of millions a year. He built many new temperature and humidity-controlled glass greenhouses.

The database grew to contain basic growing information on over three thousand different varieties of plants. After the initial software began to work, Sean turned to implementing EDI information with Hal's major brokers, allowing them to see and sell the overage online.

Sean presented Hal with the idea of using barcodes on the trays to locate them in the greenhouse for shipping or transferring to different temperature/humidity environments.

During this time of business growth, Sean also maintained a family balance. He took the family to Disneyworld in 1983, Yellowstone in 1985, and two Lake Michigan cottages in 1984 and 1985. Sean encouraged his daughter's artistic ability by taking up watercolor painting himself and painting watercolor landscapes beside her in Yellowstone and at Lake Michigan. Sean's son developed athletic skills playing soccer. Sean rarely missed a game.

[185]

Growers acquainted with Hal Jasper called Sean, expressing interest in VeriCell. Research showed over eight thousand greenhouses in the U.S., although only about one hundred were big enough to take advantage of the software.

Sean approached Hal with the idea of SMC and Associates Inc. moving on to selling and installing VeriCell to additional clients.

"Would you be opposed to others taking advantage of the processes and software you are using?" Sean asked Hal.

Hal responded. "I am not concerned," he said. "No one will take advantage of software like Jasper Greenhouses. I know that for a fact. While they struggle with the basic software, we will advance and outdistance the competition at every turn. History proves that. Go ahead, Sean, sell away. Perhaps someday we can partner up in software development."

Over the next two years, SMC and Associates Inc. picked up a client in Minneapolis, two in Florida, two more in Michigan, and one in Texas and California. Sean also installed VeriCell at client greenhouses in Scotland, England, and New Zealand.

****

Sean's son received the pass from his friend Brian, one of the tallest boys in fifth grade, who had smothered the rebound. As he had learned from Coach Martensen, his dad, the boy fired the ball across the top of the key to PJ, the third player on their CrownThree team already hustling over the take-back line. Crossing that line marked their team's possession of the ball and an opportunity, according to the three-on-three half-court rules, to shoot. PJ looked up to the basket for a shot, back at the boy for a possible pass, and then noticed Brian flashing back to the right side of the court at the baseline. PJ passed the ball to Brian, who turned and ricocheted the ball off the backboard and into the basket for a point. Two opposing team members clobbered Brian to prevent the basket but too late. Brian missed the requisite foul shot awarded to him.

The opposing team called a time-out. Brian, PJ, and the boy huddled, red-faced, wiping sweat with their CrownThree shirts. Sean stayed back on the sidelines. As much as he yearned to coach them, he realized the boys owned this game and wanted it that way. As long as they kept passing as they did on that last play, he would be happy, win or lose.

Sean had coached his daughter's sixth-grade basketball team. His daughter played like Sean, energetic to the point of schizophrenia, jumping up and down on defense, hurrying and missing a sure layup, and running full tilt back down the court on defense. Sean loved the game. He still played at least twice a week at the downtown YMCA. Former high school all-state black and white players, now in their early to late thirties, played five-on-five full-court basketball at the "Y," complete with jive talk, fights, and good-natured teasing. Sean passed the ball to better players unless he had an opening for a reverse layup from right to left under the basket, his one dependable shot. Sometimes he made a three-point shot.

He knew how to play the game and could teach young basketball players correct fundamentals and winning strategies. Tactics include passing the ball instead of dribbling to find an open teammate and the give-and-go play.

Sean's son, eleven years old, and his teammates would attend Breton school in the sixth grade in the fall. For their age, they were accomplished players.

The boy had seen his sister play and had asked Sean to coach his team. Sean agreed to coach a group of seven of his son's friends under the stipulation that they play in the downtown YMCA 3rd-4th grade league. The Forest Hills YMCA near the Martensen home, new and shiny, attracted all the white suburban tennis and racquetball yuppies. The downtown "Y" smelt sweaty, the main feature being the basketball court and the weight room. The 3rd-4th grade and the 5th-6th grade leagues consisted of black kids and one white team, Sean's.

Everyone on the team was a third grader that first year and lost every game, but they learned how to play hard and accept defeat. PJ, on occasion, provided a bit of histrionics. Competitive like his dad, PJ would wing the ball at a wall after a loss and walk in circles, pouting. His father had played college ball. PJ improved his attitude over time.

The team practiced the fundamentals once a week; shooting properly, eyes forward, head-up dribbling, and lots of passing drills. Every week they played a round-robin shooting game called Lightning.

Lightning begins with all players lined up, starting at the free-throw line and extending toward half-court. The first two players start with a basketball each.

Player one shoots a free throw and tries to make a basket. If the player misses, he must grab the rebound and score a layup as fast as possible. For subsequent shots, player one can shoot a jump shot, lay-up, or whatever is needed to win another round.

Player two cannot shoot until after player one has shot their first free throw. The goal for player two is to score a basket before player one does. If player two misses their free throw, he must rebound his miss and make a shot as fast as possible.

If player one makes a basket first, he goes to the back of the line. If player one fails to make a basket before player two, player one is eliminated (all eliminated players stand off to the side until the game is finished).

Once player one makes a basket, he passes the ball to the next player in line. That player tries to make a basket before player two does. If this occurs, player two is out. If player two scores first, he goes to the end of the line and passes his ball to the fourth player in line.

After Lightning, the boys broke into two teams and played a full-court game. Sean emphasized passing the ball down the court in a fast break style and working simple give-and-go routines to ensure an open shot.

PJ, Brian, and the boy formed the core of the team. All three boys practiced each aspect of the game. Gifted athletically, they tackled the sport of basketball as if they had already played high school ball.

That same intensity went into each sport they tried. As Sean coached his daughter in basketball, he played ping-pong each evening with his son, whose head alone rose above the table's edge. Within months the boy could return most of Sean's fast serves and tricky spin returns. They began attending Ping-Pong night at the downtown "Y," and the boy defeated a few adults. Win or lose, the boy smiled. Sean appreciated his developing skills but, more crucially to Sean, his attitude. He liked to play the game as much as his father.

Soccer captivated the boy next. Shorter than Brian by inches but just as fast, the boy's footwork with the ball appeared unmatched city-wide in third and fourth grade and beyond.

The boy turned out to be left-handed like other members of Sean's wife's family and naturally athletic like his uncles. He favored his left foot in kicking the soccer ball. A mid-fielder would kick the soccer ball to Brian, equal to the boy in dribbling, and Brian would take off down the right side of the field. Sean's son ran left, the two speedsters outdistancing the defenders.

If Brian saw an opening, he took the shot on goal. If the goalie moved against Brian, Brian would pass left over to his friend, who kicked the ball into the net. The duo scored at least six goals in every game and defeated all the other teams in third, fourth, and fifth grade.

Basketball became the next sport to master, and the trio took up golf in the summer. Sean bought the boy left-handed golf clubs, and the boys went three afternoons a week to the municipal course and played nine holes at cheap rates. The boy worked just as hard on golf as on other sports. He had a natural, left-handed swing. The golf ball sailed further and further each year. The inseparable trio, PJ, Brian, and Sean's son, practiced each sport to mastery. Sean became superfluous as a coach and mentor, but he continued emphasizing one thing with his son. Play the game for fun.

The CrownThree basketball competition included over three hundred four-man teams (three players on the court, one substitute.) Players of all ages and abilities paid the entry fee and played a guaranteed two games in the double-elimination tournament. Portable basketball hoops and backboards lined the streets of the small Michigan village, Nonagon. The players called their own fouls on the thirty, taped-out half courts. On several courts, Sean observed what he called hack-em-up basketball: in other words, streetball. The tournament administrators checked the age and experience of all players and attempted to place each team in a competitive bracket. During registration, heights were verified against the corresponding entry on the application. Elementary, high school, college, semi-pro, and all-girl teams played in the state-wide popular CrownThree. The games began on a Friday night in July. Matchups continued all day Saturday and again on Sunday.

If a team lost the first game, they played a second game in the loser's bracket. In the losers' bracket, if the team lost a second game, it was eliminated from the tournament. If they won the second game but not the first, they could continue in the tournament coming up with multiple wins to reach the finals in their bracket. The losers' bracket made for an arduous six-game climb back to the finals. Consecutive wins from the start made for a four-game path to the championship.

The team Sean sponsored had won the first game but lost the second to taller, rougher-playing sixth graders. After the first loss, the trio and Cam Sutcliff, their fourth team member, won four games in a row. They played for their bracket championship and the first-place trophy against the same black team that beat them in their second game.

Returning from the timeout, with the score fourteen to fourteen, both teams in the well-played game took the court tired but fired up. The first team to reach twenty-one points would win. His son's friends' fast passing and intelligent shot selection kept them in the game.

[190]

Most of the other brackets had either finished or played their final game. Eighty percent of the players and parents had left for the drive home. Now that the games on other courts had finished, the crowds that were left migrated over to the court where the boys were playing. Both teams' gameplay, hustle, and shots impressed the crowd.

Sean's son and PJ had both made a couple of two-point shots (shot beyond an arc at the top of the key.) Brian continued pulling down rebounds. The opposing team drove and dribbled, making great shots as well. The crowd watching had grown with each point. The two-point baskets made by PJ and the boy received oohs, aahs, and clapping. This last game involved eleven-year-old seasoned players with excellent skills.

When possible, both teams avoided hack-em-up. In short, the game excited the crowd, and as the score remained close and more people crowded around the court, cheering for each team increased in volume, upping the adrenaline of the boys on the court.

Sean watched PJ, Brian, and his son, running in sweat-soaked CrownThree t-shirts on an eighty-nine-degree day. They were up by one, nineteen to eighteen, when Brian slipped while defending his man, and the score became tied again at nineteen. Both teams wheezed with exhaustion. PJ's defense caused a missed shot by the other team in the corner along the baseline. Brian rebounded, sending the ball back to PJ, who swung the ball to his teammate on the other side. The boy dribbled left, out beyond the two-point arc by three feet. He stopped so fast that the defender sailed by two feet before recovering. The boy turned to the basket, set his feet, and put up his left-handed shot. The crowd saw the ball arc up and followed it as it dropped with a swish through the hoop for the win, twenty-one to nineteen.

Sean turned away, not wishing to demonstrate the craziness of a proud basketball father, the lump in his throat growing by the second. The crowd had no reservations, converging on the winning team, ruffling hair, patting backs, and shaking hands. Sean did not know the two men who hoisted the boy to their shoulders as the crowd congratulated the team.

The swarm thickened to the point that Sean had to step back up on the curb, fading to the outskirts of the throng. Fifteen minutes later, the crowd thinned, and the boys walked over to the trophy table to collect the two feet tall, first-place gold-colored statue of a player rising to the basket with a basketball in hand and a crown sitting cockeyed on his head.

Sean knelt and hugged his son.

"You played a great game, son," he said, "Proud of you, really proud. You four played like a team. I'm proud of you all."

"Let's go home," said the boy, "How about a milkshake on the way."

****

Harry Martensen prepared for his impending death with the same organization and aplomb he used to move through his life. There were a lot of angles to work out.

The couple had sold their home with the in-ground swimming pool and moved to a two-bedroom apartment in 1989. They cleared the house, distributing items to their children, church, and Goodwill.

Harry created ledgers for their life insurance policies, bank accounts, and small stock portfolio. Harry chose his middle child, who lived the closest in East Grand Rapids, to be his executor and reviewed with him the file drawer where he kept Harry and Sarah's wills and ledgers.

Harry's history of a pack of cigarettes every two days from the time he turned thirteen caught up with him, and he had developed severe asthma and emphysema in his late forties. That did not stop him. With the help of his inhaler, he continued with his home improvement projects, including finishing the basement, ceramic tiling the bathrooms, and adding a second-car garage. Harry always found another project. He spent thirty years as a 4-H leader and mentor, teaching Electrical, chaperoning social events, and driving to every function his children participated in.

In 1986 Harry began radiation treatment for lung cancer.

Near the end, when Hospice helped Sarah with Harry's care, Sean, who lived the closest, visited as often as possible. Stephen lived in France, and Laura in Massachusetts at the time. Robert lived in Farmington Hills, and Edward lived in New York.

Harry sat in the easy chair he had brought to the apartment from the house when his son arrived, knocked, and invited himself into the apartment.

"How are you holding up, Dad?

"Fine," said Harry, "Good to see you."

Harry's face seemed even thinner than on the last visit the week before. Harry glanced at the ring on the end table next to the chair.

"Don't forget to take the ring."

"Sure, Dad," the son said, "Let me take another look at it."

He picked up the ring, which was too large for his finger.

"I'll look at it with a magnifier when I get home. Kind of hard to make out everything written in it. I see the name Daniel and the date 1843. I can read that.

"That reminds me, Mom says there's some Cherokee in us from her family. What about your side of the family, dad?

"Hmmm," Harry mused, "Truth be told, I have no idea."

Harry went over his instructions yet again.

"This is important. You need to make sure Sarah follows through with the mastectomy operation."

"I will, Dad, promise."

Harry's left eye squeezed shut, and his lip curled up as he clenched false teeth, breathing in a rasping sound, obviously in pain. Then Harry's affable smile returned.

"Hurts, huh, Dad?" said the son.

"Not bad. The medicine, you know," Harry said, still smiling.

Father and son continued small talk for forty minutes. Sarah came in from the bedroom several times to check on Harry.

"You know, son," Harry concluded, "I've been a lucky man. Cannot complain. I've had a good life."

Sean nodded without replying. He wanted to soak in this time with his father. Harry drifted off, and they sat quietly. After a few more minutes, Harry twitched, awake again.

'I better get going back to Grand Rapids, Dad."

"Sure," Harry said, "I should get to bed and rest some."

Harry used both hands to push on the arms of the easy chair to help himself stand. His son went over to Harry, helping with a hand under Harry's armpit as he shuffled toward the bedroom. Halfway there, Harry collapsed, surprising them both. Harry's head lolled back. Sean scooped his father up, not believing he could carry the man. Harry's weight must have been less than one hundred and twenty pounds. He was no longer six feet one inch tall either. The son laid Harry in bed as Sarah came over, concerned. Harry smiled up at them both. "Thanks, son, thanks for coming down. Good to see you."

The son said goodbye to his mother. As he left, he crossed paths with the Hospice worker taking off her coat. The son introduced himself and asked if she needed assistance. Upbeat and efficient, she would call if she needed anything.

Harry died two days later, and Sarah began preparations for Harry's "Celebration of Life" at Peoples Church: the Unitarian church in Kalamazoo. Six days after Harry died, Sarah checked into the hospital for her mastectomy operation as promised. During recovery, a blood clot in her leg caused a massive stroke, and Sarah died.

Sean came down from Grand Rapids to handle the details of his parents' remains. As indicated in their wills, the ashes from their cremation would be buried beneath a purple beech tree planted in the memorial garden on the grounds of the Unitarian church.

Sean contacted his siblings with the news.

****

February: SMC and Associates, Inc. received a request for a proposal from the most significant Poinsettia cuttings grower in the United States. The company held a patent on Poinsettia cuttings. All wholesale or retail greenhouses paid royalties to Runyon Greenhouses in San Diego, California, if they grew poinsettias. Greenhouses bought cuttings from Runyon or grew stock plants to harvest them.

The proposal consisted of eighty-three pages of questions. Sean included financial documents and customer testimonials. He spent three months filling out the proposal.

At the same time, the Amway Foundation Associated Investment Capital firm in Grand Rapids became interested in VeriCell. The foundation representative suggested they might provide capital to boost the prospects of selling VeriCell to a broader market. Sean spent every spare minute on a snappy proposal with financials and sales projections to convince the panel to support SMC and Associates, Inc.

New VeriCell prospects by word of mouth had run its course. At least one hundred greenhouses in the country could afford Sean's system. The eighteen clients he already worked with seemed to be the only ones able to tackle the transition to automation. The idea of software efficiency meant working himself out of a client, except for routine maintenance. Growers liked to water plants and dig in the dirt. Punching buttons on a keyboard went against their nature.

Sean contracted with a sales representative firm in California to market VeriCell, for a percentage (a large percentage) of the initial sale. Sean had learned that he should separate the sales function from the product's engineering. He traditionally did not charge appropriately for the services of his company.

Four months after submitting his proposal to the Poinsettia grower, Sean learned that he had made the cut of the eighteen proposals considered. The company now needed to choose between two finalists. This came when Sean desperately needed a new client to support his six employees. This client would be the biggest of his career. Literally, every poinsettia sold in America put money in the pockets of the owners of Runyon Greenhouses.

After three presentations to the Amway Foundation, the investment capital company possibility went nowhere.

"Is there a way?" asked the panel, "to package your software into a standard that can be shrink-wrapped and sold off the shelf?"

Sean was at a loss. He specialized in custom software. Every greenhouse needed something different. He had core algorithms that he built up for each client. Then he would typically find a subsystem to improve. The investment capital company dropped his project.

Another two months passed before the Runyon Greenhouse vice president requested an in-person interview in California. Sean booked the flight with the last of the company cash.

Then it came time for the company payroll.

Sean had been made executor of his parent's estate when they died the last week of the previous year. He had distributed half of the funds from insurance, stocks, and bank savings to his siblings. Sean could only pay his employees for another pay period by dipping into the estate's cash balance. He did not hesitate to transfer funds to the company payroll account.

The poinsettia company had received eighteen proposals. Seventeen of those proposals were submitted by large accounting firms. VeriCell held the eighteenth spot, now competing with only one other company. Arthur Anderson Consulting versus SMC and Associates, Inc.

The tour of the company in San Diego convinced Sean that his software base fit the production processes at Runyon. With some modification, Sean's software would greatly benefit California's most significant greenhouse grower.

After returning from California, Sean agonized for weeks waiting to hear if he had landed the contract. Finally, the call came. The vice president admitted that VeriCell made the best fit for their operation. But Author Andersen Consulting had tens of thousands of employees. They offered manpower that Sean could not match, and he lost the sale.

The last straw had been broken. *What was he thinking*, Sean thought? *Would he ever learn?* Two days later, Sean called his eldest brother, Robert, and confessed to using $60,000.00 of their parent's money on payroll, even though Sean had not paid himself in months. Payroll taxes were also in arrears.

Crying, Sean asked for time to determine how to repay the money. Robert said he would contact their other siblings and see what consequences may be forthcoming.

As company president, Sean always kept his employees aware of the company's financial situation. Several employees had seen the writing on the wall and had already left. The rest of the employees left of their own accord. They thanked Sean for the pleasurable years with the company.

Next, Sean called Hal Jasper, his first and most reliable greenhouse customer. Hal listened, as always, and asked Sean for a meeting at the greenhouse.

When Sean arrived, a lawyer and Hall's brothers, partners in the greenhouse, joined the meeting.

"Did you bring a report on the money you owe?" Hal asked.

"Yes," said Sean, presenting the spreadsheet he had created. It included what he owed to his brothers and sister. It also included the amount of the back payroll taxes. The amounts did not include what the estate owed him.

"We may be able to negotiate with the IRS on these payroll taxes a bit, Hal," the lawyer interjected.

Hal looked over the spreadsheet and passed it to his two brothers.

"Sean, you have done great work here," he said. "For other greenhouses as well. Ten years ago, there was no such thing as a greenhouse plug-producing company, let alone software to run it.

"Think about this. We will buy in for fifty percent of your company. We will pay off the relatives and the back taxes. We would require signoff letters from the relatives. You can work with Jim Sanders here to help with the IRS. We ask that you keep going on our barcode location system and the other subsystems we need. A company of one, no employees, no office expenses."

"What is there to think about, Hal," said Sean. "I accept."

****

After winning the Macker in sixth grade, the boys that Sean coached participated in more basketball three-on-three tournaments. A couple of shared trophies sat on the boy's dresser.

The school boys' basketball team played several area teams in seventh grade. The boy scored twenty-three points in one game against the Sparta Middle School team. The playmaker stole the ball multiple times, racing down the court alone for a layup. He turned, caught the ball, and shot when he received a pass in the open. Two three-point shots dropped for him, and numerous two-point and foul shots.

In ninth grade, the boy struggled. He had not grown much in height, and the practices for the high school teams were brutal. The coach moved him to the third string. Sean's son developed painful shin splints and decided to quit the team. This was harder on the boy's mother than it was on Sean. Sean continued playing basketball with an unmatchable passion, knowing his son would retain his enthusiasm for the game.

Sean's daughter received an art scholarship from Michigan State University, fell in love, produced a son, and married all in the space of three years. She never stopped creating.

Sean's son graduated from high school in June of 1996. Sean and his wife acted as chaperones for the class graduation party.

Sean and his wife dressed up as a Klingon and Space Girl for the event. Before heading to Michigan State University, Sean wanted his son to enjoy this last party. He faded into the background of chaperones, watching his son from afar with an overwhelming fondness.

As a senior, Sean's son began a growth spurt. He danced that night with his date for the prom, Marianne Mosier, enjoying the D.J., taking after his father, the folk dancer. Then he sauntered off to the basketball court. Sean followed at a safe distance.

Two friends seemed to argue with him as the boy bounced the ball. After a couple of minutes, Sean held out a palm, and three boys placed ten dollars each in his hand. The boy pocketed the money. He waved his friends back and bounced the ball three or four times. He stood out of bounds, even with the foul line. He moved a step left, getting into a rhythm, then rose up high for a jump shot; a left-handed jump shot from out of bounds. Swish. The three boys could not believe it. One boy doubled over, and another pulled on his hair. The third boy wanted to play double or nothing. Sean's son, the playmaker, would not bite. He kept the thirty dollars.

****

Sean and his family traveled to Ludington, visiting the lot Sean had purchased the year before. He had spent six months designing and drawing a three-story house overlooking Lake Michigan. His crew consisted of his daughter, husband, wife, and son. The task that day was pouring the basement floor. Another squad worked on drilling the water well south of the basement walls. Sean had poured concrete with Harry, his father, back in the day on Sage Street and knew it to be hard work. He wanted to see how his crew reacted to the task.

The crew did not know what to do; they stood around while Sean worked the concrete. The concrete truck kept dumping concrete. Foreseeing a catastrophe, the plumber yelled to Sean, telling him to get his family crew moving. Finally, the family pitched in, the concrete hardening by the minute. Sean had rented a power trowel, a fan-like device that worked like the floor buffing tool he had used as a maintenance man at the spice company many years before. Ultimately, the floor turned out to be level, smooth, and he had ordered enough. The water and geothermal wells drilled by the second crew were also successful.

All the lumber required for the house arrived on pallets and skids from the state of Washington. Sean dropped off a pop-up trailer, and he and his son inventoried the wood. Over the next four months, father and son worked on framing the basement, first and second floors. When they were ready for the roof beams and the 2-

1/2"x11-7/8" by twenty-four-foot-long engineered wood I-beams, Sean hired a man and a crane to set them in place. With his son-in-law's help, the I-beam joists were light enough to be placed by Sean's three-man crew.

Sean spent twenty-two months building his house, either with or without help. Because of the limited broadband service in Ludington, Sean had to travel two hundred miles southeast from Ludington to Jasper Greenhouse. He would work there and stay in Hal's spare room. Sean put in forty-three hours in three days and then drove back to Ludington. He would rest one day and then work three days on the house, spring, summer, fall, and winter.

The second summer, while Sean worked at the greenhouse during the week, his son and son-in-law built treated lumber stairs down the one-hundred-foot steep embankment to Lake Michigan. This herculean task involved carrying bags of cement down to where the post was set. A platform would be built connecting the uprights and stringers running back to the previous landing.

****

Ryan Martensen, Sean's son, completed the steps to the beach and sided the entire house with three-inch nominal vertical cedar siding. That task took two months of constant work. From that point on, Sean knew not to worry about Ryan, a capable man in his own right. The house had been Ryan's Bush Voyage, and Ryan had proved capable.

Ryan went to Michigan State University and grew to six feet three inches. He sometimes played pick-up ball with members of the MSU basketball team and held his own.

Upon graduation, he moved to Chicago. Not finding employment in his field of study, sociology, Ryan found work in the service industry as a waiter and bartended. His gregarious nature aided his new profession. He met and joked with movie celebrities and politicos.

In Chicago, he met Susan Reed, a companionable waitress. They were married in 2000 and moved back to Michigan. In 2002, Ryan's son, **Logan Martensen,** was born.

****

Sean's marriage fell apart. He sold the house he had built and finalized his divorce in 2002. Sean's former wife moved to Europe and found peace with her new flame.

4

ANALYST

*Some ants take over and enslave other ants. Honeypot
ants even enslave ants of the same species, taking individuals
from foreign colonies to do their bidding.*

2028

Fall colors appear to travel south to north in Michigan. Along
the I94 corridor between Detroit and Chicago, the red leaves of the
sugar maples tune up the last week in September, giving a
command performance. The following week, the color orchestra
moves north along the I96 corridor between Muskegon and Flint,
adding yellow and orange hues to the brass section.

Color dances across the upper half of the lower peninsula two
weeks after the lower half of Michigan. The Ludington, Michigan
area and points north provide a somber arrangement of dark green
conifers, brown silver maples, and yellow and red sugar maples.
The upper peninsula color bloom plays an encore even later in
October.

Logan lived in a two-bedroom condo recently built on the east
side of M116 in the old sand pit north of first-curve in Ludington.
The condominium kitchen view of the state park provided the
season's color. The deck off the split level's living room
overlooked Lake Michigan's expanse across the summer-busy
highway. Set back from the road and buffered by a Michigan sand
dune hill, the stream of cars cannot be seen or heard from Logan's
living room.

Logan had signed the lease on his home in the off-season with
an eight-month option to buy. His salary as the analyst at Data

Futures Inc., the second largest server farm east of the Mississippi, provided for the luxury living arrangement.

Today, Sunday, he threw on his swimsuit, stepped into his beach shoes, grabbed a towel, blanket, and his current Michener novel, and started for the beach. He hiked across the road, swishing through the dune grass to his favorite spot. Spreading his blanket in the seclusion afforded by an overgrown Russian olive bush growing at the water's edge. On this rare day in Michigan, no clouds interrupted the dome of blue sky. Thankfully, this time of year, there would be few, if any, people walking by, either in or out of the water.

A slight breeze caressed his face, and the waves lapped the shore in an easy hypnotic rhythm. In fifteen minutes, Logan fell asleep with his open book on his chest.

In a dream state, a weight lifted from his chest. Logan, groggy, opened his eyes and saw a pair of stunning woman's legs, reaching up to the crotch of a black one-piece bathing suit. Topping the swimsuit, a swirl of shoulder-length hair framed the silhouette of a woman's face, backlit by the lowering sun.

Possibly a dream? What a dream! Logan glanced down at his suit and the start of a ballooning bulge. He grabbed his towel for cover. The woman leaned over and indicated Logan's red shoulder.

"You are going to be sore tonight," she said, pointing to where the book had rested on his chest, "Except for the superhero insignia in the middle."

"Wow," Logan said, "How long did I sleep?" He stood, never taking his eyes off the slender woman. He waded to his ankles in the lake before turning back and asking her name.

"Harper Lawrence," she said.

Now Logan could see she had sandy-colored hair matching the beach. Her cheeks seemed to become rosier as they spoke. Hazel-eyes watched him intently, unafraid. Logan somehow had to stop staring.

"Glad to meet you, Harper," he said, "My name is Logan Martensen. I live in a condo across the street." He turned to see if he could see his balcony from the beach. He could not, but at least he was not staring at her incredible cleavage.

"Nice," Harper said, "I better keep walking."

"Thanks for rescuing me from turning into a lobster."

"That is OK; I've been there, done that. I could not walk by imagining you suffering tonight," said Harper.

Harper walked away.

What to do, a beautiful girl like that. Oh, hell, nothing for it.

Logan trotted up to Harper.

"If you would not mind, I could walk the beach with you. Of course, if I am intruding…"

Harper laughed, "No, I've been walking alone all week up here. The company would be great."

They settled into a comfortable pace walking just at the water's edge; the sand there was wet but wave-hammered hard and smooth. Easy walking.

Harper Lawrence had traveled from southern California but was born in Cambridge, Massachusetts. Her parents both worked in research at M.I.T.

Logan liked the way Harper glossed over her important and brilliant parents.

Since both of his parents were long since deceased, Logan mentioned his grandfather Sean Martensen.

"Papa has been quite a mentor for me. I was eighteen when the Covid-19 pandemic hit. At eighteen, staying in his small house and not visiting friends or girls felt like solitary confinement. Papa helped set up all my senior year internet school content. When I looked bored, he began teaching me programming skills and set up a college-level Systems Analysis course. I guess I became a programmer by osmosis."

"Funny you should say," said Harper, "I'm up here testing a motherboard and microchip I designed in one of the labs at the Data Futures Inc. server farm outside of town.

"I just turned in my doctoral thesis, so I'm also vacationing for a week."

"By coincidence," Sean said, "I also work there. I am the analyst that handles the maintenance programs for all the production servers in the warehouse. I have developed several programs that watch for server malfunction or foreign or domestic invasion. My work redirects criminal program operations to honey pots that gather evidence for prosecution.

"The place is huge, and there are labs at both ends. We just have not run into each other yet."

Logan looked down as they walked to avoid rocks or driftwood, having left his beach shoes with his blanket. Those moments offered opportunities to glance at the woman's legs. He shook his head slightly.

"I guess," he began, "you might hide among all the white coats at the warehouse. Out here, you stand out in that black suit like a model on a New York runway."

Harper kept walking.

What an idiot, Logan thought, *totally inappropriate.*

"What about your thesis, practical or theoretical?" Logan asked, trying to backpedal.

"About half and half," Harper said, seeming not to mind Logan's swimsuit comment, "I interned at Klux Technology, Inc., a Silicon Valley company working on nanoelectronics. The company has the latest scanning probe microscope available.

"My work is an extension of my parents' research. They combined the chemistry expertise of my mother with my dad's electronic engineering background to advance nanotechnology.

"I'm carrying their work forward to the commercial production of nanocomponent logic processing. That is what my thesis is about."

Logan followed her explanation reasonably well. A crazy thought occurred to him. *We could be a team; what a partner.*

"Your lab at the server farm also has a Klux SCM," Harper said, "My work might triple the storage capacity at your facility."

The couple turned back, walking in silence, enjoying the waves. A freighter far out on the lake, silent at this distance, headed in the opposite direction. Sandpipers crisscrossed the couple's path, flying a few feet ahead to stay out from underfoot.

Logan picked up his book, towel, and blanket, slipped on his beach shoes, and walked Harper to her rental car.

"Could I get your cell phone number, Harper? How about dinner? I know the only three places in town that serve decent meals."

"I'm beginning to get hungry," Harper said, "Have you made plans for tonight?

Thank you, God, Logan thought.

"Where are you staying," said Logan, "I'll pick you up at six." Harper wrote down her phone and room number at the Holiday Inn.

At five after six that evening, Logan used the house phone at the reception desk of her motel to call Ms. Lawrence's room. Minutes later, Harper walked into the lobby dressed in a little black dress that contrasted with the color of her hair which she wore down, fluffing around her shoulders. Her skin had a pink glow from the afternoon walk in the sun. She wore three-inch heels. Harper knew how to emphasize her long as stilts legs. She carried a sweater over her arm. A small purse hung from a shoulder strap down to her waist. Perhaps because of her easy stride and smile, she pulled off looking dress casual. She walked up and said hello to Logan, standing eye to eye with his six feet one-inch height, which would make Harper at least five feet eight inches tall, a lot of it leg.

Logan wore lightweight gray wool slacks, a maroon V-neck sweater over a white collared shirt, top buttons left unbuttoned, and polished black leather half boots. He decided on one of the brewpubs on James Street. They started with drinks at the bar. Harper ordered a glass of Cabernet Sauvignon. Logan ordered a Glenlivet on the rocks.

When the couple moved from the bar to their booth, Logan ordered a bottle of the Cabernet Sauvignon. Harper requested a

Caesar salad topped with Salmon. Logan chose the spinach salad with crispy chicken.

They settled into social conversation, covering the weather and the category-five hurricanes that set records that summer, reaching further inland than any storm thus far recorded. The evening felt like a college date, even though Logan's twenty-eighth birthday had been in May. Harper's birthday next month would be Harper's twenty-seventh.

She had not dated much, staying focused on her undergraduate studies, research, master's degree, and doctoral thesis. Logan had a girlfriend in high school, but then the pandemic hit. Logan's grandfather's underlying conditions, age, and atrial fibrillation dictated that the family unit became isolated at home. Sean Martensen and his first wife divorced in 2002. Even so, the pandemic became very personal when Logan's grandmother died from the coronavirus.

Gen Pa youth learned anti-social behavior that stuck with them for years after the Covid-19 vaccine became universal. Logan, for instance, did not take his mask off in social situations until mid-2023. Two more years passed before he felt comfortable standing closer than six feet to another person. Hugging went away entirely, along with shaking hands. He still would not fly commercially, preferring to drive with an open window. Logan homeschooled from the day of the first stay-at-home order on through his undergraduate degree in science and his master's degree in information technology.

Remaining in the small town of Ludington to see to his grandfather, Logan had little chance of interaction with post-pandemic women. Data Futures, except for the labs at either end, consisted of row upon row of server racks, reaching twenty-two feet toward the ceiling. Robotic lifts provided upper-tier access. Sometimes days passed when he did not see another person as he worked.

Harper also had a hunger for close contact. She had been an outgoing hugger in her early days. Harper internalized her predisposition to intimacy during the pandemic, and when it seemed universally safe, around the year 2025, Harper made plans to cut loose. Men had looked at her for so long from a distance with polite hands off; she gained a reputation as too beautiful and cold to handle.

"Harper, what would you say to a wee dram of scotch at my house. I would love to show it to you. In fact, I have a second bedroom and separate bathroom you might consider for your return trips to the warehouse."

"I thought you'd never ask," said Harper, "You must have an incredible view."

Logan waved at their waiter, paid the bill, and went for the car, pulling up at the restaurant's front door and hurrying around to open the passenger door for Harper.

He unlocked the front door at his house, turned on the hall light, and let Harper precede him. Harper took two steps in, turned around, and embraced Logan. She somehow backed him against the front door and switched off the light, sustaining her kiss. Logan, breathless, found the zipper of her dress at the back of her neck and pulled it down to her hips.

Their eyes adjusted to the light pouring in from the nearly full moon high above to the east on a cloudless night. The moon, visible from all the windows on the east side of the condo, lit a path from the front entry down the hall to the bedroom. Logan turned Harper, took her hand, and led her to the bedroom.

When Logan dropped her hand and turned again, Harper let her dress drop to the floor, pulling her camisole over her bra, crossing her arms, and shimmying the satin material around her face and hair. Logan helped disentangle the camisole and tossed it on the chair.

He crush-kissed Harper, one arm holding her around the waist, his right hand unclasping her black lace bra. He stepped back. The moonlight lit the upper curves of her breast and one stiff nipple, leaving the shadowed curves of her bust to explore.

In seconds Logan threw his sweater on the chair with the camisole, unbelted, unzipped, and discarded his pants and underwear on the chair.

"God damn, Ms. Lawrence," he said, admiring the tall and proud model before him.

"Damn, back at you," said Harper. Logan, the computer nerd, played basketball like his playmaking father. They matched. He swept the decorative pillows off the bed, pulled back the spread, and bowed to Harper, enticing her with a gesture to lay down. She did, slipping her long legs under the sheet, outstretching both arms for him to join her.

He did. Leaning on his right elbow, he cupped Harper's breast left-handed and kissed her, softly but lasting. He moved his hand slowly down her torso, rubbing his hand in a small gentle circle below her navel.

Harper used her hands to break his kiss and direct his mouth to her left breast. Harper pushed Logan's hand down to the wetness between her legs with her right hand.

Logan was in a slow hurry. He gave her nipple a flick with his tongue and then shook his head.

"There is a condom package on my nightstand; give me a minute," said Logan.

"I'm on the pill, Logan, and trust me, I haven't been with a man in years."

"I haven't been with a girl since before the pandemic," he said, "but out of respect…."

Harper smiled in the moonlight and pulled Logan down to her again. At dinner, the couple talked about the thousands of servers under Logan's supervision and the nano-world inhabited by Harper's watchful eye. Their worlds were united in interests, honesty, and trust.

In the afternoon and evening, the couple sought to overcome their self-imposed distancing from years lost to post-pandemic stress.

Logan teased; Harper urged.

When Logan could stand his tightness no longer, he mounted Harper, rocking, gauging her rhythm, kissing her neck beneath her ear.

Slow down, hold on, Harper, please, he thought.

Harper thought, *faster, harder, faster, faster.*

Logan exploded, the ecstasy sweet, the after-pain excruciating. Sweating, he fought through the moments of aching to keep going. He sensed her need to continue. Within minutes, Harper let out a whoosh of breath, shuddered, then relaxed. Logan raised up with both hands to look at Harper, smiling and content.

After a time, he rolled off, looking at the ceiling, suppressing a laugh. *At last, a partner,* he thought, *please God, let her feel the same. Give it everything you have.*

The next day Logan found time to visit Harper in her lab for a tour and a demonstration of the scanning probe microscope. She worked in a clean room within the lab wing. Logan stripped, showered in the locker room, and added a starched white lab coat and white booties to the laundered scrubs provided. Putting on the surgical mask and hair cap, he entered the double swing doors to the clean room, crossing the tacky mat to pick up dust particles from his feet, and found Harper. Air constantly circulated among the stacks to maintain a positive pressure in the room, disallowing germs or other corrupting particles near the subatomic experiments.

The three-foot-tall, twenty-inch diameter stainless-steel instrument in front of Harper, crowded with cables and tubing entering the core cylinders, also sported multicolored wire groups attached to electronic controls and a computer. A flat-screen display presented a large-scale view, the nanoscopic switch so small it could not be seen in the viewing glass of the instrument.

Harper spent a half hour describing the various inputs and outputs of the instrument, the function of the robotic arm, and the controls. Then she demonstrated her next attempt at twisting subatomic particles on a graphene surface.

"Every day, I think I'm getting closer and closer," Harper explained. "The benefit of this research will be a practical four-way switch capable of doubling the storage of the binary switches used in computers to date. This could be accomplished in nanoelectronic components, a hundred times smaller than the smallest microchips today."

"So that's how you will double the warehouse's storage capacity," Logan said.

"Logan, we probably will increase the warehouse capacity ten times or more."

"What's your prediction as to when this technology will be in production," Logan said.

"This nanoscience began in the late sixties," Harper said, "Nanotechnology is already in use in biochemistry and medicine.

"I'd say no more than two years from now, we should perfect the production of nanospin switching. After that, the chip manufacturers like Intel and AMC will produce the microprocessor generation using the nanospin components."

"I followed some of your explanation," Logan said, "Tomorrow, I'll show you my side of the warehouse. How soon will you be done for the day?"

"Let us meet in the parking lot in half an hour," Harper said, "How is that?" said Harper.

Logan hurried back to the locker room, changing into his street clothes. He took the robotic tram to the opposite end of the warehouse. Deciding to straighten his desk and check his email, he also jotted a note as a starting point for the next day. His most pressing thoughts were on Harper.

In the parking lot, Harper leaned against her rental car. Logan suggested they walk the Island Trail in the state park, followed by dinner at his house. Harper agreed. They stopped at her motel to drop off her car and give her time to change into jeans and walking shoes. She put on a collared blouse and a pink V-neck sweater. She also wore a packable dark green jacket and carried a small backpack. "Necessaries," she said.

This time of year, the State of Michigan did not charge an entry fee to the reserve. They drove to the Hamlin Lake beach area in the park. Looking at the posted map of the five-thousand-acre state park, Logan chose a three-mile route and started across a bridge to the first island.

They walked in single file, Harper setting the pace. Logan pointed out the sand dunes on the north shore of the man-made lake. He talked about the canoe trip Papa Martensen, and he had paddled in Canada when he turned fourteen. Papa, sixty-eight then, still handled the canoe as he did in his youth.

Harper learned of Logan's affection for his grandfather and Mercedes, whom Sean Martensen had married in 2005. Logan hoped Harper could meet his grandfather before she left for California.

They sat on a bench overlooking the lake, and Logan picked up her hand, kissed her wrist, and hung on. He wished like hell they were back at his condo, remembering Harper standing naked when he turned to her in his bedroom. He would never forget that moment.

At the approximate halfway point on the walk, Logan turned to her.

"Halfway there," he said, "Here is your halfway kiss!" He kissed her in a standing embrace, his hands pulling her hips to him. She messaged his back as they clung to each other. Comfortable.

Returning to Logan's condo, Harper grabbed various vegetables from the fridge, chopping and dressing a salad. Logan, meanwhile, sautéed two thin sliced chicken breasts. Setting the chicken aside, he sauteed two cups of halved cherry tomatoes in white wine vinegar and water with lots of parsley, salt, and pepper.

Harper opened a Chardonnay from the wine rack above the refrigerator and poured two glasses.

After dinner, Logan sent Harper out on the deck. He loaded the dishwasher, washed, and dried his stainless-steel skillet, and brought the wine out on the deck to refill their glasses. Harper sat at the high-top deck table. Logan donned a windbreaker and offered a second jacket to Harper. She set the covering across her lap, preferring to absorb the breeze in her sweater. Standing behind her, Logan massaged her shoulders and upper arms to ensure she stayed warm. The sunset cast a tinge of pink over the Lake Michigan sand dune rolling toward the beach.

The breeze blew Harper's hair as if in a storm. She reached into a pocket and pulled out an elastic hair band. Reaching up and back to gather her hair, her chest stretched her sweater tight, driving Logan mad.

Harper wore beauty without arrogance, smiling at the sunset, the beach, the condo, and Logan. *Casual, class,* thought Logan. He reached around with one arm just below her breasts, kissed her neck, and hugged her. Harper turned her head to him, and they kissed; Logan moved his hand to lightly massage her left breast.

Harper stood, took Logan's hand, and moved to the deck rail. She offered an embrace and a long kiss. Logan mentally screamed at the sun to finish setting. When it did, when the last pink and orange streaks shot across the sky overhead, when Venus winked on, Logan could wait no longer. He pulled her sweater off over her head at the deck rail, watching the goosebumps rise around her bra. He kissed as many as he could find, hugged her tight, rubbed her back, and released her bra clasp, discarding the brassiere on a chair in the living room as he tugged her into the bedroom.

Their remaining days together spun so fast Sunday, and her flight back to California had the feeling of a funeral, too final. Logan had run out of time to introduce Harper to Papa Sean and Mercedes, leaving a meeting for her next trip to Michigan.

Sitting at the breakfast counter while Harper showered, Logan filled out his absentee ballot for the 2028 presidential election. President Joe Biden died from a stroke following an AFib attack. After being sworn in, Harris appointed Cory Booker as Vice President.

Harper came to breakfast, a towel wrapped around her head and wet hair. Looking over Logan's shoulder, she saw his filled-in checkbox for Harris/Booker.

Logan decided to broach the subject.

"When I turned eighteen in 2020, I voted for the Biden/Harris ticket. My family has been Democrats for generations, according to Papa Sean. This time I am voting for Kamala Harris. She is rated favorably by a small percentage of Republicans, which is saying something for her ability to push legislation. Democrats, of course, think she is great. I do, for sure. Last year she settled the uprising in El Paso, Texas, in two days."

"I feel the same," said Harper, "someone who believes in science gets my vote again as well.

"The new Office of National Elections has quashed the crazy theories about voting irregularities, ballot dumping, and foreign intervention."

"Yes," said Logan, "The teaching moment filmed by Warner Bros. Entertainment presented as a public service announcement has helped people believe in the science of elections."

The federal election system controls the master barcode list of every ballot printed. Each ballot has a unique number. Ballots submitted with a number, not within the proper range in the master database are fake ballots marked for removal and not counted. Scanning the legal ballots and comparing the numbers to the master list highlights groups of missing ballots. The nationwide federal election ballot is tied to a state/local ballot in the voting booth or via the internet. The national identification card quieted the rest of the controversy.

The political polarization in America, however, continued to grow. After the Democrats won both houses and the presidency in 2024, the Republican Party turned more to its roots of lower taxes and less regulation of businesses while working on expanding the loyalty of the growing Hispanic population of voters.

Democrats hoped the Return to America (RTA) party would pull votes from a revitalized rational Republican Party enough for the Democrats to win again.

The RTA party espoused the populist views left over from the Trump presidency and the Make America Great Again (MAGA) voters of 2020.

Logan had two weeks of vacation available at the end of November, and he and Harper discussed a trip to California. Thinking of maximizing his time in November with Harper, Logan booked a round-trip flight to San Jose, California, for November 16th, overcoming his fear of a germ-filled airplane. At the airport Sunday, the couple said their goodbyes. Logan hugged and kissed Harper in an extended embrace. When he pulled back, he put a hand to her chin and held her eyes with his, memorizing her every feature.

"Now, if you change your mind about me coming," Logan stammered, "Let me know, please; I will understand. I had a great time, the best."

"Logan, I would not worry about changing plans," said Harper, "My mind is made up about many things."

Arriving in San Jose, California, at Gate 25 on United flight 557 from Chicago O'Hare Int., Logan's jitters finally subsided, the ground again solid underfoot. Harper met him in the baggage claim area for the flight. After an initial tentative embrace, they walked arm-in-arm to the terminal exit. Logan pulled his carry-on, hard-side spinner. *Warm weather in November*, Logan thought, stepping into the sun from the airport terminal. He pulled his suitcase along, following Harper to her car.

Harper drove Logan straight to her home at Madera Apartments in Mountain View. Located equal distance from Intel, AMD, and Google, Harper could walk six blocks to Klux Technology, Inc. She leased a luxury two-bed, two-bath unit. Her collaborative parents visited often.

During the guided tour through the apartment's various rooms, Harper explained the photographs and artifacts. A teak bookcase covered one wall in the living room. Logan paused and scanned the titles and authors on the shelves extending up eight feet in the two-story space. A credenza held her treasured tchotchkes. A two-inch Petoskey stone from Michigan sat among other polished and unpolished mineral stones in a clear glass bowl.

Logan picked up several of the twenty-five miniature guitar pins. The souvenirs had been purchased in the many places she had traveled since the international vaccination sweep. Several states, as well as Mexico and Costa Rica, were represented.

Harper favored contemporary furnishings, a sectional in the spacious living room, a teak bed in the bedroom, and comfortable leather chairs, but no recliners. The granite tiled floor incorporated radiant heat, warm to bare feet or stockings. The mirrors and paintings hung in various rooms were painted with teal and dark blue hues. The photographs highlighted the fog and mist of San Francisco in the valley and the peaks of Mount Boardman.

"That's the grand tour," Harper said, "We have reservations for eight o'clock at La Fontaine, about a five-minute walk. I want to change."

"Sounds great," said Logan, "mind if I take a quick shower to wash off the plane flight?"

"Sure, take the other bedroom to unpack. The shower is in the second bathroom," Harper said.

"I'll be ready in fifteen minutes."

The corner two-top table at the French/Italian restaurant accommodated quiet conversation. Logan ordered the Appetizer-for-Two bruschetta and beat salad. For his entrée, he decided on the Cordon Bleu with sauteed vegetables. Harper ordered her favorite menu item, Beef Wellington.

After dinner, the couple settled in at the bar. The bartender brought a Glenlivet for Logan, Baileys, and coffee for Harper.

They walked back to the apartment at midnight.

By one o'clock, Harper and Logan were asleep in each other's arms, reacquainted.

"The agenda for today is a San Francisco site seeing trip," Harper proclaimed over a bagel and crème cheese breakfast in the morning. While Harper continued getting ready for the day, Logan poured another orange juice and watched streaming news at the kitchen bar. The news anchors focused on the few glitches in the national election on the seventh. The Democrats controlled the Senate and presidency without contentious arguments or recounts in any state. The majority in the House, however, shifted narrowly to the Republicans. As Logan had predicted, the Return to America (RTA) party had split the Republican Party giving Democrats an easy victory. When interviewed, the RTA presidential candidate vowed to consolidate the Republican Party and take the presidency and Senate in 2032. The anchor then interviewed Russel Gresham, a first-time Democrat in the House.

"What do you say in response to David Breton's vow to consolidate the Republican party and win the presidency four years from now?" the news reporter asked.

Russel Gresham lifted both hands toward the camera, pleading, "The Republican party cannot let that happen," he said.

"America scarcely recovered from the 'Make America Great' and 'Make America Great Again' faction of the 2016 and 2020 elections.

"In 2024, the RTA did not exist, yet this year their third-party candidate pulled twelve percent of the vote for President.

"People must see through this right-wing faction and its slogan: 'Return to America.' This title is simply a veiled way of saying 'Return to White America,' just as 'Make America Great' meant 'Make America White,' or 'Make America White Again.'"

Harper came out of the bedroom ready to go, catching the last bit of the news report.

"I'm afraid we'll be hearing more about the RTA party from now on," she said.

"Please, God, no," said Logan.

They were off to Fisherman's Wharf in San Francisco.

The couple toured Alcatraz and walked the beach beneath the Golden Gate Bridge. In the afternoon, Harper suggested a bike ride through the grounds of the Presidio.

"I don't ride bikes, Harper," Logan said, "Maybe we could walk the path?"

The statement caught Harper by surprise. *Don't all kids ride bikes*, she thought, *and most adults if they are in as good a shape as Logan.*

"Is this another phobia left over from the Pandemic?" she asked.

"Uh, no, unrelated," Logan said.

Harper could tell that Logan wished not to be pressed on the issue. "Alright, we'll walk," she said, "then we'll take a cable car. Driving home, we'll take Lombard Street. That is always a scary treat.

"Tonight, we're dining with friends from work. Two couples that I hang out with as a fifth wheel most of the time. I can't wait to show you off."

"That sounds excellent, but I'm no prize," Logan said, smiling.

The Black Sheep Brasserie in San Jose, where the three couples met for dinner that evening, featured an elegant mural on the south wall. The monochromatic painting featured a crowd of fifteen white sheep. One black curly-haired ewe, proud and beautiful, stood in the midst.

When the other two couples arrived, Harper and Logan enjoyed a drink at the bar. Barbara and Bob Creatin, the first couple to enter, worked in her wing of Klux Technology, Inc., albeit on a different approach to microprocessor miniaturization.

Jürgen Klomp arrived with his wife, Pam. Jürgen worked in Human Resources at Lux. Pam taught third grade at Trace Elementary School.

Her old friends seemed clearly happy Harper had a new friend. Teasing Harper, they referenced the desperate state of her lonely existence. Barbara listed Harper's three dates over the last two years, describing the shortfalls of each candidate.

Logan left the comparisons alone, feeling self-conscious. He tried to steer the conversation onto Klux Technology.

"Harper tells me Klux should produce chips within a couple of years. It sounds like the chips will incorporate the nanocomputing components she is working on with her experiments," Logan said. "Would you be able to patent any of your work?"

"No," Harper said, "Not a chance; our development is owned by Klux according to our employment contract. However, we also have performance milestone bonuses guaranteed in the contract."

"What about Klux?" asked Logan, "Sounds like a pretty cool place to work."

"For the most part, yes, it is," said Bob, "For the last year, it has become much more intense. Management is pushing us for a marketable component. That could lead to missteps."

Logan directed a question to Jürgen, the HR man at the table. "How about Harper perhaps working out of our server farm in Michigan. Might that be feasible at some point?" he asked.

"Are you kidding?" Jürgen said, "Sixty-four percent of our employees already work remotely. Since the Pandemic, remote work has increased by three hundred and fifty percent. It is a new workforce model that has proven to be as successful as remote learning.

"Once the kids developed at-home study habits, their academic scores improved by seventeen percent. Eliminating the Teacher-fed content allowed individual progress to march at a quicker pace. Teachers can spend time on the learners falling behind. The faster students get together for science experiments, theater, the arts, music, and sports.

"In Silicon Valley alone, I read that school boards have collectively saved over three billion dollars in unnecessary new school buildings, renovations, and maintenance since the Pandemic hit. At-home work and study brought our economy back, for sure."

Harper smiled at the exchange between Jürgen and Logan. She had already broached the subject of working across the country with Jürgen. She would probably have to commute back and forth for another year because of the different sets of equipment available in the two locations.

"New subject," said Barbara, "How about the new Vice President of Manufacturing, Jürgen? I think his name is Geoff Hunter. Is he leading us into trouble, as Bob suggested?"

"Can't say, won't say," Bob said, "HR confidentiality. Oh, hell with it. Watch out for him. He is different down to his core from the rest of us at Klux. He is bringing two scientists with him as well. He was given stock options, and he bought more. He is loaded, and I suspect he is backed by additional money potentates."

Pam wanted to know more. "Come on, Jürgen, give us something. What is the problem? If he is rich, I think that would benefit the company. Is he black, from China, Russia perhaps?"

Jürgen and Barbara both chuckled. Barbara answered Jürgen's question, "Oh, he is white, to be sure, whiter than this tablecloth and just as stiff."

Barbara met the Hunters at a tea for selected employees and their wives.

"Hunter's wife's name is Shelly," Barbara said, "She makes no apologies for her RTA allegiance. I suspect he has similar propensities."

Jürgen put a hand over Pam's, giving her a look to be quiet. "Those types of questions," he said, "are out of bounds from an HR point of view. We don't know, but his money is a huge shot in the arm for us."

Harper worked about half the days of Logan's two-week vacation. He made it to the beach on his own and tried surfing. He took Harper to a Golden State Warriors basketball game. The opponent that night happened to be the Detroit Pistons.

The couple toured two wineries and the San Francisco Zoo. Alone again, Logan toured both Google and Apple.

Logan tried to return to the apartment each night to make dinner for them. On nights that Harper did not work, they went out to restaurants.

They spent excessive time in bed, enjoying the excitement of new love. Logan could hardly wait the next time he saw Harper walk naked across a room. She demanded a lot from a lover, and Logan rose to each occasion. He liked it soft; she liked it hard. They accommodated each other, their bond continuing to cement friendship and love.

When his time in California ended, Harper drove him to the airport, kissing him goodbye.

"Harper," he said, "I want you in my life. I want you to meet Papa and Mercedes. I want everything with you."

Tears rolled down her cheeks. "I want everything with you too, Logan. Apart from you, I will spend time preparing my experiments that depend on the equipment here at Klux. Then we can see what is next for us. Is that OK?'

"More than OK, my love," Logan said, "Thinking about you in my bed already. Goodbye."

The cell phone buzzed on the nightstand. Logan glanced at his clock radio, 2:18am, May 23, 2029. Startled from a dream, Logan reached for his Pixel 6a and swiped to answer.

"Hello," he said, "Harper?"

"Hello, Logan, this is Mercedes. Sean had a stroke; could you meet us at Corewell Health Ludington Hospital?"

"On my way."

Fifteen minutes later, Logan rushed to the desk in the hospital lobby.

"Could you tell me where Sean Martensen has been taken? He is my grandfather, and he must have arrived minutes ago. I understand he had a stroke. Can you direct me?"

"Yes sir," the desk nurse said, picking up her phone, "He has been rushed to emergency surgery. Mercedes is with him. I will have someone come for you. Please stand by while I call the ward's nurses' station."

After a moment, the nurse hung up the phone.

"Someone is on the way."

Logan used the minute to prioritize his questions, trying not to pace, forcing himself to calm down. A man with gray hair wearing a lab coat and blue gloves approached Logan from the hallway. He was not in a hurry.

"Hello," he said, "My name is Dr. Halstead, ER attending."

"Logan Martensen," said Logan, "I understand my grandfather had a stroke."

"I'm sorry, Mr. Martensen, your grandfather has passed. Sean and Mercedes are good friends of mine. Apparently, Sean went into Atrial Fibrillation about six hours ago. Mercedes called the ambulance at the first sign of a stroke, and the ambulance arrived in minutes. He passed here at the hospital twelve minutes ago."

Logan steadied and said, "How is Mercedes doing? Can you take me back to them?"

"Certainly, come with me."

Logan walked granite-faced next to Dr. Halstead, trying to remember if Sean would turn seventy-nine or eighty in June.

Seventy-nine, he thought, *sure, seventy-nine.*

Mercedes broke down at Logan's approach. His grandfather lay on the bed next to her so still he could have been part of the furniture. *There was nothing for it.* He took Mercedes in his arms and gave her an iron grip hug, letting her cry on his shoulder. Minutes passed, and Mercedes finally pulled away.

Logan had seldom seen Mercedes sans makeup. Beautiful with or without makeup, tonight she looked her age, seventy-five. She wore her hair long; a brunette with gray highlights; slim and trim, still exercising daily. Sean and Mercedes were known in town as 'The Walkers.' Neither she nor Logan could think of where to begin.

"Can I bring you some coffee, Mercedes, from the café?"

"You know," she said, "I'll get it. I need some fresh air as well. Your grandfather,,, the love of my life." Mercedes hurried out the door, not looking back.

Logan moved to the side of the bed. He looked down at the wrinkled cheeks and the crow's feet at the corners of the eyes. The intense light of the room reflected off Sean's bald, shining head, and the dimple in the center of his chin, as always, made Logan smile; Logan had the same dimple. Sean needed a shave now, though he still looked decent with his light stubble. *No doubt, Papa had died.*

Something about the skin, a relaxing, a paleness, an eeriness that Logan could not take. He put a hand over Sean's hand. Room temperature, not cold, not hot. *Papa, I love you. I know how much you loved me, always. Thank you, you saved me.*

Logan bent over the bed and kissed Sean Martensen on the forehead; done. He left the room and headed for the desk to plan arrangements.

Harper arrived in Grand Rapids, Michigan, three days after Sean Martensen died. Logan spotted Harper walking down the concourse to the baggage area at the Gerald R. Ford International Airport. When Harper saw Logan, she tossed her carry-on bag and coat on a chair. She ran to him, and he carried her momentum around in a circle, lifting her off her feet and kissing her with a dizzying spin.

At baggage claim, Logan pulled two large suitcases off the conveyor. A letter file-sized box, a book box, and a third box of equipment completed Harper's cargo.

"I'm sure I didn't get everything I need. I scheduled my vacation/remote work experiment for July 1st. Jürgen helped me move everything up so I could attend your grandfather's memorial.

"Just so you are here," Logan said, "You will still meet Mercedes. She is a gem. My Great aunt and uncle are here, along with a few of Papa's nieces and nephews. For better or worse, right? I hope you find them 'better.'"

No casket graced the front of the funeral home where Mercedes held Sean Martensen's celebration of life. Sean had requested that his body be used for research and education, followed by cremation. He had asked that his ashes be buried beneath a newly planted sugar maple. Logan picked a spot in the corner of the Data Futures property south of Ludington; Mercedes agreed.

Mercedes offered a short elegy.

"Most of you know Sean's lifetime accomplishments. The residences he designed and built, the software he created for the greenhouse industry, and the fiber optic cable he spearheaded for the community college. His watercolors. Everything he did speaks for the man I married and loved so dearly," she said, "He liked a good party, one that involved a game or friendly contest. He loved architecture, live theater, and art. He loved to dance. We danced at every opportunity, frequently the first couple to take the dance floor.

"Devoted to his daughter and deceased son, and to his grandson Logan; he tried to let his offspring live their own lives and make their own mistakes.

"Sean never stopped learning new life lessons. With all you see around you, he thought of himself as a very private man who struggled to make and maintain friends. He told truths as gently as he possibly could.

"He was my best friend. We walked, talked, and loved each other dearly to the end. I often heard him say he had lived a fulfilling life with few regrets.

"Sean's grandson Logan and Kelly, his daughter, would like to say a few words."

Kelly and Logan rose and stepped to the podium.

"My dad made me feel special whenever he spoke," said Kelly, "He recognized my love for art at the age of four. On family vacations, we packed paints, sketch pads, and easels. I remember hiking in Yellowstone Park, stopping in a field overlooking a meadow and painting what we saw for an hour or more while Ryan ran around and hit targets with stones. How many fathers painted watercolors with their daughters? He was my inspiration."

Logan bent the mike in his direction.

"Most people here know my parents died when I was ten. Papa, Sean, and Mercedes gathered me up, parented me, and comforted me. During the Pandemic, Papa Sean helped school me. He used the internet to research job skills, ideas, and viewpoints and encouraged me to do the same. For a ten-year-old who prefers basketball, studying independently from teachers made for a difficult time. Papa Sean never let me escape my studies and scrutinized my milestones appropriately. When I looked bored, he taught me programming, encouraging me to write gaming software with him. I can point to my satisfying career and give Papa credit for getting me started.

"Make no mistake, Sean was not a perfect man. He told me so. Many of you do not know of some of the dark things Sean did. He was a man of the '60s, freewheeling, unapologetic, and rebellious. Sean would say it took him a long time to grow up. That finally happened when he turned fifty and met Mercedes. I lived with them. I saw his devotion to her. He never let a door go unopened for her. He never shirked chores. Hell, he built a house for her. I will miss him dearly, but what he taught me will stick. Thanks, Papa."

Logan escorted Harper around the room, introducing her to acquaintances and family. The funeral concierge requested Logan's assistance, and he went off toward the office.

Laura, Papa Sean's sister, took the opportunity to approach Harper.

"I'm Logan's great aunt; your name is Harper. I am so glad to meet you," she said. Laura, four years younger than Logan's grandfather, Laura, with a dancer's grace, like Mercedes.

"We Martensen's tend to favor intellect. I hear you are a research scientist. Logan did let it slip that you were beautiful as well as brilliant. He did not miss the mark there, either. My husband is a physicist."

Laura paused for a moment, deciding what to say next.

"Logan told me last night he is in love with you," Laura said, "When his parents died, Sean and Mercedes pulled him through. She became his mother, and Sean tried to keep up with him on the basketball court like Logan's father."

Harper grabbed the opportunity to learn about Logan's parents. "I was surprised at what little mention there is of Logan's mom and dad, either in the pictures or program," she said.

Laura looked around the room and steered Harper to a side alcove for privacy. Said Laura, "I believe Logan is a very well-adjusted individual for having gone through the experience of his parent's death. He does not like to talk about it, hear about it, or dwell on it."

"How did they die? Were they murdered?" Harper asked.

"Not quite," said Laura, "Ryan and Susan were getting in the car to go shopping. Logan was ten years old. He hopped on his bike, said goodbye, and pedaled away. The propane tank in the garage exploded, destroying the garage and the car and killing Ryan and Susan. The explosion could be heard for a mile. Logan returned to a charred and flattened garage, blood everywhere, and my nephew's hand lying in the driveway."

"How awful," Harper said, sighing. She stayed quiet for a minute to digest the news. "That must be why Logan won't ride bikes."

"Oh, I did not know," said Laura, "but understandable. Regardless, Harper, he will be a wonderful partner and father, but he knows your career is important to you; he told me that also."

"I love the man very much as well," said Harper, "We'll have to see."

They wandered back into the gathering room, found the cake and punch, and Harper searched for Logan.

The reception at the Ludington Boat Club involved music, dancing, and drinking. Papa Sean's brother Stephen and his sister Laura played a CD of international folk music and taught Logan, Harper, Mercedes, and Laura's children Swiss, Israeli, Japanese, and American swing dances. Logan and Harper danced afterward together as a couple, learning that they fit together in dance as smoothly as they did in making love.

Harper's parents visited from Cambridge in late August, staying in Logan's second bedroom. Joanne and David Lawrence spent two days in Harper's lab, verifying her progress and asking for recommendations from Harper on their own projects. In the evening, Joanne and David, Harper, and Logan sat at the dining table amidst stacks of notebooks, lab printouts, and scattered notes, trying to evaluate her nanoscopic switch. Logan offered suggestions for the application software needed to manage the controller. His neophyte knowledge of nanotechnology controls came from studying Harper's doctoral thesis.

On the morrow, the three returned to the lab. Bob Creatin had flown in from Klux Technology, Inc. in California. He had been elevated within the company and now must manage Harper's work and his project. Bob reported to Geoff Hunter, Vice President of Manufacturing. Before he flew back to California, he spoke to the three scientists in a conference room at Data Futures.

"Progress is obvious," Bob said, "The data looks encouraging. Harper, you have outlined a sequence of systematic experiments. We are probably five to seven years away from a reliable working nano-switch."

"I guess that sounds about right, Bob, possibly sooner. Mom's biological material has to be stable as well." Bob did not look happy. Harper suggested speeding up the experiments by skipping iterations to possibly narrow the field.

"Hunter is pushing for this work to move to production in three years," Bob said, "If we find the right solution, great. If we do not hit on the right combination, we can go back and give a try on the sequences we skipped." Harper promised to redouble her efforts.

That evening over Sportsman's takeout pizza, Harper relayed the new deadlines to Logan.

"No pressure, huh," he said.

[227]

"Right, none," Harper said sarcastically.

David Lawrence, returning to the table with another piece of pizza, stood behind Harper, rubbing her back. "Harper, you must be close to burnout on this thing. What can we do?"

"I just have to get the work done. I have to defend my paper at UC Davis College of Engineering next month as well," said Harper.

That night, after Joanne and David retired to bed, Harper put on a jacket and stepped out on the deck. The moon shone high overhead again, just as when she first met Logan the previous year. Logan brought two mugs of hot chocolate out on the deck. Harper sat at the bar table and drank cocoa, the white caps crashing ashore. Logan held his drink in his left hand and massaged her back with his right. The wind whipped clouds across the moon like a fast-forward weather report.

"Harper," Logan said, "I can see you will be stressed these next few years. I know that. I will be as well. We are beginning a significant change in the warehouse's server hardware. Eight hundred seventy-five installation swaps and updates.

"Yes, we have stressful jobs; that is why they pay us the big bucks, I guess.

"But when I am with you, in your bed at night, all that stress disappears. I want the feeling of you to be with me always."

Harper stood and walked to the deck rail. She turned and leaned back against the railing, beckoning Logan into her arms. Logan kissed her longingly. Then he pulled back.

"Harper, do you feel the same?"

"I do, Logan, you know I do," she said.

"Then let's get married," said Logan, "Will you marry me?"

Harper sighed. She embraced Logan, seeking his warmth and strength. They kissed, then Harper pulled away.

"I want to marry you, Logan. I do. I do. I have wanted that from the moment you chased me down on the beach.

"Hell, what's a little more stress."

Logan, smiling, gloriously happy, ran to the bedroom and returned with a small box wrapped in a bow. The titanium ring inside contained a medium size diamond surrounded by twelve small diamonds.

"Logan, I love it. It fits. I love you."

"I love you as well, Harper. I vow to help with dinners, washing, and cleaning. We can manage the stress together."

****

Harper's leapfrog sequence testing paid off on May 14, 2030. That day, she successfully stabilized a combination of Jane Martensen's nano biological material with a nanoelectronic two-nanometer switch.

Five-nanometer switches were standard in the industry, but three-nanometer electronics to date could only be generated using a $250,000,000.00 scanning probe microscope. A company must bring five hundred scanning probe microscopes online to scale production. Five hundred scanning probes would be required to create the millions of microprocessors a company would need to sell in a year. The profitability economics of such a chip might provide a return on investment in thirty-five years.

Harper Lawrence's concept involved coating the surface of a microprocessor chip with nanobiological material. Interaction between the spinning electron switches in the coating with embedded two-nanometer spin-switches accommodated millions of four-way storage space on a single microprocessor chip. In addition to the exponential increase in storage space on the nanobiological coated chip, Harper discovered an additional benefit from her process.

Nanoelectronic switches could be programmed via induction from a transmitter next to the conveyor, moving chips to quality control. A controller cable attached to the transmitter provided a program to be relayed to these nanoelectronic switches on the chips. Once the transmitter stores the program, the controller is disconnected from the transmitter and moved to another assembly line, to another Klux plant, or stored in the company vault.

Harper constructed two controllers. One for production runs and the other as a backup that could be used for experiments. Only a nanotechnologist using the scanning probe microscope could program the production controller. The experimental controller incorporated dials for year, month, day, and time in hours and minutes. An "on" or "off" setting could be sent from the controller to the chip passing along the conveyor. This setting determined what action would occur on the chip when the date/time armed on the chip timed out.

The manufacturing process required one expensive scanning probe microscope that could work with a two-nanometer probe.

After receiving and storing the program in the reserved nanoelectronic switches on the chip, the program cannot be reversed or revised but is forever armed. Thus, the program capability of the nanoelectronic device is limited to very low-level functions such as counters and set mathematics.

Harper asked Logan to come over to her lab. She was excited to show off her finished experiment. After Logan arrived and changed into the clean room garb, he entered her workroom.

"It works," Harper said, "My nanoelectronic component works, finally. And it is stable," Harper high-fived Logan, "I have repeated the sequence 85 times today without a single failure. Of course, I will set up an automated test now to achieve millions of successes, but I believe the mean time between repair (MTBR) will be minuscule." Harper looked like she might jump out of her skin in her excitement. Logan sighed, happy for his fiancé and excited for the resulting stress relief for both of them.

"Let's see it," he said.

"Alright, the program is simple. Using the controller, I set up a timer to flip the nanoelectronic switch on at 1:00pm." Harper explained that the controller and transmitter were ready to go.

She put a chip on the conveyor, turned the conveyor on, and the microprocessor chip moved passed the transmitter. She turned the conveyor off, picked up the microprocessor, and pressed the chip into a mockup motherboard on her desk, turning on the power. Another program on the chip contacted the Greenwich standard time clock via the internet. It displayed the time on a 6-digit digital clock on the motherboard, adjusted for Eastern Daylight Savings Time. The display showed the time and counted up the seconds. Harper and Logan only had to wait four minutes, but as the clock changed to 1:00pm, the counter stopped, and a small red led light attached to the motherboard lit up.

"There," said Harper, "Proof."

"Fantastic, Harper," Logan said, "Congratulations, Lover. Months ahead of Bob's and Geoff Hunter's expectations. This calls for champagne at Arcadia Bluffs tonight."

"Deal," Harper said, "I've got to call Bob."

"No, you don't. Wait on that. I am giving you three days off. Spend tomorrow setting up your automated test and let it run for two more days. Go back over your notes, and contact your mom and dad. Bounce everything off them, then report to Bob Creatin."

"You're right. I am too excited now. I call it an SG1 switch."

"Tomorrow, said Logan, "I will help clean up the lab while you organize your notes. I can help with programming the clock motherboard to automate the test run."

The couple moved their wedding date to Saturday, June 15th, 2030. Logan arranged the ceremony with the senior minister of First Church of Boston, a Unitarian Universalist church located a block from the Boston Public Park. The plan suggested the wedding be held in the Park by the lake if the weather permitted. Otherwise, Harper and Logan would be married in the sanctuary of one of the oldest churches in Boston, dating back to 1630 AD.

Seventy-five friends and relatives attended the ceremony on a cloudless day at the water's edge in the park. Harper Lawrence's sister Morgan acted as her maid of honor. Best woman duties were handled by Mercedes Martensen, Logan's seventy-six-year-old stepmother.

Logan Martensen kissed his bride, Dr. Harper Martensen, walked her back through the guests to the trellis, and kissed her mightily again.

The couple honeymooned in Portugal for ten days, followed by three-day rail tours of Spain, France, and Italy.

Harper continued her employment at Klux Technology, working in Ludington and flying to Silicon Valley every three months to meet with Bob Creatin. Occasionally she met with Geoff Hunter.

Ten months later, in 2031, Klux Technology, Inc. broke ground for the new plant in Mountain View. Harper flew out every two months at that point to view the progress of the equipment installation. Harper worked with mechanical and electrical engineers to convert her working assemblage of prototype components to plant production scale at the Klux manufacturing plant.

Klux upper management negotiated an exclusive contract with Micro Nano Circuits Inc. (MNC,) which began constructing a facility on the outskirts of San Jose. Harper heard rumors associating Geoff Hunter and his financial backers with MNC. The two engineers working the closest with Hunter departed Klux and went to MNC. The plan seemed to be that MNC would buy the microprocessor chips produced by Klux and build commercial products based on the chip: notebooks, servers, cell phones, etc.

MNC aims to undercut current market prices in end-user devices while increasing its products' speed and storage capabilities. The new nanoelectronic chips from Klux Technology, Inc. made MNC's mission feasible.

Logan completed the server swap at the server farm in February 2032. He began planning for the next generation of systems, the transition to start in 2038. Data Futures, Inc. commenced a warehouse expansion that would increase the company's storage space by fifty percent. Logan oversaw the expansion as DFI's liaison with the construction management team. Checking and rechecking the dimensions and clearances of the drawings with the actual building.

****

Henry S. Hunter, sitting in his antique leather club chair, waved his empty rock glass at his son. Seventy-eight years old and the richest of the four rich men and one rich woman in his study, Henry tapped ash from his cigar to an ashtray. On his lap, he held the year 2032 calendar open to March for reference.

Geoff Hunter turned back to the bar, watching a rare late March Kentucky snowfall through the window above the bar. It began to pile up on his Mercedes AMG S 63 Coupe. He grabbed the Blanton's Single Barrel Bourbon and poured another shot into Henry's glass.

"Does anyone else need a refresh," Geoff said, displaying the bottle.

"Thanks, Geoff, over here," said T.J. Melton, the majority stockholder of Coolidge Brokerage. Geoff crossed to T.J.'s Chair and poured two fingers into his ice water corrupted glass.

Cynthia Keller and Marvin Laughton waved Geoff away. Cynthia, the youngest in the group, younger even than Geoff, at fifty, wanted more details on the unique equipment being installed in the Klux plant.

"Geoff," she said, "What makes you think you can control this 'nano science' woman's process. You say she is the only one who can work the controller and scanning probe microscope."

"In the first place," said Geoff, "she will have no idea of the intent of what she is setting up. We will call it a long-run trial. When she trots off to lunch, we will install a duplicate virgin controller and have her arm the transceiver for the production run for the chips sold to MNC."

"I can't believe she won't be curious and muck things up," said Cynthia.

Geoff poured himself another Blanton's, neat. "I doubt we'll have a bit of trouble with her. Last year she married a Michigan man and moved out of California. A baby is in the works."

"Who do you have that can monitor her, Geoff," said Henry.

"Dan Creatin, a fellow scientist, is her supervisor. He reports to me. He bought a house in Mountain View, way above his station. He receives special bonus money from my pocket to watch over our gal. He's learning her techniques as fast as possible."

"What are the numbers again for the two operations?" Mr. Laughton asked.

"As you know," Geoff said, "Klux will produce two nano-componentized microprocessor chip generations.

"The standard generation (SG1) chips will go to MNC and make each of you five times richer than you are today. The Klux production lines can handle anything from a forty-pinout CMOS to an eight or sixteen-core Qualcomm Snapdragon format. The nano transceiver will arm the chips with the Klux SG1 logic.

"The SO (Switch Off) chips can be produced in the same variety of sizes and formats. The nanobiological coating at the tail end of the line passing by the nano transceiver will SO arm the chips. These chips will be dumped by the millions on the black market in China and North Korea. History would indicate the Chinese will illegally duplicate the chip, but I believe the effort will be in vain due to the nanoelectronic components we use."

T.J. laughed, "That should ruin their economies for twenty years or more. The stock market will go crazy for American products when it happens. Only we will know the how and the where. Have you decided on the when Geoff?"

"Henry and I have thought long and hard about that," Geoff said, "Sometime in the next decade or two. The further out it happens, the less chance any of us will be thought culpable. Also, the fewer people who know the details, the less likely there will be a danger to us."

"Geoff's right," Henry said, "I may not even be alive by then, but I believe the world will be far, far better off.

"We're agreed?" asked Henry.

Everyone held up their glass, a unanimous 'yes' vote.

"In preparation for that day," said Henry, "I nominate Cynthia as our candidate in 2036."

Henry had already written off the 2032 election coming up in November. Poles showed that his party would lose. He expected that. The margin is what interested him. He had future plans.

Cynthia, outwardly flustered at the proposed nomination, inwardly acknowledged how perfectly she had manipulated the men in the room. *I did it without spreading my legs, too,* she thought.

****

Harper and Logan welcomed a baby boy on June 20th, 2032. Healthy, energetic, and fussy for the first two months, Logan basked in the warmth of his son and wife. He walked the baby when he cried and rubbed Harper's back each night. He reveled in simply walking the Lake Michigan shoreline, Harper at his side, baby carried against his chest. Harper's nano microprocessor chip bonus from Klux had supplied a healthy down payment on the purchase option of his Lake Michigan condo. Logan babysat his little boy while Harper visited the health club at the community college three days a week. In October, Harper, looking incredible, flew out to San Jose to view the progress on the nano transceiver section of the production line. The portion of the production line that she designed would be ready in less than three months. Geoff Hunter planned the production line start-up for March 2033.

The election, the first week in November 2032, sent another Democrat back to the White House, but it was close. Not contestably close, but closer for the RTA party than ever before. They garnered thirty percent of the vote against a robust fifty-two percent for the Democratic candidate. The straight Republican ticket captured only ten percent of the votes. The Republican party of the last half of the 20th century no longer existed; at least, it had no base to speak of. The populist, isolationist, and outspoken racist rhetoric of the Return to America party now had the ears and hearts of a large spectrum of voters again. The rest of the American citizens, and for that manner, the rest of the world's population, be damned.

****

The group of five met again at the home of Henry S. Hunter in December. The group laughed at such a world full of rubes all the way to the bank.

Henry caught Geoff's eye and smiled. *When Cynthia loses in 2036, another certainty,* he thought, *Geoff would finally be in a position to be the RTA candidate in 2040, and he would win.* Even if Henry weren't alive, he knew his puzzle pieces fit together perfectly to ensure his legacy through his son. Geoff assured the group that their patience would pay off in March, putting money back in their pockets.

****

The Martensen's settled into family life with all eyes on the growth stages of their son. Crawling, walking, and talking were all recorded on Facebook, Snapchat, and Instagram. They lived a near-idyllic life on the shore of Lake Michigan.

Harper quit her job at Klux Technology after her extended maternity leave expired. She remained on retainer as an exclusive consultant for Klux. As such, she remotely conferenced with Dan Creatin or Geoff Hunter every other month.

Harper spent her spare time at home writing and editing her textbook on nanotechnology. She received advance payments from her agent as she met chapter deadlines, finishing the book by Christmas 2036. She then turned the book over to the publishers for final editing. The publisher sent an advanced copy to Dan Creatin at Klux Technology, Inc. for review.

****

To Henry S. Hunter's surprise, Cynthia Keller won the election for President of the United States in 2036. She won on the campaign promise of bringing water to the southern band of states from Lake Michigan. California and Arizona have dealt with drought conditions for over three years since the 2032 election. Democrats lost the majority in the Senate, and the RTA candidates also gained a majority in the House of Representatives. The twenty-two incumbent Republicans in the House began to align with Democrats on issues of police and gun reform and voting rights.

Henry S. Hunter rushed to the White House after the inauguration. He reset his sights on Geoff Hunter's future and secured the Secretary of Commerce post for his son. Geoff estimated the Klux black market chip might now be embedded in more than a million computers in China alone. As Secretary of Commerce, Geoff accessed detailed domestic and foreign import and export data of manufactured goods and Agriculture. He could track the trade deficit daily.

Geoff regretted arming the SO chips for a date so far in the future. He was ready now.

Cynthia Keller met with her private group of advisors and Geoff Hunter, Secretary of Commerce, the only official cabinet member in the group. Marvin Laughton, T.J. Melton, Henry S. Hunter, and an uncomfortable Dan Creatin sat in wingback Victorian chairs in the Lincoln room of the Presidential suite in the White House.

President Keller's first hundred days had marched along as she fulfilled her campaign promises. Over five million Latino immigrants had been shipped south. The border wall neared completion. The Army and Navy blockaded Palestine so effectively on land and sea that the Muslim population was starved down to less than a million.

[237]

Despite the violent protests in Illinois, Michigan, and Wisconsin, Cynthia Keller's National Guard construction crews completed the freshwater pipeline to Arizona in eighty-eight days. The construction companies laid a five-foot diameter steel corrugated pipe down on the ground with pumping stations to conquer the elevations of foothills. The line crossed public and private lands. Court cases and injunctions were declared moot by President Keller, who claimed a multi-state emergency in the face of the southern water shortage. The National Guard patrolled the entire two-thousand-mile length of the pipeline. The 'ugly water sucker' (UWS) blighted the landscape, ignored environmental laws, and provided one-third of the relief needed in Arizona and California. The RTA took credit for a swift drought solution.

"So far, so good," proclaimed Cynthia, so excited she refused to sit down. Instead, she stood behind T.J.'s lounger and sucked down her gin and tonic.

"I want to take the SO operation to the next level, "she said, "Geoff, can we make more SO nano chips?"

Geoff nodded at Dan for a report.

"At Klux, we can make as many chips as possible in every configuration you want. We have been doing that. We have an inventory ready for distribution.

"We cannot set a different SO date on those chips. Nor can we eliminate the SO date. The chips are sealed in blood, so to speak. I have studied nanoscience for over five years. I have read Harper Martensen's textbook, an excellent source for a sophomore-level course. I am not even close to understanding how she programmed the transceiver. With the help of the scanning probe microscope, she achieved electron alignment in the nanobiological material coated on the chips. You can make as many chips as necessary incorporating the initially programmed date."

"Thank you, Dan," Geoff said, shooing Dan out of the room, "You are excused. I'll Zoom meet with you after you are back in California."

After Dan left, Cynthia mixed herself another gin and tonic and, still standing, addressed the group, "So Geoff, that guy is a bit of dead wood. There is no one else better?"

"Madam President," Geoff said, "We don't need to change the date. We need patience. The more time we have, the more the rogue states suffer on the SO date. We can keep sending the SO chips out."

"Alright, Geoff. Here is the thing. I want Iran taken out. If we did Saudi Arabia as well, that would be a gold mine," Cynthia said. Then she laughed, "I should say, oil mine.

"Lebanon, Iraq, Jordan. Take them all out. We will have to leave Russia and Israel alone. We need someone to blame this on."

"I'll handle it, Madame President," said Geoff.

"Alright," said Henry S. Hunter, "is everyone happy? MNC has moved me up on the Forbes list to number six. When the SO date hits, I'll fight to be number one with y'all."

Dan Creatin's Jaguar slid on an oil slick heading down from Mount Boardman three weeks later and catapulted into the valley five hundred feet below. The hole in a brake line went undetected.

****

As the dune grass turned green again in the spring of 2037, the servers entered service in the new addition to Data Futures, Inc. warehouse. Logan used his bonus to take his young family to Yellowstone National Park in July.

In September, the Martensen's son boarded a bus and headed off to Kindergarten at the elementary complex on the corner of Bryant and Jebavy in Ludington. Harper spent the next two months reviewing the changes suggested by the editors of the nanotechnology textbook.

Harper toured for three months with her publishing company to the various textbook shows along the east and west coasts to promote her book. In the last week of April 2038, Harper arrived back at the condo, exhausted. She spent the afternoon jumping rope and playing four square with her son. Logan requested they dine out that evening, and the family drove to Sailor's Peace restaurant.

The couple willed their son to sleep after Harper read him seven Dr. Suess books. Logan read the next chapter in *The Shy Stegosaurus* by Evelyn Sibley Lampman.

Logan coaxed his jet-lagged wife into a beach walk. The babysitter app on his cell would notify them of any emergency at the condo or if their son woke up crying. Flashlight in hand, they picked their way to the beach, walking along the wave-lapping shore on sand sparkling in the moonlight. He planned to keep the walk short for the benefit of his jet-lagged wife. Logan stopped and pulled Harper to him, embracing her and offering one long kiss. Then he stood with her, an arm around her shoulder, her arm around his waist, looking out at empty water. The lulling noise from the stir of the waves washed away their separation over the book tour weeks.

"I love you, girl," he said, "Missed you terribly. We both did."

"I missed both of you as well," said Harper, "I believe we wrote eight orders on the west coast. I do not know how many we wrote on the east coast leg. I guess the tour paid off."

They started to walk back. Logan stopped and squatted to test the water with his hand. "Cold, fifty-five degrees, I bet," Logan said.

"The bed will feel cozy and warm," Harper said, "Thanks for watching the little man for so long."

"We had a great time, Hon," said Logan, "A couple of times, I took him to the warehouse, and he found places to hide I didn't even know existed.

"He said he liked the sound of all the server fans."

"The boy seems to like playing with computers," Harper commented, "Anything electronic, for that matter. Do you think he may have picked that up from us?"

"Probably. So, what is next for you? I have my next three years mapped out," said Logan.

"Now that you mention it," Harper said, "Remember I said Melvin Thompson of MNC called me twice while I worked the booth in LA. He called again on my flight home. The message he left hinted at a job proposal.'

"And if he offers?"

"Depends, I guess. Could you wait another couple of years for the boy's baby sister?"

Logan knew how much fulfillment Harper received from her work. In the field of nanotechnology, his wife probably topped the list of potential prospects in the country.

"I can handle it, Harper."

"My prerequisites for the job are pretty extensive," she said, "Work from home, part-time, high retainer, flexible hours, and benefits.

"Mostly something that interests me. I will see what Melvin says tomorrow. It will be easy to turn down. We do not need the money beyond the book royalties that might provide vacation funds."

"Agreed!" Logan stopped her for another kiss to seal the deal.

In the bedroom, Harper found a very sheer negligee lying across the chair in the bedroom.

"What is this, Logan?"

"Oh, that," Logan said nonchalantly, "I just thought you needed a welcome home present."

"You did, did you," said Harper, holding up the see-through thigh-length nightgown, "I think this is a present for you, not me."

"What," Logan said.

"I'll freeze in this."

"If you do, I'll help you remove it and give you a rub to warm you up."

Logan dimmed the lights and switched-on soft jazz, pulled back the bedspread, and lay down, one leg under the covers, one leg out. Harper returned from the bathroom wearing the nightie. Only her extended nipples touched the sheer material as she stood at the foot of the bed.

"A little twirl, if you please; I want to make sure it fits," Logan said.

"God, you are one-tracked," Harper said, but she turned all the way around. She grabbed the nightgown's hem between her thumbs and first finger in each hand and curtsied. Then Harper crossed her hands and pulled the nightgown up to her waist.

Her torso was now covered with her crumpled nightgown; Logan's heart thumped in anticipation. *Those legs,* he thought, *I married the best set of legs east of the Mississippi.*

Harper wiggled her hips, lifting the nightgown off and throwing it on the chair. *I dream of those tits.*

"Come here, girl," Logan said, "You will get everything you deserve." Harper leaped into bed and Logan's arms.

Harper placed a call to Melvin Thompson.

"Hello, Harper; how did your book tour go?" Thompson asked.

"Very well, I think," replied Harper, "I have no idea, but the publisher was encouraged."

"Harper, I'll get right to the point. I want to hire you away from Klux Technology, Inc. to work for Micro Nano Circuits, Inc."

"Mr. Thompson," Harper said, "That's too broad a statement. What is the job?"

Melvin Thompson read from his notes, "Quality control of the microprocessor insertion portion of the line. Consultant's wages, once a month, or whatever you need out here or there in Michigan. I want a report once a month on what you find; in spec, out of spec +- margin of error. I want to know we are using the best chips possible in our products."

"Are you still using Klux nano chips?" Harper asked, "They're the best in the world, in my opinion. You don't need me to tell you that."

"That is the only gotcha, Harper," said Thompson, "You will have to take off your Klux hat, work for me exclusively and start wearing your objective hat. I have known you to report and state the truth, even when it hurts. I need that kind of help. I believe I can trust you. I will tell you I had my doubts about Dan Creatin."

"I heard about Dan's horrible accident. That was terrible," Harper said.

"Harper, I'll have my HR department work out the details to your satisfaction. Let us know in a week, OK? I hope to bring you on board."

"OK, Melvin, I will think it over. Thanks for the opportunity. Goodbye."

On May 20th, 2038, Logan signed a two-year server purchase agreement with Virama Technology Labs Pvt. Ltd. of Mumbai, India. The contract facilitates the replacement of the current generation of computers at the Data Futures Inc. server farm. The new servers offer computing speeds five times faster. They hold eight times more data in the same space. The MTBF for the servers exceeds his currently installed servers as well. The installation plan spelled out ongoing work for Logan and his crew for the next three and a half years. The target completion date of the transition: June 2042.

Logan's family spent the summer of 2039 on the beach at their condo in Ludington. The walk to the beach was now eight hundred thirty feet beyond the shoreline as it had existed just three years previous. The Arizona/California freshwater pipeline had seen to that. Less water in the big lake resulted in warmer water temperatures, a luxury for swimming along Michigan's northern west side beaches. Overall, the summer temperatures in the Mitten state averaged eight degrees warmer than just fifteen years ago.

Ludington that summer escaped the national violence that sprung up in Chicago, San Francisco, and ten other cities in northern and western states. Violence also erupted in Houston and Jackson in the South. Protestors burned nearly thirty acres of Jackson, Mississippi (over 30% of the city.) The fires and resultant shooting of uniformed civil servants occurred in protest of Keller's executive orders for mortgage reparation. The RTA party had passed the FMF bill (Forced Mortgage Foreclosure Bill) that legislators claimed would reduce the national debt by a significant percentage. President Keller quelled the worst of the protests with federal troops in Mississippi and Texas: two hundred thirty people of color died in Texas, nine hundred sixteen in Mississippi. Real estate shell companies traceable to Cynthia Keller, Geoff and Henry Hunter, and other real estate magnates in Mississippi bought the property in the burned areas for pennies on the dollar. Massive evictions, begetting unrest, burning property, and inevitable violence became an ugly, repetitive pattern. The pattern precipitated the arrival of Keller's federal troops, commanded to shoot suspicious rioters (most likely persons of color) on sight in federally designated hot zones. A two-star general at the Pentagon, sympathetic to President Keller's ambitions, updated the map of hot zones across the fifty-one states weekly.

Cynthia Keller's real estate holding revelations contributed to the tight presidential race in 2040. The disaster in September on the east coast that brought Hurricane Valerie's storm surge inland proved to be the nail in her coffin. The flood wiped out Boston, Long Island, Atlantic City, and most of Philadelphia. For the RTA administration, ignoring the rising sea level and defunding the efforts of the Paris Accord of 2016 and the China Accord of 2032 proved fatal.

Luckily, Harper's parents had retired in 2036, sold their property in Cambridge, and moved to Grand Haven, Michigan, near Harper and their grandson. Hurricane Valerie wiped out their former home.

Democrat Olivia Roelof won the presidency and, along with fifty-eight-year-old Vice President Pete Buttigieg, promised a humanist perspective for American citizens in the face of exponential world population growth and shrinking natural resources.

Reacting to the riotous summer violence President Roelof followed through on a campaign pledge for gun control. The

Preventative Human Safety Initiative (PHSI) bill sailed through the House and the Senate.

All guns, rifles, and automatic and semi-automatic weapons would be retrofitted with PHSI microchips and radar human target analysis.

A microchip's body recognition logic, used in all weapons, would only allow firing if the radar system on the side of the barrel picked up a non-human silhouette. Weapons would not fire if the fingerprint reader on the grip could not resolve the gun holder's print as the gun owner. Target shooters and hunters could enjoy their sports worry free from lethal accidental shootings. Suicides by way of firearms came to an end. The microchip on weapons of licensed police and armed forces allowed for overriding the microchip restrictions. The law called for the completion of the retrofit of all guns and rifles by midcentury.

****

The week before Christmas 2040, Harper received a text from the QC department of MNC. She was asked to go online and examine a nano microprocessor chip off the production line that struck the technician as wrong.

When Harper went online and manipulated the 3D view of the microprocessor, rotating the chip on its three-axis, she could not see the problem. The chip had the correct size dimensions to spec, and the pinouts also looked right. Then she saw the SO1 stamp on the side.

What the hell, she thought. She called the technician at MNC.

"Where did that chip originate from, Louise?" Harper asked.

"I have been trying to track that using the serial number, but it almost had to have come from Klux. Maybe a mixed-up shipment?"

The chip should have included the SG1 stamp, not SO1. As far as Harper knew, only one nanobiological coating and one nanoelectronic armed switch existed, based on the work she had finished at Klux in 2030.

[245]

"Louise, send that chip to me overnight. I will look at it under the scanning probe microscope at Data Futures, Inc. tomorrow. I want to know what we are dealing with. Could it be a clerical error in labeling at Klux? I doubt it. Good catch, Louise. If I need anything further, I will call you.

"In the meantime, you better start tracing the serial numbers of the end products with this SO1 chip. Maybe it's a one-off mistake."

"Harper, I can tell you there are at least five thousand end products with this type of switch. The barcode scanner equated these SO1 switches to corresponding SG1 chip bar codes and let the products sail through QC. Of course, we store the chip packing slips and empty boxes for six months so we can trace faulty components. We will be able to trace them. So far, there have been no reports of malfunctioning microprocessors, so maybe we can just let it go."

"Not a chance, Louise; if we need more tracking help, I'll authorize temporary hires."

****

When Geoff Hunter looked out his office window in the Department of Commerce building in late January 2041, the White House to the northwest seemed not more than a stone's throw away. Yet, in another sense, his ambition to live there seemed elusive again. Cynthia Keller had blown it. The bitch had the subtlety of a rhinoceros in heat. She hurried the RTA agenda. She should have spread out the RTA policy implementation into her second term. Now it would be up to Geoff in 2044 to win the White House back and prepare America for the imminent collapse of the eastern hemisphere.

His files and belongings had been packed by his secretary, ready to be shipped back to Klux Technology.

The assistant commerce secretary Tim Colter knocked on Geoff's door and entered the office.

"Here is your last import report," Colter said, "I highlighted some disturbing news on page three.

"Apparently, a customs agent in Wilmington, Delaware, and an officer of CV International have been arrested for importing black market microprocessor chips into the United States. You might recall this violates the import restrictions the President put in place at your suggestion. The FBI estimates one and one half billion dollars worth of chips have been shipped into the States over the last eight years.

"You have asked me to watch for import/export matters concerning technology. Today I found this."

Geoff's hand shook as he picked up his mug of coffee and sipped once, twice, thrice, to cover his countenance losing all color. *On his last day? Really?*

"Have they confiscated the contraband?" Geoff asked.

"Yes," said Tim, "With your background at Klux, I thought you might be able to make recommendations on what the FBI should do with the chips and how far they should take the investigation."

"Good thinking Tim; let me know when they arrive."

"The FBI agent in charge, John Beresford, is down in the lobby, ready to show you a box of the microprocessors."

"I'll see him now; get him up here."

Alone in the office, Geoff buried his head in his hands, pressing his palms into his eye socks. *It is nothing,* he thought. *The chances are negligible. Keep cool.*

When agent Beresford entered and set the plain cardboard box on the desk, Geoff identified it as a Knox packing carton.

"Alright, Mr. Beresford, let's see what you have here."

The FBI agent opened the box, and Geoff picked out a forty-pin CMOS chip for scrutiny. It took him five seconds to identify it. The tiny SO1 stamp in front of the serial number on the side of the chip said it all. He did not let on. Instead, he flipped the switch over and found another tiny ID stamp on the socket for the chip between the pinouts. Made in China.

The churn in Geoff Hunter's stomach kept rising, even as he had to keep his cool in front of his assistant and the FBI agent.

"I guess," said Geoff, "we'll have to leave the decision on furthering the investigation with the next administration. Out of courtesy, Mr. Beresford, could you include me in what they decide, at least for the next few months during the transition?"

"Certainly, Mr. Secretary."

****

"Hello, who is calling, please?" the nine-year-old son of Logan and Harper asked the voice on the other end of the cell phone conversation.

"Can I speak to Harper Martensen?" said the voice.

"Yes, here she is," the boy said, running to her study alcove and handing the cell phone to his mother.

"This is Harper Martensen,"

"Hello Mrs. Martensen. My name is Marilyn Davies, Assistant Secretary of Commerce for the government. I would like to know if we might hire you to consult with us on a matter that arose in the last month of the previous administration."

"I am not sure I can help you," Harper said, "I have an exclusive contract with Micro Nano Circuits Inc., and I've signed a nondisclosure agreement with the company."

Marilyn had already spoken to President Melvin Thompson of MNC. Thompson had told Marilyn Davies that he would waive the nondisclosure agreement in the interests of national security. "He left it up to you, Mrs. Martensen, to determine if the investigation might expose a level of danger to the country."

Marilyn sent a box of the border-confiscated SO1 chips to Harper. The box contained the same type of mislabeling as the chips of her ongoing investigation for MNC. The chips were in a much different format, however. These chips were for cell phones.

"We are still investigating where these microprocessor chips end up," said the Assistant Secretary of Commerce.

"As it happens," said Harper, "I have been studying chips with this nomenclature for about six months."

"Have you had any success?"

"So far, I have found a date marker on the chip."

"When do you anticipate completing your investigation.

Harper decided to keep her investigation sketchy until she could nail down the who, what, and why of the chips. The 'Made in China' stamp on the chips socket indicated a need for as quick and thorough an answer as she could manage.

"The work I'm doing," Harper said, "involves reverse engineering nano paths at the subatomic level."

Marilyn flattered Harper while asking her to keep up the vital work. "You come highly recommended, Mrs. Martensen. Madam President is informed of our inquiries and will hear of your work. The CIA and the FBI are also running parallel investigations. They will speak to you if they develop a clue that may assist your task. Thank you. I hope to hear from you soon."

Logan listened that night over pork chops to his wife's progress at MNC and the call from the Commerce Department.

"So, what have you got so far," Logan said.

"I know it is a date marker. I have the year of the date marker; 2050. I am working on permutations for the day and time. There is a Made in China stamp that may or may not be pertinent to the why. I know the chips exist here in the United States and are also abroad, perhaps worldwide.

"Logan, tell your son to eat his broccoli, or he will not get a cookie for dessert."

Logan reached below the table and squeezed the boy's thigh, making him squirm from the tickle. "Broccoli, young man, you heard your mother. Eat your vegetable."

"Ah, Dad," the boy said, but he ate the broccoli.

"How about shooting baskets and maybe a game of pig after supper," Logan said, watching his son's smile widen. The weather in May accommodated many nights on the court near the shared condominium area pool.

Harper brought up the subject while the boy took his shower.

"I need more clues," said Harper, "I am sure I could save time if I talked to Pam, Barbara, or both at Klux. I should probably speak to Geoff Hunter. I know he is back at Klux Technology Inc."

Logan mulled that over but did not answer Harper until they readied for bed, the boy already asleep.

"Harper here is my take," said Logan, "Something is going on. You know that much.

"It must be high-level shit for the FBI and CIA to be involved.

"Geoff Hunter, think about his contributions to Cynthia's fascism. You can't trust that son of a bitch."

Harper stayed quiet until after their goodnight kiss.

"Logan," Harper said, "I should have the complete date in a few more days, two weeks at the most. Then we'll decide what to do."

"That sounds right to me," Logan replied, "let me know if I can help in any way."

****

Whenever Geoff Hunter turned on one of his personal devices, his heartburn began to crush him, and his stomach flip-flopped. He pulled apart and examined his cell phone to find the tiny letters SO1 in the upper left corner of the chip. He wished to ignore the problem and tried to forget it. His stomach ulcer wouldn't let it go away.

He wanted to confide in someone but did not know who that could be. Harper Martensen had the expertise, but for all he knew, she might be actively providing information to the FBI for his indictment.

Night after night, he suffered. Finally, to release tension, he called up T.J. Melton for a scotch at the bar and a game or two of racquetball.

T.J. spoke about the world retirement cruise he planned after the big day, the SO day. Geoff could not bear letting him know things were turning sour. He did not mention the FBI investigation.

Instead, he chugged another scotch.

On the court, Geoff began to loosen up. For a minute or two, his heartburn eased. Then he bent over double as his heartburn came back with a vengeance. Not heartburn. A heart attack. Geoff Hunter died on the court.

Many friends and relatives gathered at Geoff Hunter's gravesite a week later to send him off. Cynthia Keller, T.J. Melton, Henry Hunter, and Marvin Laughton sat at the bar afterward to commiserate.

"Well, I guess we can't run Geoff for President anymore in 2044," said Cynthia.

"Who? The country club, president," said Henry, confused.

"Keep your voice down, Henry," said T.J., "What's the matter with you."

Henry became angry, flailing his arms over his head, nearly falling out of his chair.

"When was the last time y'all saw Henry," Marvin said, "He has dementia."

Cynthia sat up, alarmed and wide-eyed.

"He has to remember the SO date," Cynthia clutched the old man's arm, "Henry, tell us the date you and Geoff agreed on for the SO1 chip."

Henry brushed off Cynthia's hand and flailed some more.

"What the fuck are you talking about, woman? Don't touch me."

Seeing his employer flustered, Henry's personal nurse approached the table. "I better take Henry home now. You understand. It has been a trying day for him."

Cynthia had not completed her interrogation. "Young man, we are asking Henry about an important date only he knows. If he talks about a date, please be so kind as to write it down and call me. Will you?"

"Yes, Madam President, he sometimes has a very lucid day."

After Henry left, the three decided the only way they could regain control of their project would be to enlist the aid of the original scientist involved in the nanotechnology project.

The short straw went to T.J. Melton.

Harper leaned back, closed her eyes, and rubbed her forehead. She had been staring into the scanning probe microscope for half an hour, moving the probe along another of the nanobiological areas of the microprocessor. The secret of the SO1 chip seemed close at hand.

She turned at the sound of a knock on the door of her lab at Data Futures, Inc. Through the glass, she recognized Melvin Thompson, president of MNC. The gentleman with Melvin Harper had never seen before. Rather than allowing their entry and contaminating the clean room, Harper motioned the two men to wait in the outer office, and she would be with them shortly. Seeing Melvin surprised her. He had never met with her in Ludington, always preferring her to report to him in Mountain View.

The threesome moved to a small conference room. Melvin introduced T.J. Melton of the Cross Group, a venture capitalist specializing in nanotechnology investments.

"Mr. Melton, pleased to meet you," Harper said, shaking his hand before she sat down, "What's up Melvin, nothing better to do than fly cross country for a meeting?"

"T.J. and I just finished twenty-seven holes at Arcadia Bluffs, so this meeting wasn't the only reason I flew out."

Mr. Melton remained quiet while Melvin Thompson explained, "Harper, I'm starting to get desperate for an answer on those chips you've been investigating. I have had to field a half dozen letters from major stockholders demanding answers. The yearly corporate meeting is scheduled for next week. What have you found; are you close to an answer?"

Harper looked over at Mr. Melton. She began to feel queasy about the unexpected meeting. She wished Logan could help her navigate this charged political encounter.

"Are you a stockholder, Mr. Melton?" she asked.

"Potential investor, Mrs. Martensen," T.J. said, "and the name is T.J."

"OK, T.J.," said Harper, "Melvin, I am close to an answer. I have come up with a date. There is a date/time stamp on the chip. Now I am working on why the date/time stamp is part of a nanoelectronic switch within the nanobiological spin field. It will turn something on or off. I still have more tracing, but I am close to the complete answer."

T.J. Melton leaned in so close to Harper she thought he might slip off his chair. "and what is the date you found, Harper?" Melton asked.

"I plan on presenting my report along with the complete answer at the yearly stockholder's meeting next week, T.J. I believe I am already on the agenda."

Melvin Thompson sided with Harper, "That is right, Harper. Best present to all the interested stockholders. T.J. buy in now or after the stockholders meeting when the stock goes up. Just because you let me beat you by five strokes this afternoon does not transfer to special stock treatment, sorry."

"No worries," said T.J. Melton, "Well, Melvin, I guess I better let you catch your plane. I fly south in the morning. A pleasure Harper; nanotechnology fascinates me."

"I'll walk you out, T.J. Great game today."

They left Harper pondering the strange meeting: the timing, the flight from Silicon Valley.

I have to talk to Logan, she thought. *That could not have been weirder.*

Harper spent twenty minutes writing her notes in her journal, including her day's progress.

Another surprise awaited Harper in the parking lot. As she opened the car door, T.J. Melton hailed her.

"I didn't mean to startle you, Harper. But I did have one additional fundamental question for you."

The man stepped closer to Harper. *This is not good!*

"Really," Harper said, "I can't imagine what question warrants being accosted in a parking lot."

"Please," said Melton, "I represent a conglomerate that will give you a two-year guaranteed contract and a two hundred fifty thousand dollar signing bonus for jumping the MNC ship. Same duties and research you are doing now, just three times the money. We need your expertise."

Harper laughed. "Let me think about that, T.J.," she said and counted to ten, "There, I thought about it. It is a big no. Now, I have to get home. It has been a long day."

T.J. Melton shrugged, resigned. He said, "I've been around long enough to know when someone means what they say." T.J. held out his gloved hand, as did Harper, and they shook hands goodbye.

Harper stopped at Luciano's in Ludington, washed talcum off her hands in the restroom, picked up a pizza, and went home to discuss the strange day with Logan.

Logan saw Harper stagger into the living room with the pizza box. She crashed into the leather chair, dropping the container and slumping over the backrest.

"Honey, what is the matter," said Logan. He panicked, "Harper," he shouted, "Harper." Logan gathered the pizza box off the floor. The scent of tomato sauce, garlic, and basil filled the living room. Harper had snacked on one piece on the way home, about a four-minute drive. Her head lolled left, her face bathed in sweat., spittle gathering on the arm of the chair. Logan ran for a cool, wet washcloth while he dialed 911.

"911 emergency services, how can I help you?" the operator calmly asked.

"Food poisoning. I need an ambulance now; my wife is losing consciousness," Logan said.

"The ambulance is on the way via GPS. Do you know what she ingested, sir?" said the operator.

"Pizza, a slice of pizza. Please hurry that ambulance."

"Stay on the line, sir. Try to remain calm."

"Should I make her throw up?"

"The ambulance indicates a six-minute arrival time. If necessary, the drivers have several antidotes for poison on board and a stomach pump."

Logan stayed on the line offering the exact address of the condo. His tow-headed son rushed through the door, smelling pizza. Logan had laid Harper out on the living room floor.

"Mom, what's wrong, Dad? Is she OK?"

"I don't know! The ambulance will be here any minute. Go out to the sidewalk and lead them in. No time to waste. Hurry, son. Leave the front door open."

Within three minutes, the ambulance siren wailed in the distance, louder by the second. *Hurry,* Logan thought. Harper's arms and legs jerked violently as the two medics entered the room.

Logan pointed to the pizza box with the missing piece. The medic looked perplexed but opened his bag and pulled out a syringe package and a small glass vial.

"Sedative," the Medic said, "Is she allergic to anything? Could she have been stung?"

"I don't know! She came in the room and collapsed."

Harper's convulsions calmed soon after the medic gave her the shot. Looking over the medic's shoulder, the boy sighed in relief as his mother calmed down, even though she lay unconscious on the area rug.

Logan followed the ambulance to Corewell Health Butterworth Hospital, dropping the boy off at Mercedes's apartment. He arrived minutes after the ambulance wheeled their patient in for admittance. The emergency room lobby had not changed since the last time he walked in, worried about his grandfather.

The nurse directed Logan to the helicopter pad; Harper would be airlifted to Grand Rapids for specialized treatment.

Outside of the emergency operating room in Grand Rapids, Logan paced, sat, paced, called Mercedes, walked, sat, and waited. The doctors had no answers. EMT doctors pumped Harper's stomach and tested her for allergies and various food poisoning possibilities, yet she remained in a coma. The lab at the hospital had found nothing wrong with the pizza the medics brought along.

The EMT staff intubated Harper, attached a sedative drip to her arm to maintain a medically induced coma, and moved her to a bed in the critical care unit.

Logan never left her side from that point forward. A nurse would bring him a meal; otherwise, he sat and held his wife's free hand. *Get better, dearest; please get better.* Over and over, minute by minute, hour by hour, Logan stayed relaxed and offered the meditative mantra; *Breathe, get better, darling.* She did not. She expired four days later.

Mercedes arrived from Ludington. Logan's son, **Martin Martensen**, entered the room where his dad still sat, holding his mother's hand. Harper, peaceful, neatly tucked in.

Logan looked at his son and began to cry. Martin put his arms around his father's neck, not really comprehending. Logan sobbed, his chest heaving wildly, the four-day vigil of steadfastly remaining calm giving way; the love of Harper pouring out of him. Martin hugged him tighter.

****

In 2046, the waves of Lake Michigan hit the shore in front of the Martensen condo fifteen hundred feet further off the pre-pipeline tree line of 2036. The shutoff of the freshwater pipeline after the election won by the democrats in 2044 finally stopped the depletion. The huge osmosis plants offshore from Los Angelos, Ca., now produced enough freshwater from saltwater to balance what the pipeline provided. What helped Lake Michigan caused damage and depletion of the Pacific. Politicians kicked that can into the future.

Melvin Thompson had never acknowledged the meeting with Harper the day she went into the hospital. He and T.J. Melton had entered Logan's huge server farm unseen. When boarding the plane for San Francisco International, Melvin had his suspicions.

Harper had hedged enough in the meeting that he knew there were problems. Her report would mean trouble for him, ten times worse for the company, yet Melvin had no idea what the report might contain. He did what any top CEO would do. Melvin Thompson protected his million-dollar bonus for 2041. He changed the agenda of the stockholder's meeting, eliminating Harper's report and telling the few worried stockholders that the rumors had proved unfounded. No one knew he and T.J. had been in Michigan except the Arcadia Bluffs golf course pro.

MNC Inc. never had any problems or major complaints about its products. At the memorial service, Melvin asked Logan about Harper's final report. Logan told him she had not begun the last write-up.

Logan studied his wife's journal for eight months after her death, determined to learn the science she specialized in. He made significant progress in comprehending nanobiological science and nanoelectronic circuitry. He decided obtaining his wife's expertise would take many more years.

After concluding that he might never be able to grasp the nanoscience that he now suspected had killed his wife, Logan began to use his own expertise in logic to come at the problem from a different angle. He spent three more months rereading the now-dogeared notebook.

Within the text of the journal dating back four months before her death, Harper Lawrence's notes began to reference the year 2050. Time and again. The words 'date' and 'time' might be circled in the text. The circled words became heavier in the last month of her life as if she must have been close. Explanations became cryptic, and abbreviations began to pop up as if Harper feared the corporations she represented.

A week before she went into the hospital, and five pages back from the last entry, Logan found the words 'switch off' circled at least four times. He knew that her nanoelectronics allowed for on/off elementary logic with nanobiological responses. The journal had the answer; he just had to accept it. The clue indicated that the nanoelectronic switch embedded in the chip would switch off the subsystem.

Logan paired his conclusion with what was written on the last page. Two words, the letters drawn three ruled lines tall: **Technological Cataclysm.**

Three days later, while in bed, nearing sleep, Logan again went over the notation of the year in his mind that appeared multiple times in the body of her notes. Harper somehow spoke to him. Logan navigated in the dark, turned on the desk light, and thumbed through the journal for nearly the hundredth time. Harper dated her entries in the top left or top righthand corner above the page number. Starting from the journal's beginning, Logan found a consistent sequence of dates. Five pages from the end of the journal, the date 07/01/2050 jumped off the page at Logan. Notes afterward returned to a typical ascending date sequence. Logan's logic concluded that on July 1st, 2050, all SO1 nanoelectronic circuits would turn off.

Logan thought through the consequences of the SO1 shutdown. Harper had not exaggerated.

P aranoia dictated all Logan's actions from that day forward. He no longer trusted Data Futures, Micro Nano Circuits, or Klux Technology. He thought of the billions of dollars the SO1 chip represented. Harper had learned that this Klux SO1, probably duplicated in China, India, and perhaps North Korea, eventually to be shipped back into the United States by the millions, posed an incomprehensible threat.

Could he sound the warning? He could try, but without another five years to study nanoscience, he may be wasting time. He had no evidence. The chips worked perfectly and would continue to work until the trigger date. The nanobiological coating and the nanoelectronic spin switch could only be seen with the help of electron microscopes that could distinguish a two-nanometer object, 10,000 times smaller than the circumference of a human hair.

Logan's son, Martin withdrew from the world after his mother died; the picture of her convulsing on the living room floor haunted him. Only his father could reach him. They played basketball together, including pickup games on the middle school outdoor courts. At fourteen, Martin had developed competitive skills matching anyone in his age group. He remained quiet. Whenever he spoke with a classmate, visions of his mother moved in the way, and usually, Martin would walk away. Mercedes died in 2043. He missed his great-grandmother almost as much as his mother for the comfort she gave him the year after his mother's death.

On Martin's birthday in June, he unwrapped a present from his dad: A Bear 60" Super Kodiak Recurve bow and a set of arrows. Logan set up a target in the dunes to the side of the condo and, surprisingly, strung a duplicate bow and began teaching Martin the fundamentals. From then on, after dinner and before basketball, they developed their aim for half an hour. Logan remembered his time with his grandfather, an expert marksman. Now, he passed on everything he had learned to Martin. Somehow, Martin understood the seriousness of the practice.

One day in late July, Logan, sweat dripping off his nose, the basketball wet from his sweating hands, stopped for a time before handing the ball back to Martin. "I'm thinking of signing up for Martial arts lessons. That is a challenge we could both work on together. What do you think?" Logan asked.

Martin liked the idea. From the first class, Martin saw Logan's dedication to studying the sport. They both increased in rank that first year, and the following year they began competing competitively in Karate and Jujitsu tournaments.

Logan seemed to withdraw as much as Martin. He continued to mourn the loss of his brilliant, beautiful wife. Logan missed her shapely legs, the size and feel of her breasts, the scent of her hair, and her laughing eyes. He had only a few casual friends. Women were not on his radar.

Logan resigned and walked out of Data Futures, Inc.'s server farm for the last time on April 1st, 2048. The year before, he opened up over 50 random servers throughout the facility. Logan had finished the overhaul of the servers six years previous in the winter of 2042. All the servers he opened up had SO1 nanobiological chips installed. It would take fifty staff working three shifts a day to replace the chips again in time, assuming SG1 chips were available. Logan had better use of his time. Logan ordered a box of the now scarce SG1 chips from Klux to accommodate his subbasement storage batteries.

Six months before leaving, Logan hired out-of-town contractors to modify the warehouse.

He told one contractor he needed a new trench and six-foot pipe to extend underground for one hundred feet to the rear of the building. The communications tunnel would connect to the subsequent expansion of the warehouse and house fiber cables and electrical connections. A second contractor installed a monorail track and a small rail handcart in the pipe. A third contractor dug a double-deep basement foundation in the dune next to the open end of the connecting pipeline to the warehouse. The fourth contractor poured a concrete foundation and four walls. A fifth used a crane to lay concrete planks wall to wall as a ceiling for the lowest basement and a floor for the upper basement. Four more concrete walls rose from the concrete planks. Logan bought the land where these basements were poured. He paid the contractors from his wife's bonus savings and bank account. (Each contractor worked independently on only a portion of their project requirements. They had no real idea about the overall scheme.)

A sixth contractor constructed a door in the outside wall of the server farm building that swiveled on a center axis. With the door closed, the plastered door face blended seamlessly and invisibly into the wall. A unique key in the form of an abstract turtle could open the door from the outside. The four feet of the turtle fit four indentations on the outside wall. Turning the turtle with its feet in the indentations released the door. Logan left the turtle hiding in the dune grass next to the door.

[260]

Logan had worked out worst-case scenarios for the **Cataclysm.** Now he only had twenty-seven months to finalize his and Martin's preparations.

Martin would turn sixteen in June. According to Logan's plan, he and Martin needed to learn how to survive.

Martin could not have imagined a sixteenth birthday stranger than his own. Martin's surprise did not include a car (electronic vehicle components were complicated.) Logan knew an automobile would not work in the event of an electromagnetic pulse. The impending microprocessor cataclysm would create the same end result.

No sixteenth-birthday car. Horse riding lessons, yes.

Instead, Martin took his son to the site of the basement foundation. All evidence of the lower basement had been hidden with the sand backfill.

"You and I are going to build a cabin on this foundation," Logan said.

"Wow, Dad, kinda cool. How long will that take?" asked Martin.

"About twenty months," said Logan, "It has been a while, but I helped your great-grandfather remodel his retirement house in Ludington, where he and Mercedes lived."

"What about winter? Will we work out here then?"

"Yup," Logan said, "I'll need to home-school you for the next two years while we work.

"We'll skip the usual curriculum and work on practical skills, cooking, sheltering, mushroom and herb identification, etc. I'll be learning right along with you, so lots of Internet research."

"But what is going on, Dad? Why?"

"That, my dear sixteen-year-old son, I will tell you over a steak dinner at the brew pub. The story involves your mother and why she was murdered." Logan looked up the hill at the Ludington Pumped Storage Plant. Perhaps his beloved wife's discovery and his own assumptions would prove false. If true, however, he planned for Martin and himself to survive. He put an arm around Martin's shoulder, gripping his arm.

"Happy 16th Birthday."

****

The skills Martin learned on the way to his eighteenth birthday seemed incredibly challenging at the time. Looking back, he could not be prouder of what he and Logan had accomplished.

The cabin construction had become a work of art and a place to wait out whatever turn of events played out in ten days. *Maybe nothing would happen. Maybe Mom and Dad have it wrong,* he thought, *Maybe.*

They had worked through the first winter, some days fighting sub-zero gale-force winds sweeping Lake Michigan. They had made mistakes, occasionally tearing out whole walls and starting over. Martin learned how to hang drywall and sweat copper. Logan taught Martin to wire three-way switches, install electrical boxes and run Romex.

Logan and Martin had reworked the remote access to the sub-basement twice. A concealed stairway and false wall from the cabin's basement led down to the sub-basement.

The windows on the south side of the cabin looked out on a porch and an old orchard of cherry trees stretching further down the dune. The overhang would shield the place from the overhead sun in the summer and allow the low winter sun to warm the cabin in the winter.

The floor plan featured a twelve-foot by fifteen-foot living room space next to the entry vestibule from the porch. A small, four-top table and dining area also served as a secondary food prep counter. The kitchen contained minimal appliances, a stove/oven combination, a side-by-side refrigerator/freezer, and a small microwave. The bathroom with shower backed up against the kitchen. A single bedroom along the entire west side might be divided in two if Martin married.

Windows in the west-facing bedroom looked out toward the reservoir. North windows overlooked an old apple orchard and provided cross ventilation. One basement wall contained a built-in shelving unit that held a couple of boxes of canned goods and bags of bulk goods. Tools and a box of Christmas ornaments help disguise the hidden wall behind the shelves.

Stairs to the sub-basement led to an all-purpose survivalist's dream room. One area held a rack of bows and arrows. One whole wall contained historical textbooks and every imaginable science reference book. The science bookshelf included Harper Lawrence's book on the fundamentals of nanotechnology. The reading wall was completed with a shelf containing over a hundred novels for winter reading and a section of how-to books on farming, building, and survival skills.

A twelve-foot partition that ran the length of the sub-basement closed off the grocery store containing enough canned and dried goods, powdered milk, soda, orange juice cartons, gin, vodka, bourbon, and other additional foodstuffs to last at least ten years for two people. A jack-hammered opening in the foundation floor, four feet by ten feet, allowed access to a rock-lined, six-foot-deep space that served as a root cellar kept to fifty-five degrees by the surrounding sand.

They reserved an entire closet for medical supplies. Penicillin vials, syringes, antibiotic salves, itch, eye, headache, and stomach relief medicines. Splints, crutches, and cases of toilet paper filled another large closet.

A workbench and an extensive collection of hand tools adorned another wall. A pool table for recreation in the center of the space, a sectional for lounging, and two single beds completed the safety room. They moved all the supplies in during the third shift at the warehouse under the cover of moonless nights. No one knew they owned a cabin, let alone where it might be; absolutely no one. Logan still owned his condo. *Would he ever be able to return to a semi-normal life?* Logan's experiences during the pandemic thirty years ago prepared him to sit out this subsequent trial in possible isolation. Logan wondered how well Martin would take to quarantine. All the supplies had been moved into the cabin. The sub-basement oozed functionality but looked homey at the same time. A four-foot shaft rose from the sub-basement behind the secret access wall above. Through a series of mirrors, the duct allowed a periscope view through a window to the outside world underneath the front porch. The chimney ran next to the shaft and backed up to the fireplace chimney in the living room.

Throughout the two-year building project, father and son spent an hour at lunchtime, rain, shine, or snow, sharpening their archery skills. After dinner, they would roll out a wrestling mat and work through karate and jujitsu exercises.

On his eighteenth birthday, Martin matched Logan in height (five feet eleven inches) and shoulder width. Although he weighed fifteen pounds less than Logan, he could flip Logan over his right or left hip during mock jujitsu scrimmages. His strength matched Logan's.

Beginning with a birthday dinner that evening Logan had even planned these last days leading to the first. They rented clubs and played golf., as well as body and boogie board surfing. They crammed in as many activities as possible before the date everything might change. They tried skydiving and bungee jumping. They went to a couple of premiering movies.

Ending up at a bar in Manistee with two nights to go, Logan ordered two beers and pushed one over in front of Martin. After two more refills, Logan left the table for the restroom. On the way back to the table, a girl touched his shoulder and asked Logan to dance. A slow country ballad played after the rock number, and Martin danced close with Shirley. She wore a way-above-the-knee, low-cut dress. Logan could feel every curve of her through the thin material. Shirley and her mother, Sandy, came over to Logan's table. For the next hour, the two couples spoke about anything but politics. Shirley announced she had to work in the morning. Sandy told Shirley she should not drive home. Logan held out the keys for Martin and suggested he transport her home.

Shirley moved closer to Martin in the car than when they were dancing. She made no bones about wanting to sleep with Martin, the hard-as-rock, blond-haired, agile dancer.

The whole time Martin undressed the redhead standing before him, he could not help thinking, *this may be my one and only time*.

Martin, inexperienced, made the most of it.

2050 – July 1st

Logan and Martin hunkered down in the sub-basement at eleven o'clock Eastern time. They listened to a classical music station on the radio. A silver-framed picture of Harper sat on the table. A photo of the three of them taken on the beach with the big lake in the background on Logan's birthday in 2039 stirred silent melancholy memories.

At twelve o'clock, the radio stopped working. Father and son waited to venture up from the sub-basement. The electrical appliances no longer worked. Outside on the porch, Logan no longer heard the hum of the six pump turbines of the Ludington Pumped Storage Plant.

"I guess this is it, Son," Logan whispered, "Harper, God bless you."

****

Nearly all the people heading out to lunch (a minute before noon) walked in bunches toward the downtown restaurants in Grand Rapids. Brian Calpain happened to look up at the sky as he came through the revolving doors of the Fifth Third Center. What he saw would have made him turn and run if it had not happened so fast. A commercial aircraft flailed downward in his field of vision. Seconds later, the airplane crashed. A moment later, Brian felt the earth throb from the impact and heard the explosion. Women screamed around him. Northeast of where Brian stood, smoke and fire rose from the crash site high above the two-story buildings crowded between two thirty-story office buildings.

Brian had not taken two breaths when, to his left, a second plane dove nose-first into the Union Square Condos, ripping through the top six stories. Again, the vibration, again, the echoing crash noise. Two seconds later, Brian felt the ground shake again, and he heard the echo of a third crash, not knowing where it originated. Yet a fourth crash way off to Brian's right sent the rest of the women and some men screaming on the run in all directions, bumping and trampling into each other and the cars on the street. Most of the vehicles had either rolled to a stop or crashed into the stopped car in front of them.

In the next two hours, panic ruled. People ran but did not know where to go. Nothing worked. Men stood under building awnings angrily punching their cell phones, popping the backs off, and pulling and replacing the battery for a reboot.

People caught on the non-working elevators soon began to cry and call for help. The elevator phones worked, but the switchboards did not, so the calls never reached the elevator emergency response centers. The same situation epitomized fire stations and police stations. Not only did their communications not work, their police cars, filled with microprocessor gadgets, stopped working as well. Anything that used a microprocessor built, replaced, or upgraded in the last eighteen years stopped.

The SO1 chips shut off the power to the equipment. Pulling out the chip did the same thing. Replacing the chip with a new SO1 chip also would not work for the same reason. Examining the nanobiological coating on the chip, impossible without the scanning probe microscope, would take a monumental effort by experts. Very few experts in nanotechnology existed; if they did, the nanoelectronic switch would take months to find, as Harper had learned.

The plane crashes occurred all over the planet. The stoppages, the lack of communication, and the panic swept the globe. The stock market did not crash. It just stalled. Chicago's greater metropolitan area witnessed forty-five airline and twenty-two small plane crashes in the first minute of the cataclysm. The ghastly destruction and far-flung body parts from the plane and train crashes, the heart attacks and hospital equipment that stopped functioning, utter despair began to strangle people's humanity.

The infrastructures of China, all the countries of the middle east, and North Korea were devastated. The SO1 chip, however, had been released into the wild nearly two decades ago. The chips had crossed borders into every country in the world. Companies had purchased the chips on the black market and sold them back to legitimate businesses in countries such as England, the European Union, and the United States. South American countries were not spared. Russia was not spared.

The plan of five rich people to take over the assets of the third world by devastating those economies backfired. The Band of Five's acquisitions dwindled every second beyond the trigger date/time of the cataclysm.

T. J. Melton called Cynthia Keller from the Data Future's parking lot after meeting with Harper Martensen and Thompson. Together, they decided the cabal must be protected if they could not find the date. Thus, the VX nerve poisoned dust on T.J.'s glove after his last-ditch effort to compromise Harper Martensen in September 2046.

By 3:00 o'clock on July 1st, 2050, panic settled in, and looting and rioting began, worse than anything humankind had seen. The guns in the states and adopted worldwide, all outfitted with PHSI microchips and radar human target analysis, failed. Police picked up crowbars as their weapon of choice to be met by looters with the same idea. Blood and death could be found on most of the streets in big cities all across the globe. People stole large flat-screen TVs that did not work and would never work again. Everything from washing machines to Apple cell phones flowed through the broken-out storefront windows. Commuters could not decide whether to hoof it home (without their car) or hole up in the city with their loot.

People became hungry. The hoarding of food began. Everyone older than thirty remembered the pandemic and looted toilet paper, flour, and yeast, whether or not they had ever baked bread.

Once the panic calmed, the populations in the cities split into two factions. The largest category included the looters, murderers, and the addicted. The other class of people found their way to the parks and stadiums to seek or give aid. Red Cross workers slowly but steadily brought in and set up tents and supplies on hand carts. Without operable cars and trucks, the rescue associations took ten times longer to set up and begin to be beneficial for the sick and hungry. Charitable organizations had no idea when fellow volunteers from other cities or states would arrive. Limited communications hampered relief efforts (landlines worked, but ninety-five percent of the world's population had abandoned landlines decades ago.)

Violence, lawlessness, and inhumane behavior occurring in the city centers fanned out to the suburbs and satellite cities, and townships in an ever-increasing radius of despair. Inhumanity became the new normal.

Small rural cities and towns like Ludington remained more lawful than the greater Grand Rapids area. Hoarding began, but dairy and frozen items became problematic with no operating refrigerators or freezers. All the ice bags in Ludington vanished within three hours. Without working freezers, the bags of ice melted in hours, and cold storage ended. Thirty-year-old solar-powered home generators directly connected to a refrigerator or freezer offered a limited solution. Cities banned natural gas connections to gas stoves, furnaces, water heaters, and generators in 2035 in an effort for the country to meet the requirements of the China Accord of 2032.

The locals of Ludington attempted to adjust to their circumstances, as impossible as that might be. Tourists walked in family groups south on US31, trying to return to their homes, savings, and civilization, even though civilization as they knew it had dissolved.

Father and son Martensen stayed in their cabin for thirty-five days. Logan wanted to observe and experience the life they would now lead. No one came to the Data Futures, Inc. server farm. Logan moved through the tunnel from the cabin to the server farm. He inspected his old facility, observing the acres of stacked servers, now dormant.

Martin's curiosity began to eat at his patience. They had neither seen nor heard of an automobile, truck, plane, or train. Venturing up to the reservoir, Martin spied a 28' Hunter sailboat out on Lake Michigan heading north, too far away to distinguish a crew.

Logan decided to head into town. They donned mostly empty backpacks and began the seven-mile walk to town. They brought a small amount of sausage, cheese, crackers, and three water bottles in one of the backpacks. Logan planned to walk to the condo north of town to check on his property and perhaps retrieve a few more pictures and mementos. They walked at a leisurely pace. They crossed the Pere Marquette River by using the US10 bridge. That is when they began to see people, lingerers getting a late start walking home downstate. One man walked next to his wife, leading his family of ten-year-old twins and an eight-year-old girl. They looked hungry and tired already. The girl whined. The man told Logan they were from Muskegon, sixty miles away.

Martin suspected the man sniffed the sausage in the backpack, but he did not bring up the subject of food. The wife looked perplexed as the backpackers headed toward town. Martin noted her expression. "We're local," he said and walked on.

The town seemed deserted. The welcome sign coming into town had been splashed with so much paint only the letters "LUD" remained readable. They spotted movement and flashlights waving inside as they passed the Wesco gas and convenience station. Three teenagers, Martin's age, chucked a small bag of contraband out a demolished window and stepped through. Spotting Martin and Logan, they fanned out. They each wielded long, heavy flashlights, holding them like weapons. The one in the center, the eldest, nodded at Logan.

"Hey, old man, whatcha got in the backpack?" asked Center Boy.

"Just a little travel snack," Logan said.

"Well, hand it over. We are collecting."

Logan decided the time had come to find out if his son could survive the age of the cataclysm. He nodded to Martin, who winked back. They both took off their backpacks, and Logan approached Center Boy. Martin held his pack out to the kid on their left. Before handing over the bag, Logan dropped it and used a swing kick to the boy's chest, knocking the wind from him, the flashlight flying. At the same time, Martin karate jabbed the second boy, blocking the downswing of the flashlight with his left forearm and, with a twist, flew the boy over his extended hip to the ground. The third boy ran off behind Wesco out of sight in seconds, abandoning the loot and his friends. Disarmed, the two boys stayed on the ground recovering until Logan and Martin left the site.

During the walk along the main avenue in the town, Martin kept a watchful eye on the minimum movement he saw in some of the stores. The few people on the street, almost zombie-like, made a wide berth, even crossing to the opposite sidewalk to avoid Martin and Logan. They shuffled along, peering in windows, trying to determine if anything of use or to eat might be left inside.

In another hour, Logan unlocked the door of the condo. So far, it had not been touched. Everything remained in place.

They decided to stay the night.

At the shore after dark, father, and son stripped down and skinny-dipped on Martin's favorite beach. The night sky offered up a million more stars than Martin or Logan had ever seen. Unhampered by the city lights of the town as well as a dark Chicago across the lake to the south and a lights-out Milwaukee beyond the horizon to the near northwest, the cleansed heavens above sparkled like an all-white Christmas tree.

Logan thought of Harper, rubbing the back of his neck as he silently walked the dune toward the condo. Martin remembered when he stepped on a cropped dune grass stalk that pierced his foot. *Must have been six, maybe seven,* he thought. Harper had carried the crying boy back to the house and sprayed cooling Bactine on Martin's injury.

Logan awoke around ten o'clock to insistent knocking on the front door.

"This is the police. Open the door," a voice said in an even, loud voice.

Logan looked at Martin, who had hurried into the hallway, shaking his hands at Martin as if to say, 'What do we do?'

"Police. Open the door. We have a warrant for Logan Martensen. Open the door. We have a side arm and will fire a warning shot if necessary," said the same voice.

Logan turned to Martin and shrugged, "Martin, lie face down in the living room. Hands in plain sight.

"Alright, officer, coming. I am unarmed. Please, no shooting; my son is with me," Martin said.

Martin unlocked the door. The two state police troopers walked in. The first trooper to enter held a long-barreled revolver at his side, pointing at the floor.

"Mr. Martensen, please help your son sit on the couch," the gun-toter said.

"What is the matter, officer," Logan said, "I own this place, and I can prove it if I can look in the file in the alcove."

"Not necessary, Mr. Martensen. My partner is Officer Reed. I am Officer Rillema. Let me serve this warrant, and it may clear things up.

"This is a federal warrant, served with the cooperation of the Michigan State Police. The orders are to locate Logan Martensen, 3045 N. Beachcroft St., and accompany him to the Grand Rapids Police Department – State of Michigan, to be transferred to the care of Lieutenant James Palmer of the United States Army."

Logan seemed only slightly confused as opposed to Martin, who stood. "What is the charge. All we have done is defend ourselves," Martin said. He assumed the three teenagers had filed assault charges.

"Sit down, son," said Officer Rillema, "Your father is not under arrest. As it was explained to me, and believe me, it is way over my head; the feds need your help, Mr. Martensen.

"The FBI has documentation of you writing and meeting Representative Olmstead from your district in January 2043. Apparently, you attempted to warn the government of a July 1st, 2050, plot involving computers that would devastate the United States."

Martin had never heard mention of Logan's trip to Washington.

"I admit I tried," Martin said, "Everyone looked at me like I was deranged, suffering from the death of my wife."

"Yet, here we are," said Rillema, "Look, the FBI research this past week has focused on your wife. As I understand it, Harper Martensen is a nanotechnologist dealing with unseeable particles used in the engineering of microprocessors."

"Was, officer," Martin said, "She was murdered September 10th, 2041."

"Well, the government is asking for your help now," said Officer Rillema, "Back in '43, you mentioned using a scanning probe microscope. The armed forces have a laboratory equipped with such a microscope at Wright-Patterson Air Force base in Dayton, Ohio. That is your final destination. We will commandeer a bicycle in town for you. It is a four-hundred-mile trip. We will hand you off to Lieutenant Palmer in Grand Rapids."

"And what if he doesn't want to go," said Martin.

"He will go; that is our order," said Officer Reed, sounding burly.

"Look," said Martin, "I spent years trying to solve the problem of reversing the nanobiological/nanoelectronic switch-off that caused this catastrophe. My wife was the genius, not me; I'm just an analyst that figured out the conspiracy."

"Mr. Martensen, you may not be a genius," said Rillema, "but you may be the best man available. At least you have a head start on the research. Which will it be? Will you come with us, or do we handcuff you to the handlebars?"

Logan looked at his son, but only for a moment. Any longer, and he would have collapsed, crying.

"I'll go with you," he said, "But I do not ride a bicycle. I'll walk."

"Four hundred miles?" asked Officer Reed.

"He doesn't ride bikes," Martin stated, turning to his father, "I'll go with you, Dad."

Martin stood. "Can my son go too?" he asked.

"It is a long way," said Officer Rillema, "We will get you as far as Grand Rapids safely, maybe. Things are boiling over downstate. The trip will be dangerous. Luckily, the GR department found this old 38 Special that never received the PHSI microchip retrofit."

"I need to talk with my son, Officer," said Logan, "Can you wait outside?"

The two officers dressed in their official dark blue, short-sleeved uniform shirts and dark blue dress pants, their ties tucked through the third and fourth shirt buttons to prevent them from flapping in the wind. They circled Martin and Logan as they plodded up to the top of the US31 escarpment on the way to the Hart, Michigan State Police post for a meal and overnight accommodation.

Logan had agreed that Martin could accompany him as far as Hart. He took advantage of the seven-hour walk to review all the warnings, procedures, and skills they had learned these past years to survive.

"Give no quarter," Logan would say, "Remember the boys at Wesco. Strike first if the situation looks dicey. Avoid the confrontation if possible. Do not take the highway going back. Stay close to your new home. I will try to send news."

"I'll remember, Dad."

The foursome made it to Hart without incident, but Officer Rillema received a warning from the commander at the post of significant trouble in the Muskegon outskirts.

In the morning, back at the highway, Martin hugged his father. "Goodbye, son," Martin choked out. "With the world as it is, we may never see each other again. Please do not dwell on it. This is your life and your world now. Make something of it."

"I'll see you again, Dad; that is a promise," said Martin, "I'll be fine. I'll do my best."

Logan and the two troopers turned south. Martin turned north. Martin forced himself not to look back as he came to a hillcrest.

Logan refused to look back as well.

5

FILTRATOR

The years following the KT extinction event are believed to have been a time of incredibly rapid speciation and worldwide expansion for ants, marking a rise to ecological dominance.

2063

Martin Martensen dug out two objects from his denim jacket and a third from the back pocket of his jeans. He laid all three things on the counter.

"Just a minute," said the counterman, "I got to talk to the boss about these. They look computerlike."

"No worries, I can wait," said Martin.

The counterman returned accompanied by James Lash, the owner of the salvage company. The poster above and behind the counter presented a picture of Lash. At the bottom of the poster, a pitch in bold type said, "We pay purple tickets for diamonds, even more for gold.

The proprietor took a long look at the artifacts. Picking up the middle piece, a solid-state drive, Lash turned it in his hand, wiped it down on his dirty sleeveless t-shirt, then set it back down. Next, he picked up an item, the size of his fist, judged its heft, and said, "Three purples for the heavy thing: transformer maybe. One red for the smaller piece. This third thing doesn't weigh shit. I'll throw it in with the other two pieces."

Martin shook his head, making a show of returning his billfold to the back pocket of his jeans.

"I don't have that much; next trip, maybe," Martin said as he left. He turned to the proprietor, "I've got a lonely silver piece in my pocket if you would take it for the lighter piece."

Lash laughed. "Let me guess, trying to piece together a real computer, right," the man said, "you fellas never stop trying. Let me see your silver."

The third article, the heat sink, should have been priced at three purples, thus Martin's misdirection of focus to the two heavier objects. Martin exchanged the nickel in his pocket for the heat sink and left the shop. Outside, out of sight of the shop, Martin scuffed the heat sink, threw it in a mud puddle, dried it, and tucked it in the corner of his backpack. He picked up two crushed and rusted bean cans that had floated to the street drain. Martin threw those in his pack as well.

He headed for the city-state gate. Martin had spent three days searching twelve junk yards in three slum sections of Graapids before finding the treasure he now carried. The sooner he left the depressing city-state, the sooner his mask would come off.

When the city-state of Graapids formed in late 2051, the mayor, a disciple of Van Andel, had asked her CSG (City-State Guard) to gather all the residents on the east shoreline of the Grand River. Speaking through a bullhorn from the opposite bank of the river, four hundred feet away, Mayor DeClark reviewed the new laws she enacted to prevent the chaos prevalent in Dtroit, Chitown, and Philly. All two hundred thousand survivors of the Microprocessor Cataclysm stuck within the city-state fence listened to the mayor optimistically. They would be fine.

Nine months after the mayor's speech, the Meijer stores' food supply dwindled. The trickle of rationed food created so much strife that CSG stopped all distribution. Rioters, beaten and thrown in jails around the city, never received another meal, dying by the thousands. The stink permeated the detention centers. The fetid conditions caused the locals in the surrounding buildings to abandon their homes, except for the 'high-heads' in Nirvana. The slums and their death toll did not faze the guarded Herihill area.

The lucky rich who lived there had transferred their holdings to gold.

Martin approached the officer at the gate. He shucked his backpack, expecting a search. The sentry held his M6 Scout rifle to his shoulder with the barrel pointing to Martin's shoes. An eight-foot tall, razor wire topped, chain link fence stretched out of sight east and west. Sentries stood guard outside the border every three hundred yards to prevent unregistered entry. The guard tower beside the entrance remained unmanned due to the personnel shortage.

The chain link fence contained crudely patched holes at ground level. At night, men and women risked being shot as they cut through the links from the outside. Spaced so far apart, the guards gave intruders little doubt about their success. The single shot M6 could be reloaded quickly, but travelers still took the chance.

All automatic and semi-automatic weapons produced since 2040 contained microchips affected by the cataclysm and could not be fired. Newer rifles had long since been scrapped in favor of CSG-confiscated antique M6 Scout rifles, among other pre-PHSI weapons (Preventative-Human Safety-Initiative.)

The torches spaced fifty yards apart along the fence caused checkerboard shadows on the ground beyond, but large swathes of shadowed darkness covered the trespasser's approach in between. Every few months, the sentries would re-space further apart. The precious .22 hornet rifle bullets were redistributed to each guard. The M6 Scout rifles carried by the guards now held just five shots in the rifle's stock storage, which, fully loaded, could contain fifteen shells.

Guard duty pay remained low; four red government punched food tickets per week. The mayor periodically ordered the spacing between guards to be increased as many deserted for lack of ammunition and the increasing risk of interloper attack along the perimeter of Graapids. Amidst the ongoing security concern, constructing a second fence encompassing a shrinking city-state area neared completion. Within weeks the sentries would be moved back to the inside fence, the outside fence dismantled and reconstructed one hundred yards inside the recently completed barrier. A vicious shrinking circle in a decaying city-state. Life within the boundaries of Graapids mirrored existence in the overgrown countryside; starvation, freezing winters, and sickness. For most, the city-state offered a symbol of better opportunity rather than the reality of a slum.

Under no such illusion, Martin would return north after a freezing bath in the Grand. He would pay the exorbitant bribe to the gatekeeper to leave, just as he had paid to get in.

The officer waved his rifle at Martin's backpack on the ground, so the traveler unzipped the front panel and emptied the contents on the broken asphalt, neatly lining up everything in a row. A tightly rolled tent, sleeping bag, change of clothes, an open mess kit, and of course, the two empty bean cans and the heat sink completed an inventory of Martin's belongings.

The guard bent over and nudged the heat sink with the peep sight of his rifle.

"What about this," the guard said, raising the rifle to point at Martin's chest.

"The slots will conveniently hold my tickets. No moving parts, as you can see. I've got a red ticket for you, but if you'd rather have the gadget," Martin said.

"Naw, worthless, but you better have two reds, or you ain't getting by me."

Martin had been through the exit negotiation before. He dug a crumpled red ticket out of his front jeans pocket and found his reserve red coupon in the backpack pocket.

The guard stomped on the empty backpack, proving it held no hidden treasure. Then he took the two red tickets Martin produced and opened the gate. Martin repacked his belongings and set off toward the river.

The road led to the one remaining navigable bridge across the river, but Martin would not attempt that crossing. He planned to avoid the possibly harmless man walking across the bridge.

Bandit, drug dealer, undercover CSG? Martin planned to cross by wading the river upstream at the crumbling fish weir.

When the man up ahead reached the end of the bridge, another man leaped from the shadow of the structure like a troll. The ensuing scuffle caught Martin's attention. Too far away to be any help, Martin watched the ragged man beat the innocent man to the ground with his fists. The felled man grabbed the shirt of his attacker and pulled himself up. Realizing that his life depended on staying upright, fending off the troll, and running for the gate, he returned blows to the rag man's head and ears.

Amidst the close-quarters struggle, Martin heard a gunshot and looked back to the gate. The guard held his rifle to his shoulder, pointing toward the two men.

Turning back to the scuffle, Martin saw one of the men fall to the ground, his head a mess of spurting blood. The guard must have fired to protect the man trying to cross the bridge, but his aim had been inaccurate due to the struggle. The bridge troll crouched over the dead man, rifling his pockets and stripping the bloody ripped shirt away from the victim.

Another shot echoed off the bridge, and the troll dropped across the body, dead as the first.

Martin hurried north from the guard's twitchy trigger finger under the cover of a row of two-story buildings.

The river curved around the west side of Graapids flowing westward to Big Lake, a half-moat buffer for the city-state. Martin waited in the dark underneath a willow until the first quarter moon rose in the east. He watched for strangers and ogres but, so far, had not seen any signs of activity. He waited fifteen more minutes to be sure. The river spilled over the weir, gurgling and roaring in hypnotic repetition. Martin wished he could camp at the weir. The ambient sound of a river always made for a restful night's sleep.

Too restful, too dangerous. Martin stripped off all his clothes and stuffed them in his backpack. Wearing only his boots and hefting the bag high overhead, he waded into the cold river, trying not to gasp as the water hit his balls. The water, decades clean from industrial pollution, had no smell. In the moonlight, Martin could see to the bottom. Walking in the water, he used his free hand to wash the city grime from his armpits, groin, and butt.

When he was knee-deep and near the west side of the river, Martin tossed his backpack ashore, kneeling down to wash his face. He ducked underwater, kneading feather light brown hair hanging in his eyes, covering his ears, and extending halfway down his neck to his shoulders. Standing again to his full height, shy of six feet by an inch, the man climbed the shore and swiped excess water from his body. Since his father's arrest, he had walked everywhere in the new wilderness, his legs now long and muscular. Martin had an iron stomach, no butt to speak of, but broad-shouldered from over twenty years of working construction and farming alone.

He airdried under the branches of another tree before he dressed. From the river, he walked northeast by the radium glow of his compass, picking his way among empty suburban homes until he reached a third-growth forest. Too dark to pitch the tent, Martin unrolled his sleeping bag underneath a silver maple and went to sleep hungry. The horror of the city-state is soon to be forgotten in sleep.

At dawn, July 9th, Martin trekked north again. Just before noon, he spotted the church steeple, his navigational landmark. Reaching the steps of the abandoned church, he turned due west toward the forest. The small graveyard, overgrown by the woods, hundreds of years older than the church, contained only twenty-two gravestones. The names and dates on all the markers had weathered away to gouges, unreadable. Martin went to the second to last headstone in the second row, moving a large pile of brush and leaves aside.

His takedown, fifty-pound, twenty-eight-inch draw, recurve bow had not been touched. Neither had his hip field quiver with twelve stainless steel, razor-tipped arrows. A tightly bound waterproof bag held a choice of three freeze-dried dinners, two cans of green beans, and a can of peaches for dessert: pears for another night. A large canteen of water, a pot to mix the dinners, a porcelain cup, and a large spoon completed the supplies in the bag. Martin strapped on his ankle holster and sheathed his hunting knife. Patting his rumbling stomach, he sat down on a headstone to mix the beef stroganoff dinner with water in the pot. He knew better than to attempt to smuggle any hidden items into the city-state. The articles would have been confiscated, and he would have been jailed. Jail meant death, not detainment.

Finished with his cold casserole, beans, and peaches, Martin buried the empty cans. He washed his mug with sand, loaded his backpack, clipped the quiver to his belt on his left side, and proceeded north, carrying his bow in his left hand. Turning west, Martin traveled on the grassy edge of gravel roads, zig-zagging past Sparta and Ravenna. He neither met anyone nor heard any human noise the entire day. He camped back in the woods, figuring he might be more than halfway to the big water.

Before turning north at the edge of the deserted suburbs and lowlands of Muskie, Martin spotted another man in a white t-shirt and shorts walking toward him. *Not exactly camouflaged*, Martin thought. Martin moved to the forest's edge but stayed in plain sight of the approaching man. If necessary, he could leap into the cover of the woodlands. The man stopped in the middle of the road and held his palms out, unarmed. Martin hammered his heart twice with his right hand, then extended his right arm full length, palm open.

The man on the road duplicated the gesture, the sign of the Independent. He moved on, his back to Martin, never looking back. Martin returned to the edge of the road and turned north toward Whitehall.

Martin's stomach tugged and growled with hunger before dawn. He sat perched in an apple tree, waiting for daylight, the path below him peppered with black turkey scat. Midmorning, six hens clucked down the track, followed by a colossal tom neck jerking with each claw forward. Martin drew his bow, bringing his arrow to point, and shot the turkey. The turkey let out an involuntary squawk and died.

Martin pulled the bell rope next to the gate in front of the Lebanon Lutheran Church of Whitehall, Lakeshore. Two minutes later, he heard children shuffling in the courtyard beyond the gate. Pastor Tim Corallina helped his wife, Pamela, swing the solid oak gate in. Both smiled.

"Good day to you, Martin, welcome, welcome. Please do not stay away for so long. It is three months, I think, since your last visit," he said.

"I purchased a significant piece in Graapids," Martin said, "and you are on my route home."

Martin swung the big turkey off his backpack. Pamela hefted the thirty-pound bird by the rope that bound its claws. With many thanks, she hustled off to the kitchen.

Pastor Corallina locked the solid oak gate, took Martin by the arm, and gestured for him to sit in the Adirondack chair on the patio. Then Corallina went to a second chair and pulled it close to Martin. At that point, three of the youngest children swarmed the visitor. Shaking them off momentarily, he set his backpack, bow, and quiver on the picnic table.

Martin spent the next half hour bouncing each child in his lap, letting them safely fall through his legs after a big bob. Then he joined the older children in the line for a game of four squares. Martin let the rubber ball that found his square pass him on the third attempt, signifying defeat. He returned to the back of the line.

Pastor Corallina rescued him from the game, and they sat again to chat.

"Were you followed?" Pastor wondered.

"No," said Martin, "I circled your block twice to make sure."

"Good," Corallina said, "Then I will call the rest of the children."

He left the courtyard, returning a minute later, followed by six more children, two Latinos and four Blacks, all under ten years old.

"Come here, Lincoln," the Pastor said, "You remember Martin?"

"Sure," said the ten-year-old.

"Thank you, Lincoln, for keeping the others corralled until we knew it to be safe for you.

"Martin, we are never safe now that the city-states are beginning to crumble and the militias are gaining more power."

Martin knew what he meant. In one way or another, the Microprocessor Cataclysm caused the death of billions. The world population dropped from ten billion in 2052 to the 1900 level of one billion five hundred million people within two years, and millions still die each month.

For the most part, however, due to PHSI weapons, people do not shoot each other with guns. Lawful, humane societies formed post-MCC but collapsed under the economic law of supply and demand, specifically food supply. In a world that traditionally lived off fast-food counters, hunger, and barbarism now overshadow altruistic intentions. Most militias are comprised of outlaws. They developed other means of control and torture without working guns, using chains, ropes, knives, spikes, and crossbows. Militias subjugate, kill indiscriminately, and declare war on rival militias. In place of undrivable microchip-filled gas and electric cars, the return to a horse and saddle transportation network limited the geographic realm of any given militia. Militias could command a larger territory than all but the largest city-states of LA, Nueva York, or Miami, which continued to shrink like Graapids.

Just like with the ancient realms of kings, many families lived within the boundaries of a militia's territory without ever encountering the wrath of a militia or the CSG.

Ogres, trolls, and bandits roamed, stole, and scrounged; typically murdered by the first person they crossed. Trolls lived under highway overpasses or in large storm drains. Trolls dressed in never washed rags could be identified by stench long before an attack. Starved and weak, they were only an occasional threat. Ogres tended to be dumb brutes that lived by intimidating travelers they met on well-traveled thoroughfares. Ogres were dangerous but slow, typically easy to outrun. Bandits tended to be subtle and deadly. They did not bother with masks or disguises, sometimes traveling in small groups of not more than three. Running for cover may be the only remedy if a bandit or anyone in a group of bandits brandished a weapon. If necessary, take an alternate route, stay hidden, or prepare a defense. Ogres and trolls desperately needed to be in mental institutions, of which there were none. If not killed on the road, ogres, trolls, and bandits risked jail, the house of death.

Independents would have nothing of either the militias or the city-states. By definition, they chose a self-sufficient lifestyle, hidden away in wilderness areas or abandoned villages, respectful of each other's space and property but isolated from most human interaction. These survivalists, subsistence farmers, expert hunters, and monks moved if threatened by militia encroachment. Martin, proud to be Independent, would describe his lifestyle as ideal. Never bored, willing to try new techniques, Martin helped a fellow Independent when asked; otherwise, he kept to himself.

"Is there anything else I can do, Tim?" Martin asked.

"The Lebanon Lutheran Church is grateful for your efforts, Martin. Some of the children are old enough now to help in the garden. The generous Independents in our area also assist. We will be fine.

"I only worry about the children of color. The cleansing war that raged after the MCC has dissipated; there is not much left for the militias to purge. Militias enslaved blacks for mule slaves, killing all but a few stud men outright. The women are whipped to pull the plows like horses on the plantations east of old Cincinnati in the Smoky foothills. When they are not slaving in the fields, they are slaving in the beds of the militia's upper echelon."

After enjoying the offered soup and bread meal sitting among the children, Martin attached an old tarp from the garage to a hay bail. He pierced an apple with a stick and stuck the apple to the center of the makeshift target. The children gathered behind him on the opposite side of the courtyard twenty yards away. He asked the children to raise their hands if they thought he could hit the apple. Only three raised their hand.

Martin drew the bowstring back to his anchor point, the arrow's nock brushing the dimple in his chin. He released the shaft, and the apple exploded. The children begged to see if Martin could repeat his performance. Pastor Corallina stuck another apple to the target.

The archer backed up another ten feet, waved the children to the rear again, and asked for raised hands of those who thought he would hit the apple. Eight children raised a hand. The skeptics still outnumbered the faithful. He split the apple again. Not wanting to push his luck, Martin packed up to leave. When asked how he could hit an apple so far away, he replied, "Practice, kids, a half hour a day since I turned sixteen. Two hours a day since I turned eighteen."

Potholes, encroaching weeds, sprouting bushes, and even trees broke up the pavement of the ten-foot-wide historic trail to Hart. The path still provided a beautifully peaceful, relatively easy walk enveloped by oak, various species of maple, poplar, aspen, and white and jack pine. On this cloudless day in September, Martin relished the afternoon sun shooting through the leaves, warming his left side as he walked north.

Martin's destination, a giant server farm built in 2026, six years before Martin's birth, now serves as Logan's manor in Butters, Lakeshore. The vast data storage warehouse covers an area equivalent to three football fields.

The building, constructed in the middle of a 100-acre apple and cherry tree orchard, is missed by travelers along the old highway. Butters, Lakeshore could be called a one-horse town. The gas station, convenience store, and two homes built upon completion of the warehouse are now deserted.

The site had been chosen for its proximity to the Pumped Storage Power Plant on Big Lake. The freshwater reservoir, two and a half miles long, one mile wide, and one hundred ten feet deep, provided cheap green electric power to the grid. The six turbines that generated electricity and pumped water back into the reservoir at night fell silent on the day of the Microprocessor Cataclysm.

In addition to tapping into the generated electricity from the power station, the warehouse, built in the lowland below the reservoir, also powered the building's geothermal heating/cooling system. Before the Cataclysm, water circulated down the hill from the pool to the data depot. The facility had been named one of the twentieth century's most environmentally friendly and power-efficient projects.

The Microprocessor Cataclysm instantly knocked out nearly six hundred servers in the data warehouse. The computers still operated; they did not compute. Soon the power grid ran out of emergency power, the turbines of the pump storage station shut down, and everything went deathly quiet. The microprocessor controllers for the solar power panels on the warehouse roof suffered the same MCC fate.

Later that year, as migrating populations searched for food and treasures, a wave of looters swept through the warehouse, hoping to find stores of food. That not being the case, the angry mob did what angry mobs inevitably do; destroy everything in sight.

Most solar panels were smashed, and many server racks were overturned. Then the throng continued marching up and down the coast of Big Lake. Thousands died of starvation or the fatal fights over the small food stores the gangs did discover. The hordes split up. Thousands returned to the new city-states for protection, and the rest joined militias.

The Microprocessor Cataclysm occurred on July 1st, 2050, eleven days after Martin's eighteenth birthday. This year he had turned thirty-one. After his return from Graapids, Martin spent two days cleaning his home and weeding the garden. In the mornings, he arose at sunrise and walked to Big Lake to swim and wash up. Martin had no clocks in his home. Still, he woke up every day, all summer and fall, and went swimming. Routine, the secret of sanity.

After breakfast, he entered the details of his trip to Graapids in his journal. He used an old mechanical typewriter from Historic White Pine Village. The village contained several buildings replicating the early life in the town to the north. In many ways, the village again represented life in Butters, Lakeshore.

After journaling, Martin studied for the rest of the morning. He continued with his textbook on the solar system and the applicable laws, theories, and myths of physics that applied.

After lunch, he practiced archery for two hours and then an hour on jujitsu. He used a weighted, straw-stuffed dummy as his sparring partner, flipping, chopping, and punching it until it felt like he had killed it. Repeating his father's mantra. Stay cautious, practice, and be ready.

In the late afternoon, Martin went hunting. With no automobiles smacking into them, and few hunters, an abundance of deer could be found along one of their north-south pathway trails or as they headed down to the lake for water, except for yesterday and today. No deer! Unusual but not unheard of in the eleven years Martin had been culling the deer herd in the area. Martin thought of traveling south to hunt, which troubled him because he would have more work transporting the field-dressed deer back home. Today, he decided to take his fishing gear to Big Lake and catch dinner.

After breakfast and making a short journal entry, Martin decided to seriously hunt game south of his property. He took off midmorning, carrying his bow, his hip quiver attached to his belt. He swung his pack on his back. The backpack contained lunch, a first aid kit, water, tools to field-dress a deer, and tools to make a travois if necessary.

In the vicinity of Bass Lake, he found an abandoned blind and decided to try his luck waiting there. An hour later, Martin heard a rustle somewhere behind him. Seeing another man parting the brush, Martin stood in the hunting blind ready to shoot.

The other man also held a bow, but the two men were somewhat out of range of each other. Instead of drawing the bowstring to point, Martin spread his arms apart with palms up, the sign of the Independent. The other man did not draw either. Instead, he pounded his heart twice with his right hand, extending his right arm full length, palm open; a fellow Independent.

The other hunter approached. Three deer sauntered along the path at the same time. The hunter on the ground drew back and fired, dropping one deer and scattering the other two. Before gaining speed, Martin shot a second deer in the back of the neck. Two hunters, two kills; a good day.

"Hell of a shot," said the hunter on the ground, "I thought sure those two would get away."

"Now the work begins," said Martin, "let's drag them both over to the clearing and dress them there."

The esprit de corps of Independents grew year by year after the Cataclysm. Once recognized, an Independent typically participates in a brief social exchange with a fellow Independent. The downside of the Independent lifestyle is loneliness. Martin had calculated on one depressingly cold, snowy day that he had been in the company of other humans for seven hours in the years since his father walked south on US31.

Martin did not know Logan's location and could not find out or communicate with him. He only knew that the world had not changed. Logan had evidently not been able to reverse the effects of the Cataclysm, at least not to date.

The two men conversed little as they went about dressing their kill.

"How has your summer been going, Indy?" Martin asked, hopeful the other hunter would not be reticent.

"Best one so far. The weather has been great. Wife is due in August," said Indy, cutting off his own laugh.

Martin saw that Indy had decided he had said too much. Independents were notoriously protective of their private life. The security of an Independent's family and home depended on secrecy. The cruel slaughter and plunder of Militia, outlaws, mercenaries, and sexual deviants hinged on tortured Independent confessions to find their next victim. Unspoken laws developed among Independents. They were already considered social miscreants for abandoning the communal groups of towns and villages at the expense of managing every aspect of their lives alone.

Rule 1: Never reveal the location, size, amenities, or lack thereof of your home or family. Never ask another Indy for this information.

Rule 2: Never ask or offer names; given or sur.

Rule 3: Offer or receive aid graciously as long as rules one and two are respected.

Martin sawed down a couple of saplings and formed a crude seven-foot crisscross triangle tied off with rope. The short end of the triangle, two feet across, created a bed for the strapped-in meat. The crossing yoke fit around his head and rested on his shoulders. The rope attached where the branches crossed hung down his chest. Granny knots in the rope formed hand holds for Martin to pull the heavy load the one and three-quarters miles back to his estate.

Martin assumed by the whiff of the man that hygiene might be difficult for him wherever he hid his family. He stretched the rules a bit, "I understand Pastor Corallina's wife Pamela provides midwife duties if you can make it down to Whitehall."

"Yes," said Indy, "she has helped before, but I have heard a rumor about an attack on their church. A militia out of Ohio looking for black refugees found their compound."

"Shit," said Martin, "I just visited them a week ago. I'll have to travel down there and see if they need help."

Indy looked down at his deer while shaking his head, "Hard to say if there is anything left," the hunter paused, "Well, Indy, I will be off."

"Yes, Indy," Martin said, deciding to shake the hunter's hand, "Safe travels, stay safe."

Two days later, Martin found his way to the old Hart trail and began the walk to Whitehall. The course, overgrown, still provided a narrow, clear space, straight as the paved-over train tracks that in the past had brought freight and people north from the lower eastern coast of Big Lake.

Martin saw the party heading his way along the path from a half mile away. They made no attempt to walk or speak softly, crashing through the overgrowth and laughing as if they owned the trail. Only militias believed they owned the land they traveled. Even City-State Guards journeyed cautiously outside their fenced limits. Militias traveled boldly.

Martin melted into the woods lining the trail. He took up a position on a hill overlooking the path in a group of apple trees, just in arrow range. Their group consisted of six men, bows slung over their shoulders, armed with field quivers full of arrows, a crowbar hanging from their belts. Two other men wore beaten-up army slouch hats and tan denim jackets, somehow proving their superiority over the other men. One of the archers held his bow with a notched arrow pointing at two women as they stumbled along. One woman was black, the other white. Both women had their hands tied together. Their knees were joined with a short length of rope. They fell over often and were prodded to get up and keep plodding. Running away would be out of the question.

The group stopped, presumably for lunch. The women dug a pit, scrounged wood around the trail, lit the fire, and fixed a pot of coffee for the soldiers and the officers. The soldiers passed a flask of alcoholic drink. They became louder in the time it took the women to prepare the lunch. The group ate chunks of hard bread and salami like Martin.

Martin took a closer look at the two women through his binoculars. The sun was behind him, so no reflection from the glass eyepiece gave his position away. Both women were beautiful. The white woman looked young, probably early twenties. When the black woman stood, Martin decided she must be five feet eight inches tall. Her legs were exquisite. Martin remembered the many times Logan had commented on how beautiful his mother's legs were. This woman had gorgeous legs as well. She wore a blouse that had been ripped in half and tied up from her waist to expose her midriff, flat and muscled. Her chest created instant heat in Martin's crotch. Her right breast, showing for the delight of the officers, swayed when she walked and dropped down as she bent over in the direction of the soldier she served. Two soldiers reached to grasp her breast, but she moved too fast for the oafs sitting on the ground.

The woman's hair was long, extremely curly, and tied back in a ponytail. Her face reminded Logan of his mother. Perhaps the high cheekbones and softly rounded chin contributed to her beauty, just like his mom. The woman's demeanor remained non-plussed in the face of the teasing, reaching, and abuse she put up with. *Smile,* Martin thought; *I wish I could see you smile.* She must be around his age, the white woman much younger in comparison.

The officer with a feather-plumed hat approached the woman and pinched her cheeks together. Then he gave her a slap which Martin plainly heard. He must have commanded her as well because she smiled through the pain. Brave girl. The officer commanded more, and the woman smiled more broadly, rubbing her cheek. Martin, enraged, resisted charging down to the trail and knocking the bastard's teeth in. Logan spoke in his head, "Avoid fighting if at all possible,"

Martin tried to put his need for companionship in perspective. He could shoot three of the six before the group caught on. He faced trained soldiers. The remaining officers would split up, surround, and descend on him. He would surely die in the exchange.

"No," he said to himself, "Martin, stay back, stay safe; your day will come."

Yet he wanted more than anything to rescue this woman. Perhaps she would like him. Maybe love him. *He would never know.*

Martin walked on to Whitehall and cautiously approached the Lebanon Lutheran Church. He had not slept well the night before, worrying about what he might find and exhausted from hauling the deer. Yesterday Martin carved tenderloins, steaks, roasts, and stew chunks. He prepared ground venison, wrapped all the meat in plastic wrap, and placed them in cold storage. He would worry about freezing some of the pieces when he returned from the Lebanon church.

An alley a half block from the compound and a dumpster allowed Martin to observe the church compound. His binoculars did not reveal any movement outside the walls. He heard no sounds rising from the courtyard. Martin waited another hour before approaching the gate. He rang the bell as loudly as possible five times, then retreated to the dumpster. He let another hour pass before he passed through the gate.

Bodies. Children's bodies hither and thither; blood-colored sand or cobblestones, slashed stomachs and arms, decapitations, gruesome. Martin swallowed hard and moved through the carnage. The finality of the view saved him from retching. His stomach flipped at each turn in the courtyard and building as he found more bodies. The scene was days old and over. Nothing for it. He ended up in the kitchen. There, propped against a wall, he found Pamela; her dress ripped down from collar to waist, naked breasts limp and shrinking, a slash halfway through her neck, her head canted almost to her shoulder. She still held the handle of a pitchfork in her right hand. Her weapon?

By the look of the massacre, the Corallinas had been caught off guard. The militia had stormed the walls in unison, slaughtering whomever, making their way through the compound, leaving no one alive and nothing to chance. Pamela must have been trying to protect someone.

That trap door is here somewhere, thought Martin. He had to move Pamela's body before he found it. Her spread skirt had hidden it from the marauders. After lighting a candle, Martin descended the ladder into the darkness. In the corner, he found someone curled up, boy or man, somewhat comatose but alive.

Martin splashed water from his canteen over the dehydrated lad's face. Then he lifted his head and forced water down his mouth and throat. After three harsh slaps, the boy tried to raise his hand to brush Martin back. Martin forced more water down him in sips.

Martin dragged the boy up the ladder by his shirt collar. He located Tim and Pamela's bedroom and cleared two eight-year-old girls and boys' bodies outside the courtyard. Then he lifted the teen he found and placed him on the bed, covering him with a blanket.

Stretched out, the boy looked to be twelve or thirteen. He may have been the blackest black-skinned person Martin had ever seen. The black population in the north mitten had been scarce during Martin's youth. The joke before the Cataclysm had been that diversity in the area meant whether one hunted with a rifle or a crossbow.

Martin fed the boy small bits of bread and sausage from his pack. The boy recovered. There had been some rations in the cellar hideout, water too, but it had run out two days before Martin's arrival. Although the boy still struggled, Martin pushed the boy to walk in the morning. Together they walked out of town toward Butters. Martin knew of a deserted hunting shack about a mile off the country roads accessible through overgrown asparagus fields and a chestnut tree orchard. The boy made it that far, and Martin allowed another two days for him to recover further before they traveled on.

The boy dressed before dawn. He folded his blanket. The shuffling awakened Martin, who sat up in his sleeping bag, scratching his neck.

"Mister, I am ready to go," the boy said, "I have lost too much time already."

"Oh," Martin said.

The boy had been ready for an argument. Martin's nonchalance put the boy off a bit.

"I did want to thank you, Sir," he said, "for finding me. I guess I got lucky you showed up."

"No worries," said Martin, "so what is your plan?" Martin used his knife and flint to light the kindling he had prepared the night before in the fireplace.

"I've got to find my mother, Sir."

"Where do you think she is? Which way will you go?" Martin asked.

"I thought I would go back to the church and look for clues there," said the boy.

"Listen, son, I know these parts pretty well. Why don't you tell me about your mother and how you wound up at the Lebanon Lutheran church? I knew the couple that sheltered those kids at the church. Good friends of mine. I would really like to take the mother fuckers down that killed them. Maybe we could help each other." Martin threw a branch on the fire.

The boy's mother had escaped from the militia compound east of Day Town. The boy figured Day Town to be an eight or nine days walk south of the church.

Before her capture, she and the boy had been living in the basement of the family farm. A neighbor told the militia soldiers about their secret and tortured his mother's friend for harboring blacks.

His mother escaped with the boy from the militia base two weeks ago. They traveled north to the Big Mitten as fast as they could, hoping to cross to Canada. A passerby informed the travelers about the church in Whitehall. That is where they went for sanctuary.

The militia scouting party, gaining on the black deserter, found and tortured all the travelers they met, learning about the Whitehall church.

The boy assumed the scouting party would return to their compound in Day Town.

"The problem with that theory," Martin said, "is that I believe I saw your mother the day before I found you. Her hands and legs were bound to prevent escape, and eight militiamen guarded her and another white woman."

"Where did you see them?" asked the boy.

"That is just it; they headed northeast, not south. They are trying to find Idlewild to bring back more black women to look good to their superiors."

The boy seemed more desperate by the minute. "Alright, can you tell me how to catch up to them? Is there a shortcut you know of? Please, I have to find her; help her."

"How," said Martin.

"I am not sure yet. Probably sneak into the bastards' camp at night, cut her bonds, and escape."

"You have no knife," Martin said, "I doubt you have the skill to use a knife as a weapon.

"Further, six trained soldiers guard your mother in shifts. Guards that would be killed themselves if they went to sleep or let your mother escape.

"In short, I will not tell you which way to go. You do not even own a compass or know how to use one. I do not believe your mother wants you to come after her and get yourself lynched. Hung from the nearest oak tree if they catch you. Black women are prized by these mongrels. Black men are put to death on the spot. As you heard at the compound, these men kill people like they are stepping on annoying ants."

Tears streamed down the boy's cheeks. He dropped to the floor and buried his face in the folded blanket.

"Mother, Mother, please be OK," He cried, the blanket muffling his words.

Martin let him cry out his frustration. When he stopped, he looked up at Martin, still determined to wander off to search for his mother.

"I said I wouldn't show you the way to follow her. I did not say I would not help you."

"Really, with your help, surely together we can rescue her."

"Again, you are getting ahead of yourself. You have not heard or agreed to my conditions. Object to any of them, and I go my way; you go yours. So, think about that for a minute."

The boy cocked his head, wondering what Martin meant by conditions. Pacing in the small eight-foot square shack could not be done. The boy walked two steps, turned one-eighty, took two steps, then repeated the process.

"I need to hear the conditions before I agree," said the boy.

"Of course," said Martin.

"First, I will not fight these bastards with you until you have the training and stamina not to get killed or get me killed in the first minute. You will have to train rigorously with no objections.

"Second, you must show mastery of the skills I teach you. I will be the judge of your competency. No objections.

"Lastly, I will continually judge your character. If I have to question your integrity at any point, you are on your own, or I will kill you. Simple as that."

"How long does this training take, Sir? My mother is a workhorse and slave to the whims of these militia dogs. She cannot take it much longer."

"From what I saw," said Martin, "she has the strength to take it until she can get back to you. How long will it take? If you practice diligently for the next year and have some inherent natural skill, maybe twelve to sixteen months. Again, we go when I say you are ready.

The boy's forehead furrowed at the thought of waiting even a year. With work, the boy believed he would beat Martin's timeline.

"I agree, Mister," said the boy.

"Good, my name is Martin, Martin Martensen. Let us get to walking,"

"My name is Davion Okoye," said the boy.

"And your mother's name?" asked Martin.

"Tamara Okoye."

"Ah," said Martin, *Beautiful.*

Martin stopped for a moment on the rise to observe his estate. He swept the area with his binoculars. No signs of life or intrusion. Davion's mouth hung open at the vastness of the building housing the former server farm. From this vantage point, Davion could not see the bungalow Martin and Logan had built behind the warehouse building. Graffiti covered the entire three-hundred-foot wall facing Martin's and Davion's approach.

"What do you think?" Martin asked.

"Actually," said Davion, after absorbing all the scenes and symbols, "It looks pretty cool."

The wall had been divided into ten sections of different sizes, each painted with a different motif. Abstract, multi-colored swirls in a few areas gave way to a portrait of a man embracing a woman standing at the water's edge, waves splashing at their feet. An illustration on a sixty-foot-long section represented an apple orchard; the exaggerated green apples on the left side of the orchard changed and grew into red apples that changed again on the far right to brown shrivels. Next came a section of Big Lake and the lighthouse north of Butters, the top of the lighthouse chopped off, broken like an old crumbling castle rampart.

A group within the second horde had climbed the structure using heavy rope and grappling hooks. They broke the windows, destroyed the lens, and entered from the top, looking for nonexistent food stores.

Across all the scenes, thick lines, symbols, and glyphs in black paint added hard-edged violence to the look of the wall.

"Thanks," said Martin, "I thought it looked rather good when I finished it. Discourages other artists, no space left for them.

"That's my mother and father. I was seven years old when I took the picture."

"She's beautiful, Sir," said Davion.

"Yes, so is your mother," admitted Martin, "Tamara, right?"

Martin thought the time appropriate to begin Davion's schooling.

"Lesson:" said Martin. "Never walk to the building along the same route. I do not want anyone to think there is a path through this field leading somewhere in particular." Davion nodded, and they set off around to the south side of the building.

Again, at first glance, this building wall looked wrecked beyond hope. Initially, a hundred feet wide, a hole, perhaps a bomb blast, exposed sixty feet of the interior of the building. The roof had peeled back in the explosion approximately fifty feet.

The hole began six feet up the face of the wall, extending in a jagged and burnt array of broken concrete and hanging scorched steel struts swinging in the wind. Steel bars rose from the blasted side wall, ending ten feet above the ground. Coiled razor wire topped the bars. Passersby could not see the interior of the building. The hole in the roof extended back into the interior approximately forty feet.

"Did the hordes do this as well?" asked Davion.

"No, I did it," said Martin, "It took six months. Jackhammer and torch. The 1st horde that passed through destroyed most of the solar panels, but the wall, razor wire, and artificial look of abandonment I created have worked to discourage further marauding. My garden is behind this wall. No one sees it but the sun. Later, I'll show you the partial glass roof that turns the space into a greenhouse in the winter."

Martin continued on to the west side of the building. His cabin sat one hundred feet further west from the server farm building. Thick dune grass grew knee-high, whispering in the wind. Darion saw two Adirondack chairs on a porch on the south side. The siding all around the windows looked scorched, like the south side of the bombed server farm building. Every other window was cross boarded with one-by-six-by-six-foot boards. It seemed the cabin had survived a fire.

"So, that is where we stay," Davion assumed.

"No," Martin said, "I use the porch, though."

Davion followed Martin along the bare west wall of the building to a small copse of eight-foot-tall white pine trees. Martin threaded his way through the branches to a clearing, where he stopped and picked up a turtle from the dune grass. Martin placed the turtle against the wall, turned the figurine counterclockwise, and an invisible door opened in the wall.

"Do you want to try it?" Martin handed the turtle to Davion. He could see the impressions in the wall where the turtle's feet fit. The rotating circle surrounding the indentations could not be made out from a foot away. Davion closed and then reopened the door. A vestibule and a closet served as a final barrier to the interior. The man and boy hung up their jackets. Martin unlocked another door, and Davion passed through, eyes widening at the elegance.

Davion stood in a wood structural shell built within the Warehouse metal-sided building. Beautifully finished tongue and groove cedar siding tinted with a blue semi-transparent stain covering the cathedral ceiling. Horizontal six-inch shiplap cedar painted white adorned the east and west opposing walls while the same stain as the floor colored the shiplap cedar on the north and south opposing walls. A free-standing wall separated the bedroom and the kitchen. Above the kitchen, a second bedroom, accessible via a ladder built into the bedroom partition, would serve as Davion's guest room. A Clerestory window on the south half wall in this bedroom looked out over the garden and let in plenty of light from Martin's illusory bombed-out garden area of the warehouse building. The five-inch plank maple tongue and groove flooring, stained to a rosewood color, polished and full of character knots and whorls, ran wall to wall in the forty-foot by sixteen-foot rectangular open space. An eight-foot sliding glass door in the south living room wall led to the garden. Another entry on the east wall presumably led to the vandalized racks and damaged server junk heaped in the interior of the larger building.

Davion noted a partitioned-off bathroom with a shower and toilet next to the vestibule. A door and stairs led down to the cold storage cellar and tunnel to the cabin and subbasement safe room. Otherwise, the space utilized an open floor plan. A sectional and two easy chairs defined the living room space where Martin stood. A queen bed in the far corner of the bedroom allowed garden views out through the kitchen and living room slider. On either side of the bed, ledges built into the wall served as nightstands. Above the bed, two shelves between the walls contained Martin's favorite books and novels yet to be tackled. A lounge chair for reading sat next to the bed. A long counter with a built-in sink occupied the center of the space. Anyone washing dishes at the sink looked out on the garden through the living room. In front of the counter, a brick heatilater wood burning fireplace provided heat. Martin had installed ductwork below the plank flooring that distributed warm air from the fireplace in the winter. The chimney pipe rose through the roof between the clerestory windows. A small two-top in front of the fireplace served as a dining table. Two large fans, one in the bedroom and one in the living space hung from the ceiling. A freestanding wall with base cabinets, wall cabinets, and a ten-foot countertop housed the oven with an induction stove top and refrigerator. The kitchen area completed the floor plan a few feet north of the living room.

The server farm building was undoubtedly full of surprises. Martin suggested Davion wander through his new home while he extracted a pound of ground venison from the refrigerator and sliced potatoes for French fries. Martin asked Davion to pick a large bowl of sweet cherries from the orchard for dessert.

"Did you get settled in up-ladder?" asked Martin as the two sat down to dinner.

"The view is fantastic up there," said Davion. "The hills in the distance you don't see in Day Town unless you travel east to the foothills and the militia compound."

"I call it the escarpment," said Martin, "The Mitten land becomes quite flat south of Hart."

"Why don't you fix up the cabin again?" Davion asked.

"Because marauders have wrecked it twice. I can take a hint. The cabin is my decoy now. My dad and I framed, plumbed, ran electrical, and finished the bungalow. There is a basement and a subbasement that Dad and I hid in for a few days after the Cataclysm. I stayed there on my own for two years. I heard the first horde pouring over the server farm building, breaking in, and busting solar panels on the roof. The server racks they tipped over sounded like thunderclaps and crackling lightning. I managed to dive into the subbasement. I did not make a sound for ten days.

"The horde departed, the dead strewn in the forest, on the shores of Big Lake, and even on the roof of the server farm building, pieces of glass jutting from necks and thighs.

"They were looking for food, of course. There was a minimum amount of food in the cabin and spoiled food in the office refrigerator in the server farm building, but of course, not enough to feed the thousands of rioters destroying the cities as they moved up the coast."

"I spent the next eight weeks cleaning up and restoring the cabin. Then, one morning I heard a rumble, a low murmur. I looked north and saw the horde again heading my way, stretched over two miles. I guess they were heading back to where they came from, as hopeless as that may be. When they passed through, the cabin fared much worse. It was as if they wanted to leave nothing of value behind that someone later might come along and put to some small use. They wanted everyone to live as miserably as themselves."

Davion knew nothing of life before the Cataclysm. Bones and skulls littered his life experience as a matter of course. The house where he now ate dinner seemed like a palace to him.

They chewed on cherries, spitting out ones containing a burrowed worm.

Martin shook his head, seeming to clear the memory of those times. "What about you? How did you and your mother get along."

"Mom told me I was born ten days before the disaster," said Davion. "I was just a baby. Mom never said much about that time. I know we lived on a farm outside of Day Town. Mom and Dad owned a goat and chickens and knew how to garden and raise sweet corn and wheat for flour."

"So, is your birthday June 20th?" asked Martin.

"I don't know," Davion said, "what's June?"

"June is the month you were born," said Martin. "There are twelve months in a year. As it happens, we may have the same birthday, June 20th.

"So, do you remember your father?"

Davion looked up to the ceiling and rubbed his chin. "I guess I don't," he said, "I think I must have been seven or eight when the militia came to our farm. I do remember that. I remember the two arrows sticking out of my father's back. He screamed and kept screaming, trying to claw at his back, lying face down in the dirt, my mother screaming as well. Screaming. I remember that."

"That must have been terrible, Davion," said Martin, "I'm sorry.""

"All I really remember is the screaming."

"Yes, but from what I have heard of the purge, it seems a miracle you survived that day."

"There were at least five of them," Davion said, eyes wetting, "Someone held me by the throat from behind. I could not see him but felt a knife point pressing on my chest. The five others attacked Mom.

"She kept yelling and watching the man that held me, telling him she would do whatever they wanted if they did not kill me.

"They didn't kill me. They pulled the arrows out of my dad and threw Mom across his body, blood everywhere. I know they raped her, finally covering her mouth with one hand to stop her pleading. They did not kill me.

"They took us both to the militia compound. As I grew older, I understood why. If you saw my mother, you would understand. She was the prize of the compound. If I had died, she would have killed herself. She may still, if I can't-"

Martin did not mention his encounter with the Day Town militia and Tamara Okoye. *Yes,* he thought, *she definitely had power over men.* Martin stood and put his hand on Davion's shoulder. "Enough talk," he said, "Let me show you the subbasement safe room. You'll see how I got along these many years."

The two descended the stairs to a vestibule and a door with a small window: the root cellar. A thermometer/hygrometer mounted on the wall indicated the root cellar temperature and humidity. Through the cold storage room window, Martin pointed out the shelves containing potatoes, parsnips, onions, garlic, sweet potatoes, and various squash varieties.

On the west wall of the vestibule, a door opened on a two-foot-deep closet. A clothes hanger bar stretched across the four-foot-wide storage space. Martin slid the coats hanging in the closet to one side of the wardrobe, pressed a concealed button on the door frame, and the back wall slid into a pocket. Behind the sliding panel, a hand cart on a rail track led off down the tunnel. A vertical angle iron welded to the cart rose to wire reinforced rope running overhead wrapped around a pulley. The cart itself measured three feet by eight feet, accommodating Martin and Davion and, if need be, any cargo they may need transporting to the subbasement and cabin. Martin pulled on the rope, and the cart started the one-hundred-foot journey to the cabin subbasement.

Once they arrived at the subbasement, Martin walked through the space, pointing out the study area and textbooks Davion would be scrutinizing to catch up on his education, which was nonexistent at the militia compound. When Martin came to the section on survival skills, he pulled the relevant books from the shelf and set them on the desk. He opened one book and told Davion to read the page out loud.

"I can't, Sir Martin," said Davion, "I don't remember. I understand the pictures."

Martin grabbed a children's book, *The Shy Stegosaurus*, from the shelf. "One of my favorites. See if you can work through it with me tonight before bed. I need you to be able to read and write the messages, danger signs, and maps we will use when your training is complete."

Davion nodded, and they continued the tour. They inspected the medicine closet.

"Case in point," Martin said, "If I'm down and need medical attention, you might need to fetch the right medication. You have to be able to read the labels, or you might kill me with the wrong item. Get it?"

Davion nodded again.

Next on the tour, Martin showed off his grocery store. Logan and Martin had planned for the foodstuffs on the shelves in this area to last the two of them ten years. After the Cataclysm, Martin understood the seriousness of the food situation. He conserved his food stores, figuring he could last thirty years on the canned and dry goods he and Logan had reserved. He replaced or added to his grocery store on trips to Graapids and other communities. With Davion in the house, the grocery store would be depleted twice as fast.

Martin pointed to his supply of toilet paper, "Go easy on it. It's a luxury," he emphasized.

The workbench wall came next with its impressive array of hand tools, clamps, and saws.

Finally, Martin came to the weapons wall. Thirty bows and crossbows hung unstrung on the wall. The rack upon rack of store-bought hunting and target arrows made of aluminum cores wrapped with carbon fiber outer jackets impressed Davion with their beauty. Cabinets stored fletches, razor-sharp points, nocks, arm guards, and finger guards. The foot-pedal-powered lathe could turn wooden arrow shafts when needed. A fletching jig attached to the workbench held an arrow shaft ready for feather gluing.

"When you lose an arrow," Martin said, "don't go to bed until you come here and make a replacement."

Martin asked Davion to stretch his arms out from his sides. Martin measured from Davion's left fingertip to the right. Then he selected one of the recurve bows, strung it, and taught Davion how to pull the string to his chin.

Unsatisfied, Martin grabbed a second bow from the rack, strung it, and Davion repeated his pull position. "That's the right length and pull weight," Martin said. Next year you will likely be able to use that first bow. For now, I do not want to see this one more than five feet away from you at all times, day or night."

The archery instructor handed his student a field quiver and filled it with a dozen target arrows.

"Tomorrow, rain or shine, we start."

"Sir Martin," Davion said, "What will you be doing?"

"I'll practice for two hours every day right with you," Martin replied.

Six weeks passed before Davion lost an arrow he and Martin could not find. They spent an hour looking. It had probably found its way into a chipmunk burrow, buried beyond the nock.

Martin found Davion to be a pleasant student, absorbing everything Martin presented like a natural sponge. At the compound, any disobedience courted a severe beating. Davion followed orders. His mother had taught Davion to respect their dangerous captors. As Davion made his way, the agony his mother put up with kept his stomach in constant churn.

Tamara hugged and reassured Davion when he was a small child when they were alone. She never spoke of the weight of despair their situation engendered. As he grew, Davion looked to his mother's strength, able to tolerate the injustice his mother experienced daily by becoming strong in his skin.

At night when their cabin door creaked open, and a soldier or two crossed to his mother's bed, the boy wrapped his blanket around his head and turned toward the wall. The men's final grunts or yells penetrated Davion's blanket muffler. He waited for the door to creak again before straightening his blanket, feigning sleep until he heard regulated breathing from his sleeping mother. She never made a sound when the men were in the room.

Tamara never talked about their condition, ever. Instead, she informed Davion of his ancestors, his father's good nature, his grandparent's farm, and hard work. She aspired to give Davion hope, and she always spoke optimistically. They kept each other optimistic, and as Davion grew, they complimented each other in that strength.

When Davion met Sir Martin, he began to see a man whose nature seemed totally at odds with the soldiers and officers at the militia compound. Davion's need to rescue his mother drove an obsessive work and learning ethic every waking minute.

Martin admired Davion's drive for one so young. The look in Davion's eyes during martial arts instruction, archery practice, and survival training never lost focus. At times Davion's intensity frightened Martin. Tamara had raised a son that Martin could respect. Davion's reading and writing abilities progressed rapidly. Martin used the novels on his wall to stimulate Davion's imagination and an expectation for a better world than he had thus far known.

The more Davion told Martin about his mother, the beautiful long-legged black beauty he had seen through his binoculars, the more she grew in stature in his estimation.

Tamara had run competitive marathons in college, thus the legs. She raised a child in the most unimaginably terrible situation, yet Davion did not spit hate, only quiet determination to provide a better life for his mother.

Martin joined Davion's quest to rescue Tamara and others at the compound. He found in Davion companionship from the loneliness he kept at bay out of necessity in his Independent lifestyle. Martin had to acknowledge the toll isolation took on his own psyche. When he met a fellow Independent on the road, the hello words he croaked out sounded foreign and strange to his own ears. It may be months before he hears another human voice in winter.

On a late fall day, Martin looked at the boy eating dinner across the table and decided he could handle the next advancement in his training. More intensity, more challenging goals, and expert skills. After Davion went to bed, Martin read in his bedroom for a while. He broke off from reading at the end of the chapter. *Yes,* he mused, *companionship had been worth the risk. This time.*

Six years ago, the last time, in 2057, Martin was not so sure.

****

He thought, *"Face your own self, Martin; you are lonely as hell.* Martin walked along Old 31 from Kazoo. There he had found a ransacked sporting goods store. The store had no armaments, but

Martin discovered a door and stairway to the basement where an extra stock of arrow parts and Dacron bow strings had been overlooked. His backpack packed, his bow in his left hand as he walked, arrow nocked; he walked at the edge of the gully twenty feet from the highway. He had scoured the deserted Kazoo area without meeting another soul. Up ahead, someone waved to him.

Upon approach, Martin found a slim, shapely woman who must have crossed the highway from a parallel road to the east. She did not know the sign of the Independent. A sweep of the open landscape on both sides of the highway assured Martin that the woman traveled alone. He stopped an unsocial ten-foot distance from the woman holding out her hands to show she had no weapons.

"Hello," Martin said, "I will put down my bow if you turn around for me to see if you are armed."

As the woman turned, Martin noted a sheath attached to her belt in the center of her back, holding a long stiletto.

Martin reached down and unsheathed his own knife from his ankle. "Hold it right there," he said. "Shall we both place our weapons on the ground? What is it you want?"

The woman reached behind, extracted the knife from the sheath, and laid it two feet from where she stood on the ground. Then she turned to face Martin.

He thought *this woman was the stupidest person he had met since the Cataclysm*. She was one of only three women he had spoken to since then. Now she stood unprotected before a man who might overpower her at a moment's notice. Unless her skill in hand-to-hand combat exceeded Martin's, she would be helpless in seconds.

The woman wore jeans and heavy boots. The top two buttons of her brown corduroy shirt were missing. Nice cleavage. Her yellow nylon jacket would do nothing to keep her warm on even a mild night. It would, however, draw immediate attention while traveling on the highway. Thus, Martin had spotted her. The more he looked the woman over, the more temptation burned in him.

"I'm hungry, of course," said the woman with green eyes. She seemed to be Martin's age or a bit older. "My name is Constance Gilman. Call me Connie."

"I have a bit of food to share," said Martin. He dug out his bread and a can of spam.

They headed north together, neither asking where they were heading. In four hours of walking, Connie chattered the entire time, while Martin remained quiet for the most part. He liked the sound of her voice, any voice for that matter. Martin listened intently and nodded, showing interest so she would continue talking. He had a comfort level with Connie he had not known could be possible in the new world. He kept working his odds out in his head as they walked.

By the time they reached the cut-off to the server farm building, he had decided the odds were in his favor.

"I have a warm shower," Martin said, "and an extra bed, and a great meal lined up at home, if you want to see it.

"Well, I may not stay," Said Connie, "but I would like to see your place."

Martin's dwelling within the Server Farm building had unfinished stud walls and a particle board subfloor. The kitchen functioned, and the fireplace worked if needed. Martin politely locked his bow, knife, and Connie's stiletto in a closet. The conversation centered on pre-cataclysmic times and events. Nostalgic and comfortable, two lonely souls, now sitting close together, drinking wine, and talking about their parents and siblings. Connie had a brother out in the wild she had not seen since the Cataclysm. Martin spoke of his father.

The wine bottle was empty. Martin accompanied Connie up the ladder to the loft. They said good night, and Connie hugged Martin in thanks for his hospitality.

An hour later, Connie entered the bedroom and stood at the foot of Martin's bed. She wore only her shirt. "Couldn't sleep," she said. "I'm cold, lonely, and horny as fucking hell."

"Connie, I can warm you and keep you company," said Martin. "I'm ready to explode."

Martin held the bedspread back while Connie unbuttoned her shirt and threw it on the chair. Martin drank in every curve, muscle, breast, and thatch, trying to find a flaw. Not possible. The couple made love as if they were the last two people on earth. Martin scarcely let her rest before ravaging Connie again as if she were the first woman on earth. She responded, and while shuddering, Martin rose up and joined her orgasm.

Minutes later, Connie shook Martin's shoulder, "I'm heading back to the other bed. I will sleep now."

Martin thought about objecting but discarded the prospect of cuddling in the crooks and crannies of the woman, staying in contact with her soft skin. *Take it slow,* he thought.

Martin woke up at dawn. He planned on milking the goat, gathering eggs from his chicken coop, and making breakfast for the soft-skinned woman asleep in the loft. Martin climbed the loft ladder to view a woman sleeping under his roof. If she woke up, he could ask about her favorite breakfast, scrambled, poached, or an omelet.

The empty bed alarmed him. A search of the house, a look in the garden, and leaning out the turtle door convinced Martin she had left. *Why?*

Martin ticked off the possibilities:

- She did not like him, politely leaving an awkward situation.
- She did not wish to become entangled.
- She did not want to be tied down.

But the overriding reason, the dangerous one that spurred Martin to action:

- She now knew about his estate and could report the information.

Martin dressed, gathered his bow and quiver, filled his water bottles, threw on his backpack, and started following the swished-down path of dune grass leading southeast.

He could not estimate how much of a head start he needed to overcome. Martin stopped at the side of the highway a half hour later. He noticed that Connie's left boot impression in the soft ground of the gully revealed a worn edge along the first inch of the heel.

The pavement ended the possibility of finding additional tracks. Martin headed south, back the way the couple had traveled the day before, watching the east side for evidence of the woman's travel. Luckily, he found such evidence twenty minutes later. Another path through a field again heading southeast over the escarpment. Easy to follow. Martin started off on the run.

Perhaps he could convince Connie to return with him, he thought. He hardly knew her, but the thought of her rigid pectoral muscles leading to those soft pear breasts and jutting nipples washed in and out of his thoughts as he trotted. They had talked. He could almost hear her voice, the accent, southern?

An hour later, he came to a wide trail leading due east/west: no visible tracks. He took off at a jog, watching both sides of the path for her cutoff. The farther he followed, the angrier he became. *She should have been man enough to tell him of her displeasure.*

There, he thought, *the boot marks heading south into the woods.* A narrow, barely used path. Martin followed on the run. Then he spotted the yellow jacket, one hundred feet ahead, approaching a clearing in the woods. Aghast, he saw a militia scouting party eating breakfast around a campfire. Seven men were identified by their colorful armbands and the crossbows propped against the logs they sat on. Connie stopped fifty feet short of the clearing and hailed the group. One man stood and moved to greet her. They kissed briefly, and Connie pulled the man by the elbow back into the privacy of the woods forty feet from the fire.

The two ardently tussled briefly before Connie broke apart and began her story. Martin's heart hardened. He estimated his distance to the couple at thirty-five feet. He checked the wind, closed his eyes to settle, then drew to a point, aiming for the traitor. Simple shot.

Martin relaxed his pull and knelt in the forest undergrowth. He could not do it. His father's mantra about survival came to mind. He remembered each moment of the four years he spent building a safe haven. Martin's hands shook as he recalled the woman's betrayal.

God damn it. God damn it. He breathed deeply. His hand stopped shaking as he stood and brought his arrow to point. The woman in yellow had turned and pointed in the general direction of Martin's home. Martin could not understand their words, but he heard their laughter.

His arrow pierced the woman's neck and tipped her away to her right, blood erupting. The man, shocked, caught her fall, lowering her to the ground. He recognized danger but instinctively stood to get his bearings, attempting, perhaps, to determine the origination of the arrow. Mistake. Martin's second arrow struck through the man's heart, and Martin was already off and running. No sound had broken the forest's quiet except the soft whistle of an arrow's flight and the thud when it found flesh.

Now he ran a zig-zag pattern through the woods. He recalled the often-experienced nightmare of running away from the horde, waiting for a spear to sail through the air behind him, and waking in a sweat just as the point touched his back. This time it would be a crossbow shaft.

An hour passed, and his heavy, sweaty clothes chafed his sides and crotch. He proceeded at a slow jog with labored breathing. He dared not stop. If he could make it to Lud Town, perhaps he could lose the militia scouts in the burned wreckage of the buildings and streets. He dared not go directly home.

Martin made it via a circuitous route through Lud Town to the beach and the break wall and lighthouse with the broken off top. He hung his bow across his neck and under his arm, stuffed his shirt into his quiver to avoid losing arrows, and breast stroked across the channel to the sand beach on the opposite shore. Martin walked from the beach to the power reservoir and home. As he stripped for a shower, he began shaking and threw up in the toilet. He used every drop of his precious hot water to calm the pinpricks and shakes.

****

Martin and Davion had adequately prepared for the coming winter. Vegetable harvest completed, the glass ceiling hand-cranked to cover the garden, and greenhouse plants seeded. Tomatoes stewed, and bottled, potatoes filled the root cellar, along with parsnips, squash, and sweet corn. There were enough chickens to meet their winter needs. Plenty of deer around; the cars did not cull the herds anymore. Trees had been cut, the logs sawn, split, and stacked to dry along the north side of Martin's home inside the server farm building. The already dried logs from the previous year were restacked near the garden's edge, within reach of the slider.

Winter comes early, close to Big Lake. Typically, wet and cold, Martin and Davion kept practicing. Martin emphasized the need to control accurate shots under extreme conditions, freezing hands, rain dripping in eyes, snot thumb-blown and wiped away, and concentration imperative.

Martin attached the eight-inch weighted foam ball to the clothesline cord, wrapping the other end around a tree branch twenty feet off the ground. After climbing down, Martin stepped off twenty paces and instructed Davion to swing the ball to form a pendulum in the target range. Martin timed the swing in his head and shot the foam ball as it crossed the center point of its swing. He notched a second arrow and followed the swing of the foam ball as it arced toward Davion, again hitting the moving target.

"That's your next goal," Martin said. "On a stationary target, you are my equal, ten for ten at twenty, thirty, and fifty feet. When you can match me on a moving target, we will go find your mother."

Davion spent the day trying to hit the moving foam ball, missing it every time. During the next week of practice, Davion hit the moving target three times. Many days his hands were frostbitten after two shots. Davion never complained. He blew on his hands between arrows and continued. Martin held his hands over a fire waiting for his turn. They would trade places, and Martin would practice; he missed very few attempts.

After a lunch break, the two would venture back outside for more combat training in brutal conditions. At this point in Davion's training, his moves and balance equaled Martin's. He just needed to grow into his skills.

Winter seemed conducive to relaxing at night, listening to the crackle/snap of the fire, and playing games. Card games included pinochle, gin rummy, and double solitaire. Davion learned how to play checkers and then chess. They worked on one-thousand-piece puzzles, which Martin had put together often on his own.

Some nights they moved the table aside, brought over the easy chairs, sat by the fire and talked. Martin opened up about his fears for his father. There might be a chance the militia officers at the compound that imprisoned Tamara might know of his father.

Davion kept asking about Martin's estate.

"Where did you find the wood to build this place," he asked, "How did you get it here? How did you reach the peak to put the ceiling in?"

Martin put off his explanation week after week. One night, he pulled out his building journal, reviewed his timeline, and spread his journal and drawings on the table.

"At the beginning, I guess I did nothing. I stayed in the subbasement. As I mentioned, the first horde wave came through, heading north, wrecking the cabin. When the tens of thousands of men, women, and for a while, children moved north from the cities in the south of the state, they ran out of steam at the northernmost point of Big Lake and turned back. I had heard the wrecking power of the rioters moving north, but I only saw through the subbasement's periscope window. When the thinned-out horde returned from the north, I saw them and barely reached the subbasement and safety.

"For two years after that, I lived in constant fear. I could not think beyond staying hidden and safe in the subbasement. I bet my skin looked as white as clean sheets, dangerously anemic. Then the second horde came. They were more scattered than the first horde. Two hundred ragged people came through, then none for a day and then seven hundred, then nothing for two days, then five hundred. Always different size groups. Sometimes two groups would meet, and the fighting left bodies scattered on the highway. I searched the pockets of many bodies in between the waves of people. This horde had traveled up from Chi-Town, Indian Polis, and other places, including Day Town. The crowd consisted of truly diverse factions. More people of color than I had ever seen in my life.

"Then the militia came on the heels of the horde. There were only three or four hundred soldiers, but many were on horseback. The cavalry carried swords and beheaded, trampled, or sliced those in their way. The foot soldiers carried crossbows, killing anything in their path, targeting black men. The horde thought to escape over the long bridge up north, but the mammoth, dynamited section of the bridge a quarter of a mile offshore stymied that. Escape meant a swim across cold, dangerous waters and death by drowning. Those that turned back met the militia head-on with perhaps hammers and crowbars for weapons. More death, more bodies. Black women were corralled, raped, and prized.

"The Cataclysm created terrible turmoil. People had become dependent on the drug of fast food, cell phone, social media escape, and computers. A few controlled the many, from traffic and air control to energy management and cheap overseas goods. A few lived a rich, easy life; the many scraped by.

"A disaster of this magnitude illuminated the decaying social structure and polarization of the world's societies. It only took a year or two before groups turned on other groups. Mobs formed, ogres, trolls, and bandits became commonplace.

"In short, humanity lost to barbarism.

"Hundreds of millions died of hunger. Billions, I suspect, died from murder, cannibalism, and the color of their skin."

Martin stared into the fire, lost in the red glow of the cinders. An ache in his chest over the demise of the world. A former world that Davion would never know.

"You don't have much hope for us, do you, Sir Martin," said Davion.

"On the contrary," Martin replied, "When I look at you, I hope with every cell that our future will be bright. That is why I finally got off the couch, put down my books, stopped being afraid, and began planning.

"Let us leave this on the table. Tomorrow you will see what one man can accomplish, even without a McDonalds every five miles."

"What's McDonalds, Sir Martin?" asked Davion.

"Ancient history, Davion, ancient history. Not something you will need to learn."

The next evening, while Martin prepared dinner, Davion examined Martin's drawings and thumbed through the journal.

Martin saw the militia heading back south from a high branch in a three-foot-thick oak tree in the middle of the apple orchard. Even the militia seemed forlorn now, disheveled, slogging along without purpose. The purge could not be sustained. No one left to kill.

On a whim, Martin counted more than a hundred bodies strewn about in his field of vision. He stopped counting. Two days passed after the last of the groups of militia stragglers passed through the orchards. *It is probably over,* he thought. Martin went back to the subbasement and continued with his plan.

He had burned out at about the same time the militia appeared again, heading south, back to their base, wherever that might be. *Sick of this shit,* he remembered thinking. *I am through with this basement.*

Martin figured there were now very few survivors within a fifty square mile area. Survivors were so scattered that they would not be worth even a militia scouting party to find. His chances for survival after the purge had improved. Martin figured the probability of him being discovered might be 1 in 10,000. Still, he remained cautious. He spent an hour every morning scanning his vistas with binoculars for stragglers.

To live above ground, in the light of the new world, Martin sought to make his existence as invisible as possible. That meant creating an environment that looked not worth the bother. No food here, nothing of value, no warmth, no hospitality.

Martin drew up a map of his proposed estate, the orchards, the server farm building, the cabin, and the immense pump storage reservoir. He decided he would not build fences. A fence is an invitation. There must be something of value on the other side. No, he would not create a wall. He would invite cursory scrutiny of a burned-out building and cabin. He came up with the idea of a home encased by the half-demolished server farm building. The server warehouse could scarcely be glimpsed from the highway, and its proximity to the Pump Storage Reservoir would provide a source of nearly unlimited water. The fields from the road to the building left unplowed and unmanicured, had succumbed to invasive Russian Olive, the thorny branches providing a partial barrier and a definite discouragement to exploration.

Graffiti seemed an appropriate disguise for the server farm building. Vandals and spray paint went hand in hand. Artists would move on after their graphics were finished. If done right, the building would look totally abandoned.

The graffiti idea helped generate the rest of the details for the creation of Martin's invisible home.

Home, what should that look like. What should it involve? How could he best live? Martin took a step back to understand his goals and the complete picture.

Sustainability meant not starving. Isolation engendered safety. Comfort, where possible. These were the three maxims he wished to live by, at least until the crazy world of the Cataclysm righted itself and people became human again. Based on his experience so far, Martin estimated the age of sanity might be decades away.

An assessment of the server farm building established that just three fifty-foot-long rows of server racks had not been pulled down. The generators running the backup uninterruptable power supplies lasted three days, but the servers did not work even when they had backup power. The SO1 microprocessors shut down the computational capability of the motherboards. Rusting racks, smashed servers, and broken motherboards littered the floor everywhere.

The labs on either end of the building had not fared any better. Many of the windows were smashed out. Chairs thrown through windows must have been a favorite game. Damaged equipment clogged the floor between the lab tables. The darkened windows of the clean room that housed the scanning probe microscope had somehow avoided destruction. Martin could not tell if the microscope had been destroyed or not. It looked intact. Although not operable, the automatic sliding glass doors leading to the clean room had been overlooked by both hordes, offering possibilities.

The exterior of the building consisted of concrete blocks up to fifteen feet. Corrugated steel siding ran vertically from the top of the block to the roof. The siding on the building's east, west, and north sides remained intact.

Martin recalled the night of the explosions. Following the 2nd horde invasion, the militia placed dynamite on top of the block of the

[316]

south face of the server farm building. The ensuing blast blew a forty-foot-wide hole above the block wall up and through the roof. Thinking there may be horde members huddling inside, the militia threw another bundle of dynamite into the space. This charge ripped a forty-foot by thirty-foot jagged hole in the concrete floor and killed no one. Martin felt the tremor in the subbasement as he played solitaire, hoping the rioters would not find him tucked away in his secret lair.

The somewhat bent but still usable extension ladder lying near the maintenance room in the southeast corner allowed Martin access to the roof. Again, out of one hundred fifty solar panels that Logan had installed to supplement the electrical usage of the servers in the farm, only forty-three survived undamaged. Logan had installed the silver-carbon battery packs for the solar system in the vestibule outside the subbasement just before the Cataclysm. They still operated, although Martin needed to put them to use. He took the time to consolidate the functional panels, leaving a broken plate or two in between to disguise the importance of the ones that worked. He rewired the working panels, checked the inverter and controller in the subbasement, and monitored the charging of the batteries. The system would supply enough AC electrical power for his conservative requirements at full charge.

For the first time since the Cataclysm, the two-element induction cooktop and steam/convection oven installed in the subbasement kitchenette operated. Martin's LED lights could again supplement the periscope light shaft allowing nighttime reading time.

Living off canned and freeze-dried food would continue as he developed a self-sufficient food supply. Isolation became an even stricter mantra for venturing into the outer world; Martin's bow and arrows provided security.

He relocated the free-standing wood-burning fireplace from the cabin to his new home for comfort. He ran a pipe from the reservoir to procure gravity-fed fresh water to the new house. He calculated the amount of electricity he could generate and store with the remaining solar panels and battery packs. He reinstalled the small refrigerator/freezer, the induction cooktop, and the steam/convection oven from the subbasement in the new home.

Three solar panels would be used for on-demand hot water for the shower. A small supplemental tank on top of the walk-in shower could be filled with water heated on the wood stove during sustained cloudy days and the bitter winters of Butters, Lakeshore.

Someday he would erect a wind turbine on the bank of the pump storage reservoir to harness the great wind from Big Lake for more power options.

It would be simple to hook the new house sewer system to the existing waste system and septic tank used by the server farm building. The hand crank washing machine would also move over from the subbasement. Led lighting and natural light would be part of the design. Two-by-six studs would accommodate loads of insulation to help minimize the home's heat loss and increase efficiency.

Martin worked out some rough sketches of the space, minimizing energy usage by compacting the living area. Living off-grid would demand compromise, no clothes dryer, hair drier, TV, radio, etc. Many of the conveniences of his teenage years would be abandoned. Still, he would live in relative Cataclysmic comfort with proper planning and building techniques.

To build, Martin needed to first demolish. He destroyed the drywalled partitions in the north and south laboratories with a crowbar and claw hammer. After stripping off the drywall, Martin attacked the stud walls. He banged the top plate off all the walls, knocked the studs off the bottom plate, and used the crowbar to pry the bottom plate loose from the ramset attachment to the floor. Martin denuded all the wood of drywall screws and tenpenny nails, stacking all the studs among broken server racks. He salvaged the sliding glass door panels from the clean room. The horde attacks had also spared eight three-foot square framed glass windows. Martin set those aside as well. He left the rest of the mess in place: the broken equipment, chairs, busted-up desks, scattered drywall pieces, broken server racks, and motherboards. The site looked like the beginning of a city construction dump.

The bombed area of the concrete floor did need to be cleared. Martin decided to try and locate a few more basic tools, a wheelbarrow, pulleys, rope, fresh tenpenny nails and paint for the graffiti. With his bow in hand, quiver on his hip, and backpack empty except for a water bottle and snack, he set off on his first trip to Lud Town. Martin arrived in town at dawn. He saw no one.

The hardware store had been ransacked and stripped of just about everything functional. Martin did find a spare wheelbarrow wheel in the rubble. Out of a small barrel of rusting bulk tenpenny nails, Martin threw several handfuls into his backpack. From the Sherwin-Williams store down the way, Martin found plenty of paint. Many paint cans littered the floor, and vandals had opened many of the cans and splashed the walls and floors with a kaleidoscope of colors. He could only carry two-gallon cans in his backpack and three cans of spray paint.

Over the next two weeks, Martin made many more trips to town to bring back more paint, and scrounged tools, arriving at the server farm building by nine o'clock in the morning. He had not seen a soul. Martin built a wheelbarrow using the wheel and cleared more of the concrete away from his future garden area. He would garden around the large pieces he could not move. He retrieved soil from a low-lying area south of the cherry orchard and filled and leveled the dynamited hole.

Logan had foreseen the need for a sustainable garden and stocked the subbasement with various seeds. About a mile away, across the highway, Martin visited one of the larger farms in the county, now abandoned. In a closet in the farm office, he located enough seed varieties to supplement his own seed store for many years. He brought the seed packets to the server farm building to store in the subbasement.

Before planting his garden, Martin journeyed to the Home Depot store in Lud Town. Almost everything in the store had been plundered. Some items had been challenging to pick up and run off with. Two people could carry off a stove/oven combination, but the refrigerators were tough to move without an operable pickup truck. The same held true for many of the construction supplies. Panicked rioters had grabbed the easy items, destroying other things out of frustration. Martin found enough particle board and plywood sheets to sheath his house. He just needed to get them back to his site.

[319]

He did find a roll of 1-1/4" potable poly pipe light enough in weight to carry home, along with fittings for his irrigation system. He squirreled away rolls of red and blue PEX pipe and all the proper fittings and PVC pipe, glue, and fittings for his home's sanitary system. He hid his supplies under a tarp in a dark corner of the store. He would return for these supplies later in his building process.

Martin ran the flexible poly pipe from the pump storage reservoir down the hill to the server farm building and buried it three feet in the sandy soil. Three feet below the lip of the pool, he dug down and drilled through the asphalt/clay, threading the poly pipe into the water and sealing the opening around the pipe. The eighty-foot drop from the reservoir to the server farm building made for a near-perfect gravity-feed freshwater system to the garden and the reverse osmosis filter for cooking, drinking, and showering.

No strangers had wandered in range of Martin's arrows. In fact, he had not seen anyone for over six and a half months since the militia marched south. He began to feel he had the territory to himself. The stench of the hundreds of corpses had subsided. Just as he left the demolished building alone, he left the bodies to the crows and raccoons. The bones and skulls would serve as additional deterrents to uninvited guests.

With the garden coming along, Martin built an eighteen-foot tall, eight-foot by three-foot-wide scaffold that he could easily dismantle and move along the east wall of the warehouse. He projected his grid points on the building and painted an orchard scene. Martin finished the orchard story in five weeks and laid out the lighthouse scene's grid points. From the top of a rise halfway to the highway, he inspected his orchard scene with approval. A mix of realism with abstract giant green, red, and brown apples. Martin appreciated his accomplishment and suntan, much preferred over the anemia he had suffered during his years in the subbasement.

It took six weeks to finish a lighthouse scene with a broken-off top. Martin felt confident at that point in tackling a picture of Logan and his mother on the beach. While he worked on it up close, the painting consisted of lines, curves, and colors. In late October, with the scene completed, he stood on the hillcrest and cried. It was like his parents had come for a visit. His mother's sun-bleached brown hair flowing in the wind created a lump in his chest. Martin did not often cry in his lonely world, but on this day and future days when he wanted company, he would walk to the rise and visit his giant parents.

Yet he continued to paint. For three more weeks, Martin used black and dark brown paint to deconstruct the prettiness of the scenes he had created by applying giant glyphs, paint splotches, and abstract symbols. He used his propane torch to scorch large areas of the exterior and interior walls on all sides. The building exuded a look of disrepair, decay, and abandonment. Success!

The garden grew so well that Martin decided it needed further disguising. The dynamited hole on the south side of the building began at a height of ten feet. Martin scavenged pieces of the rebar strewn about the gap, positioning them in hollows of the broken blocks' tops and cementing them vertically. The owners of the large farm where he had found the vegetable seeds had held off the first horde with helical razor wire and pitchforks.

After many bloody scratches carrying a roll of the barbed tape home, Martin installed it along the top of the jagged block. He attached the dangerous material to the jutting rebar. He could not see over the broken wall from the ground, and a climber would have to contend with the wire to investigate further.

The garden produced potatoes, carrots, onions, beets, and parsnips for his root cellar. Bicolor white and yellow corn graced his table. He bottled stewed tomatoes, green beans, and zucchini.

Martin finished chopping, sawing, and splitting the wood he needed for the cold winter months, stacking it all in the subbasement.

The snow in December found Martin ready to meet the challenge of the winter months better than at any time since Cataclysm Day. He still ventured outside to keep his archery aim sharp. Martin hunted abundant deer and wild turkey. He exercised on the elliptical bike and lifted free weights to stay in shape.

Martin anticipated beginning construction on his new home within the server farm building in the spring. As the snow deepened, he had time to plan, spending weeks at his drafting board creating working drawings from his crude sketches. Using the scaled detailed floor plans and elevations, he worked out a material takeoff, listing in detail the required lumber, sheathing, and finishing supplies.

The new house, though small, would be a more significant challenge than the cabin for two reasons. Materials were scarce and could not be dropped off by a supplier. Martin would need to trek everything to the site. Logan and he had built the cabin together. This time, Martin had to do everything alone. Building a house with two workers took considerable thought regarding safely placing roof trusses, applying the sheathing, etc. Logan and Martin had used a block and tackle to set parts of the roof structure of the cabin. Martin wanted to find one other such device to simulate Logan's help.

Doing all the necessary tasks alone meant planning in even greater detail. Martin had completed all the necessary building tasks on the cabin with his father. All the tasks to build his new home would need even more careful planning. He would take complex processes one baby step at a time. If Martin lost control of something heavy or fell from a high point, no one would tend to the resulting injury.

Martin traveled his territory with the material takeoff, noting the materials he found and their locations. He had stashed many essential materials under a tarp at Home Depot. He listed the paint store as another resource. His most exciting find involved two luxury lakeshore home construction sites that had just finished framing at the time of the disaster. The residences had been started by a contractor and were in staggered stages of completion. At one site, he found a stack of tarp-covered drywall. Three inches all around the edges of the pile were soaked. Martin would cut off those areas and use the good leftovers for interior walls. The second site had a stack of plywood sheathing and enough 2-1/2"x11-7/8" by twenty-foot-long engineered wood I-beams to use as floor and roof joists. The two construction sites were less than a quarter mile from the reservoir and at the same elevation above Big Lake. Transportable.

Now that snow blanketed the highway and roads in Lud Town, Martin figured a sled would efficiently get needed materials to his site. The sled he built could hold a four-by-eight sheet of plywood. The evening of the next fluffy snowfall, Martin pulled his sled to one of the residential construction sites, stacked three drywall sheets on the sled, and dragged it home. Since the contractor building sites were close in elevation to the server farm building, Martin skirted around the north side of the reservoir and made it home, bathed in sweat. He made ten more similar trips with drywall and another twenty with plywood sheets. He built a special jig to prop up the twenty-foot-long I-beams on the sled. Martin used the wheel from the wheelbarrow attached to the dragging end of the I-beams to bring four joists to the site at a time. During a snow shower, he transported material with the sled; his tracks, sled runners, and wheel rut were covered with new snow as he trekked.

By the middle of March, Martin had stored all the materials off his list in the server farm building. In the quiet of the dawning day on the 18th of March 2056, Martin hand-ramset the baseplate perimeter of his new home on the concrete floor. The frame became a forty-foot by sixteen-foot rectangle.

His plan called for an eighteen-inch insulated crawl space. He built the crawl space wall sections and nailed them to the baseplate. The whole time he worked on the crawlspace, Martin fretted over the noise he made, attracting too much attention with the echo reaching across the field toward the highway. He decided to switch from hand-nailing tenpenny nails to three-inch deck screws and his cordless drill and impact driver to build the house frame.

The four 18v lithium-ion battery packs hold a day's worth of working cordless tool charge. The lithium-ion battery packs can be recharged at night via the silver-carbon battery array in the subbasement vestibule. Martin's and Logan's cordless tools included a circular saw, reciprocating saw, impact driver, and drill. The impact driver and drill motor were much quieter than a hammer and nails and could not be heard outside the server farm building.

Martin laid the I-Beams on sixteen-inch centers across the sixteen-foot span. He attached the rim board to the ends of the I-beams and then laid down the plywood floor sheathing.

A double wall on top of the sheathed floor took advantage of the abundant two-by-four studs recovered from the laboratories. By staggering the two four-inch walls on a two-by-six-inch plate, more insulation could be put in the wall. The break between the two sides from the inside to the outside world soundproofed the house. The west wall of his home abutted the west wall of the server farm building, so he kept that wall simple. He would fill the gap between the two walls full of insulation. After the perimeter walls were completed, Martin used turnbuckles and steel wire to tie the two side walls together.

As the structure stretched upward, Martin began using his block and tackles to hoist material in position. He erected his scaffolding on the structure's interior so that he could stand and adjust the I-beam rafters. He built the second-floor pitched sidewalls for the east and west elevations. The lone carpenter fastened a post within each side wall to hold a doubled wood composite I-beam along the peak between the framed slanted sides. Again, using the block and tackle, Martin attached I-beam rafters 24" o.c. over the double I-beam angled down at an approximate 6" in 12" slant to the south wall of the house's first floor. Plywood sheathing screwed to the rafters completed more than half of the roof.

Next, Martin built a knee wall across the top of the I-beam rafters to accommodate twelve feet of framing for four-foot by three-foot-tall clerestory windows from the laboratory wreckage. More I-beam rafters were laid in a steep run from the top of the knee wall down to the house's north wall over the future bedroom. Interior stud walls enclosed the bathroom and separated the kitchen from the bedroom.

According to the house plans, the electrician (Martin) ran Romex in the walls, floors, and ceiling. The HVAC ducts were run in the crawl space from the center of the home to the two future registers in the bedroom and two in the living room. The ductwork would connect to heatilater ports after the installation of the fireplace. Martin rough-plumbed the PVC pipe for the bathroom, kitchen, and vent through the roof sheathing. He ran the water supply PEX blue and red flexible tubing.

With the framing complete, Martin sheathed the exterior walls with plywood on the outside and drywall up to a height of seven feet on the inside. He left a foot of the perimeter wall open for filling with insulation. Martin completed the rough framing and rough utility installation in mid-November. He installed the eight-foot sliding glass door that looked out into the garden. With the clerestory windows installed, the house became enclosed.

Winter would be at Martin's doorstep soon. He spent three weeks preparing for the cold weather. The wood for the fireplace in the subbasement needed to be chopped, sawed, split, and stacked. The root cellar required tending.

With the winter preparation tasks complete, Martin began to strip the corrugated steel siding from random areas of the west exterior wall of the server farm building. He used the rusting steel sheets to cover the plywood sheathing on three sides, camouflaging his new home.

In the darkened interior of the server farm building, the house looked like an extension of the warehouse, dirty, rusting, and not worth investigating. Martin enhanced the effect by piling wrecked server racks, concrete chunks, tree limbs, weeds, and motherboards against the house's exterior walls. He threw large branches on the roof of his home as well. Even in the daytime, the interior of the server farm building seemed intimidating and treasureless.

Beautiful, Martin thought.

Martin worked all through a frigid winter on the house. He installed four stairs from the vestibule up to the main floor. He found a building supply warehouse in Hart that the hordes had missed entirely. Martin piled eight bags of cellulose insulation on his sled and hauled them back to his house, a two-day trip in subzero cold. A second trip three days later completed his acquisition of insulation. The warehouse also contained shiplap siding and five-inch plank maple tongue and groove flooring, prestained. When he discovered the beautiful rosewood-colored flooring, Martin did a little jig in the warehouse. After four more two-day trips, Martin had enough siding to cover the house's interior and floor.

Martin shoveled cellulose into the walls and crawl space while the siding and flooring acclimated to the house's interior. Then he patched the walls with drywall.

Using the scaffolding, Martin installed the shiplap siding across the I-beam rafters to form the ceiling, filling the twelve-inch cavity with cellulose as he progressed. The floor came next. Martin hand-hammered the floor along the tongue with hardwood floor nails. He slammed the grooved side of the next piece tight to the last plank and continued nailing.

In the end, Martin calculated he had hand-hammered over 22,000 nails into the first floor and loft: all in the quiet of his soundproof home. Shiplap siding covered the drywall.

Spring weather came early. Martin spent the first warm day outside in the sun. He sat down at his favorite hillcrest and saluted his mother's and father's billboard-sized images on the east wall. Martin climbed the big oak tree in the orchard and scanned the horizons and the highway to the east. Then he ascended to the top of the pumped storage reservoir, sat down with his binoculars, and watched the coast of the Big Lake to the south, sweeping 180 degrees and ending on the sight of the broken lighthouse to the north in Lud Town.

The air smelled of the lake, with a whiff of white pine sap when the wind gusted offshore. The Big Lake water level had returned to the pre-pipeline shoreline. Smog no longer blew up from Benton Town or Chi-Town. In the six years since the Cataclysm, the ozone layer had been restored, the environment had freshened, and the earth and all the animals that roamed the sparse man-inhabited land breathed easy.

Martin mused about the finishing tasks left on the house. He would move the wood stove from the subbasement and connect the ductwork. He would install the kitchen counter and breakfast bar. The sinks and toilet, and shower needed finishing. All the light switches, outlets, and LED lights could now be wired in. Martin could now haul up the induction stovetop, refrigerator, and oven and move them to their proper place. Kitchen cabinets need to be scrounged and installed.

Martin shook his head. *Four more months of work*, he thought.

He had spent two years building the house. Today, though, Martin concentrated on breathing the new world's air and enjoying his accomplishments.

It was a good day.

****

Three years after Davion came to the estate, Davion realized how much Martin would stake on Davion's ability to hold his own in a skirmish. He had trained harder without being pushed, adding free weights to his exercise regimen. The duo ran two miles along the beach and back before breakfast. Martin, turning thirty-five, became winded before Davion, who would be seventeen in June.

Davion had shot past Martin in height to over six feet, still growing. Martin never knew Davion's father. He assumed Davion took after both his tall parents.

The teenager could best Martin in a jujitsu match fifty percent of the time. He remained untested in his karate skills. Davion could hunt and track as well as any Independent. His archery skills, even on moving targets, matched Martin's. He could throw his knife into a target ten feet away. His favorite books were *Hawaii*, by Michener (C) 1959, *A Promised Land*, by Obama (C) 2020, and *Equal Justice*, by B. K. Thompkins, (C) 2046.

Through Martin's tutelage, Davion had an equivalent college education in math, physics, and social science. He understood his mother's book *Basic Nanotechnology*.

Not only are the winters colder, but spring and warm weather seem to come along late at the latitude of Butters, Lakeshore. Davion and Martin relaxed for a stretch after their morning run and swimming on a sunny day in late May. The swim had been more of a dip: in and out, lather up, dip in and out.

"Sir Martin," Davion began, "I am ready for any test you present. If my mother still lives, it is time to find out."

Martin smiled, laid his head on the beach towel spread on the shore, and watched a wispy cloud overhead. "You have been ready, Davion," said Martin. "You have already passed or surpassed every test I have conceived. I have been working on a generalized plan and hoping for summer weather. Let's go up and start laying out our trip."

Davion wanted to wait until after archery practice to hear Martin's plan. After training, Davion set out plates and food for lunch. He also cleared the table and sat back down, clasping his hands.

"I'm ready," said Davion.

Martin took a few moments to look his young companion in the eye. He noted his determination, which had not faltered since their first meeting. He also noted the boy's relaxed confidence. Except for the uncertainty of Davion's handling of stress in actual combat, Davion equaled Martin in capability. Martin worried more about his own response to the dangers of a skirmish than Davion's.

"Alright,": Martin said. "First, the general approach."

****

On the twentieth day of their walking journey, Martin began seeing signs for Day Town (Dayton.) Martin assumed the city of Dayton, Ohio, circled on his dogeared atlas equated to Day Town, post-Cataclysm. Logan had included the atlas in the survival library collection in the subbasement.

Davion and his mother had traveled north after escaping the militia compound near Day Town. The distance and travel time north to Whitehall, where Martin had found Davion, matched the travel time down to Dayton from Butters, Lakeshore.

The weather had been favorable for the journey this summer, dry, with clear days and cool nights. The further the couple traveled from Big Lake, the less cloudy the days were. They stuck to Martin's rules of travel.

Their established routine began with walking three hours before sunrise on the highway. As soon as dawn broke, they moved off the thoroughfare along the gully of a secondary road. Finding a forest or scrub brush to use for hiding, they slept between ten and six o'clock in the evening. On moonless nights they rose and walked on the highway for three more hours, then rested until their predawn trek. The moon, when available, allowed an extra two hours of relative danger-free travel time. Davion or Martin kept a nocked arrow at the ready, trading that duty with the other traveler at hour intervals. One carried the food pack strapped to his back, shifting his backpack to the front. They took turns with this duty as well.

Before approaching the city center of Day Town, Martin turned east, heading for the Wright-Patterson Air Force Base. It seemed logical to assume that a large militia compound might be located in that general vicinity. Davion sighted the runways and cautioned Martin about the lookouts and guards ahead.

The plan called for Davion to remain out of sight while Martin approached a guard seeking membership in the militia. If accepted, Martin would investigate the compound and shoot an arrow into the building where Davion waited. If Davion did not find his nightly arrow three nights in a row, Davion should assume the mission a failure and move forward with a life on his own. If Martin discovered Davion's mother, he would fire two arrows. Davion would wait for the dark of night to reconnoiter with Martin at the corner of the tall building across the airfield. They would figure out the final strategy for rescue at that time. Three arrows meant "HELP."

Martin walked deliberately toward the front gate of the airfield without Davion. No guard appeared to challenge him. Martin walked the perimeter of the airfield fence. The second guard station was not occupied either. A ten-minute walk across the airstrips and an investigation of three buildings in the complex convinced Martin the military base had been abandoned.

A man popped out from the cover of a doorway fifty yards ahead of Martin's position, offering the sign of an Independent before ducking back to cover. Martin returned the gesture and approached with hands outstretched. Martin ended his approach thirty feet from the doorway, staying halfway covered by an old cargo cart.

The glimpse he caught of the man in the doorway suggested an unkempt, bearded man with shoulder-length ratty hair who wore filthy, holey army fatigues, carrying a crossbow, shaft in place, but with a bowstring broken in worthless strands hanging to the ground. He could not have fired on Martin in any event.

"Hello," Martin said. "What happened here. We expected a militia presence. Is there anyone else around?"

The ragged man tried to speak, coughed, tried again, cleared his throat, and finally croaked a reply.

"I'm the - I'm the only - I'm here," said the wretch.

"Do you know how long the militia has been gone?" asked Martin.

"No," said the man, still staying in the cover of the doorway, "they left before the winter. No, they left two winters ago."

"What have you been living on?"

"C-rations, K-rations, and rat meat stew. Are you hungry? Can you stay for supper?"

"Do you know where the soldiers here went?" asked Martin.

"Which ones, the real ones or them that came after?" The man worked his jaw back and forth, up and down, getting used to the sound of voices, including his own.

"Both."

"Well, the real ones just dispersed. Threw down their worthless rifles and went home to their families, except for a few of the asshole officers. They figured they owned the place. Thought it might make a great base for starting their new order. They hustled around Day Town in small groups finding crossbows and machetes. They killed just to add to their weapons arsenal. They created the militia and allowed others to join or die. They were the ones that chained the women. Those fields you see to the south of the last airstrip. They used heavy rope against the backs of the women if they rested from pulling the plow or stood during planting or harvesting food for the officers."

"What happened," said Martin.

"Two things, the drought here in 2062 scared them, and when the west militia came through, half of them died before they escaped to the foothills and forests east of here. Picked a spot called Clear Creek where they could hide and rebuild their forces. It is a lush area, good soil."

"Did they take the women with them?"

"Does a bear shit? Of course! Mostly blackies, strong good looking workers."

"Could you guide me to their compound?"

'Not on your life, mister. I am lucky I found a way, in the end, to meander off unnoticed. I am not ready to suicide myself yet. I have a good thing going here. Last a long time. Here, not there.

"You can find them militia. Head due east. Maybe they will find you."

Five days walk later, Martin and Davion made camp just inside the edge of the great forest stretching as far north and south as they could see, leaving the flat fields, abandoned farms, and burned-out towns behind them. They did not build a fire or set up their rain shield, opting for piling leaves beneath a large maple tree for softer beds. They unrolled down bags and slept. In the morning, after cleaning up the campsite, Martin cautiously led the way on a two-track he noticed from the highway that cut into the forest. Even though overgrown with weeds and bushes, the two-track showed evidence of trampled travel on one of the ruts. The terrain began an upward slant, evidence that Martin and Davion traveled the foothills of the East Mountains. They reached a meadow and threw down their packs, using them for backrests. They each closed their eyes to rest.

Davion first heard a commotion somewhere in the woods; he could not pinpoint the source or direction. Martin hurriedly packed the gear, and they moved fifty feet off the path into the forest. The sounds increased in volume, and Martin identified the sounds of multiple travelers perhaps walking the same route they had chosen. He looked over at Davion, who had pulled his bowstring to point and looked determined to hold it until the travelers passed. Martin motioned to Davion to kneel and be patient.

"Maybe we can follow them," said Martin softly.

Minutes later, a party of seven militia soldiers jostled and laughed along the path, oblivious to the world around them. They

[331]

wore fatigue pants and black ankle boots. They wore identical t-shirts with the head of a snarling timber wolf screen printed on the front. Scars on the soldiers' right triceps looked like stylized lightning bolts or crooked S's. It looked like a brand, not a tattoo.

After they went by, Davion seemed ready to explode. "I knew two of them. We could have killed them. Three by me, four by you," he said.

"Stop that talk, Davion," Martin said. "If you can't stay focused on rescuing your mother, I will turn around, and you will never hear of me again. We probably have a one in fifty chance of succeeding. Don't fuck up what little chance we have."

Davion settled quickly. "I understand," he said.

Martin and Davion followed the group, staying at least one hundred feet behind on the same path. Within two hours, Davion heard one man in the group loudly hail someone ahead of the group, yelling at the top of his voice.

"Jim," said the man in the front of the group. "Norcross here. There are seven of us coming through."

"Fine, Lieutenant, come on in."

Martin grabbed Davion and pulled him off the path, deeper into the woods. He pointed to the trees in front of the group where a guard station, fifteen feet off the ground, held the sentinel. Davion and Marten faded away more than half a mile among the trees and set up a cold camp, again with no fire.

They reviewed Martin's plan to infiltrate the militia, essentially the same strategy they had devised at the airfield. Davion would stay outside the compound, providing cover, only approaching the buildings on an emergency arrow signal from Martin.

Martin climbed a tall chestnut oak, surveying the compound, fence, and buildings. Ten buildings, the first painted bright red, the next painted blue, then red, and so on. The complex of buildings had been located two hundred feet from the surrounding ten-foot-tall perimeter fence in a ten-acre flat, grassy meadow. The most prominent building seemed to be the mess hall. Three Quonset-type buildings were probably the soldier's barracks. Between the fence and the buildings to the north, fifteen cabins, ten by ten-foot square and painted white, formed a line five feet apart.

South of the compound's buildings, the meadow stretched out to encompass twenty acres of cultivated fields where women of color dug in the dirt, pushed plows, or picked produce. All the women wore the same exposed right shoulder and right breast shifts. Soldiers in groups of seven sauntered casually in and out of the compound at the five gates and guard stations spaced evenly around the perimeter fence. Patrol seemed to be the only apparent duty of a soldier.

Davion suggested the compound seemed less than half the size he remembered. The West Militia had taken a toll on the Wolf Pack. The two conferred on a rendezvous place and signal arrow location. They crept up close to the fence.

"Hold it, Davion," Martin whispered, grabbing Davion by the collar and stopping him. "There is a trip wire here. It looks like it runs around the whole perimeter a foot from the chain link fence.

"That must be a signal system, but how they made it without electrical power is beyond me. I guess we stay away from it.

"If you have to come over the fence for any reason, you better throw our rain guard on the fence and not touch the chain link, just in case."

****

"Mister," said the sentinel, "you got twenty seconds to say what you want here."

"I'm looking to join the Wolf Pack," said Martin. "I hear you guys are the best. At least until I came along."

In response to Martin's boast, the guard let fly the shaft in his crossbow. It landed one foot in front of Martin's left boot.

"One warning, go," said the guard.

While the man in the tower reloaded his crossbow, Martin drew back his bow and shot the bell ringer of the alarm bell hanging six inches from the guard's head. Martin had another arrow nocked and drawn while the guard struggled with the crossbow.

"Do not raise that crossbow if you wish to breathe," said Martin. "I want in, you need me, and your superiors will appreciate the skills I bring."

"You may be right, dickhead, but if you are wrong, it will be my pleasure to cut off your nuts and make you swallow them, one at a time. The recruiting station is straight ahead. You can see the blue sign from here."

In response, Martin walked toward the buildings two hundred feet ahead, waiting for a crossbow shaft to penetrate his back and pierce his heart. Same old nightmare. He reached the office door with the blue "Recruitment" sign and walked in.

The man at the desk did not look up from his solitaire game. Martin counted to five before saying, "I'm joining up."

The desk sergeant picked a sheet off the top of the pile on the corner of the desk. "Sign it. Read it if you want," said the sergeant.

Martin skimmed the document. He had two thoughts. One: The last paragraph indicated that Martin would die for the privilege of serving the militia. He would be killed if he disobeyed an order.

Second: Martin believed that these days most of the young recruits probably could not even read the document they were signing.

Martin signed.

"Forgot to mention the test," said the desk sergeant, still not looking up. "See the sergeant of arms in the long building through that door. If you survive, you are in."

Martin started for the door, then stopped. "That red eight of diamonds plays on the nine of clubs in your second column," he said.

The man finally looked up, picked up the red card, and set it down on the black nine. "Thanks."

The next building had a shooting range with targets set up fifty, seventy-five, and one hundred feet downfield. The soldier in charge must have been three inches taller than Martin. The man could have burst out of his Wolf Pack t-shirt. Martin noted the red marks at the end of the sleeves due to bulging biceps. The double "S" scar within a circle looked smudged. The big fellow must have shifted just when the brand had been applied. Martin decided the man might not be as formidable as his intimidating physical appearance.

The man tried to hand Martin a crossbow and a shaft. "See if you can hit the first target," the instructor said.

Martin judged the distances of all three targets. No wind would alter his arrow's flight. He waved off the crossbow offered, drew back his bow, and hit the bullseye. As the instructor stared downfield at the accuracy of Martin's shot, Martin pulled back and shot the bullseye on the second target. In a blink, he drew back on the third target, one hundred feet away, and hit that bullseye dead center.

"Hey, I didn't tell you to shoot again," the man said.

"Sorry, what target do you want me to hit next," said Martin.

"Alright, the next target, hit the next target."

Martin did not split his first arrow like the scene in the old Robin Hood movie he so enjoyed as a kid, but he came about as close as possible to doing just that. He pulled back and repeated his accuracy with the third target at the soldier's request.

"Think you are pretty sharp, huh? Let's get to the next building. I would hate to break that fancy shooting arm when you have no mat to fall on. Lead on, there is the door."

Martin started walking toward the door at the opposite end of the building. The soldier followed for about five feet before viciously striking Martin with a powerful right-fisted blow to the muscle in his back protecting his kidney. Martin sensed the impact coming without turning, so he leaned forward before feeling the excruciating pain in his back. He fell to the floor, thinking only about the kaleidoscope of stars and pinpricks, tears flowing down his face. Martin lay curled on the floor while the monster walked around him one full circle, looking for the next place to deliver a killing kick. Martin still could not see the man smirking at him, but he could hear him. He calmed and ignored the pain, kneeling with his arms and hands still on the floor, his head resting on his arms.

When the man drew his leg back for a kick, Martin straightened his torso and punched upward with his left leg, connecting with the soldier's chest with full force.

Now the big man lay on the floor coughing for breath. Martin went to him, boxed his ears, and chopped his collar bone with his bow, hearing a sickening crunch and then a scream from the soldier. Martin retrieved his precious arrows and went through the far door to the next building.

More card players, three of them.

The middle soldier looked up, "Where is Brick?"

"The big man," said Martin, "He will be here when his ears stop ringing. He will not be much help for about six weeks. His collar bone is broken."

"Who are you," the spokesman said.

"Recruit," Martin said. "As far as I am concerned, I passed the test."

"If you say so," said Middleman. He looked at the two other card players, who both shrugged. "Sit in the chair over there, Cowboy; time for the initiation."

Martin took a seat. The spokesman went over to the charcoal grill in the corner, stoked the crimson briquettes, and withdrew the branding iron from the center of the red-hot coals. The iron looked quite beautiful, ranging in color on the tip from white to yellow to red-orange and then blue fading to black. Waving the smoking iron before Martin, he asked him to shuck his shirt. Martin did, beads of sweat forming on his forehead. The two card players strapped Martin's wrists tight to the chair.

"Last chance," said the middleman. "On your say so, we will unstrap you, and there is the door. You are welcome to chicken walk right out of here."

Martin thought *an arrow in the back would surely follow such a chicken walk. The nightmare for real. Contract fulfilled.*

"Get to it," Martin said, clutching the chair, nails digging into the wood, pain running up his arm, *distracting, hopefully.*

[336]

One of the card players went around to the back of the chair, putting his arms through open spaces in the chair's back. He pulled Martin back in the chair and locked his hands together.

As Martin expelled air twice like a bellows, then held his breath. Spokesman pulled the reheated branding iron from the fiery coals, turned, and pressed the iron into Martin's arm, hard.

My fingers hurt, thought Martin. *My nails are breaking. He is pushing that fucking thing right through my arm.* "Argggrhhh," Martin screamed, hoping to scare the enemy into stopping. Spokesman pulled the iron away. The soldier on the right dabbed a towel on Martin's upper arm, extinguishing the smoking fire.

"You did good, Cowboy," said Middleman. "You are in. A clean symbol. Bill, you and Larry better see to Brickman. You should probably head to the base hospital for a bandage Cowboy. See you at the dinner bell."

The hospital consisted of a room in the next building with one wall of medical supplies and medicines and three beds, one occupied by Brick, who looked none too happy to see Martin.

The doctor on duty already had bandages and salve on the desk, ready to administer to Martin. Brick turned his head to the wall, not moving his shoulder. The pain in Martin's right side felt like the branding iron still stuck out of his arm. The doctor gave Martin a shot of morphine, rubbed salve gently on the burn, and bandaged his arm.

"Your arm will hurt like hell until the morphine kicks in," said the Doctor. "Otherwise, you are much less beat up than most of the recruits who meet Brick. Tables were turned, I see."

"Thanks for patching me up, Doc," said Martin. "Have you got any antibiotics for later?"

"We have all the supplies from every hospital within a hundred miles," said the Doctor. He went to the next room and brought back a small bottle. "Take two pills three times a day until they run out. That will prevent your arm from getting infected.

"Over the years, these pills have been losing their potency. That is why you want to take two at a time."

"Again, Thank you, Doc."

"Have you heard about your reward for the branding?"

"No, not yet."

"One hour with a black bitch of your choice tonight. That should perk you up.

"Let me look at the schedule. Cabin four is open at ten o'clock. Carolyn, what do you say?"

"Say Doc," Martin said, "I've heard about what a good time a gal named Tamara gives out."

"Really, she is older, about your age, I guess; still in high demand. She is a good pick. She does not have an opening until 1:00am in the morning. Cabin eleven."

"Perfect," said Martin.

The doctor directed Martin to the next red building, the quartermaster's office. The quartermaster issued Martin some used black boots in his size, fatigue pants (washed and crisp,) and a new Wolf Pack t-shirt. Upon looking at his logbook, the quartermaster assigned Martin cot thirteen in Barrack B and directed Martin to report to platoon leader Ronald Shepherd. Salutes and formalities were not in the lexicon of the Wolf Pack. Recruits were 'Cowboys,' experienced soldiers had nicknames. The word 'Sir' never seemed to be used. Martin saw someone receive a hard kick in the butt when an officer's request went unheeded.

Shepherd assigned toilet cleaning and bathroom mop-up. Typical recruit duties. Martin would be heading out on patrol at ten o'clock. No introductions to the rest of the squad ensued.

The bulletin board in the mess hall where Martin went for dinner notified the men of upcoming events. The notice explained that one of the events, actually labeled 'A Panty Raid,' would be coming up. Half the camp would encircle a town to the east known to harbor blackies. The flyer promised a good time for all.

Martin's full name graced another document posted on the board. Disgusted, Martin stood in the chow line, received his ladle of stew, and sat down to eat. The platform at the front of the mess hall held the officer's table, where ten comrades jostled and joked over their officer's special chicken dinner. A man in a white shirt and brown pants ate quietly toward the end of the table, scanning all the tables as if he were looking for something or someone.

Martin's heart skipped when he realized the bearded man was his father, Logan. At the same time, Logan locked eyes with Martin; he must have noticed Martin's name on the recruits list. Neither thought it the time to connect. Martin surmised that Logan must hold some esteem as a science officer with the militia. He would seek him out on the new day. Tonight, he had to deal with his first priority, Tamara.

Arriving at cabin eleven at 1:00am, Martin debated knocking, rejected the idea, and stepped through the doorway. Moonlight revealed two beds on opposite sides of the small room. At a loss, Martin spoke gently, "Tamara Okoye."

"Who is there," a voice said from the bed on Martin's left. "How do you know my name."

Martin presumed the other bed to be occupied by another slave. He had to be careful. "Who is in the other bed?" Martin asked.

"None of your business; get over here; clock's running."

Martin closed the front door and walked to the bed, sitting close to Tamara's shoulder. "Davion sent me," Martin said

Tamara exploded, "What, Davion, is he here? Both of you get out of here. Go away. If he gets caught, everything is for nothing."

"Tamara, be quiet. I will explain. First, Davion can care for himself and you when we get you out of here."

Martin went on to explain his infiltration of the militia. Tamara barely listened before interrupting, "You must be crazy; never in a million years will you be able to get me out of here. I will not endanger my children by trying.

"You do realize the fence is electrified. Do you not?"

"How can the fence be electrified? Where does the power come from?" asked Martin.

"The professor rigged it up. A battery-powered surge is released to the fence if the trip wire is broken. The professor connected solar panels that charge up batteries."

Martin smiled in the dark. There could only be one explanation for the fence. "Is the professor's name Logan," he asked. He could not see Tamara's nod in response. "That man is my father.

All the unusual commotion woke up the occupant of the other bed.

"Mommy, what is a in… what is a filtrator," a tiny voice sounded.

"I guess a filtrator is someone who will help us," said Tamara.

"That is right," said Martin. He knew his task had just become ten times more complicated. "Now, do you ever have a night off from,,, appointments?"

"Tomorrow after the meal, we girls line up for a shot from the doctor, and then we have a night off. I usually spend the time playing dolls with Alyssa ('uh-lee-suh.')

"Well, tomorrow night, instead, we're all leaving this place. Do you have anything I can write a note on to Davion?"

Tamara had a notebook and pen she used for a sanity journal. Martin ripped a sheet out and wrote instructions to Davion. He took his arrow repair kit out of his quiver, glued the note's edge to an arrow, and wrapped it tight with string. Martin said goodbye to Alyssa and Tamara and left. He had never gotten a good look at either of them. He ducked into a moon-shadowed corner of a building and fired off his signal arrow to Davion.

The patrol duty consisted of seven men carrying crossbows or compound bows or, in one case, a powerful recurve bow strolling through the woods on a well-worn path straight out from the third gate. Martin and his six companions walked within thirty feet of Davion's camp: oblivious. Patrols intended to capture, question, or torture strangers, Independents, ogres, or bandits. Discovering an Independent's dwelling. Surprising and corralling Independent women make the exercise worthwhile. The scouting party made enough noise that anyone with half an ear could escape captivity. On this day, the group saw only birds and a red fox on their round. They returned to the compound in time for lunch.

Martin's squadron leader gave Martin a note ordering him to appear at the commander's office. Before Martin could address the sergeant at arms, Logan came out and hustled Martin into his own office.

Once the door closed, Logan opened his arms, and Martin approached his father for a hug, melting away sixteen years of longing he had for his father.

"We shouldn't spend too much time together," said Martin. "I intend to break out of the compound tonight with my young friend Davion, his mother Tamara, and her daughter Alyssa. Of course, I hope you want to come along. This place is horrid. Have you been here all this time?"

"No time to explain," Logan said. "I was under Base arrest for years, then the militia formed, and they also wanted the nanochip shutdown reversed. For ten years, a guy holding a machete guarded me in the same room where I worked. I have had relatively more freedom in the last couple of years. They tend to forget about me. I try to stay valuable by offering little conveniences to the commander occasionally. Just a little night light on his bedside table allowed me to bargain a reduced sentence for a woman due to be whipped for stealing a bunch of grapes for her wee little one."

"The fence. That is your work as well, I presume," Martin said. "Yes," said Logan. "The trip wire triggers a surge applied to the chain link. That will bite you. Put you on your ass."

Martin shook his head, his task getting more complicated by the minute. "You're saying I can't go out over the fence. That means going out by way of the guard station."

"Nah," said Logan, "I have put duplicate controls in my laboratory. If I turn off the trip wire alarm and the corresponding power surge breaker, we will be good to go at the fence."

"Will you come with us then? I have an extra breakdown bow in my pack. Is there any reason you would hold us up?"

"I'm sixty-six, son, but I'm in good shape. I have been exercising. I knew I would have to leave soon. I will go with you on one condition. Someday I want to return and wipe out this inhuman blight of nature."

Martin agreed. Based on his militia infiltration, he did not think it would take many men and women with expert commando skills to liberate the rest of the women and destroy the Wolf Pack criminal organization.

That evening as darkness approached, the women's work crews came in from the fields. Alyssa was too young to work, but she had to play with her dolls on the side of the meadow while her mother worked. The workers and children stopped at the mess hall for soup and bread. Then all the women visited the doctor's office for their venereal disease examination and possible medication. The women marched to their cabins in the dark. Tamara and Alyssa played with her straw dolls waiting for the signal, a knock on the door.

Martin had gone to bed, his clothes neatly folded in a bundle under his cot. No one had noticed he had left his bow and quiver hidden outside under a corner of the nearest red building. At his guess of midnight, Martin crept out of the barracks, put on his clothes, and reclaimed his bow and quiver. Logan waited for him at the last building nearest the white cabins. Martin circled wide of the guard sitting on the porch of the white shack. Killing the man had to be done. Coming at the man in the chair from behind, he smothered the man's mouth and reached around, plunging his knife into the heart and dragging his body off the porch to the side of the building.

He went to cabin eleven and tapped on the door. Tamara emerged, carrying Alyssa. They headed for the closest guard station, joining Logan, who had successfully dispatched the guard on the other side of the white cabins.

As they approached the guard station, a soldier leaned forward in the darkness, trying to discern what animals were skulking in the compound. Finally, he reached for the alarm bell. An arrow through his heart ended his attempt at warning there was trouble in the complex.

Davion already had the rain guard over the fence, which was unnecessary since Logan had turned off the electric fence. Martin climbed up to the top. Logan handed Alyssa to Martin, who handed her down to Davion on the other side.

"Meet your sister, Davion," Martin said. Logan climbed the fence, followed by Tamara. Tamara hugged and kissed Davion for a full minute before Martin urged the group's departure. His plan called for getting as far away as possible from the compound in ten hours of double-time marching. Martin stopped long enough to put his spare takedown bow together and hand it to Logan. He dug out his extra jeans and flannel shirt from his pack and gave them to Tamara. He offered a spare bowstring as a belt to hold the jeans up. She thanked him.

All four adults took turns carrying Tamara's three-year-old. Two leg holes were cut in one of the backpacks. Alyssa sat in the backpack which the adult wore in front. She would tuck her head into the neck of the carrier and wrap her little arms around their neck.

The escapees jogged, walked, jogged, walked, rested for two minutes, then repeated the routine.

Walking in the group's rear, Martin hailed the band to stop and rest. Joining the group, he finally got a look at Alyssa and Tamara. They were both beautiful. Alyssa is angelic; Tamara is an athletic model with high cheekbones, a soft round chin, and large, unusually blue eyes. Tamara sat with Davion on one side and Alyssa tight on the other. When Martin approached and sat down next to Alyssa, he saw the jagged scar on the left side of Tamara's face, running from above her left eye, down behind her cheek, all the way to her jawbone.

The most astonishing thing to Martin was that Tamara paid no attention to it, did not try to shield it from his view, ignoring the disfigurement, almost as if she took pride in it. *That is one hell of a woman,* thought Martin.

Based on years of experience at the compound, Logan and Tamara suggested that the patrol squads were probably already on their trail. Perhaps less than two hours behind. In this case, the dogs would have picked up the scent at the compound and proceeded straight to the escapees. Multiple scouting parties would be sent out along the spokes of a virtual wheel in case the first trail turned out to be a decoy.

The search party would have seven soldiers. When captured, the soldiers would have orders to kill everyone except the woman. She would be used back at the compound as an example to the rest of the women in the camp, disfigured again, just as Tamara had been cut after her previous recapture.

"How are you doing, Dad?" asked Martin.

"Fine, son, feels good; ready when you are," said Logan.

Martin studied the members of his group. "We have three expert archers to their seven. If they swarm us, we also have three combat-ready men."

"Give me a knife," said Tamara. She yanked Davion's knife from his ankle sheath and stood in the center of the clearing. "I will show you combat-ready."

Alyssa hugged her leg. "Mommy,' she said, "is Filtrator going to kill the man that got in my bed?"

Martin's heart dropped. A small child should not go through what Alyssa had suffered, and probably Davion before her.

"I promise, Alyssa," said Martin. The circumstances and odds of success had shrunk. Without his sixty-six-year-old father and three-year-old Alyssa, his band would have consisted of two trained commandos and a marathon runner. Martin had been sure the three could elude the militia back to Butters, Lakeshore.

"Ideas?" asked Martin, "I don't believe we will outrun the patrol if they have dogs."

Davion figured it out. The first meadow they crossed, Davion and Martin would circle back wide and await the patrol. They would eliminate the dogs, elude the soldiers, and double-time back to Logan, Tamara, and Alyssa.

The fugitives would put as much distance as possible between their party and the patrol party. They would ignore Martin's travel rules and take to the roads, zig-zagging in a northerly direction. As they traveled, they would look for a place with higher ground to hide and ambush the patrol squad.

Davion heard someone approaching through the forest from the west. Whoever it was made no attempt to be quiet.

"You there," a voice said, "Will you allow approach. I am alone and Independent."

The voice may have been connected with the militia. Logan and Martin looked at each other, and Martin shrugged.

"Approach where we can see you," said Martin.

Shuffling resumed through the woods until a woman appeared in view and stopped, offering the sign of the Independent. Martin returned the gesture, thumping his chest with a closed fist and spreading his arms in welcome.

"Thank you," said the woman, approaching closer, bow lowered with no nocked arrow. I have been tracking you for half an hour. Heard your conversation. Trying to elude the Wolf Pack, huh?"

She was tiny, barely over five feet tall, but smartly dressed in jeans and a clean dark green hooded sweatshirt. Her black hair was close-cropped, and she wore a knife sheath on her belt, knife safely holstered.

"We do not have time to become acquainted, I am afraid," Martin said apologetically, "you understand?"

"Sure, I would offer you shelter, but you know the rules," the woman said.

"No worries, we will be on our way." Martin would not ask where she sheltered, nearby he suspected. *How did she elude the dogs,* he thought?

"Sure," the woman said. "I could tell you are not from around these parts. The accent is wrong. "Have you heard of the AIR Corp?"

"No," said Logan.

"Stands for Alliance of Independent Resistance," she said, pointing to her white armband. "If you make it to the city-state of Columbus, the AIR Corp may be able to help."

"How do we contact your organization," Logan asked.

"You don't," she said. "There is no organization. We would not be Independents if there were. Someone will be watching. Please do not count on it, but a call to arms happens occasionally. Best of luck. Nice to not meet you." The woman turned and faded into the woods, this time without a sound.

Fifteen minutes ahead, they crossed a meadow ideal for Davion's plan. The scrub brush grew low to the ground in the field, and only a few trees were sprinkled through the ancient pasture. The group continued for twenty minutes before Davion and Martin circled back. The two men hid on opposite sides of the meadow at least seventy-five feet off the path.

Davion and Martin waited two hours before they heard the wail of the hounds. Martin could not tell how many dogs were leading the pack. He took three arrows from his quiver and stuck them in the ground within easy reach.

Seventy-five feet and a moving target. Martin's hands' sweat. He wiped them on his pants. He had no time to worry about Davion. The search party broke into the meadow on Martin's left. There were three dogs held on leashes by two men. There were the requisite seven men in the squad.

Martin breathed, drew his bow back, and shot the lead hound dog in the neck. He did not wait to see where the shot landed. Instead, nocking his second arrow, he drew back and was about to release when he noticed all three dogs were down; Davion's two shots had taken out both remaining dogs.

"Damn fucker shot my dog," said one soldier, still holding a slack leash. "God damn, he can shoot." Those were his last words. Martin's arrow entered the right side of the soldier's ribcage and passed through his right lung, stopping after puncturing the man's left lung.

Martin turned and ran, again zig-zagging to make a difficult target. After a while, he turned back to the path and kept running. In a few minutes, he heard heavy breathing behind him. Martin turned back, facing the course, and drew his bow. Davion came into view, and they both took a minute to catch a breath, bent at the waist, hands on knees, wiping forehead sweat with their shirtsleeve.

"Good shooting, boy," squawked Martin.

"You as well, Sir Martin," Davion breathed.

Both men straightened and jogged to catch up to Logan, Tamara, and Alyssa.

The refugees reconnected in two and a half hours. The group pressed on, taking to the highways in a random northwest pattern toward the outskirts of the City-State of Columbus. Exhausted from the ten-hour double-time march, they sought rest in Three Creeks Park. A gazebo situated at the convergence of the Alum, Big Walnut, and Blacklick creeks offered shelter. One person, standing guard, could defend the pavilion from an eastern attack. The three rivers provided warning and security from the north, south, and west compass points.

In the morning, Logan pointed to the ten-story building at the park's north edge off Williams St. next to Big Walnut Creek. "I don't see how the patrol could have followed us," he told the group, "but if we spend a couple of days laying low and watching for them, we may be able to declare that we lost them for good."

Martin agreed, "That building has open space from the parking lot to the park. We would see them coming."

A consensus was reached; the refugees crossed to the abandoned building. They circled the building once and found two main entrances. Glass doors, broken out, allowed entrance from the park. On the opposite side of the lobby, the main entrance from the parking lot also allowed unrestricted access through broken glass doors. A third door on the east side of the building could not be opened, at least from the outside.

The cornerstone of the building gave the address of the 'Worthington Tower" as 4049 Williams Road. The architect, Olsen Associates, AIA, and the main contractor, Thornton Construction, Inc., were listed under the year of construction, 2047.

The sixty-foot square tower of polished vertical stainless steel panels featured three twelve hundred square foot offices, an elevator, and a restroom core. The second floor housed the corporate headquarters of a bank. Martin favored the three separate offices on the third floor. A balcony jutted out from each side of the building on all the levels.

The three men could defend the building from the balconies, and Tamara could watch for an eastern approach across the river and warn one of the archers. The dormant elevator would cause no concern. The group made a barricade of office furniture in the hall at the top of the stairs. With extreme rationing, Martin estimated they could hold out for three more days. After that, they would have to take to the streets no matter what.

From the top floor, Martin and Logan surveyed the city-state. Martin's binoculars picked out the city-state fence and gated approximately a mile away. The wall seemed to surround the high-rise district of the city center. Surprisingly, neither Martin nor Logan could spot any CSG personnel. People were inside the fence, too far away for Martin to determine their condition, but seemingly going about their business purposefully. By tracking the people, Logan decided they were heading to or from Franklin Park Botanical Garden or one of the city parks to the west. Logan concluded that the parks had been turned into fields of fresh produce to provide for the citizens still occupying the city.

In stark contrast to the decaying city of Graapids that Martin avoided, the city-state of Columbus had taken a humane approach.

The citizens had decided to get busy in the post Cataclysmic world and grow sustainable food. The city-state could therefore support the people who wished to remain within the fence.

Who protected them from marauding militias, bandits, ogres, and trolls? If their own group survived the chasing Wolf Pack, Martin and Logan felt it worth the risk to find out.

On the morning of the third day of their Worthington Tower occupation, Davion came rushing into the conference room where Martin and Tamara were washing up the breakfast dishes at the kitchenette in the corner.

"They are here," he said, gathering everyone on the balcony to see for themselves.

Martin took the binoculars. The patrol he spotted had already progressed halfway across the park. *Where had they gotten the dogs,* Martin thought. Then he sussed it out. Behind the first patrol came a second patrol, following the patrol with the dogs. The patrol whose dogs he and Davion had killed had met up with a second patrol and found their trail again, leading them to the city-state of Columbus. Martin turned to the group.

"Two search parties," Marti said. "Fourteen soldiers. What do we have, thirty arrows?" Alyssa sensed the growing tension and started to cry. Tamara tried to console her. Martin kneeled and took hold of both her shoulders. "Do not worry, little one," he said. "Your mommy and I will not let them hurt you. You must be unafraid now and let the grownups protect you. OK?"

"Yes, Filtrator," said Alyssa. "What should I do?"

"You must protect your dolls," said Martin. "Stay in this room under the table and guard your dolls. Do not come out until Mommy comes and gets you. Can you help Filtrator and do that?" Alyssa nodded.

The adults took to their posts. The dogs were leading the patrols straight to the Worthington Tower. Davion, Logan, and Martin stayed out of sight behind office chairs on each of the balconies. The soldiers had not thought yet to surround the building. Martin realized his advantage and called Tamara to retrieve Logan on the north side of the building to join Davion on the south side. He rushed to join Davion as well. The first patrol had almost entered arrow range. A long, difficult shot. When the patrol stopped seventy-five feet from the tower, Martin, Davion, and Logan stood and fired. Three soldiers went down. Chaos among the patrol sent soldiers scattering as the second patrol closed in.

The second squad seemed more disciplined, staying about one hundred feet from the building. Martin took aim at the soldier straggling last. Down went the militia man.

Davion and Martin followed Martin's strategy. In this manner, they picked off two additional soldiers. Tamara's call sent Logan and Martin to their original posts. Davion stayed on the south balcony. Arrows hit the walls underneath his position. A projectile shot from a high vantage point, such as the third-floor balcony, provided much greater accuracy than the opposite, shooting up from the Worthington Tower lawn.

Martin shot another soldier coming around the corner of the building. *Was that six,* he thought, *eight left, against three.* Of the mercenaries still attacking, Davion watched five of them enter the building and exiting again, throwing chairs and tables ahead of them on the lawn. Then the five, probably under orders to lay siege and not allow escape via an unknown entrance, ran and crouched behind the pile of chairs. They returned to shooting upward at Davion's position. Davion shot another archer. The man had remained still behind two chairs interlocked together. Davion breathed deeply, aimed at the man's button visible through the openings aligned in the two chairs, and released. The soldier toppled backward, an arrow cleaning slicing the button, blood flowing out on the grass from the belly wound.

Tamara yelled again, "The stairs. The Wolf Pack is at the barricade."

Martin could see no one in his quadrant of the tower grounds. Neither could Logan. What militia men were left, besides the three that had come into the lobby and set up the chair barricade outside, had climbed the stairs to the third floor.

The four wild-eyed, snarling Wolf Pack men pushed the barricade into close quarters with Martin, Logan, and Tamara. Martin grabbed the arm of one soldier, chopping the man's wrist and, at the same time, throwing an elbow into the man's chin. The mercenary dropped his knife. Martin hauled the man over the barricade and flipped him on the floor. With a thrusting karate kick, Martin broke the man's neck.

Logan struggled with another soldier.

Martin, out of the corner of his eye, saw another soldier step back far enough to cock his crossbow.

Davion came around the corner. "Help is here," he said. The Wolf Pack soldier outside the barricade lifted his crossbow to shoot. An arrow whistling up from the stairs hit the soldier in the shoulder, spinning him around and down.

Four women and two men, wearing white armbands, members of the AIR Corp, finished climbing the stairs proclaiming victory over the militia scouting party. No other patrols had been spotted in the vicinity. The group spent several hours dragging all the bodies to a corner of the park where leaves and brush were piled. The victors cleared a space, piled the bodies, and covered them with a heavy layer of leaves, then brush, then heavier branches. A hasty grave; the raccoons would have a feast, and the crows as well.

Two of the AIR Corp party (they refused the term members) invited Martin's expedition to join them in the city-state for dinner. The atmosphere in the dining room of the old Victorian mansion where the group ate sent Logan back two centuries, candle chandelier and all. By the time they sat down to the grilled chicken and salad dinner, Martin, for one, felt weak with hunger. He asked the somewhat older woman he sat beside to explain why and how the city-state seemed to be doing well.

"Compared to Graapids, I would say it is the climate. We began to convert the city parks to community gardens shortly after the Cataclysm. Our more extended growing season gave us a head start in subsistence farming.

"Of course, many people would not participate in the work required, no tractors, for instance, and left the city to starve on their own."

Martin thought back to the smell, violence, and despair of Graapids. "What keeps you people safe?" he inquired. "The militias capture anyone of color, such as yourself. They kill the men and boys. The Ogres would be as dangerous. You have no guard patrols."

"We have the AIR Corp, as you know," the woman said. "Actually, we have many Independents living in the city. I have no idea where they live. I see them, and then they are gone. They are very private but seem to be around when needed.

"By the way, if you need food for your trip home, you can get a basket at the OSU golf course. The food requires three hours of work in a city garden."

The group volunteered to work the entire following day in the garden. They camped in another gazebo on what used to be the seventh tee, surrounded by knee-high corn.

In the morning, they stopped at the thrift store. Tamara picked out ladies' jeans that fit, as well as boots, a belt, a proper-sized bra, underwear, a shirt, and a blue jean jacket. Alyssa had never seen racks and racks of clothes, let alone children's clothes not made by her mother. Tamara helped her pick out jeans for the trail and underwear, a belt, boots, a shirt, a jacket, and a soft light-yellow cardigan sweater that Alyssa fell in love with. Martin also bought a new outfit, dumping the Wolf Pack t-shirt in the trash in favor of a long sleeve wool flannel shirt over a long sleeve thermal tee. Tamara may not be self-conscious about her scar, but Martin did not appreciate people staring at his branded arm. Logan purchased a backpack to help carry food.

They paid for the clothes with tickets received for working in the garden, stuffed the backpacks with food and their belongings, and began the long walk home.

****

Martin stopped on the rise at the edge of the estate with his father, Tamara, Davion, and Alyssa at the end of the walk from the city-state of Columbus. Tamara and Alyssa gasped at the three-hundred-foot mural. Logan cried at the sight of his tall and beautiful wife on the section of wall in front of him. He sat down, weeping, and told Martin to go ahead, "I want to stay here a while," Logan said.

Later, when Logan finished Davion's grand tour that day, he put his arms across Martin's and Davion's shoulders.

"You have done a fine thing here, Martin," he said. "Visible but invisible. Perhaps someday, this deception will no longer be needed."

Logan, Martin, and Davion set about adding a small bedroom to the house. They also divided the bedroom in two, allowing Martin and Logan their rooms and privacy. All the extended family worked in the garden, milked the goats, and helped pluck the Sunday chicken.

Martin commenced work on the wind turbine he had dreamed about so often. Martin and Logan ventured into Lud Town for raw materials. They built the tall structure at the top of the Pumped Storage reservoir and tied the current generated into the silver-carbon battery packs in the subbasement. The whoosh of wind channeled up from Big Lake Bay drove the wind turbine non-stop.

In the evenings, Martin sat on the sectional next to Tamara with her daughter on his lap and read to Alyssa. He began with *The Shy Stegosaurus,* followed by A. A. Milne's poems and stories of Christopher Robin, Pooh Bear, and Piglet. In time he held the book in one hand and rested his other hand on Tamara's knee.

Martin attempted to describe his feelings to Tamara. He wanted to care for her, Davion, and Alyssa. One day he made a half-joking remark, "I think I am in love with you."

Tamara had looked him straight in the eye. "Well, are you or are you not," she said.

[353]

It took four months for Tamara to appear relaxed in Martin's home. One evening Tamara and Martin were the last two awake in the house. Martin took her by the shoulders and gently kissed her on the mouth. She did not cringe. Martin thought that a good sign. She went away to sleep with Alyssa and Kagiso, born seven months after the menagerie found their way back to Butters, Lakeshore. Three nights later, Martin kissed her again.

"I do love you, Tamara," he said, "I want to spend my life with you. I have been lonely to the point of craziness. I will be happy if you agree to stay with me, sleep beside me in my bed, and tell me your concerns."

Tamara took Martin's hands in her own. "Martin, I have been incredibly lonely since my husband was killed.

"The Wolf Pack! I see their faces in the dark. The phantoms and the ghosts of them haunt even my waking world.

"Every day, you have helped them go further away. I do not know about love yet, but you are my medicine and hope for my children."

"Yes," Martin said, "I understand, and I want your children to be my children as well."

"Martin, let me try to sleep in your bed for an hour each night to allow Alyssa time to get used to sleeping alone. If that works, well, we will see."

Six months passed. Alyssa slept through the night. Tamara cuddled with Martin. Martin, on occasion, would stroke Tamara's smooth as silk thigh once, twice, or thrice as she slept, imagining her great-looking legs under the covers.

One night, as they were about to get into bed, Tamara kissed Martin passionately, broke off, and said, "It is time, Martin."

Martin did not argue. He pulled her nightgown over her head, tossing it on the foot of the bed. Martin took off his t-shirt and slid his boxers down to the floor. He kissed her, pressing his body as gently as he could stand into her body. Chest to breast, penis to her mound, already in agony.

Martin wanted to prove that he was different than the others. Patient, kind, and gentle.

"I have wanted this," Martin had said, "since the first moment I saw you, Tamara. Your legs, your breasts, and now these lovely dark nipples. You are beautiful."

"You have never said anything about my scar," Tamara said.

Martin had reached up and traced the jagged line from forehead to chin. "Like you, I never will. Your pride and stature speak for you," he said.

He kissed her in as many places as possible, then lifted and laid her on the bed. Tamara ignored all the historical nightmares and concentrated on pleasing Martin. Martin continued his gentle caresses, softly stroking her, increasing her excitement, and entering her carefully.

Martin had been right to remain patient all these past months. Tamara confirmed her love that night. Together, their marriage was consummated.

Martin wiped Tamara's forehead with a cool, damp washcloth, then kissed her cheek. She smiled. Martin leaned over the bed and kissed his son, Dakari Martensen, on the tip of his tiny ear. Seven-year-old Alyssa stood at the foot of the bed, waiting her turn to hold the new baby. Two-year-old Kagiso napped in the other bedroom. Logan stood in the corner of the room by Davion, Martin's adopted son.

Dakari's light skin, at birth, might turn as dark as Davion's if he took after his sister Kagiso. He was small but active within the warm blanket wrapped tightly around him. He had not opened his eyes yet. Would they be blue like his mother's, hazel like Martin's, or brown? Dakari's hair, black, shiny, and plastered on his little head, already seemed to curl in swirls.

Logan spent his days working on the reversal of the SO1 shutdown. He had theoretically solved the problem many years ago in 2067. The scanning probe microscope at Wright Patterson Air Force base had been broken beyond repair in 2054. That was when the legitimate officers left, and the psychotic militia formed. For a couple of weeks, the militia smashed everything, including a few all-important components for the microscope. From that point on, Logan faked half of his research findings. His legitimate endeavor, trying to reverse the effect of the SO1 chip, required the scanning probe microscope sitting unused at the server farm building in Butters, Lakeshore.

When Logan finally succeeded in the reversal, he spent a year writing everything down, basically a sequel to his wife's book: *Basic Nanotechnology*. Half of the book discussed how to manipulate nanospin components. The other half of the book presented a philosophical argument for leaving the chips alone.

Logan believed the world's dependence on microprocessors had nearly annihilated the human species. At the very least, the madness behind developing the SO1 chip had inadvertently reset the human/planet equation. Chapters in the book included his perspective on what turned out well because of the Cataclysm versus the inconveniences of a subsistence lifestyle. The dependence on technology contributed to the impossibility of the common man to understand the workings he depended on. For example, Logan listed the PHSI (Preventative-Human Safety-Initiative) as good. The loss of the power grid and worldwide communication was unfortunate.

Logan gathered Martin's family at the Sugar Maple tree, where his grandfather's and Mercedes's ashes had been scattered. Thirty feet away, his wife's Purple Beech tree already matched the maple tree in height. Thirty feet to the north of the Purple Beech, Logan pounded a stake to represent his own sugar maple resting place. As the family listened to the wind clattering the leaves, Logan told some of the stories of his ancestors, the shipmaster, the scout, the horse handler, the homesteader in Canada, and the radioman. Martin had never realized he was named after Martin Martensen, who had sailed across the ocean around 1800. Logan also produced the ring engraved with Daniel Martensen's name, the scout of Logan's story, and the year 1843. He requested Martin give it to his first-born son, Dakari, when he became an adult. Dakari would be entrusted to carry on the lineage of the Martensen family line.

Logan decided to continue to record what knowledge he possessed. Others: experts in medicine, communication, transportation, etc., would do the same. Perhaps future generations would build measured, thoughtful, and humble foundations for human/planet symbiotic progress. Baby steps, understood, instead of the lightning adoption of technology for human convenience. Logan wanted to reintroduce libraries and begin capturing and distributing advanced concepts in all disciplines in the new world.

This notion became Logan's Johnny Appleseed approach to post-cataclysm in his senior years. He would help Davion and other young pioneers conquer what might initially seem like impossibly complex science.

Reading had become a passion of Davion's since Martin had taken him in. He was in his twenties and had devoted the past year to dragging a museum-obtained printing press to the estate, refurbishing it, and printing the first edition of *The Independent News*. He worked on sand molds of each letter and set up a forge to melt automobile body parts to pour over the sand, creating metal press letters.

The Filtrator went on ever-widening expeditions with the AIR Corp to wipe out even the notion of militias. Militias and ill-fated city-states were dying as fast as the world of Independents expanded. Tamara helped organize the Gathering of Independents in 2070. She chose the neutral location of the Lebanon Lutheran Church compound in Whitehall, Lakeshore. Forty Independents nervously attended. Martin spoke of the importance of the AIR Corp.

During the Gathering, Martin and Tamara had wed in a handfasting ceremony. Davion gave the bride away; Logan was Martin's best man. Alyssa threw rose petals in front of Tamara as she walked to the front of the church. She had sewn a beautiful blue gown for herself and Alyssa, dyed to match her eyes. Martin wore a white shirt, again sewn by Tamara and clean jeans. The ceremony, per the Independent's Rule 2, had been conducted entirely without revealing any names of the participants.

This year, 2076, Tamara expected over two hundred people at the Gathering of Independents. *The Independent News* had circulated as far east as East Big Lake, southeast beyond the city-state of Columbus, and southwest around the bay of Big Lake. Tamara planned workshops on canning, sewing/knitting, seed propagation, animal husbandry, wind power, homeopathic curatives, and more.

Davion printed the *Declaration of Independents*, a one-page flyer to be posted and distributed at the Gathering. Logan kept the wording to a minimum. He argued that the amendments added to the pre-Cataclysm constitution over the previous three hundred years should be consolidated. The document should be fresh and simple.

Declaration of Independents
August 2076

We, the Independents of this abundant planet, choose to live separately in harmony.

Accordingly, the rules of an Independent lifestyle are as follows:

Rule 1: Never reveal the location, size, amenities, or lack thereof of your home or family. Never ask another Independent for this information. This principle assures that no one, Independent, friend, or stranger will covet the lifestyle of another Independent.

Rule 2: Never ask or offer names; given or sur. The anonymity tenet provides security for all Independents. Torture is thus rendered unproductive and ineffectual.

Rule 3: Offer or receive aid graciously as long as rules one and two are respected. Do for a neighbor as you one day may need yourself.

Rule 4: Independents strive to leave as little a mark on mother earth as possible. The air, water, and land will never again take second place in existence or for the exclusive benefit of Independents.

Rule 5: Discrimination of and or oppression of any group or individual based on sex, age, race, ethnicity, nationality, disability, mental illness or ability, sexual orientation, gender, gender identity/expression, sex characteristics, religion, creed, or individual political opinions will not be tolerated.

Rule 6: The Alliance of Independent Resistance (AIR Corp) forms in emergency protective situations to assure adherence to Rules one through Five. The AIR Corp disbands when security is restored.

Author Request:

Please rate and review *FILTRATOR* on Amazon USA.

https://www.amazon.com/dp/1732603472

or on Amazon UK

https://www.amazon.co.uk/dp/1732603472

Please participate in the author's quick, eight-question survey at:

https://www.surveymonkey.com/r/CRY39PS

Author's Blog and Website: https://johngerts.weebly.com